Kat Richards █████████████████████████ ped Los
Angeles in the 9 ██████████████████████ Seattle with
her husband, and a crotchety old cat and two ferrets. She rides a
motorcycle, shoots target pistol and does not own a TV.

Visit her website at www.katrichardson.com.

UNDERGROUND

A GREYWALKER NOVEL

KAT RICHARDSON

PIATKUS

PIATKUS

First published in Great Britain in 2008 by Piatkus Books
First published in the US in 2008 by ROC,
A division of Penguin Group (USA) Inc., New York, USA

A CIP catalogue record for this book
is available from the British Library

ISBN 978-0-7499-0873-7

Data manipulation by Phoenix Photosetting, Chatham, Kent
www.phoenixphotosetting.co.uk
Printed and bound by Clays Ltd, Bungay, Suffolk

Papers used by Piatkus Books are natural, renewable and recyclable
products made from wood grown in sustainable forests and certified
in accordance with the rules of the Forest Stewardship Council

Mixed Sources
Product group from well-managed
forests and other controlled sources
www.fsc.org Cert no. SGS-COC-004081
© 1996 Forest Stewardship Council
FSC

Piatkus Books
An imprint of
Little, Brown Book Group
100 Victoria Embankment
London EC4Y 0DY

An Hachette Livre UK Company
www.hachettelivre.co.uk

www.piatkus.co.uk

FOR JIM, FOR EVERYTHING.
AND IN MEMORY OF JAY MEZO:
"EVERYTHING'S BETTER WITH BACON!"

Two people in particular made this book work, and to them I owe huge thanks: Rick Boetel, chief historian of Bill Speidel's Underground Tour in Seattle, and Fran Fuller, of the Seattle Mystery Bookshop, who introduced me to Rick and vetted the first draft. Without their help, the setting of this book would never have come to life. However, I must also apologize to Rick for taking tremendous liberty with the real-life layout and access to the underground. All I can say is, "The story made me do it."

I'd also like to mention my agent, Steve, and my editor, Anne, who made fun of the monster at the proposal stage and thus made me swear it would work. All the funny bits are because of them. Special thanks to my mother-in-law, Sandy, who let me cast her as a homeless woman—she's way too good to me. And many, many thanks to the Western Washington Urban Fantasy Posse: Cherie Priest, Richelle Mead, Caitlin Kittedge, Mark Henry, Lilith Saintcrow, and member-at-large Jackie Kessler.

The usual suspects also deserve many thanks, but the list is so long I can't name them all without boring the pants off you. Family, friends, fans, fellow authors, certain booksellers, RAMs, agents, editors, my incredible cover artist, and that husband fella: You guys rock!

A final good-night to Jay Mezo, Boyd Grice, and Soren Pedersen. And the pirate kitty. You'll all be missed.

PROLOGUE

If ghosts and monsters had someone else to harass, my life would have been a lot quieter, like it was before I died. But something happened while I was gone for those two minutes—something no one has been able to explain to my satisfaction—and now I not only see ghosts and monsters and things that go "bump" in the night, I seem to be some kind of stepsister to them. I'm a Greywalker: a dual citizen of the regular world and the Grey—the creepy interference fringe between the normal and the paranormal. The Grey overlays the normal world, invisible to most people but there nonetheless. It's a place of misty shapes and memories, shot with hot lines of living energy, layered with time and magic, where ghosts, vampires, and monsters are as real and common as dogs and cats and just as likely to bite.

I'm a private investigator. I like the job most of the time, but I have to admit it isn't a great occupation if I want to have a reasonable social life, even at the best of times and without the complication of a client list that reads like the cast of a gothic horror novel. My profession and my ability to work in the world of ghosts and magic seems to have tangled me up in the needs, cases, causes, and disputes of every undead thing in the Pacific Northwest. They aren't very good at taking no for an answer and they don't stick to office hours, either. As much as I might want to leave that part behind, it's a job I can't quit and it's hell on my love life.

It's my bad luck, I suppose, that I met a great guy just when my life was being turned upside down by my own death and a permanent residence halfway into the uncanny. I've never been able to explain it—I don't even try. Most people can't really swallow the idea of murderous ghosts, helpful witches, uncanny artifacts, living energy, necromancers, vampires, and psychotic poltergeists. They are even less inclined to accept that those things are all part of my daily life. I have a few friends and acquaintances who know, but they aren't exactly life-mate material and some are downright nasty. It's not surprising that my life and relationship are both pretty messed up.

My boyfriend, Will, and I were giving it another go over the holidays. A pretty rough go, I'm afraid, what with ghostly things demanding my attention whenever they took a shine to the idea. Thanksgiving had been OK, but Christmas hadn't gone so well. By the second week of January, both the weather and my relationship got hit with an unexpected cold snap. And that was when I made the acquaintance of my first frozen corpse.

ONE

My knee ached in a way my physical therapist called "good" but I called "annoying." Of course I might just have been annoyed with Will Novak and working too hard on the knee I'd messed up running from a murderous poltergeist in October. The lower leg lift I was concentrating on hurt like hell—who'd have thought that straightening my knee a paltry thirty degrees against a mere twenty pounds' resistance would be so hard? But a lot of things are harder than they seem at first glance. What was hardest at that moment was holding my temper.

Will sat on the weight bench to my left, watching me. Resistance machines clanked and groaned around us, and free-weight lifters snorted like bulls amid the smells of rubber and sweat. "I still don't understand how you managed to tear that knee up so badly," he said. "What were you doing?"

"Working," I said, grunting from the strain of the weight as I lowered my leg slowly, and muttering under my breath, ". . . three, four . . . five." Two more reps and I could give the knee a rest while I worked on my shoulder—also a bit banged up from October's ugly case.

I ignored Will while I finished the knee lifts. Then I slid out of the machine and sat down beside him. It wasn't my favorite gym, but the pre-Christmas windstorm had knocked a tree into the front of the one I preferred, so I was using the gym near Will's hotel. Downed power lines and damage were still widespread in outlying parts of Seattle and King County, so the facilities that were functioning were packed, and the moment I vacated the machine, another customer rushed to use it.

At first, Will had taken the hotel room so he wouldn't presume on my hospitality when he'd come back from England as a Thanksgiving surprise. Somehow the right time to move his bags to my condo had just not come around—and I felt guilty that I didn't want it to. He'd been lucky to keep his room at the hotel, since the city had been flooded with people who needed accommodations while their all-electric houses were unlivable during the power outage. It was expensive, but it had working plumbing and heat, which even my condo hadn't had at one point.

Right behind the wind and rain had come an epic cold snap, and the current daytime temperature hung two to ten degrees below freezing—not cold in the Midwest, but plenty cold enough for a coastal city whose winter daytime temps usually ran in the mid-forties. The bizarre weather had killed people: nine deaths by asphyxia—people trying to heat their homes with barbecues and open flame heaters; two by falling trees that crushed motorists; and one by drowning in a flooded basement office. I was lucky to have been too far away from any of those events to feel them propagate through the energy grid of the Grey—I'd felt the delayed shock of one person's death earlier that year, and I hoped to avoid ever feeling such a thing again. Even without that it had been a rather grim holiday season and the cold wasn't letting up now that it was January.

"I was chasing a killer," I continued. I'd said it before and I was a little galled at having the conversation yet again. In fact, I'd been running away, but the circumstances of that weren't something Will would be able to swallow. I had been running with the intention of leading something into a trap—chasing it from in front, in a way.

"It's not your job to chase murderers. That's what the cops are for. You aren't a cop. You don't have to do that."

"Sometimes I'm not in the position of saying 'That's not my responsibility,' Will. I can't arbitrarily stop at the legal limit and ignore what's morally right. Come on . . . you were at the final hearing—the guy was a whack-job. Should I have let him get away to kill those other people?"

I could tell he was trying to find a way to say yes without sounding like a jerk. I can be selfish, but not that much, and I didn't want to hear that I should be, so I tried to redirect the conversation. "Would you get me the five-pound hand weights off the rack?"

Will sighed and went to fetch the two small rubber-coated barbells. I admired his bright silver hair and his lanky frame as he loped across the room, but I still found myself heaving an exasperated sigh of my own. Where we once struck sparks, it seemed we could now only strike prickles. It didn't help that I could see his frustration with me—it radiated around him in spikes of orange and red energy visible to my Grey-sensitive sight.

I couldn't shut the Grey out anymore; the best I could do was keep it enough at bay to know what was physically present to normal people and what wasn't—I didn't want to fall over real objects to avoid unreal ones. As a result, the gym looked to me like a steamroom haunted by layers of history and gleaming with a light show of neon energy and emotional sparks. I paid no attention to a bloated specter that lurked near the pull-up bars, but I also refused to use them.

The ghostly world was always with me and it was yet another chafing veil between me and Will—him so normal and me so . . . not. I'd tried to tear through some of those layers over the holidays, but it only made me seem crazy, which increased the distance between us. Neither of us were happy with that and unhappiness had soured into an abrasive that chafed Will into wrongheaded prying and me into silent resentment.

Will returned with the hand weights and I started doing slow lateral lifts to rebuild the muscles of my injured shoulder. I did the other arm as well, figuring I might as well get my money's worth out of the gym time. It wasn't as convenient as running, but it was more comprehensive—and seeing all those trim and toned gym rats plucked at my competitive side and reminded me of my athletic past.

Maybe Will was more in touch with the Grey than I'd credited and had picked up on my thoughts. As he watched me work out, he said, "If you keep this up, you could go back to dancing professionally."

"Too old," I said, panting between lifts.

"You're thirty-two."

I puffed and put the weights down for a short rest between sets. "For a pro dancer, thirty's old. Thirty-five is ancient and forty is the walking dead. Baryshnikov and Hines might have been able to dance in their fifties, but they danced continuously from the age of nine. I started younger, but I quit when I was twenty-four. I never wanted to make a career of it and I've only kept up my moves as an amateur."

"You could teach. . . ."

I glared at him. "Will. Let it go. I worked hard to be good at my job—the job I chose to do—and I'm not going to give it up over a few injuries and freaks." I picked up the weights again and started on my last set. Any exhilaration I felt from working out had burned off under the heat of my growing irritation. Leaving professional dance was no loss to me: I'd hated it. It had been my mother's dream forced upon me from the time I was little. Useful but not beloved, and I didn't miss the pain, the paranoia, or the dieting.

"I'm not asking you to change jobs—"

"No. You're *hinting* that I should." Breathe, Harper, nice and slow, I reminded myself—it kept both my temper and the Grey in check enough that I could keep going. "You get me as I am or you don't get me at all." I finished my set and took the weights back to the rack. I didn't even limp, which was my consolation prize, I guess, since the day itself was starting out so crappy.

Will stayed where he was and watched me. I knew he didn't like that I'd been hurt and I knew he was confused as to why I'd want to stay in a business that had suddenly turned violent after years of routine. He didn't understand all the strangeness that collected around me. How was I supposed to explain that I didn't have a choice about it? That it was better for me to stay in my job, where I had the autonomy and skills to maintain my independence and keep at least some of the Grey things in line, than to end up a pawn—or dead—by some monster's whim? And I liked my job, damn it—most of the time.

I walked back to Will and looked up at him. "I have to shower and get to work." I schooled myself and waited. I didn't want to upset him, no matter how irritated I was. It wasn't his fault. Was it?

"Mm," Will grumbled.

"Hey, at least it's safe and boring—just a bunch of witness backgrounds for Nanette Grover and some financials." I put my arm around his waist and turned toward the locker rooms. I hoped he'd take the gesture as a sign of truce, even though I wasn't feeling very peaceable. At least I was trying.

"Yeah . . . I have to do some work, too." Will laid his arm over my shoulders, careful not to put any weight on the dicey one, and walked with me.

At the doors he stopped and turned, putting both arms around me in a loose hug, looking down from his six-foot-plus height and making me feel delicate. The overhead lights glared off his eyeglass lenses. "Maybe we could get together for a late lunch?" he asked.

I pasted on a smile. "OK."

He leaned down and kissed me. "I'll come by your office about . . . two?"

"Two's good. I'll see you then."

"I'll call you when I'm close." He kissed me again, squeezed a little, and stepped back. I turned away, feeling odd, and went to shower.

I washed and dressed and headed out to my old Land Rover to drive to my office in Pioneer Square, thinking about the strangeness. The rhythm of our relationship hadn't ever been truly on beat—we'd always had some personal concern between us or some distance keeping us apart. The togetherness that I'd hoped would put us in sync didn't seem to be doing anything of the kind. It was like trying to dance samba while the band was playing "Dixie"—you can almost do it, but it's uncomfortable as hell and you look like an idiot.

On the drive, there was ice on every horizontal surface. The roads were mostly dry enough to negotiate during the day, but inside my parking garage, the floors were slick. I had to place my feet with care as I walked from the Rover to the sidewalk.

It didn't help that Pioneer Square is the most haunted area of Seattle, and the ice hid under a silver fog of ghosts and memory. I walked flat-footed and slowly and made it to the doors of my office building.

I considered using the elevator and giving my knee a break, but I still don't feel quite comfortable around the old-fashioned lifts since I was killed with one. Double gates and polished brass give me the creeps now. I walked up and was grateful to sit down in my desk chair once I reached it. Some days the climb is nothing to my bum knee, but with the cold, it seemed much worse. Even my shoulder was twinging a bit. Between the physical discomforts and the emotional ones, I was glad to have work to distract me and I plunged into it.

I didn't notice the time so, when someone tapped on my door, I assumed it was Will and called out, "Come in!" without looking up. My cell phone buzzed on my hip as the alarm went off, telling me the door was open. I turned it off and looked up, smiling, faking a bit more enthusiasm than I felt, and then frowning with surprise.

Quinton put his backpack on the floor and shot me a crippled grin. Like Will, I'd met Quinton when my world changed. Since he'd discreetly and quietly installed the office alarm, he'd become my regular go-to guy for anything electronic, especially if it was odd or hush-hush. A little secretive, quirky, distinctly geeky, he fit well with my own taciturn nature and we'd been instant friends— and unlike with Will, I didn't have to hide the creepy stuff from him. Now he stood just inside the doorway and looked as if he wasn't sure of his welcome.

"Oh. Hi," I said, letting my curiosity draw a little silence between us.

"Hi," he said, shifting from foot to foot. His usual ease had been replaced with an unhappy nervousness and a swirling mist of smoky green, mottled like some kind of sick mold, wrapped around him in the Grey, clinging to his long coat. "Umm . . . Harper. I—there's a—err . . . Can you come look at something?"

"Now?" I asked, glancing my watch. It was 1:12. Less than an hour until lunch with Will.

"Well, yeah. Now would be good. This is kind of important."

I found myself standing up and reaching for my own coat without giving it any thought. I owed Quinton, I liked him, and I'd only seen him nervous and jumpy once—not even vampires caused him to lose his cool—so whatever was bugging him had to be nasty. "What's the problem?"

"I really want you to see it first—before anyone else gets to it. I don't want to give you false information because I don't know what's going on myself."

"All right. Where are we going?"

"The train tunnel."

"Oh, goody," I said, grabbing my bag. "Frozen gravel and garbage. My favorite." In spite of my cynical tone, I felt a little tickle of pleasure at getting out from under the paperwork on my desk.

"Uh . . . Are you carrying?"

"Is that going to be a problem?"

He looked relieved and hiked his backpack up on to his shoulders. "No, no. I just want to be sure. Just in case."

That piqued my caution and curiosity. I followed him out the door and paused to lock it behind us. "In case of what? Is this going to get hot?"

"Shouldn't, but . . . I don't know what's going on, so I figure it's better to be prepared."

I nodded and we went downstairs and out of the building.

Quinton hurried me along but said very little as we wound our way through the historic district and down to King Street Station. Since lunchtime was over and the commuter trains hadn't yet started the evening runs, the train yard and rails near the station weren't busy. Quinton led me up to the Sounder train entrance at Fourth Avenue north of the train station.

"Why here?" I asked as we worked our way down the stairs toward the platform. My knee felt stiff but it wasn't throbbing, and I thanked my foresight in putting on the goofy-looking elastic brace under my jeans.

"It's closer to the tunnel than going through the station, and the platform personnel won't see us if we swing around the bottom and stay behind the stairs while we walk. They don't care that much since there're no freights at this time of day, but they're supposed to run you off if you're down on the grade."

"I don't think anyone's going to come out of that nice warm station if they can avoid it."

"Probably not," he agreed, "but we don't want them to get interested in us."

"You're being very mysterious about this," I commented, ducking around the bottom of the stairs and onto the tracks in his wake. He kept his personal life to himself, but this sort of dodginess was unlike him and it intrigued me even more than what we might be approaching.

We began crunching through the gravel and cinder toward the mouth of the Great Northern Tunnel, our breath coming up in puffs that vanished rapidly in the cold, dry air. It was a distance of about a block, but it felt longer. There were concrete walls on each side that held up the streets and buildings above and made the stretch from the stairs to the tunnel mouth seem close and claustrophobic even with the blue-white winter sky above us. A few crows cawed at us from the street railings, but the area was surprisingly uncluttered with Grey things.

"Have there ever been any accidents in this tunnel?" I asked as we neared the portal.

Quinton looked back at me, startled. "Only a couple that I know of. Nothing spectacular and gory, though. No deaths or fires. Why?"

"I don't see anything—that's strange. This tunnel's—what—a hundred years old or so?"

"About that," he replied, ducking into the darkness.

I followed him, putting my left hand on the cement wall as I went. The cold was shocking, but not preternaturally so. I wished I had gloves on. The interior of the tunnel was like a freezer and I shivered as I went forward.

Once we were a short distance from the station, I heard Quinton's coat flap and rattle. A light snapped on and he directed the beam against the corner where the wall met the floor. A few feet farther away a dark stain seemed to have grown on the wall. As we got closer, I saw it was a hole.

The cement lining the tunnel was about four feet thick at that point, but someone had managed to make a hole through it about two feet across and three feet high. Lying at the foot of the hole was a dead man, scruffily bearded and dressed in ragged layers of filthy clothing. One of his legs was missing from mid-thigh down.

I stepped back, repelled. "Damn, Quinton . . . He must have been hit by a train." I've seen bodies before, but this one upset me more than I cared to admit. There was something wrong about its disposition that unnerved me and urged me to flee.

Quinton shook his head. "I don't think so. There's no blood. And if you look at the wound . . . it kind of looks . . . chewed."

In spite of myself, I moved forward and peered at the poorly illuminated corpse. The leg ended in a gnawed stump, and though
it was hard to be sure with the amount of dirt on his clothes,
there truly didn't seem to be any blood. He stunk of filth and
smoke, but the guy hadn't been dead very long. Even discount-
ing the cold and the darkness and the indifference of the station
crew, someone would have spotted him if he'd been lying there
for more than a day. He also had a shroud of Grey clinging to him
and raveling away into the hole.

I took another step closer and looked harder at the hole, professional curiosity fully engaged. The edges flickered with ethe-
real strands of something Grey, gleaming with a soft white and
pale yellow luminescence. Although the pall of energy lying over
the corpse was suitably black—black for death, I thought—the
strands that led away from it and into the hole were a neutral gray
that looked as soft as angora. I shuddered at the idea, but I reached
out and rubbed a bit of the nearest strand between my fingers. To
me, Grey material usually feels icy cold, alive, and electrified, but
aside from a cottony sensation, I couldn't feel anything this time.
I touched my finger to one of the brighter bits adhering to the
broken edges of the cement and got a mild tingle from it as it
wriggled aside like a worm on a sidewalk. I tried to look into the
hole, but I couldn't get my head craned around far enough with
the body lying where it was.

"It goes all the way back into the basement of the building on
the other side," Quinton said, watching me.

I glanced at him. "How do you know?"

He turned his face away from mine. "I crawled into it."

"All right," I said, straightening up. "I'd like to know how you
happened to find him. This isn't exactly a public thoroughfare."

Quinton kept his mouth shut.

I sighed and thought of Will's admonishments of the morning. "I'd better call the cops."

"I'd rather you didn't just yet."

"What?"

A rumbling sound started far away and a rhythmic vibration set the gravel on the tunnel floor to chattering.

"Train. C'mon!"

Quinton grabbed my wrist and hauled me along as he started running back the way we'd come.

We dashed out of the tunnel and cut to the side, pressing ourselves to the wall outside the opening, just a few feet ahead of a shrieking freight train. Something pale flipped and tumbled through the air from beneath the engine's wheels, landing on the gravel barely a yard from us. It was an arm.

Quinton's eyes widened and he looked sick. I wanted to gag but swallowed the urge. There was something particularly awful about that mangled, lonely limb lying on the gravel outside the Great Northern Tunnel, but puking wasn't going to improve the situation.

"That's it," I said, pulling my cell phone off my belt. "I'm calling the cops."

Quinton clamped his hand over mine. He was sweating, though I didn't know how anyone could in that cold air. "No! Not now. Please."

I shook his hand off mine and gaped at him. "Why the hell not? That's a dead body—a dead person—in there—"

"He's not the first!"

Damn it, I thought. I clipped my phone back on my belt and crossed my arms over my chest, glaring at him. It seemed like a better idea than screaming and trying to run away. I had trusted Quinton with secrets and lives—including mine—but I realized then that I knew very little about him. And now he was showing me bodies in tunnels and saying they weren't the first. . . . I let one hand drift down my side toward my holster. "Talk fast," I said.

"Just give me a chance to get out of sight," he said. "I don't want the cops to know I'm connected to this."

"Connected to what? And what is it with you and cops?"

He looked around, but no one was coming out of the station to investigate us, nor was anyone stopping on the icy sidewalk above us. Any pedestrians were too anxious to get out of the cold to pause and look down at the gravel by the tunnel mouth. "Look, this guy, he's not the first dead body to turn up around Pioneer Square since the big storm. I knew some of them. And there was that article in the papers about the leg found in that construction site near the football stadium—you read about that, right?"

"Yeah. They never found the guy it came from. So?"

"Something nasty is happening and I'm afraid they'll connect me to it."

"Why? You wanted me to see this, but you don't want it reported. What kind of connection do you have to this? What the hell is going on?" I generally prefer anger over fear.

"I don't know what's going on, but I want it to stop and I don't want the cops digging around in the underground over this—or at least not digging around me."

"If you think someone is killing bums, that has to be reported to the police. That's what they do—find the people who prey on other people."

"What if it's not a person?"

"What?" I demanded, feeling colder inside than out.

Quinton started to reply, but my phone burred and cut him off. I swore and snatched it from my belt, glaring at Quinton and pointing at him with my other hand. "Hold that thought."

I flipped the phone open and answered it.

"Hey, Harper, it's Will. You ready for lunch?"

"Will?" Crap. I sneaked a look at my watch. It was eight minutes past two. "I'm at the train station—"

"I'm just outside Zeitgeist. I'll walk down there."

"No!" But he'd hung up already. Zeitgeist Coffee was two blocks from the tunnel. With Will's long stride, it wouldn't take five minutes for him to reach the train station. He'd spot us on the gravel as soon as he came around the corner. And he'd spot the arm.

I jammed the phone into my coat pocket with stiff hands and looked at Quinton.

"We have a problem if you don't want the cops all over this. I have to run into the station. You stay here and block the view so no one sees that arm. I'll be right back and we'll pick up where we left off. Don't ditch me. If I have to hunt you down to get the rest of this story, you won't like it."

He nodded and shuffled closer to the arm as I scuffed back through the gravel to the station as fast as I could.

Will was just coming into the rotunda as I trotted across the main floor. He caught me by the shoulders as I reached him and frowned at me.

"Harper, you're limping. Are you OK?"

"I had to take a look at something down here and the ground's pretty rough. I lost track of time. I'm sorry." Apologies don't come easy and it must have sounded as strange to Will as it did to me.

His frown remained as he stared into my face. "You're skipping out on lunch, aren't you?"

I pulled in a slow breath. "I have to wait for the police."

He blinked. "Why? What's happened?"

"I can't tell you yet. I have to talk to them first. I'll call you when I'm done and we can do dinner instead."

"I can wait with you."

"No—" I stopped myself. If I just told him to go, he'd get balky. "It may take quite a while. It's going to be ugly work and I know you don't like this kind of thing. I'd be happier if you didn't waste your day hanging around here."

"How long will it take, this mysterious, ugly thing?"

"I don't know. If it's quick, then that's great, but I just don't know."

Will sighed. Déjà vu. Just like our first date, with me running out on him for some mysterious errand. I knew it ticked him off and that ticked me off. "This job of yours . . ."

My turn to sigh. "Yes. I know. You wish I did something else."

"No. No, I just wish—" He stopped and shook his head. "Dinner. We'll get together for dinner. It's fine."

"Fine" it obviously wasn't, but I'd have to deal with that later. Severed limbs and Grey holes in concrete walls had a higher priority to me than Will's sense of betrayal over a missed lunch. Dating sucked.

"Thank you, Will." I locked my arms around him as he started to turn away and pulled him down for a kiss. "I'll make it up to you. I promise." I felt like I was kissing ice that only started to warm up and flow at the end. Then he stepped back and walked off, giving me a quick wave and a thin smile as he went. My shoulders slumped and an unpleasant pricking of tears started behind my eyes.

I growled at myself. "Don't be a jackass." I straightened up and hurried back to the tunnel.

Quinton was crouching near the arm, facing away from it. He was tense and the Grey gathered around him in clinging sulfur-colored ropes. His expression was an anxious frown as he watched me return.

"So?" he asked, straightening up.

"I am going to call the police, but if you explain this to me, I may keep you out of it. Tell me why you don't want the cops to know about you and what your connection is to the dead man."

He drew a couple of long, deep breaths before he began, the tension in his face easing.

"I know him—knew him. There've been several deaths down here since the weather got crazy. They've all been homeless, street people, undergrounders like that guy in the tunnel. And I know them because I'm one, too. An undergrounder, that is. Homeless by choice."

"Fugitive?" I asked. I had to wonder who I'd gotten hooked up with.

"Kind of. Fugitive by conscience, you could say. Certain government people don't like me and I don't want them to find me now, but I don't want to see more of this stuff. Dead people in alleys and sewers and in the subterranean places. I want to cover my ass, but . . . not at that cost. Most of the deaths have been written off as accidents—just old drunks and nutcases who didn't come in out of the cold and died of exposure. I don't think they've connected the leg in the construction site to the bodies in Pioneer Square alleys, but I saw those, too. All the things I saw looked like that guy—bitten on. Chewed. With the bodies, the cops said it was dogs, but you saw that guy's leg—that's no dog bite. The leg in the construction site was the same way. Something is eating these people."

TWO

Monsters in the sewers . . . As I waited for the police, I knew I wasn't going to try that idea on them. There was an undeniable Grey element to the body in the Great Northern Tunnel, but I knew from experience that wild stories attributing crimes to the paranormal wouldn't endear me. I wasn't sure how I was going to keep Quinton out of it—or why I'd agreed to try—but I'd do my best. I didn't think he'd had anything to do with the body other than stumbling across it, and I didn't see much to be gained in alienating him by siccing the police on him. The thing I couldn't answer for myself was why I was waiting around at all. It was freezing in the frost-bound shade of the train yard, below the street level, and I was shivering and stamping, trying to figure out a plausible story to tell the police when they arrived, and guarding the arm from a small murder of curious crows—the biggest crows I'd ever seen.

Three of the birds had swooped down to walk around on the gravel and assess the situation. They kept themselves spaced around me so I had to turn constantly to keep one from darting in while I tried to keep an eye on the other two. One of them cocked its head and glared at me with a baleful yellow eye, cawing and clacking its beak.

"Shove off, Lenore," I snapped back. "Not only 'nevermore' but never at all. Go bother a poet somewhere."

I heard something scuffling through the gravel behind me. The crows shouted their disappointment and jumped into the air with a clatter of wings and beaks. I turned to see a small procession of Seattle PD and rail yard employees approaching my position. I stifled a despairing groan at the sight of the man in the lead: Detective Solis.

"You talk to birds?" he asked as he drew near.

"Only when they talk to me first."

I respect Solis; he's smart, he's honest, and he's tenacious. Everything I really didn't want to face right then. My only consolation was that the wiry Colombian looked even more miserable in the cold than I felt. I hoped I could use that to my advantage. He grunted in acknowledgment and glanced around me.

"This is the limb?" he asked, spotting the severed arm by my feet.

"Yeah."

He motioned for one of the men to come forward and deal with the sad scrap of flesh and bone while he started to walk me to the side of the scene. "How did you come to find it?"

Showtime . . .

"I was crossing the bridge up there," I said, pointing up to the street, "and I saw it flung out from under a train."

"Why did you come to look at it? Why not keep going?"

"It was freaky. There was something wrong about the shape, and when I looked harder, I saw what it was. I couldn't leave it lying there. So I came down."

"Have you been standing here the whole time since you called?"

"Since I called, yes. But I started to go up the tunnel before I realized I shouldn't. So I came back out and went into the station."

"Why did you go into the station?"

I sighed, feeling uncomfortable and reluctant to stray too far from the facts, but equally unhappy about speaking some of them. "I had to meet my boyfriend—we were supposed to have lunch— but I had to break the date to wait for you guys. He wanted to argue about it and came down here. I didn't want him to come out and see the arm and freak out, so I went in to him. He left after a couple of minutes and I came back out."

I glanced back toward the arm. The man Solis had directed to it was laying markers on the gravel around the severed limb and playing with his camera. I turned my head back to Solis.

He frowned. "And the arm was just as you'd left it?"

"Yes. I wanted to check farther up the tunnel, but once the crows came down, I thought I shouldn't leave."

"What is up the tunnel?" Solis asked.

I snorted. "I have no idea, but the arm has to have come from somewhere nearby or it would be a lot more ripped up by being caught in the train's wheels for any distance—the tunnel's about a mile long, so I'd guess the arm got under the train somewhere in that distance. Has anyone from the station reported an injury on the train that came through or any accidents in the tunnel?"

"I can't say. Yours was the first report we've had." He raised his head to look toward the opening. Then he glanced around the gravel and tracks nearby, seeming to take a quick survey of the situation.

The large-sized gravel wouldn't show any footprints, and it hadn't developed much of an ice coating to trap fibers and blood on the surface. There wouldn't be much physical evidence out here. If Solis was going to get anything useful, he'd get it from the hole in the wall or the slab-cold tunnel floor. I doubted he'd find much, and there would be pressure to close the file quickly once they realized the victim wasn't a taxpayer—unless he turned up as a missing person, which would change everything.

Solis looked back at me and sighed. "This has been an ill season. Like the weather, it seems people have gone mad. I could wish for less of this kind of thing to go with all the rest." He shook his head. "You can go, Ms. Blaine. I know where to contact you. Unless there's anything else you want to say now?"

I resisted an urge to be flippant and shook my own head. "No. I just want to get inside where it's warm and thaw out."

A little scowl and a flare of orange annoyance prefaced his nod of dismissal. I wasn't too proud to scurry for the nearest heated room and leave Solis and his minions to the cold work of scouring for evidence. I knew he'd take my hint and go into the tunnel to find the body—he's thorough and he probably would have done it anyway. I was glad I wouldn't have to look at it again and see whatever grisly damage the train had added to what was already there.

This time, I didn't take the stairs but went through the lobby of King Street Station. Outside, I glanced back toward the tunnel and saw Solis standing at the mouth of the hole bored through the hill. He was talking to one of the train yard men, and their conversation sent ripples of red fear or anger through the layers of the Grey around them. At my distance, I didn't know which one of them was causing the disturbance. Solis was usually contained and quiet, but I'd seen his bright orange frustration earlier, and this wasn't the right color. Maybe the yard man was obstructing him, or perhaps it was the yard man who was angry.

Before I could speculate further, I heard the hoot of a train and saw one of the Sounder commuters edging forward to begin its afternoon run north. It must have been after three, and I realized that Solis might not be able to secure the scene much longer. In the collective mind of the railroad and Sound Transit, I imagined, dead bums took a backseat to middle-class working stiffs at rush hour, and even the SPD doesn't tangle with the transit system— and its politically powerful management—if they can avoid it. Even cops have to pick their battles at times.

I turned my back and walked west, squinting into a sudden beam of the early sunset that cut between the buildings. Standing in the cold had made my knee stiff and I found myself limping as I walked the six blocks back to my office.

I didn't feel like dodging the first-round drunks on Second, so I walked over to Occidental and went up the broad, car-free boulevard that had once been the heart of Seattle's vice district. Now it housed quaint galleries and shops and overpriced "pubs" whose "bangers and mash" were actually CasCioppo Brothers Italian sausages with a side of skin-on red potatoes mashed with garlic. The last bastion of Seattle's original sin on Occidental was Temple Billiards, where lately the coat racks had begun to sprout leather jackets with designer labels more often than those with studs and chains. I was tired, and although it's not the safest street in Seattle, "Oxy" was one place it was safe to let the Grey come upon me as it would, so I could relax my usual efforts to differentiate the normal from the Grey and just walk.

Even with gentrification, Occidental Avenue hadn't changed much physically since the city finally finished the streets and sidewalks in the early 1900s. During some later civic fit of historic preservation, an open park paved with reclaimed white bricks as big and uneven as giant's teeth had been added at the north end where there once was a parking lot. The rest of the three-block stretch above the stadium had been restored to its original bricked and cobbled plane to match, so I ran no risk of suddenly stumbling into a Grey gap between the old street level and the new. The most dangerous things were the ice-slicked bricks and the possibility of running into someone—Grey or normal—with bad breath and a chip on their shoulder.

It was getting dark between the rows of historic brick-and-stone buildings, and the quaint three-globe iron streetlamps were powering up to cast oblong pools of light onto the cobbles. Even in the gloom I could see the transparent memory-shape of a statue that had stood in the middle of the mall during the 1990s: a life-size bronze cow with a howling coyote perched on its back. Crowds of ghosts moved up and down the mall, mostly men going in and out of the former saloons, box houses, and brothels. Dim signs advertised various services from assaying to while-you-wait tailoring—though there were an awful lot of those for such a sleazy district, and I had to wonder what exactly was being "altered" in these catchpenny shops.

I paused by the shadowy cow and watched the ghost of a Klondike-era whore stroll eternally up and down the brick sidewalk. She paid me no attention, nor did most of the other specters: they were no more than recursive whorls of time in the city's memory of itself.

Most ghosts are like that, just memory loops or fragments of time, having no will and no volition. It's the other kinds—the thinking and acting kinds—that cause trouble. Which brought me back to the problem of the dead guy in the tunnel. There hadn't been a ghost attending him, no sense of shock, or even a lingering presence of death except in the color of the Grey material that clung to him, and his odor had been a perfectly mortal stench, not magical corruption. I'm no necromancer, so I can't pick up information about someone's death from the atmosphere or objects. If they've died violently where I'm standing, I may feel shock and pain, but unless there's a repeating time loop, I can't get more than that—I don't *know* anything. But there'd been nothing to know as well as nothing to feel. It was as if the man had died elsewhere and been carried to the tunnel, or had somehow simply ceased to exist without any shock of death at all and left his body behind, missing one leg. It was confusing and I didn't like it.

Maybe it had been his leg found in the construction pit near the football stadium, I mused. That site was just a few blocks south of where I stood near the former bronze cow. But the leg had been found weeks ago and the body hadn't shown signs of decomposition that I'd noticed—he'd looked like he had been dead a day at most. It was cold now, but it had been warmer and wetter when the leg was found. If it was his leg, there should have been rot whether he'd been dead or alive when he lost it. If the leg wasn't his, where was his own? And who or what had made that hole in the side of the tunnel?

I wandered forward, toward the park and my office building beyond it, thinking more than observing. Had he just frozen to death? When was the leg removed? Who was he and how did Quinton come to know him?

Movement among the shadows drew my attention back to the street. I'd come to the Main Street intersection without noticing. The open space of the park with its two avenues of plane trees lay just across the brickwork road. Clusters of men and women gathered under the square glass shelter on the south end or stood in knots near the totems on the north side, jigging and hugging themselves against the cold. Fires had been started in trash cans, but those wouldn't last long before the beat cops or the firemen came by. The figures were all bulky and brown in layers of old clothes that no amount of washing would ever make bright again. Even at a distance I recognized a few of them. I saw them around the Square and near my office all the time. Denizens of streets and alleys, some of them drug users, many of them alcoholics, all of them homeless.

I spotted the old man I'd come to know as "Zip"—I'd returned his prized Zippo cigarette lighter to him back in October when a poltergeist snatched it to fling at me—huddling near the glass picnic house with a crowd of rough-looking younger men. They were passing a paper bag around with small, underhand gestures, sharing the bottle within but still sober enough to attempt discretion. There was the talking man who marched back and forth angrily in front of the killer whale totem, muttering in an incomprehensible language. A huge Native American woman sat at the feet of the giant carving of a female figure nearby and watched him, laughing to herself and shuffling through her bags of collected treasures before returning them to a rattletrap wire cart. A group of anonymous, mouselike people gathered in somber contemplation of their trash fire near the remaining parking lot on the east side of the park, looking as if they'd been outcast even by the outcast. Soon they'd all head for the homeless shelters and missions, hoping for food and a bed for the night. Those who couldn't get in to the crowded facilities would try to find places out of the cold to sleep until morning, or until a cop rousted them. Thinking of what Quinton had said, I wondered how many of them might not wake up, and I shivered. In a fit of pity and guilt, I dug into my pockets and handed over my change to the first panhandler who asked.

I noticed other pedestrians avoiding the park altogether, hurrying to warmer, safer places. The presence of poverty and apparent hopelessness frightened them, or maybe they, too, sensed the disturbed and conflicting emotions that roiled in the Grey over the park in combative colors and streamers of cold. Chilled through, I started across Main and through the park, keeping to the middle where the path was the most even and the eddies of Grey tumult thinnest.

I was almost to the pair of totem poles at the north end—where the talking man was pacing—when something darted out from behind the giant bear totem on my right. It cackled and giggled and I whirled to face it: a hunched figure in clothes so ragged they looked like streamers of matted fur that flowed out from under his long hair and beard.

"Lady, lady," the man called out, reaching for me as he darted closer. A Grey stink of sulfur and sewage and a hard, metallic tang like blood and steel swirled around me as he came within clutching distance, creating weirdly twisting vortices in the layers of Grey that blanketed the park.

I gasped and jumped back with a shock of recognition. This man—this thing—had come running for me before. In an alley nearby, he—it—had asked if I were dead and tried to drag me into the Grey, back when I didn't know there was such a thing. The last time I'd seen the . . . whatever it was, I thought it was just a drunk in an alley, but now I knew the Grey better and I could see it wasn't a real man at all—not a ghost but some more corporeal eldritch thing. I reached for a fold in the Grey and yanked it between us, making a shield against the creature.

Where other things would and had fallen aside, its hand pushed through my shield as if it were no more than mist. I felt its cold fingertip touch my hand. It stopped without apparent momentum and raised its head, breathing a reek of rot into my face. Beneath its dreadlocked mane, the face was now half destroyed, twisted with barely healed scars on the right side that almost hid one terrible emerald eye.

It stared at me and I stared back, unable to fight it this time as its uncanny gaze held me. It peered at me as if it could see into my soul—if I have one—sighing as though relieved of some pain.

It drew in a deep breath and said, "Dead enough, lady. Yes." It moved its filthy hand to my chest and made a patting motion of satisfaction. I felt the touch ripple through my rib cage and down my limbs. Then it laughed and scampered away in its queer, hunched posture, showing a back as recently and horribly scarred as its face.

I stumbled back and felt the cold bricks slipping under my boots as I started to fall. A quick scramble kept me up inelegantly, and I caught a mouthful of icy air, not realizing I hadn't breathed during the encounter. I looked around, but there were no other strange creatures lurking nearby to ambush me, and none of the pedestrians hurrying away from the cold nor the homeless people huddling over their fires had paused to stare at the scene. The only person showing me any attention at all was the massive woman under the female totem, and she merely guffawed and waved as if my near pratfall was the funniest thing she'd seen all day. In spite of her merriment, I felt shaken and had to stand still a moment before I could continue the last block to my office.

The creature hadn't hurt me—and I had no idea what it had wanted either time we'd met—but I was still unnerved. I couldn't imagine what its sudden appearance meant, but I was pretty sure I wouldn't like it when I found out. I tried to put it out of my mind as I climbed the stairs to my office, wincing as my knee complained. Discomfort quickly got the upper hand on speculation, and by the time I sat down to call Will for dinner, I'd pushed the incident aside but not completely out of my thoughts.

Will answered quickly, but he sounded a bit annoyed.

"Hi. Am I calling at a bad time?" I asked.

"Harper. No." He took an audible breath and mellowed his voice. "I'm down under Alaskan Way at an old friend's shop. It's just—" Something crashed, sounding like a load of timber falling on a wooden dock, and a distant voice cursed. Will muttered something away from the phone before returning to our conversation. "I think he's just broken a vintage phone box. So. Are you free for dinner?"

"Yes, I am. How 'bout you?"

"Not only free, but eager to get out of here and meet you."

I smiled a little in response. "How 'bout the Bookstore?"

"I thought you wanted food. . . ."

"No, silly man. It's a bar in the Alexis Hotel lobby at First and Madison. Good pub food, lots of old books on the walls, nice old wood furniture . . ."

He made a disgusted noise. "I hate places that use books by the yard as 'interior decoration.' "

"They're real books and you can take them out and read them—they'll even let you buy them. Phoebe told me they bought them out from under her at a liquidation sale when one of the other used bookstores went out of business."

"Well . . ." he said, still sounding dubious about it. "OK. I guess I can try it. I'll meet you there in . . . fifteen minutes?"

"OK," I agreed, but I found myself frowning as I hung up and started to gather my things together.

Will and I both liked old things and I'd thought the tiny bar and restaurant full of good old wood furniture and books would be pleasant, but now I wasn't so sure. I didn't remember much about the decor of the first place we'd eaten together—I'd been too interested in Will and thankful for not being hit by a car to care about it. It was frustrating to be always just a bit off—had he always been so picky? I didn't think so. . . . But maybe dining together wasn't our best skill, considering how often our meals had coincided with various unpleasant events.

Knowing I might not find a better parking space closer to the hotel, I walked down to First and caught a bus. I saw Will going into the restaurant as I got off at Madison.

Inside, I found Will seated at a small wooden table in a nook near the back—where the heat was. Even with double glazing, the tables near the large front windows were too cold to sit next to. Will grinned at me and I smiled back on the sudden surge of remembered giddiness I'd felt when we first met. It was a sweet, warm feeling I wanted to hold on to a little longer. I shucked off my extra layers and sat down across from him as the waiter handed us menus and left us alone.

"Hi, there," I said.

"Hello, beautiful."

My face got hot. I'm way too tall and tomboyish for that description, but the warm setting lifted my spirits more than I'd expected and I took the compliment as a sign there might yet be hope for us.

"How did your day go?" I asked.

He smiled at my corny question. "It was pretty good. I visited a friend in the business and he asked me to look at some stuff for him. And we found this."

He picked up a white plastic bag from the seat beside him and handed it to me. "It reminded me of you."

I made a mock frown and took the bag, reaching inside to pull out a wooden ball about the size of a large grapefruit. Then I really did frown. There was something strange about it, but I couldn't figure out what—it didn't have an obvious Grey gleam or anything like that; it was just . . . odd. The surface was covered with sharply etched rectangular segments, and as I turned it over something rattled inside. I noticed a little threaded cylinder inset into the ball to screw it onto a post of some kind.

As I was staring at the ball, the waiter approached and I put it aside to order. As soon as he was gone, I picked the ball up again.

"What is it?" I asked.

"It's a puzzle box," Will replied. "Charlie found it in an old house he was taking apart up in Leavenworth. Someone had used a pair of them for decorations on the newel posts of a staircase. Neither of us had ever seen round ones like that before and it was kind of a strange way to use them, so he asked me about them. But I couldn't tell him anything except that the wood seems to be teak and the threaded cylinders are much newer than the boxes. Charlie gave me that one for my time and I thought you might like it—kind of mysterious and pretty with some kind of secret inside."

"What's in it?"

"Don't know. We couldn't get it to open. But, you know . . ." he added, blushing a little and shifting his eyes away, "I've learned that not every secret has to be revealed." He let his gaze move back to mine.

I looked back down at the round puzzle box. "So . . ." I started, "umm . . . this is the Harper box?"

He looked so nervous that I started to giggle. Then we were both laughing, and he reached across the table and took my hand and kissed the back. The gesture was so overtly romantic and so out of character for the recent state of our relationship that it startled me. The arrival of the waiter broke us apart and covered my bewilderment.

Conversation became more mundane while we tended to our food. We were almost done and waiting for coffee when curiosity got the better of him.

"So," Will started, "what happened at the train station?" Then he added very quickly, "You don't have to tell me. This is just like, 'Hey, honey, how was your day?' "

I shook my head, still smiling a little. I didn't mind that he was interested. I just wasn't going to tell him the whole truth, and that I did mind. "It wasn't too bad, so long as you don't mind the high ick factor," I replied. "Some homeless man turned up dead in the train tunnel. I found him while I was looking for someone else and I couldn't leave until the police got there and we discussed it. I'm sure the railroad isn't thrilled about it, but the SPD didn't order me to keep it quiet, so I guess it's just a sad accident."

"In the tunnel." He looked a little green.

"Yeah. I figured you didn't need to see it." I let the subject drop and changed direction. "I like your day better. How 'bout you tell me more about puzzle boxes?"

"That one's really unusual," he started, pointing at the ball on the table beside me. His eyes began to shine as he went on. Will loved these sorts of odd old objects—and it had been the more accessible mysteries of things like this that had taken him to England and away from the uncomfortable quandary of my strangeness. "Most puzzle boxes are square- or cube-shaped, and the famous Japanese ones have intricately inlaid surface patterns to obscure the moving parts. Normally, I'd call something like this one—a round one—a burr puzzle, but those aren't hollow and puzzle boxes aren't usually round, so this is a hybrid."

I sank into the warm rhythm of his speech, watched his pleasure in the conversation turn the aura around his head a bright gold, and didn't think about dead men in tunnels for a while and wished this quiet moment wasn't doomed to end.

THREE

As we left the restaurant, stepping back out into the deepened cold made more frigid by comparison with the cozy warmth we'd left, I tucked the puzzle ball into my bag. Beneath the restaurant's doorway lights, a handful of moths trailed ghostly doubles in front of my face, making hash of my vision as we stepped onto the sidewalk and I slipped a little on the icy cement. Will caught my arm and kept me upright, the warmth of his touch spreading through me. The flutter of moth wings sounded like spectral whispers in my ears.

"Can I give you a lift back to your truck?" Will offered. "Mine's just under the viaduct."

I'd have been foolish to refuse a two-block walk to a comfortable ride in favor of walking the six frozen blocks to my parking structure or standing in the cold waiting for a bus. And having put a few patches over the rough spots of the morning and afternoon, the rest of the evening looked encouraging. I accepted and we began walking toward Elliot Bay.

The viaduct's elevated double-decker road looms over the

flatland of the waterfront like a concrete house of cards waiting to collapse onto the desolate parking lot wasteland beneath it. Blocks of old warehouse buildings on one side face the patchwork quilt of the waterfront businesses on the other. Crazed, pitted blacktop, striped with parking stalls and lane markers, stretches the width of the missing city block between them. An uneven fringe of stunted shrubs marks the edge of the old trolley line, but nothing else grows under the viaduct's unloved shade.

I batted at the moths that muttered around my head and nearly missed the small animal that darted out from the scruffy hedge. Wan yellow light from the streetlamps on the waterfront gleamed on its russet fur. Doglike with huge pointed ears and a brush tail, it ran into the empty lane and then darted a few steps toward us before it cast a look over its shoulder and bounded away into darkness, dragging a shadow behind it.

Will stared after it and asked, "What was that?"

"A . . . fox, I think." I didn't know why, but a shiver of dread swept over me.

"Fox?" he questioned, taking a couple of steps away from me, following the vanished animal. "Where did it come from? We're a long way from the zoo to be spotting an escapee."

I turned to look where the fox had glanced and saw two vaguely human figures emerging from a shadow that should have been too small to hold them. The world around them boiled in the Grey and heaved layers of time like stacked plates in an earthquake. I faltered forward a step, and the figures moved into a thin slice of streetlight.

In the ordinary light, they looked like two men dressed in rags, stumbling a little from drink or debility, but as they moved forward into shadow again, they shed their normal aspect in my eyes. One was the shaggy creature that had braced me in Occidental Park and it was leading the other, shambling and putrescent, toward me. The clinging cowl of black threads and Grey strands like spiderweb wasn't necessary for me to know that the thing was dead—a walking corpse. I gagged on the stink of decay the zombie carried with it.

The hairy man-thing held out a hand to me. "Help, lady. Free—"

Will pulled me back and stepped between us. "Don't touch her," he warned the scarred creature. "We don't have anything for you. Go your way."

"Will," I started.

He put a protective arm up in front of me but kept his eyes on the two creatures. I knew he didn't see what I did. He must have thought they were just a couple of bums panhandling a bit aggressively.

I began objecting again. "No, Will. Don't!"

Will tried to push me back. The matted hair on the furry one's head and neck rose like hackles on an angry dog. It lowered its head and growled. "No. Need lady!" Fury sparked in its green eyes and it jumped at Will, butting its head into his midsection.

Will tumbled backward and both the monstrosities rushed for him, voicing weird cries. Bright lines of Grey energy rippled around them as the three figures tangled on the ground, thrashing.

"No!" I shouted, plunging into the fray. I didn't want to touch the Grey things and I didn't want them to touch Will any more than they had. I grabbed onto him and hauled backward as hard as I could, pushing back on the Grey as I went. I shoved the edge between us and the shambling, furious things that flailed at Will. "Stop it!" I yelled at them. "Stop!"

Will's hand connected with the zombie's face and a chunk

of rotten flesh fell away, trailing Grey strands on Will's fingers like glue. The dead man's jaw sagged open, unhinged on one side. Will recoiled with a shout, stumbling back and staring at the gaping thing and its feral companion. His shout turned into inarticulate sounds of horror, but I didn't look back at him. The shaggy thing lurched forward again and I slammed my forearm across its chest, shuddering at the touch of its matted hair and knotted body.

"Stop!" I ordered. "Stop now or I won't help you." I was panting from the adrenaline surge. "That's what you want, isn't it? My help?"

The thing whimpered with frustration but turned its gaze to me at last. "Yes. Help," it whined. It reached for the undead man and drew him closer to me. "Trapped. This spirit, tangled here. One of my people, before your kind. Free it."

I peered at the standing dead man and saw a tangle of Grey threads, yellow, blue, and black under the unnatural spiderweb of soft Grey—similar to the stuff I'd seen in the train tunnel—that seemed to bind the rotting flesh together. The threads were inside the body, but the rot was well advanced and only the web of Grey held it to form. I'd pulled a living Grey thing apart before, deconstructed it by force, hating every burning instant. As I looked at it, I could make out a shadow of a face amid the tangled strands of energy and magic, a face that suffered and implored with a look where voice had long failed.

It was disgusting and repellent, but . . . I'd have to make the best of it. I didn't know if I wanted the blue strand or the yellow one, but if I pulled them both out, I could disentangle them more easily. This old corpse shouldn't have been walking around for any reason—he'd been dead a long, long time and deserved to lie down for good. My stomach lurched, but I braced myself to do it, sending a muttered "Gods help me . . ." to the sky as I pushed my hands into the rotten flesh.

The threads of spirit felt like live wires and burned my fingers. I gasped and bit off a yelp of pain as I hooked the living energy in my fists, squeezed my eyes closed against the coming flare of agony, and pulled. Fire and electric shocks jolted up my arms and down my spine, raging through my chest. And then the stands broke free. I staggered back, opening my clenched fists and closed eyes.

The zombie tumbled to the ground, decomposing as it fell. The energy strands slid apart and for an instant two faces looked at me. I gasped. Two? That was all wrong. I stared at the faces—one pleased, one furious—and wondered why the angry one seemed familiar before it flashed away. The other was an Indian—some kind of local Native American, I would guess—and he looked on me benignly for a moment before all cognition faded. He didn't say anything, didn't smile or nod, just slowly vanished leaving a sense of profound relief in his wake.

My shoulders sagged and I let my head fall forward as I exhaled. Could have been worse, I supposed. I heard a noise behind me and turned, having forgotten about Will in the pressure of the moment.

Will was staring at me, breathing in panicky pants. "You . . . you killed that man."

"Shit," I muttered. "No, Will. He was already dead." I tried to close the distance between us, but he backed away from me, so I stopped. "Look at the body. Just look." I turned my head back to see the rotten pile moldering into dirt as we watched. I glanced at my hands and then at his. A thin greasy dust clung to my fingers where the dead man's remains had already dropped away. But I saw a knotted thread of blue energy clinging to Will's fingers and wrapping around his arms where he'd touched the zombie.

I walked toward him again, reaching for his hand to brush the energy strand away, but he jerked back, staring in disbelief at me and then at the pile of dust and dirt beside the now-docile hairy creature. I didn't know how much of the Grey he could see by dint of the tangle on his hand, but it seemed to be enough. Or maybe he could only see the absence of a body, but that would do. He looked sick and his skin was slick with fear sweat that gleamed in the jaundiced light. He started shaking his head in a stiff manner that signaled the edge of hysteria. I kept my hands where he could see them and stood very still.

"Will," I said in the calmest tone I could muster. "I didn't hurt anyone. And I wouldn't hurt you, either."

"They attacked you. You—you attacked back!"

"No. They wanted help."

"You tore that one to pieces!" he shouted, pointing at the drifting pile of dust.

"Will. No. Will, I can't tear a person up. It can't be done. The body fell apart on its own. Will. It was a zombie. It wasn't alive. It was a spirit trapped in a rotting corpse!"

I shouldn't have yelled. At the sound of my raised voice, Will turned and bolted. I tried to go after him, but the hairy man-creature loped after me and caught me, pulling me back around by the arm.

"Lady, lady, dead lady. Even now."

"What?" I demanded. "Even for what?" Exasperating thing!

It touched the scarring around its eye. "This."

"I didn't do that to you!" I cried, frustrated, horrified, wanting to run away from it, to run after Will, and knowing it was too late.

"This because of you. Scaled man struck me. Because you didn't come with me."

I stared at the shaggy thing, halted in my thoughts of Will and forced into another direction. "Scaled man?" I thought hard and came up with pieces that fit. "Wygan? The vampire? The white-haired one?"

It nodded. "Scaled man."

I swore and spit on the ground, damning him till the air quivered with my fury. Bloody Wygan! The bastard vampire who'd stuck a knot of Grey into my chest, bound me inextricably to the grid of the Grey for his own reasons and without my consent, and ripped reality in two for me once and for all. So Wygan had sent this bizarre, simple creature to do his dirty work and then punished it for failure. It blamed me as much as him. I didn't know why Wygan had done any of this and I wouldn't enjoy finding out—but someday I would.

I take vows seriously. As a kid—pushed into activities and occupations I didn't choose, forced to pursue my mother's remodeled dream without heed to my desires—I'd made a vow: to find a way to run my own life, my way. I had done that only to have it all turned on its head. And now, another: I would find out why this had happened to me and what Wygan had done.

The creature patted my chest, wresting me from my thoughts. "Even." Then it turned and loped off, vanishing into shadows of the Grey that drew around it like curtains.

I looked around, suddenly emptied of rage and action, and was taken in a fit of shaking from cold and a swift stab of despair. I was alone under the viaduct. Will was long gone, the dust of the released zombie was already blowing away in the icy breeze off the water, and even the strange moths had disappeared. I clenched my fists tight and felt as if the world was twisting and falling down around me. I stumbled on solid ground, choking on a scream I couldn't release, and forced myself to walk away, back toward

Pioneer Square, away from the empty street under the viaduct. But emptiness came with me, kindled only by the tiny spark of my pledge.

I finished the walk to my truck alone. I drove home in a daze of post-confrontation exhaustion and carried the puzzle box upstairs to my condo, shoving it into a bookshelf at random after the door clicked closed behind me.

Chaos, my ferret, rattled the door of her cage, demanding immediate release. I let her out only to imprison her again against my chest.

"What am I going to do?" I asked the ferret.

Chaos, impatient little beast, wriggled with annoyance as I tried not to break down. I gave up and let her go, dropping onto the sofa and putting my face in my hands. Hot salt water ran against my palms and down my wrists but nothing, not even breath, could pass the stone that seemed to have settled in my throat. I didn't even have the comfort of howling or sobbing, just stupid, hard tears.

I cried until it stopped hurting and put my head down on the arm of the sofa. Chaos skipped over to check on me, climbing the upholstery to lick the moisture from my face. "You don't love me, you just want salt," I muttered, letting her tiny kisses tickle my cheeks until I stopped feeling so wretched and wrung out.

"What now? I'm not ready to go after Wygan," I continued. "Not skilled enough for that yet. So . . . just pick myself up and go on like there never was a William Novak in my life? Yeah, right."

I wondered what had happened to the thread of Grey that had tangled on Will's arm. I'd have to check—

The ferret stuck her cold nose in my ear.

"Hey!"

She snorted and bounced away, busy as always. Busy.

That's what Will and I would both do. That's how we got by; working to avoid dealing with the personal ugliness. He wasn't likely to let me near him for a while—at least not until he wasn't so horrified. Much as I wanted to get at that bit of Grey, I'd have to wait and let his mind make some more comfortable suggestion of what had happened before I could. We'd have to talk and it would probably be the last time—I could no more keep on with this mess than he could, after this—and that would be my chance to fix what I could, including the strand, and let the rest go forever. But the Big Break would have to wait for calmer daylight, when there were fewer shadows heavy with reminders of shambling creatures and dark actions under the otherworldly stare of fox eyes and ghostly things.

FOUR

One of the requirements for my degree in criminal science was a psychology course about criminals and victims of crime. For a week we discussed how victims cope with the results of the crimes—everything from burglary and bank fraud to rape and the murder of loved ones—committed against them. In the end, all traumas elicit one of two major categories of response: break or cope. Breaking down is good for you, I'm told—catharsis and all that jazz—but I rarely indulge in it and never for long. Me, I'm of the suck-it-up school of coping till you crack. So after a night of feeling like a dog that'd been kicked, I dragged myself out of bed, worked out, and went back to my job. But Will was in the back of my mind and I worried in silence while I made myself work.

In between witness checks for Nan Grover, I left a message for Quinton and eventually arranged to meet up with him back in Pioneer Square about three o'clock. Quinton was standing near the bust of Chief Sealth and talking to Zip when I spotted him.

". . . Thoreau was protesting the Mexican-American War," he was saying as I approached.

Zip lipped an unlit cigarette and spoke in an impaired mumble that twitched out of one corner of his mouth. I'd gotten used to his odd speech in the months we'd been acquainted. "So he din't pay his taxes?" Zip asked.

Quinton nodded. "Yup. And they threw him in jail."

Under his flap-eared cap Zip looked thoughtful, rubbing his white-bristled chin with one hand that was clenched around his prized lighter. "Huh. So, this in't new? Tellin' the gov'ment you in't gonna pay fer a war?"

"Nope. See, man, you were the practitioner of an honorable tradition."

"Hm," Zip grunted, lighting his smoke and stamping his feet to stay warm. "Wish they hadn't thrown me in the nuthouse, though."

"Setting yourself on fire may have been a bit much, Zip."

"I come out OK." He looked up and noticed me. "Hey'm, Harper."

I had to shake myself out of my distracted funk. "Hey, Zip. Do you mind if I take Quinton for a while?"

He flipped his hand lazily at us. "Nah. Gonna get dinner in a minute. God Squad's got chowder on Friday. S'Friday, right?"

"Has been all day," Quinton replied.

"Good. 'Cause y'know, they change that on ya sometimes. Sometimes it's Wednesday halfway through, then it's Vienna sausages. Don' like them. They's like fingers. I in't gonna eat no fingers."

"Not even fish fingers?"

Zip pushed out his lips and frowned, the smoldering cigarette wobbling on his lip like a wind sock in a changeable breeze. "Fish in't got fingers." Then he huffed, hunched into his filthy layers of clothing, and marched off.

"Think he's offended?" I asked.

"With Zip you never know. So. You wanted to talk . . . ?"

"Yeah. About that incident yesterday. But this isn't the best place." I forced my wandering mind into the work at hand and looked around, letting my gaze sweep past the pair of heavily jacketed beat cops chatting up the bums on the benches in front of Doc Maynard's Public House. It wasn't tourist season and their demeanor was more solicitous than threatening, but with Quinton's dislike of cops, I assumed he wouldn't want to talk about dead men out on the street where they might hear.

"Yeah," he replied. He bit his lip and frowned a moment before continuing. "Come on. I know where we can talk and you can get a better idea of what's happening."

He led the way west toward the water. I shuddered at the memory of the previous evening, but after we'd crossed First, we walked only one more block before Quinton turned right onto Post. It's not officially designated Post Alley at the south end, but it's not much wider than if it were. It was already dark in the narrow street between the old masonry buildings, and the picturesque red brick underfoot was crusted with dirty ice. I dug my boot soles into the uneven and ghost-strewn surface with firm steps, following Quinton through the turns of the road until we reached a poured concrete wall under the Seneca Street off-ramp from the viaduct. A three-story retaining wall held back the tumble of the hill while a wide stone staircase climbed the side of the building perpendicular to it, creating a dark half room roofed by the roadbed above us. The other side of the street held the southern loading docks and dog-walking slab for the hotel tower of the Harbor Steps complex—an area I had discovered had no active history in the pit that had been gouged into the cliff edge for its foundations. Just behind us, the rich, tilting timescape of the

Grey looked like the Painted Desert done in shades of mist. Our location lay at the intersection of history and void, and I couldn't help but stare at the contrast.

Quinton touched my shoulder and startled me out of my rapt gaping. He motioned me into the darkest corner, where the retaining wall met the back of the staircase. A shallow, bunkerlike structure of concrete slabs poked out from the retaining wall. A rusted steel door had been set into the bunker wall and sported a triangular yellow caution sign with an odd symbol of spikes and circles and the words AUTHORIZED PERSONNEL ONLY.

Quinton pulled a short cylinder—about the size of a fat pocket flashlight—from his coat and pushed it against a plate above the door's lock. I heard something clunk and he grabbed the door handle that looked as if it shouldn't turn, but did. The door swung in, and he stepped through into darkness and pulled me in behind him.

The door closed with the thick thud and hush of heavy rubber seals. The lock clunked again and the lights came on. We were in a small cement vestibule that opened into a larger area bounded by old walls of stone and brick. The room was cluttered with shelves and tables made of plain boards and various containers or architectural elements that must have been discarded in someone's rebuilding scheme long ago. Electronic equipment was neatly arranged among stacks of parts, books, clothes, and canned goods. A dorm fridge hummed under one of the tables. It was like some mad scientist's basement that had been taken over by engineering students.

A crazy collection of lights hung from wires strung between the walls to illuminate the roughly L-shaped room. The walls rose to a height of about thirty feet, and we were standing right in the corner of the L with the door behind us in the short side. A bed hid in an alcove at the long end of the L. The final wall beside the bed was built of heavy timbers held together with archaic metal straps and huge bolts—not medieval so much as Victorian gothic. It reminded me a bit of a castle's massive gates that had smaller doors cut into them.

I stared around the place. "We're under the sidewalk," I said in wonder. "Or part of it . . ."

"Yeah, that wall supports the stairs," Quinton agreed, pointing toward the bed alcove. "The wooden part blocks off the old sidewalk level."

"You live here?"

"For about six years. The company that built the Harbor Steps put in the bunker as a temporary security box during the excavation and I . . . appropriated it when they were done, before anyone thought to remove it. I made sure the paperwork disappeared, and once the sign and locks were on the door, everyone seems to have figured it was someone else's problem. Especially since no one's keys work on the lock." He shrugged. "Must not be the authorized personnel."

"Where's the electricity come from?"

He waved at the concrete wall. One end was covered in electrical panels. "It comes straight off the utility grid. Just looks like more of the city works to the system. I thought about pulling cable, but it's been hard to get at without attracting attention. I use the library's system or the Wi-Fi that's all over the place in Seattle now. No water, though. I'm not too handy with plumbing."

I ignored the trivia. "How . . . ?"

"People don't pay much attention to things that look like they belong. I keep things repaired and smoothed over so no one has any reason to come and look for problems or wonder what's in here. Just a utility hole for something no one's curious about."

"So the symbol on the door . . . ?"

"Means nothing—I made it up—but it looks like something you ought to be afraid of, doesn't it?"

"Yes," I agreed, and I wondered if there were other things to be afraid of here. The diabolical cleverness of the bunker was unnerving. The situation with Will had left me raw, and the oddity of Quinton's actions the previous day had me on high alert for trouble. "Why go to all this effort, though? What are you hiding from?" I asked. I was a little afraid to hear the answer.

"Kind of a long story, but, basically, I just want my own life entirely in my own control. Or as much as I can get it." That was a sentiment with which I could concur. Not knowing my thoughts, he continued, "The only way I can see to have that is to be out of the system. So I got out of it. I don't have a social security card or a driver's license or a voter registration. I have no fixed address, no job, no ties, no bank account."

He hung up his coat and hat and turned on an electric space heater that was sitting near one of the tables.

"Sounds kind of isolated."

He shrugged and pulled the elastic band off his ponytail, scrubbing his hair loose onto his shoulders with a growl of pleasure before heading for the tiny fridge. "In some ways, yeah, it is, but it's not so lonely. There's a lot of people down here who are like me in one way or another."

"Down where?" I asked, leaning against the nearest wall with my arms crossed, still a bit unsure of the situation.

"Here. The literal underground, Pioneer Square—the skids. The homeless, the discarded, the hidden . . . we're all down here. We're our own community. And that's why I'm a little pissed about the deaths and disappearances. These guys are my friends—my neighbors. Sometimes I'm the only one around who isn't off his rocker, and I feel like I ought to do something when we're threatened."

"And of course getting me involved means that you don't have to expose yourself in order to do the right thing."

He opened the fridge and looked into it. "That sounds kind of selfish of me. And cynical of you. You want a beer?"

"Well, if you're going to call me cynical, what kind of beer?"

He laughed. "I don't know. I have one or two bottles of about five different things in here—people keep paying me for stuff in beer. Or books."

A sudden muffled rapping came from the wooden wall by the bed. Quinton kicked the refrigerator closed and trotted past me to the sleeping alcove. He pushed on something and looked at the small screen that was revealed behind it. Then he covered it up again and grabbed one edge of the wall. He pulled and it swung open. It was, as I'd imagined, a door within a larger gate that only looked like a wall. Now I knew how he'd moved in the bed, since the bunker door wasn't very large.

In the doorway stood a hunched, dark form. It leaned into the light and looked up at Quinton—he's a little shorter than I am, so the figure was hunkered down pretty small. It was a dark-skinned man, but I couldn't tell if that was natural or just dirt. He held out a metal box—some kind of electrical equipment to judge by the colored wires hanging off it. He was shaking and looking behind himself, wrapped in a twitchy haze of substance withdrawal.

"Hey, Q-man. I brought you the radio. See, I said I would. It's OK, right?"

Quinton took the radio and looked it over. "Yeah, this'll be good. Hang on." He went to one of the tables, put down the radio, and picked up a palm-sized object made of black PVC pipe with a couple of metal horns sticking off one end. He carried it back to the door and started to hand it to the man. Then he hesitated.

"You know how to use this?"

"Yeah, yeah!" the guy said, reaching out for the thing.

Quinton looked askance at him and kept the black tube just out of reach. "Sure, Lass. Let me show you, just in case. You hold the plain end and you push the button on the side, see." A blue-white ribbon of electricity jumped between the horns with a crack. "Make sure that bit's touching the bad guy when you push the button, OK?"

The hunched man nodded vigorously and accepted the shock gun. "Yeah, yeah. OK. Got it."

"No shocking Tanker's dog, all right?"

"He scares me! I don't like . . . animals," he added, shooting another glance behind himself.

"Avoid him. If you take out that dog, Tank'll take you out— zap gun or no zap gun. Got it?"

Lass hung his head. "Yeah, yeah . . . No shocking the dog. I got other ways around that dog. . . . All right. Just the creepy guys. And monsters."

"Monsters? What monsters?" Quinton asked, intense.

The smaller man looked startled and backed up a step. "You know. The things that come out of the walls, up out of the holes, the sewer . . ." Lass's voice got shrill and he started to shake harder.

"Ah. Those. Yeah. That's all right. You go ahead and shock the hell out those," Quinton said, patting the man on the shoulder. "You'll be all right."

The other man nodded and tucked the little device into his pocket. "Yeah. OK. Thanks, Q-man." He scampered off into what looked like a brick corridor beyond the door.

Quinton closed the wooden portal and turned back to me. "Want that beer now?"

"Sure," I said, relaxing into a chair I pulled out from under one of the tables. I was reassured by the little scene that Quinton wasn't a dangerous lunatic who had lured me to his lair to kill me or something. Lass would have been an easier mark and less likely to cause complications.

Quinton gave me a New Belgium Brewing Company bottle that had lost its label. "Mystery beer—figured it was a better risk than the Rolling Rock."

I made a face while Quinton uncapped the brown bottle for me. The contents proved to be Sunshine Wheat. That was fine.

"Does that sort of visit happen often?" I asked.

Quinton quirked his mouth up on one side and frowned a little. "Not quite like that. People do ask me to fix things or solve problems, but Lass's been really freaked out lately and wanted something to drive the spooks off—he's been trying to quit drinking again, and he gets jittery and crazy."

"So, he's got DTs—hallucinating and that sort of thing."

"Maybe. He's sure there's someone after him, but around here there may well be. Vampires turn up around here sometimes, hunting."

"You know, Quinton, you're pretty calm about the vampire thing. Most people don't believe they exist. Most people don't believe in anything magic or occult. People like Will—"

I caught myself before I went too far, but Quinton peered at me. "Will." He shook his head. "I imagine it's . . . hard for you . . . dating someone who isn't comfortable with those ideas."

I looked away, annoyed with myself for feeling a flush of misery and anger I didn't want him to see. "Yeah . . . well . . . I don't think we're dating anymore." I held up a hand and, shaking my head, I added, "Right now, I don't want to talk about Will and all those other people who believe in pop science and TV and what the newspapers tell them—stuff that fits in their transparent little scientific world. I thought you didn't particularly care for vampires and ghosts and witches and magic, but you don't seem to have any problem with the idea—the reality—of them. Or with me. Why is that?"

He took a moment before he answered. "I don't believe in holding on to notions that don't work, just because a majority of people prefer them. I learned that slipping into the cracks meant I had to learn to see the cracks first." He leaned one hip against a worktable supporting the carcass of a gas-powered leaf blower and sipped his beer. "Sometimes I've had to figure out that something exists by inference or inductive reasoning when—like gravity—it's not something you can see or touch. I went looking for the holes in what most people accept as reality, and where I couldn't find a solid answer just sitting there, I poked around until other things led to a conclusion that fit, even if it seemed screwy. The knowledge of those holes and cracks has helped me out many times.

"So I'm used to acknowledging things that most people don't even believe in. I can't see magic—like I think you do—but I can see evidence that there's an unexplained force in the world. Down here where anarchy is the status quo, the presence of magic and the things that go with it are a lot more obvious, if you're alert. Or unlucky."

"Have you ever seen a ghost?" I asked. It would be nice to know that someone else did. . . .

"Ghost? No. I don't think so. Weird stuff, cold stuff, sourceless movements of air or steam, auditory anomalies—yeah, plenty. Is that what a ghost is?"

"No. That's just the special effects," I replied in a dry voice.

"Magic and ghosts are two things I have to concede, but I still don't like them. I don't like vampires either, but that's a different thing. When you're one of the hidden people, you're fair game for them—no one's going to notice you're gone." The air around him seemed to curdle with his disgust, his emotional radiation going olive green shot with angry bolts of red. "The homeless are just as disposable to them as they are to the rest of society, but the vampires can get something from them before they toss them on the dung heap. I think they're responsible for whatever is happening to the homeless people and undergrounders."

"The vampires? Why?"

"Why not? Who else would be down here, preying on people? We're like the fast food of the vampire world. Just drop down to Pioneer Square after dark, find an alley or a doorway, slip down into a basement, and there's lunch. I just can't figure out why their approach has changed. They're usually careful and they don't rip into people the way most of these bodies have been. They don't chew, for one thing."

"Why haven't you asked Edward? You obviously have some clout with the . . . undergrounders." The term felt odd in my mouth. "You know Edward and he knows you. Couldn't you go to him as a neutral party, a representative of the homeless?"

Not that I thought the city's chief vampire was likely to welcome Quinton with open arms—they didn't seem to like each other—but I'd thought there was some mutual respect there, at least enough to make a parlay possible.

Quinton snorted and coughed on his beer. "Hell, no! I've gotten between the vampires and their next meal often enough to be unpopular with Edward and his friends." If he hadn't been drinking good beer, I think Quinton would have spit.

"And none of them's tried to whack you yet?"

"They've tried. But I know what their weaknesses are and how to hurt them without killing them outright—which would make me fair game. I have tried to stay neutral—it's a bad idea to have enemies down here. I used to do bits of work for Edward when I first got here, but working for him's like working for the government, and I've had to keep my distance—and force him to keep his. I'm in no position to go snooping around at the After Dark."

I shouldn't have been surprised that Quinton knew about the vampire club—he seemed to know about a lot of things I was still figuring out. I sighed. "So, you want me to go to Edward?"

"Only if it's necessary. I think it's his crew, but I could be wrong. I don't have the skills to really know what's going on. That's what I want—to know what's going on and stop it. I don't want to be lunch and I don't want any more of my neighbors to be lunch, and I sure as hell don't want anyone snooping around down here and bringing this place to official notice. Things are getting pretty high-profile now that the cops are looking into the guy I found in the tunnel, and it won't be long before other . . . people start to stir the waters. That's not good for any of us."

"All right," I said, putting down my empty bottle. "I get you. How many dead or missing are there?"

"Three dead, five missing. And the leg in the pit—which might be unconnected, but I doubt it."

"Some of the missing could have moved on to some other location," I suggested.

"One or two, but most of these guys have no way out of here. It's not like they have cars or money for fares. In this cold at this time of year, most couldn't walk far enough in a day to make it to the next place they could be assured of food and shelter. And it's not like you can continuously hop transit buses from here to

Los Angeles or someplace. Most of these people are stuck here—
they didn't come here by choice like I did—so they're already at
the end of the line. If they go missing from this community, the
chances are good they're dead."

I narrowed my eyes at him and played devil's advocate. "Some
of them do get out. They find homes and jobs."

"Some do—there are some good service groups around Seattle
helping the ones who want help—but they usually let the rest
of us know. That's not what's happening here. It's the ones who
stand the least chance of that who've been disappearing or turning
up dead: the odd men out. They haven't been killing themselves,
so someone or something has been doing it for them."

I put up my hands, conceding. "All right. Someone's killing
homeless people, and if the guy in the tunnel is typical, it's in a
pretty bizarre way. All right, you've convinced me. But I'm still
not ready to agree it's vampires. I don't really want to mess with
Edward unless there's a good reason."

"Then let's go find one. Or find something else."

Quinton stepped away from the table he'd been leaning on
and collected his coat and hat before he started for the wooden
door by the bed. I shrugged and got up to follow him.

Beyond the wooden wall was a tall, narrow corridor of brick
and stone on one side and heavy stone blocks on the other. The
surface beneath our feet was rough cement. There were no lights
except what Quinton made with a pocket flashlight.

"There aren't that many places where you can get in without
anyone knowing," he said as he led me down the cold hall. "Most
of the actual underground is closed up pretty tight if it's not in use
by the property owner. I sort of forced my way in."

"How did Lass get in, then?"

"Oh, there's a way down here where some service stairs go into the basement of the building at the other end of the block. He doesn't know about the other door. Most people don't."

I stopped and stared at the wall on the right dimly illuminated by the light from Quinton's flashlight, and I recognized the bricked-in shapes of windows and doors set above crumbled steps. "Where are we? What's this building?"

"I don't know the building's name, but if you walked through the wall, you'd be in the kitchen of Las Margaritas Mexican restaurant. Next to that is the workroom and storage space for a wedding dress boutique. From here to the hotel is the back rooms of the stores that face Post. We're under the sidewalk of First Avenue."

"How far does this go?" I asked.

"Only to the end of the block. Then you have to get back out on the street. We'll come out under McCormick and Schmick's side door. There's a lot more of these buried sidewalks, though. In some places, you can get into the basements of buildings, if you know what you're doing. It's supposed to be completely closed up, but nothing's ever totally sealed. In weather like this, people who can't get into the official shelters will look for any shelter they can get, even if it's a hole in a wall, and some of those holes lead into the underground."

I knew that there was an "underground city" below parts of Seattle—mostly Pioneer Square—but I hadn't put any thought into what it actually was or how it would be laid out. I wasn't sure of the details, but I did know the underground was a remnant of the city's rebuilding after the famous fire. The streets had been raised from the muck and fireproof stone and brick architecture mandated in place of the previous tide-flat-level roads and wooden buildings. They'd even laid a modern sewer and water supply that didn't backflush every time the tide came in. This buried corridor, formed of the building's foot and the raised road's retaining wall under the modern sidewalk, was just a part of that whole tangled, buried mess.

I'd thought the underground city was just a tourist version of local history in basements and sewers. Listening to Quinton, it seemed that there were really two undergrounds—the physical one and the hidden social structure of the economically dispossessed who lived near or in it. I couldn't help but wonder if there was more to it. . . .

I put my hand against the building's wall and relaxed, breathing in the musty smell of the space below the street. Quinton just stood by without speaking as I let the Grey come up to full strength around me.

Most of the time, the Grey seems darker than the normal world, but this time, the silvery overlay of time and memory was brighter—much brighter. The accessible layers of time at that spot all seemed to be filled with daylight. Ghosts bustled past, busy with their own long-ago affairs: women in sweeping dresses from the 1890s, men in suits or work clothes. A mob of giggling flappers stumbled through me, shushing each other in drunken whispers and going on their way just as giddily as before. I shivered involuntarily when they touched me. I looked around, expecting to see an open sky over the street on the other side of the walkway, but there was still a wall, even then. I glanced up and realized that the light poured down into the sidewalk through thick glass prisms in the concrete above. In other angles of time there was no upper walkway, just ramps that connected the upstairs shop doors to the street across the open hole and a wooden staircase at the corner.

It was like some underground mall that had collected an undue measure of history. I gave a small gasp of surprise as I realized that this now-abandoned place had been the thriving heart of the city's shopping and business district at one time, full of people at all hours where now there were only shadows and dust.

"Do you see something?" Quinton asked. I shifted my focus back to him and saw he was a little nervous at his question. I considered lying—it was what I usually had to do—but if ever there was a time to risk disclosure, this seemed like the best chance I would ever have.

"Ghosts," I replied. "Lots of the city's memory of itself."

He was curious. "The city's memory? That's a funny way to put it."

"It's the best I can come up with. The things I'm seeing here aren't aware of us. They're just like recordings. But there's a lot of them. Layers and layers. This must have been a popular corner."

"I don't think so. This end of the city was built up later than the parts around Pioneer Square, though I think the fire started near here. . . ."

"Hm."

I just looked at it a while longer, letting it flood in: the flickering images of the original buildings overlaid with the roar and rush of fire consuming the wooden city and the stop-motion play of the landscape as it became a towering canyon of brick and stone where dead generations shopped, visited, and caroused in helical time. This was not the low-down history I'd seen replayed on Occidental, but something more middle class that had risen with the streets, eventually, rather than being buried and disinterred only for tourist show-and-tell.

"Do you want to continue?"

I could feel my toes going numb from the cold seeping into

my boots and I pulled myself out of the hypnotic depth of history. "Yes. These ghosts aren't going anywhere and there's probably a lot more of them around. Let's go."

We went down the dank corridor and around a corner to a low door. Quinton tinkered with it a bit and opened it with care, looking around before he stepped out to let me through. We stepped out and headed uphill to First. The weather had driven people indoors, and none were looking out of McCormick and Schmick's windows to see us emerge. We crossed between the old and new federal buildings and continued back toward Pioneer Square.

FIVE

The streets seemed to grow darker as we went south into the older environs of the city. The roads were narrower below Cherry Street, where the city plat bent to run truly north and south rather than northwest to southeast to match the shoreline. Cherry was also the northern boundary of the historic district where the darkness I saw was not entirely due to dimmer, cuter street lights.

"Let's go see who's at BOLM," Quinton suggested. It sounded like he'd said "balm."

"What?" I asked.

"The Bread of Life Mission on Main and First. It's the smallest shelter and they only take in men overnight, but they're the closest to the Square. It's where Zip was headed. We'll try the Union Gospel Mission afterward."

"If these guys sleep in the shelters, how did they get killed on the street? Vampires wouldn't be hunting in those places," I objected.

"They weren't sleeping in the shelters. Some of them won't sleep indoors or in certain buildings—some of the undergrounders are funny that way. Others can't get in and some don't even try. There aren't enough beds—even when the Christian shelters like BOLM and UGM open the chapels in extreme weather. But there's usually more food than beds, so people come for that and maybe an extra blanket, then go out again to see what they can find. But the beds fill up fast. That's when people start getting into the staircases, doorways, and cellars if they can. That's where the bodies have been found—near the underground accesses."

"And you're thinking that the ones who disappeared were also in the underground tunnels or near access points?" I asked.

"Yeah. But I'm not sure. If we ask around, we might find out."

Even in the sub-freezing cold, there was a line on the sidewalk in front of the Bread of Life Mission. Most of the people in the line were men, or seemed to be—it was a little difficult to tell under the layers of clothes everyone wore against the cold. Quinton left me for a moment and went up to the front to talk to a man at the door. He came back shaking his head.

"He won't let us in. We'll have to talk to the people in line and try to catch the rest another time."

We started near the front, where we found Zip listening and nodding along with a woman dressed head to toe in black. She looked about forty-five, Hispanic, thin in the ropy, muscular way of people who've done manual labor most of their lives. Her clothes were clean and reasonably new, and a woolly hat covered most of her dark hair. She seemed oblivious of the rank odors that hung around the men near her, even in the cold.

". . . on Wednesday," she was saying as we approached. "And you're coming this time, Zip."

Zip bobbed his head. "Yes'm."

She looked up at Quinton and me as we stopped beside to them. "Quinton! You can help me. We're having a vigil on

Wednesday in front of the Justice Center from one to three. We need leafleteers—we have two leaflets this time, so we need plenty of help."

"I don't do leaflets," Quinton said.

The woman shook her head in sharp negation. "Nonono. You get to be my cattle prod. Some of these guys aren't very reliable," she added, giving a hint of a smile as she elbowed Zip in the ribs, "but they may show up if they're reminded by someone they trust."

"Oh." Quinton nodded. "OK, Rosa. I'll play big brother."

She looked surprised. "Well, OK, then." Rosa turned her gaze on me and I felt like I was being sized up. "Who's this?"

Quinton put his hand behind my shoulder. "This is Harper Blaine." He caught my eye and gave a small smile, tipping his head. "Harper, this is Rosa—Rosaria Cabrera."

Rosa put out her mittened hand and took mine in a quick, hard grip. "I'm with Women in Black. We organize silent vigils to remember the homeless who've died on the street."

"Does that happen a lot?" I asked, retrieving my hand.

Her face went stern. "More than you want to know. Winter's always the worst, and this one is worse than that."

"Who's your vigil for on Wednesday?"

"The dead in general, of course, but recently we lost Jan and Go-cart—Chaim Jankowski and Robert Cristus."

I glanced at Quinton. "Go-cart was the guy in the train tunnel," he said, and then he looked at Rosa. "Harper found him."

Rosa's gaze became very sharp and she shot a look between us as if she knew the truth of the matter. "How is it you found Go-cart?" she asked me.

"I'm a private investigator," I replied. "I was looking for someone else, but it was Go-cart—Robert—I found."

"Who were you looking for?"

I pulled a name out of Nan Grover's list. "One J. Walker Eddings Jr. A witness in an upcoming court case."

Rosa shook her head. "Don't know him—at least not by that name."

"Do you know if Go-cart had any family? What's going to happen to the body?" I asked. "They know the cause of death yet?"

Rosa sighed. "They don't tell us any of that. We don't even know if they're investigating his death except to relieve the railroad of any fault. Usually guys like Jan and Go-cart just end up in an anonymous grave with nothing but a number on the plot or as a box of ashes in a file cabinet, and that's the end of it. I understand he had a brother someplace in the Midwest, but who knows?" She looked back to Quinton. "Quinton, can you find out? I know you're good at that sort of thing, and Go-cart was in the military once, so he must have some records. We should mention his service on the vigil leaflet—and the memorial if the county comes through."

"I'll see if I can find out," Quinton agreed. "How many's that make in Seattle since the storms?"

Rosa rolled her eyes in thought. "Uh . . . six. No, seven."

"What about missing men?" I asked. "Do you guys count those as dead?"

Rosa looked at me like I was growing donkey ears. "No. If I wanted a shocking statistic to take to city hall, then I might, but we only count the ones we know died. It doesn't matter where they died or how. That they died homeless is what matters."

I felt a nudge and noticed that while we'd been talking to Rosa, the line of homeless men waiting for dinner had moved. Zip had disappeared inside and a new group had come abreast of us. Our witnesses were dwindling away into the food-scented warmth inside the mission. I looked at Quinton and Rosa caught it.

"You guys didn't come out here to talk to me," she said, "and I have a lot to do, too. So I'd better get to it. Spread the word, Quinton, and let me know what you find out about Go-cart."

Rosa waved and walked past us, down the line of shivering people waiting for food. She buttonholed a few as she went, telling them to come to the vigil—she didn't ask but couched it as a duty they had already agreed to perform, and each one nodded quickly, eyes downcast. I had the feeling people didn't argue with Rosa Cabrera.

Quinton and I asked the remaining men about the recent deaths and disappearances, but most knew little that was useful. As we neared the end of the line, Quinton found Lass's nemesis: a stocky, long-coated, spotted mutt named Bella who definitely had some kind of fighting dog in her ancestry. Quinton squatted down and scratched her ears and back, chattering to her.

In spite of the cold, Bella frisked around at the end of her rope leash as if it was the finest day of summer. She whined with joy, licked Quinton's face, and tried to climb up his body as if she would curl up around his neck like a cat. I supposed that if Lass were spooked by dogs in the first place, that behavior might freak him out a little. To me it was endearing, in a sort of doggy-disgusting way. All right, so I like big dogs.

At the other end of the leash, the man I assumed was Tanker gave one sharp tug on the rope. His voice was soft and slow as he said, "Off, Bella. Don't be such a kissy-face." The hood of his sweatshirt hid his face as the man put his hand down to pat the dog's huge head. His clothes were the most ragged of any man's there, and he smelled of engine grease and sweat.

Bella sat down next to Tanker at once. Her stumpy tail went

still and she looked up at her master in anticipation. Quinton got back to his feet and we all moved a foot or so closer to the door as the line of hungry men advanced.

"Hey, Tanker," Quinton started. "This is Harper. Harper, this is Tanker."

Tanker turned his head to look at me. As the light from the streetlamp fell on his face, I twitched with stifled horror. Tanker's dark face was a lumpy mass of scars that covered him from collar to crown in a patchwork of burns, grafts, and emergency reconstruction that had never been prettied up afterward. In whatever disaster had overtaken him, his mouth had been reduced to a lipless, twisted cut and his one visible ear was a misshapen knot. If he had any hair, it was on a part of his head I couldn't see.

He ignored my start and offered a massive hand covered in a brown leather glove that didn't match the blue ski glove on his other hand. "Hi."

"Hi," I replied, taking his offered hand.

"Sorry if I scared you." I wasn't quite sure from his expression and voice, but the sparks that danced around his head made me think he wasn't entirely sincere. Some turmoil boiled beneath his blank surface.

Touching him sent a feeling of disquiet through me and I released his hand. "No, you're not," I said.

He made a wheezing, barking sound and glanced at Quinton. "Where'd you find her?"

"Couple of blocks up, on the skid."

"Pig shit."

"Absolute truth. Hey, you know about the vigil for Jan and Go-cart?"

"Yeah."

"Good. Where're you sleeping tonight? It's pretty cold."

Tanker seemed to glower at Quinton, though it was hard to tell in the gloom. "Got a place in the bricks."

"You better be careful down there. That's where Jan was staying before he kicked it."

"Nothing'll bother me. Not with Bella."

"Lass is probably staying down that way, too—"

Tanker interrupted him to say, "That little turd. Better keep his distance or I'll tell Bella to rip his throat out."

"That's why I'm telling you to keep an eye open. Lass is flipping out about things following him around—"

"Man's a freak, what d'you expect?"

"So," Quinton went on as if he hadn't been cut off again, "I gave him a stunner. I told him to keep away from you and Bella, but you know how Lass gets when he's off the juice."

"He should drink till he croaks."

"Tanker, I know Lassiter's a head case, but I'm not sure he's just hallucinating. You see anything strange down there since the storms? Notice anything, anybody missing?"

"Aside from Tandy? And Hafiz and Go-cart and Jan?" Tanker asked with a snort. Then he turned aside and looked into the open door of the mission.

We'd come up the door as we'd been talking, and now Tanker stopped and looked at the mission worker inside. The man held out a small paper box, like restaurants give you for the leftovers.

"Can't bring the dog inside, Tanker," he said, looking nervous, "but we put some bacon aside for her and a couple of the guys brought some dog food samples." He held up two small bags of dry kibble with green labels declaring the food within to be "natural" and "healthy." Looked like the dog ate better than the people.

Tanker mumbled thanks and took the bags and the box and

stepped out of line. We followed him a few feet away to an alley mouth where he put the box on the sidewalk and opened it before ripping open the bags and pouring them in. Bella sat still and stared at Tanker, though her eyes shifted toward the food once or twice before he said, "OK, Bella. Eat."

Bella leapt for the food and began crunching it down. We watched for a few moments. I noticed the ease with which the mutt reduced even the hardest-looking kibble to dust and thought I wouldn't like to be on the wrong side of her jaws.

"I saw a hand," Tanker said, still watching his dog, "down in the stairs by the record shop."

"You mean Bud's? On Jackson?" I asked.

"Yeah."

"You're sure it was a hand?" I questioned.

Tanker glared at me and a swirl of black fury roiled around him. "You think I'm stupid? Think I don't know what I see with my own eyes? It was a hand, sister. A hand just like yours." He slapped my left hand with his right, and the dog stopped eating, going tense and alert, staring at us. "I seen body parts. I see body parts flying through the air like crazy birds. A freakin' hand!"

Bella had begun to growl low in her throat.

Quinton, keeping an eye on the dog, grabbed Tanker by the shoulder. "Hey, hey. She's not dissing you. She just wants to be sure. We're trying to figure out what's happening to people here. You know—like Tandy."

Tanker breathed heavily through his mouth, staring at me. I stood still and looked back with as much blank calm as I could muster to cover my wariness. As with his dog, I didn't think it would be wise to rile him. Finally Tanker waved at the dog, making a down-patting motion with his hand. "Peace, Bella." The dog sat down by the remains of her dinner, but she kept an eye on her master.

He turned his focus to Quinton, cutting me out of the conversation. "Tandy's gone, man."

"I noticed that," Quinton said. "I want to know who else you haven't seen around lately. Who's missing?"

Tanker stepped backward until he could lean against the stained wall of the alley. His breath had slowed down and the nightmare color around him had drained away, but he still seemed agitated. "John Bear. Haven't seen Bear in a while."

"Was he staying in the bricks, too?"

"Man, you know Bear wouldn't sleep inside. He's the bear, he sleeps with the bears. Crazy mofo."

"But he hasn't been sleeping in the park lately, has he? In this cold?"

"No. I haven't seen him. I seen his blanket—Jay had it."

"So Bear's missing and so's Tandy. Anybody else?"

"I don't know," Tanker snapped. "I don't know and you and your questions can go to hell! And I don't want your help!" he added as an afterthought. Then he grabbed Bella's leash and gave it a sharp jerk as he began to stalk off down the alley. "You go to hell!" he shouted back.

Quinton took my hand and pulled me away, into the street. "We'd better move on."

"What just happened?" I asked, falling into step beside him.

Quinton shook his head. "Tanker's got problems."

"I imagine most of the people down here have problems."

"Yeah. Well. Tanker's got more. He used to drive a gasoline tanker—hence the nickname—and he was in an accident that killed a couple of other people in a pretty ugly way and gave him those scars. The company blamed him, fired him, and refused to pay his medical bills. Later it came out that the company was using cheap retreads on the tractors and that was the cause of the accident, but by then it was old news and Tanker was on the skid. The icing on the cake is that Tanker got burned trying to save people in the cars, but one of them came apart as he was hauling him out—in the smoke, Tank didn't realize the guy'd been sheared in half by the steering column. He kind of flipped out after that."

The story shook me and I studied Quinton's face; he looked grim and didn't meet my eyes. I couldn't think of what to say, so we just walked on in silence.

We headed up the hill toward the Union Gospel Mission in Chinatown, hoping to catch some more of the undergrounders sitting still to have dinner.

UGM took in families and women as well as men and were a little more open to letting us come in and talk to people, though I was pretty sure they wouldn't have let me in without Quinton beside me. The volunteers running the kitchen and dining room told us we could talk to anyone in the common room, but we couldn't go into the sleeping areas and that was fine by me. I figured most of the people we wanted to see would be awake, but I was surprised by how many people had already gone to bed.

"Homeless is hard work," one of the volunteers said. "These people are on their feet all day, and having no home doesn't mean a lot of them don't work or try to get work. If nothing else, they panhandle, sweep sidewalks, wash windows, do manual day labor, and walk their rounds, looking for work, or food, or recyclables—whatever they do to put a little change in their pockets. They hit the hay while the night's still young and it's not only because the good places to sleep fill up fast. Sometimes going to bed early is the only way to get any sleep at all."

That puzzled me. "It seems quiet compared to the street and it's warm. Why don't they sleep?"

"They're worried about being robbed or attacked. Even in here where we try to make it safe."

I looked at the heaving roomful of people. In such a mob scene, where no one was turned away until the shelter was full, crimes would be easy to perpetrate. Though the theft of what these people owned was petty to the law, it would be much more important to the people who had so little to begin with. Assault of some kind would be even worse.

"They must live in a state of constant paranoia," I said.

"Yup. That's why a lot of them drink or use drugs—though we don't allow that here—so they don't have to feel so much. Despair's an easy trap to fall into."

I could see that too in the sick, sad colors that swirled around many of the figures in the room. Here and there, hot sparks and columns of brighter or crueler emotions pushed up from the low-lying fog of exhaustion. The smell that clung to them seemed to be as much despair or apathy as dirt.

"How do you keep doing this? Doesn't it grind you down?"

The volunteer gave a tired smile. "The Lord gives me strength. If I can help some of them in His name, even if it's just a night's hot meal or a blanket, then maybe they will find hope and strength to rise from this."

A child's wail distracted us. "Oh, boy . . . I'd better go see what that is. You know, if you have a lot of questions about who's doing what, you might want to talk to Sandy over there." She pointed and I followed her indication to a woman sitting against the near wall in a bright yellow energy corona that sent tendrils over everything near it. "She's a little . . . imaginative, but she keeps a sharp eye on things." Then the volunteer left me alone.

I glanced around and spotted Quinton moving slowly through the room. He seemed to be making slow progress, so I thought I'd give Sandy a try. I walked over to where she was sitting and plopped myself onto the floor in front of her. My knee complained a little at the sudden acute angle as I folded my legs.

She was probably in her mid-sixties—though it was hard to tell the ages of the homeless and most seemed much older than they had to be. Her salt-and-pepper hair was clipped very short, and she was curiously round and thin at the same time as if she'd been comfortably well off before something had changed her circumstances drastically. She had a pair of very large glasses that she adjusted on her nose as I sat down. She was still shorter than me, but not tiny, so I guessed she was about average height when standing. She was wearing a white raincoat over a collection of blue and purple sweaters and skirts and ragged work boots. She smelled of potting soil and talcum powder.

She met my eyes at once. "Hello," she said. "Do you need help?"

"Are you Sandy?" I asked.

She nodded once. "I am Sandy. What do you want?"

"The volunteer back there said you see everything that happens around here, and I'd like to ask you some questions."

"I can answer some. So long as they don't blow my cover."

"Your cover?"

"Yes. I'm undercover. Part of an ongoing investigation. I can't discuss the details. You'd have to call my lieutenant."

"Oh." She didn't sound much like any undercover cop I'd ever met—they don't go around saying they're undercover for one thing. But she seemed willing to talk if I was willing to play along. So I did. "I'll be discreet when I call. What's your full name?"

"Detective Sergeant Sandra Livengood."

"Thank you, Sandy. Here's the situation. I'm a private investigator—"

She interrupted me. "Oh, I know who you are, Ms. Blaine. I see you in the Square all the time. We've checked you out. Go on."

That startled me a little, but it was plausible that she had seen me and did know who I was if she spent enough time in Pioneer Square. Though it was strange that I didn't recognize *her*. In spite of that creepy factor, I went on. "I'm trying to discover if there's been anything . . . strange going on in the area around the underground accesses in Pioneer Square."

"Oh, that. Yes, there've definitely been more of them lately." As she was talking to me, she scanned the room, watching constantly.

"More what?"

"Zombies. I'm pretty sure some of them are recently coined, not just immigrants or plants. The new ones smell less."

"Immigrant zombies? Where do they come from?"

"Oh, for the love of— They come from China. On boats. In containers. Or they come in from Tacoma and Bellingham at their master's bidding. You can bet we'll figure out who he is someday. We can't let this zombie thing get out of hand. Luckily, they're easy to kill."

If I hadn't seen one myself, I'd have thought she was totally bonkers. As it was, I thought she was mostly bonkers. "What did you mean by 'recently coined'?"

"I mean they're the recent dead raised by whatever voodoo someone is up to. I really could wish the department was a little more on the ball about that—I know they're fragile, but that doesn't mean zombies aren't a threat for as long as they do survive. Good Lord, they're not exactly the sort of things you want crawling around in infrastructure. Next to bioterrorism, there's not much worse than a zombie in the water supply. They're no treat in the electrical systems, either."

"Could their appearance be related to the spate of disappearances and deaths among the homeless?"

"Certainly! I wouldn't be surprised in the least. Now you mention it, I think the first one turned up a few weeks after they found that leg at the construction site on Occidental South. I've found a few bits and pieces since then."

"What sort of bits and pieces?"

"Body parts. Let me think. A few fingers, a toe, a hand, a foot, most of an arm."

"Where did you find them?" I asked, leaning forward.

"Some of the fingers I found in the alley behind the kite shop. The arm was down under Jackson Street. The foot . . . I think that was up against the wall by the Grand Central Bakery's glass porch, though that might have been the hand—I'd have to look at my notes. The toe I found on Yesler in a stairwell. No—I'm confusing that with the hand. Definitely. I found the hand in the stairwell by Bud's Jazz Records. The toe was on Yesler, but it was just next to the door the Underground tour uses when they come up from the bank. The tourists probably walked right past it and didn't notice—it looked like a piece of dog dropping."

"Surely a toe looks like a toe?"

"Not really. Even fresh they don't look too impressive, and you might not notice if they're dirty and bloodless. That's a thing to note—the bodies and the parts have all been quite bloodless. The scenes aren't cleaned up, so the perp isn't wiping up afterward. There just isn't much blood."

"Which bodies are you referring to?"

"Hafiz and Jan. I didn't see Go-cart's body, but I heard it's the same way—not enough blood. Believe me—when you cut into arteries there's a lot of red, even when the body's been dead a while. Saw a man hit by a train once—God, what a mess that was."

I put a lock on my imagination and pushed that vision aside. "Any ideas on why there's so little blood?"

She frowned and finally turned to study me. "I don't like to advance theories without more evidence, so I'd rather just say something is draining the blood or keeping it from flowing. Could be a lot of factors. You need an autopsy report to know for sure."

Her attention shifted over my shoulder and the bright energy around her slammed down to a narrow yellow outline that hugged close to her body. Sandy stood up in a rush and grabbed her bag. "I have to go. My suspect is on the move." She darted off through the crowd and ducked out the front door before I could see who she might be following as her energy shadow vanished in the sea of homeless diners. I couldn't decide if I thought she'd been incredibly helpful or incredibly nuts.

I scanned the room and caught sight of Quinton talking to someone who was hidden from my sight. I eased toward him and came level with Quinton as he squatted down in front of an old, rough-skinned native man.

"No, don't think I've seen him in a while," the man was saying in a tired mumble as I arrived. He poked the food on his tray with a fork in a desultory way and didn't meet Quinton's eyes. He had a round face graced with a mouth that folded in over mostly toothless jaws, making his chin thrust forward. His hair was coarse gray strands that brushed his shoulders. The aura around his head was small and pale, as if even the energy of the Grey was running low here. "Aside from them what died, I'd guess there's a few gone missing." Cheap, hoppy beer clung to his breath and his coat had a scent of garages and motor oil to it. He looked up as I came to a stop beside them, jerking his head over to peer at me from one eye and going silent and scared.

"She's OK, Jay. This is Harper. You've seen her around the Square," Quinton said.

"I'm not sure. . . ."

"You like to sit near the first tree on the Square, near the Pioneer Building's door," I said as I recognized him. "You remember back in October when I gave Zip back his lighter when he dropped it?"

He hesitated, licking his lower lip as he thought about it. Then he grunted. "Uh. Yeah. I do know you. You gave him money, too. We had some good smokes that day, me and Zip."

"That's good. May I sit next to you?"

Jay grunted and slid over, dragging a stained blanket patterned in gray, red, and black along the bench under his legs. I sat down in the tight space between him and the next diner, who shot me a glance and hunched over his tray possessively.

Guessing, I asked, "Are you Blue Jay?"

Another grunt and a nod. "Yeah. Not a *good* name, but it's *my* name."

"Oh? Why isn't it a good name?"

"Jays. They're talkers, braggarts. Too smart for their own good, but lazy."

"You don't seem that way."

"Oh, I was. I was." He nodded to himself. "I try to be better now I'm old."

"Jay," Quinton said. "Stop flirting."

Jay blushed. "Not flirting."

"You are too, you old fox."

"No, foxes are bad—they mean danger and death are nearby. I seen a fox last night, running through the alley behind that fancy bar."

"Which bar?" I asked. It was too odd a coincidence that we'd both seen a fox on the same night.

"Oh. That martini place—with the devil on the sign."

"Marcus' Martini Heaven?"

Jay nodded. "I guess."

The bar was about three blocks from where Will and I had been confronted by the hairy creature and the zombie. At the reminder, I felt my gut wrench and had to swallow hard and clasp my hands together against a sudden cold frisson of memory and a lick of anger at Will for abandoning me there. I must have looked as upset as I felt, maybe I'd gone pale—I certainly felt chilled enough—because Quinton gave me a worried glance. I shook him off.

"I don't think anyone else died last night," he said.

"Not that I heard of," Jay replied. "But could be something else. Could be . . . another gone somehow."

"You mean missing? Like Tandy?" Quinton continued.

"Could be."

"Who've you noticed missing?" Quinton asked.

"Well, Tandy and, uh . . . Little Jolene. What's his name . . . The guy always has a forty going. . . ."

"Pranker Jheri."

Jay slapped his thigh and nodded. "Jerrycan Jerry."

"What about Bear?"

"I told you I haven't seen Bear." He plucked at the blanket and lowered his head further. "I found his blanket, though."

"I thought I recognized it. Where did you find it?"

"In the bricks." He stood up. "I'll show you."

We followed Blue Jay back out into the cold, he wrapping himself in the dirty blanket and us making due in the icy air with just our coats. As we headed back toward Pioneer Square, I glanced up and saw a ring around the moon—ice in the air. I shivered and followed Quinton and Jay through the freezing darkness and the streets empty of life but thick with the shades of the dead.

SIX

We staggered and slipped our way west on the frosted sidewalks of Jackson Street—my knee twinging—until we were a half block from Occidental where Jay took a sharp right turn into an alley beside the newly rebuilt Cadillac Hotel. Parts of the brick frontage had tumbled down in the earthquake of February 2001 and the old place had been slated for demolition. Like the titular phoenix—or "Fenix"—of the nightclub that had once graced its basement, the building had somehow risen from the ashes and reopened as the new Klondike Gold Rush National Historic Park in 2005. How a museum entirely contained in a building was a national park still confounded me, and I wasn't sure how they'd rebuilt the place from the wreck that had stood on the corner of Jackson and Second for years.

I was pretty sure that there were no unguarded openings on the building, but Jay ducked down in front of a sunken window on the opposite side of the alley, glancing up and down the brick roadway, and pulled a bit of grillwork loose. Then he disappeared into the resulting hole as slick as an eel. Quinton waved me forward and showed me the tiny ledge at the bottom of the window frame on which to place my foot. From my half-sunk position it was easy to slide down into the dark gulf below the buildings.

A rush of unnatural cold washed over me as I descended, like plunging feet first into a pool of Grey. I felt like Alice gone down a haunted rabbit hole. Quinton came down behind me, hanging onto the ledge for a moment as he pulled the grille back into place, and dropped to the floor of cracked and tilted concrete and compacted dirt.

Quinton brought out his flashlight and directed it at the ground, keeping the beam from reflecting into the glass of the window we'd entered through. I'd expected to land in a basement, but the space proved to be a gallery built of brick and rusting iron girders that held up part of the alley above. I looked around in the dim light and felt a little dizzy. Here below the street the world was in the unending grip of gelid fire and inhabited by ghosts, fairly writhing with the incorporeal mass of deceased humanity. Their phantom bodies flowed through and around us like chill water, making me shiver and gasp in their unexpected tide. Long dead men, horses, and dogs—even a mangy cat—still went about their business here while the roaring flames of the Great Fire consumed all and nothing.

Quinton's beam spotlighted a more lively animal—a brown rat that scuttled into a deeper darkness with a squeak of outrage. Then the blinding light moved over my face and quickly back down to the ground.

"Are you all right? You look sick."

"Just adjusting. The atmosphere's a little . . . heavy here," I panted, getting my equilibrium back.

Then I whispered to him, "Have you ever . . . seen any zombies . . . down here?"

He looked at me and blinked. Then he answered slowly. "If by zombie you mean ambulatory dead, then yes. I have." He fell into a wary silence, as if he wasn't sure what I was going to make of the answer.

"That sounds like a nutty question, doesn't it?"

"From most people, I guess. From you, I think it means there's something more going on. So, what is it?"

I shrugged. "I don't know yet. Sandy—the woman I was talking to at the Union Gospel Mission—said she'd seen zombies and found body parts around Pioneer Square since the storms, and I had a . . . run-in with a zombie last night. A walking corpse, to be more precise. Just before I saw it, I saw a fox—just like Jay did and in the same area. Probably the same fox."

"I thought that spooked you."

I nodded. "Here was the strange thing—well, one of several strange things. . . ." I felt myself frowning about that and shook it off.

"What strange things—stranger than zombies, that is?"

"This zombie was animated by its own spirit—or two spirits—which was trapped in the corpse by a—a kind of web." I was having a little difficulty with a more precise description without going into ridiculous detail that wasn't relevant. "Magic energy—one of those things I can see and touch. But the important point was that I found the same sort of material on the hole in the tunnel wall where you found Go-cart yesterday. I've never seen anything quite like it elsewhere, so I think it's the same thing in both cases, which would imply a connection to a common source or cause between the dead man and the zombie. And Sandy's talking about missing people and zombies made me wonder. . . ."

Jay had moved farther down the buried alley and whispered

back to us from the dark. "Up here. There's people in here. They took Bear's stuff."

Quinton linked one of my arms with his free one and tugged me gently forward. "C'mon. We'll talk about this later."

I nodded and took a deep breath before falling in beside him. Moving helped, but I was thinking as we went. If Go-cart was part of a pattern of death and disappearance, were the strands of soft, neutral Grey part of that pattern? If so, then the pattern would link him to the zombie I'd had thrust upon me the night before, and that man had been dead quite a while. Who was he before he became a walking, rotting prison for his soul, and who had been along for the ride? I shuddered and carried on beside Quinton through the unseen throng of burning ghosts.

We caught up to Blue Jay at an underground corner, where the alley met an old sunken sidewalk of rotted boards and disrupted cement. Down the sidewalk to our left there was a light and gathered around it were three people.

Jay pointed into the dark at the near corner and spoke in a raw whisper. "I found the blanket there a couple days ago. Bear's hat was there, too, but it didn't fit me, so I left it. Now it's gone. You see the man with the braids? Tall Grass."

"Did he take Bear's hat?" Quinton asked.

"I don't see it on him."

"Do you see Lass or Tanker?"

"No. Just Tall Grass and his girlfriend and . . . looks like one of the People."

I shot a questioning look at Quinton, who whispered back, "He means another Indian." Quinton peeked around Jay's shoulder and studied the group. "They look OK. Let's go ask them what they've seen. If they've seen Bear or his stuff. Or Lass or Tanker."

Jay dug in his heels. "I won't go."

"Why not?" Quinton asked.

"Moths. And that bird. There shouldn't be birds down here. That's bad."

I backed up so I could lean against the other building corner and see down the sidewalk better. Through the fog of Grey shapes I spotted the more solid, moving flickers of large moths. They were acting strange for moths—staying away from the light in favor of fluttering around the heads of the people in the circle.

"I don't see a bird," I said.

Jay pointed into the shadow where the light began to fade away into darkness again. A gleam of something dark and shiny showed me the eye of a good-sized bird. As I concentrated on it the shape became more clear. It was a small crow—much smaller than the ones I'd seen at the tunnel mouth, but still a crow. It hopped and flapped its wings, flying farther into the shadows, and I knew this was screwy—birds don't fly in the dark. The gleam of the light touched several more pairs of bird and rat eyes that blinked from the darkness.

"What is it with crows and moths?" I muttered.

"Moths carry messages from ghosts. Crows and ravens, they're 'specially magical. Those guys are talking to ghosts. I don't want nothing to do with ghosts. Bad, bad magic." Jay began backing away, past Quinton and me. Then he turned and ran into the darkness in the opposite direction.

I didn't like the feeling of being abandoned, but fleeing myself wouldn't help. There was something more than ordinarily eerie to the situation—perhaps it was the setting, though. The hidden sidewalk and its sun-deprived landscape populated by the shapes of memory and broken slabs of time over equally broken concrete had an otherworldly feel that encouraged an anticipation of something uncanny breaking through at any moment.

"Well," I muttered to Quinton, "I talk to ghosts all the time. This doesn't look too bad. You know any of them?"

Quinton pointed to each one, his voice edged in distaste as he spoke. "The woman is Jennifer Novoy—Jenny Nin. Small-time grunge rocker, got into drugs, fell out of the regular world and into this one. Whores for drugs, alcohol—you name it. Probably why Jenny's down here with Tall Grass. He's big-time trouble, small-time crook. Most of the shelters won't let him in since he's been caught stealing, dealing, and messing with the kids. Criminal record as Thomas Newman. He's from a local tribe—Nisqually—on his mother's side and makes a big deal of it when it suits him to play the victim. He's one of the most politically aware of the undergrounders, though he mostly uses it to his own ends." His tone went neutral. "That other guy—Grandpa Dan—I don't know much about him except he's older than dirt and he seems to polarize the Indians around here—they love him or hate him."

"How do you know some of this? Doesn't sound like the kind of thing most people would tell."

Quinton shrugged. "I do things. I get to know them, or I look into records. I snoop when I have to—I want to know who's going to do what. Some of these guys I know better than their parents did. I wish I didn't, to be honest."

I knew that feeling. It may be part of my job, but sometimes digging around in other people's lives seems dirty—it is dirty. Everyone in the business has a justifying excuse and some limit beyond which they won't go, but there are times when it seems there's not enough soap and hot water to remove the muck.

I stood up straight and took a long, bracing breath. Then I caught Quinton's eye. "Let's go find out what they know about John Bear," I said. "And the rest of this."

We came around the corner and began a slow walk toward the group near the light. A tumbling knot of energy rolled in the air around them, and a scent of burning wood and pot with a hint of rust and mold met us as we neared. The auras around Tall Grass and Jenny wove into each other in shades of black, blue, and green just like a bruise, while Grandpa Dan's was more like a reflective silver mist that bulged with the shapes of ghosts momentarily caught in its surface.

Tall Grass saw us coming and as his attention centered on us, it pulled Jenny Nin's gaze around to us, too. Dan, weathered and gray, pushed back into the shadows a bit more, wary at our approach and drawing himself away from our attention.

"Hey, the Mighty Quinn," Tall Grass drawled.

"I don't see you jumping for joy."

"Got the joy part covered my own self." He put his arm around Jenny's shoulder and pulled her possessively tight. She put her cap-covered head on his shoulder. The dim light of their tiny fire in a large metal pail threw a yellow shine on Jenny's unfocused brown eyes. There was something more than just pot in her blood stream, I'd be willing to bet.

"We were looking for John Bear and Little Jolene, or Lass, or Tanker. You seen any of them?"

Dan just grunted, but Jenny spoke in a slurry, waltz-time voice. "Those guys were here. We're all partying and Lass was all hitting on me and then the dog comes around the corner and—wham!—the dog's all like a rabid monster, yipping and howling, and then mean ol' Tanker's all mad. The dog's all mad and growling and we're all like, 'Shut up, man.' Tanker's all in my face and then Lass's. Then he ran off. Asshole. Didn't like our party, so he left, too."

I was confused as to which of the men was an asshole and which didn't want to party. Unless it was Bella, but it was fairly obvious she hadn't been in a party mood.

Quinton looked stormy. "Damn it. I told Lass not to tag that dog." He turned to me. "Didn't I tell him to stay away from Tanker?"

"Yes, you did," I affirmed.

"See, that's what I was afraid of. They both said they were coming down here and sure enough Lass has to act like a jerk."

"Hey, dude, don't be so rough," Jenny said, giggling, and turning the Grey mist around herself a drunken shade of magenta. "The dog started it."

Quinton sighed. "If you say so. So Bear and Jolene were down here, too?"

"Nah, stupid. Just Dan, here, and Lass and Tanker. And monster dog."

"When did Bear give you his hat?"

Jenny sat up, sending a moment's red flare into the tangled energy around them, and yanked the earflaps of the kooky leather and fur hunter's cap down so the bill rode onto her eyebrows. "Fuck you."

"Don't hassle my girl, Q," Tall Grass warned, leaning into the light so he looked like a monster from a silent film. "We found it down here with some crappy broken stuff someone dumped over there." He pointed into the dark just behind my right shoulder where the street wall was. "Isn't that so, Grandfather?"

Dan didn't actually answer, but Tall Grass took his silence for confirmation before going on. "Just keeping it until Bear comes around again. Haven't seen him in weeks. And not Jolene, either. Lot of folks gone to warmer places, I think. Bear probably got smart and went, too."

"Not hassling you, Grass. Just trying to find some people. Seems like there's a lot of people missing and dead this year."

"Well, that's sad, but it's the cycle of life, brother. Some go, some come. Like those guys with the wagon and like that crazy lady in the park—you know, the one who laughs at everything?"

"Yeah, I know. She's native, right?"

"First Nations, white eyes."

"What's with the politically correct Candianism? I thought you were a Washington Nisqually."

Grass tried to look noble but didn't carry it off. "We are all one great people, without boundaries. It's your people who want to cut everything up and make countries and territories and reservations out of it."

Quinton did not take the bait. "I just wondered if she was from a local tribe. I hadn't seen her around before Thanksgiving."

"I think she's Kwakiutl—funky accent like Bella Coola Valley. Y'know—in Canada," Tall Grass added with a sneer at Quinton.

"Dudes, you're bringing me down," Jenny whined. She pulled a sloshing bottle of brown liquid from the shadows by her side and waved it. "Sit down, drink up, shut up. Or fuck off."

"All right." Quinton squatted down near the pail of burning junk and held out his hand.

Jenny leaned forward, trashed and unsteady, and slapped the bottle into his hand. "S'better." She petted his hand a second. "You loosen up good. Hey . . . you wanna screw? S'quiet down here. . . ."

Quinton took a swig from the bottle, but I noticed he didn't swallow. "Nah. Gotta work tonight," he added, handing the bottle back to Jenny.

Jenny pouted insincerely and took the bottle, drinking and passing it to Tall Grass, who made a show of looking me over as I squatted down between Quinton and the silent Dan.

"Working," Grass said with a laugh. "That's not work, brother. That is a long, slow pleasure ride."

"Can't ride what you can't catch," I started, then was cut short by a soft snort from my left. Tall Grass just laughed, hearing nothing of the sound and not even noticing the old man getting to his feet.

He was still bent even standing and the light made red rivers on his creased face. It almost seemed as if only I could see him, for all the notice the others took. He just stared at them and then looked around at the fluttering insects and deeper into the blackness beyond the fire's light. I watched him, tuning out the conversation on my other side as I noticed a silvery shadow clinging to his form.

"Fools," Grandpa Dan muttered at last, the ghost shape gleaming on him. "The ravens say death comes here." He glared at the air. He paid none of us any heed as he started off into the dark, disrupting the fluttering moths that swung in crazy circles, making odd eddies in the Grey mist that almost took form before collapsing into nothingness. A rustle of feathered wings trailed away behind him, and the shadows of crows closed him into the dark.

I stared after him, wondering what that meant. Then I was jarred from my thoughts by a hand on my back. I turned to see Quinton, his brows drawn down and a small orange light outlining his form as he peered at me in the waning light of the fire.

"Did he say something?"

A rattle of wings from the darkness made me cover a shiver with a shrug. "Something about death and fools. I think he's unimpressed."

"Grass and Jenny and I have made a list of who's missing."

I'd lost a few minutes in my reverie. I glanced at Tall Grass and

Jenny, who both appeared a lot more trashed than before. I shot a questioning look at Quinton. He pointed at the empty bottle on the ground.

Jenny tittered. "Good stuff, Maynard."

"Jet fuel is what it is," Quinton corrected.

"S'good though," she replied, and broke into half-swallowed guffaws that sounded like whale hiccups.

Tall Grass wrapped his arm around her and pulled her into his chest, kissing drunkenly at her head and mostly getting the hat under his lips. He growled and jerked it off, revealing messy, butched-out brown locks. He managed to snare her short hair in his fist and yank her head back, exposing her thin face to his slobbering assault. They tumbled sideways into the ice-coated wall, groping and pawing at each other.

I rolled my eyes and pushed to my feet, banishing the complaints of my knee to a back compartment of my attention. I hoped those two wouldn't get frostbite or set fire to anything, but that was about as far as my concern for Jenny and Grass went. "How do we get out of here?" I asked Quinton.

"Out's easier than in." He grabbed my hand and we went the same direction Jay had taken, away from Occidental, around the Second Avenue corner, and down the short stretch of tunnellike sidewalk to a recently installed metal door with a push bar on it. The door led into a tiny space with two more doors. The one on our right opened on a modern fire stair, and we went up it to exit on Second between the Cadillac Hotel and its neighbor.

We peered out of the doorway like frightened animals and found the cold street empty of all but ice and the unearthly chill of Grey mist. Quinton nodded. "OK. Let's move. It's too cold to stand here."

We walked away toward my office. I felt a little disoriented, as if I'd missed something, so I kicked the conversation back into gear as we went. "All right. Who's on the list?" I asked.

"The first of the strange dead bodies was a guy named Hafiz. No one was sorry to see him go. The Women in Black didn't organize a vigil but just stuck him on the leaflets for the next time—that's how much people didn't like him."

"Hafiz. Was he Muslim?"

"Not that I heard and certainly not that anyone cared. Being a mean-spirited ass seems to have universal application. Then Chaim Jankowski and now Go-cart. There've been a couple of other deaths, but they were from things like heart attack and drug overdose, so I'm not counting those. Just the weird ones."

"Go on. Who else?"

"John Bear and Little Jolene, Tandy, Pranker Jheri—no idea what his parents were thinking with that name—and Felix." He pronounced it the Spanish way: Feh-LEEHKS. "There may be others, but that's for sure. None of them would just take off or had anyplace else to go, and if they moved up, they'd have told someone. The Enhancement League tries to keep track of who makes it into housing, and there's usually talk if someone's been seen in another part of town. None of that's true with those five."

"So you're thinking all of them are victims of vampires or whatever it was that killed Go-cart."

"I'm leaning that way."

We'd come to my parking garage and I stopped by the gate. "Sandy's talk about the lack of blood gives me pause, but I'm still reserving judgment on the vampires. There is something going on, creating a pattern, and that's disturbing. Even crazy ladies and homeless criminals are picking up on it—though I'm not putting too much store by any one set of remarks."

"Smart. I live with these guys and I understand them, but most of them are at least a little nuts."

"Crazy sounds like self-defense, here."

"Yeah." He looked at me for a moment in silence before continuing, his expression hidden by the shadow of his hat brim. "Better go home. It's too cold to stay out here."

"Yeah. I'll try to get some info from the medical examiner about Go-cart—Robert Cristus, right?—and look into cause of death on the others to see if there's a real pattern or just an appearance. I'll let you know what I find and see if that moves us anywhere."

"All right. Then I'll be seeing you."

"Yeah."

We stood and stared at each other for a moment. I felt exhausted and uncertain of a lot of things and Quinton seemed hesitant himself, but for a wavering second it seemed he might do or say something. But he didn't and I wondered if my disappointment with Will was making me think all men were on the verge of untoward actions.

At last Quinton turned away a little and started to walk back toward First, lifting a hand to wave. "OK. Good night, Harper."

"Good night," I echoed and lingered a few frowning seconds before going to my truck and heading home to West Seattle.

It felt much later than it was and I was tired, cold, and distracted. I let Chaos out of her cage to romp around the living room while I took a shower and warmed up some soup for my dinner. The ferret followed me into the bathroom but had abandoned her post beside the tub by the time I got out.

I found her in the living room, curled up around a squeaky toy that was shaped like a small eggplant sporting Richard Nixon's face. I scooped her up and put her in my lap while I ate dinner, but she didn't want to stay there either and slithered down the chair leg to the floor to wander off and throw herself down on the living room carpet with a sigh, doing the flat ferret thing and staring at me as if I'd let her down by spending time outside her company. I just wasn't measuring up to anyone's expectations and I found myself irritated by it. I wanted to yell at someone and tell them off about what they could or couldn't have from me. Chaos wasn't the one who deserved it, but I wasn't quite sure who did.

SEVEN

"Harper, you'd better get back down here."

It was five in the morning, so I was kind of groggy, but I recognized Quinton's voice. "What's happened?" I mumbled—the automatic response to such a statement as his.

"Someone else has found a body. Near the park."

I sat up in bed, blinking. "Which park?"

"Between Oxy and Waterfall. There's already police securing the area, so I haven't been able to find out who it is or what's going on."

"You think it's another one like Thursday's?"

"I'd bet on it."

I groaned. "Great. I'll be right there."

No time for more than a splash of water on my face before I pulled on several layers of sweaters and a wool coat over my jeans and boots. Light snow had fallen overnight, and the air seemed no warmer although the radio report claimed the temperature had risen a whopping twenty degrees. My condo was in one of the coldest parts of the city. I figured they must have been reporting from Boeing Field, where the acres of tarmac on the windless plain of the airport always makes it hotter.

I negotiated the ice-crusted streets of West Seattle and crossed the bridge to downtown, where there was no sign it had ever snowed at all. The air coming off Puget Sound was warmer but still nowhere near the usual temp for January.

There were some cop cars, an aid car, a couple of city vans, and a small ant farm's worth of busy people in official-looking clothes around Occidental Park when I arrived at my office building. I parked the Rover in my lot and walked back down the block toward the park.

Pioneer Square was deserted—too early for weekend business and too cold for just hanging out—so the unusual activity just south of the square drew whoever was around. My short walk was accompanied by Zip and one of the other homeless men I'd met the night before. Zip waved to me and I nodded back, guessing they'd come down early to scout the recycling bins behind the bars for any bottles containing a little booze or beer that had been tossed the night before—if the closing crew was in a hurry, they didn't check too closely. Zip smelled like he'd already been diving for bottles. We all walked down the block and into Oxy Park by the totems. A huge, blanket-covered lump snored at the base of one of the wooden statues, oblivious to the killing cold. Zip and his friend stopped near the sleeper, watching the cops warily as I continued.

I spotted a dun-colored van from the medical examiner's office and followed it as it pushed through the crowd toward the southern edge of Oxy Park. I stopped in the fringe of the crowd, but the van stopped where the edge of the parking lot met the wall and iron fence of Waterfall Garden Park on the southeast corner of the block. The low sun hadn't penetrated the frozen shadows on the ground yet, but the shape of a human body was discernible there in the frosted morning gloom. I recognized Detective Solis and a coroner's investigator kneeling beside it. The layers of time around the area were disarrayed and heaved up in broken shards shaggy with disrupted energy lines that were writhing around to reknit themselves as I watched. It made me feel queasy to see them moving like that, confirming that the energy grid was alive in some way.

I backed away a little, staying out of the detective's line of sight to watch the scene.

The coroner's investigator stood up, and he and the scene technician chatted for a moment while Solis continued to stare down at the body. I could see something was wrong with the shape. As Solis dropped the waterproof sheet back over it, the settling fabric fell too flat on the corpse's legs.

As if disturbed and released by the stirring of the air below the covering, a thin Grey shape coiled up from the body and held a human form like a breath in the cold. It looked confused and more vague by the moment. I thought it wouldn't last very long before it disappeared to wherever the lingering memories of ourselves go when there's no reason to stay. I glanced up at the face of the lingering ghost and felt a shock of cold as she met my gaze and then faded from sight, leaving a flashbulb vision of what lay beneath the sheet: Jenny Nin, the hat gone and her right arm ended too soon—the hand that had offered Quinton a bottle and lingered over his own hand was missing, the stump short and gnawed; ragged legs hung in space below the rest. Something clung to her shape like a shredded shawl and her face was blue, twisted with surprise. I felt her go away and hoped I wouldn't see her again in any form, but especially not that one. But I'd have to get a look at the body itself before I'd be sure.

I saw Solis stand, returning his attention to the scene and the removal of the body. By the pulsing line of color around him I knew he was more upset than he let on. I'd have to dodge him, since I couldn't answer the questions he'd surely ask. I turned and stepped behind the orca totem. Then I walked straight from it, keeping the tall wooden figure between me and Solis's sharp eyes until I was too far away to recognize. Then I turned the corner and hurried back to my truck. If I could get to the morgue faster than the ME's van, I might see the body brought in and that might tell me enough.

The slippery road was tricky driving. I wanted to gun it up the hill to Harborview, but I knew the wheels would only spin on the icy bricks and asphalt. Luck was on my side: I had a small head start and just beat the van to the parking lot. Since I didn't have a clumsy gurney to unload, I made it into the building and down to the basement ahead of the ME's men and their burden.

The morgue always has its compliment of ghosts, though there were fewer this time than the last time I came and they ignored me. None of them seemed aware enough to want anything from me on this occasion. The area's always a bit unwelcoming—old and sterile and furnished in institutional patchwork—and no one particularly notices the drafts, cold spots, and general sense of being in the presence of the unseen. In this dour atmosphere, the night shift was drawing to a post-Friday-night close. Looking drowsy and haggard, the night crew wasn't terribly worried about me as I made my way toward the desk at the pace of a winter tortoise.

The elevator opened behind me and the men from the van came in with their gurney. They stopped at the desk and I stopped next to them. As they handed over paperwork, I stared hard at the bag enclosing the remains of Jennifer Novoy.

I couldn't see through the plastic but there was enough of something clinging to the bag itself to know I'd guessed right. Soft strands of Grey curled from the zipper like fuzzy threads. The same sort of thread I'd seen on the hole in the tunnel wall and on Thursday night's zombie. I hoped it wasn't having the same effect on Jenny that it seemed to have had on him.

I needed to find out and took a risk.

"Hey," I said. "Is that Solis's Jane Doe from Oxy Park?"

The three men around the desk looked back at me, startled.

"Uh, yeah," one of the gurney men replied. "Why?"

I pulled out my license and flipped it past them fast enough to blur the name. "I have a related case. Solis said I should take a look."

The two men with the body glanced at each other and shrugged. The man behind the desk sighed. "Let's get her in the cooler first, huh? Richards will be pissed if she stays out here any longer than necessary."

The men with the gurney agreed and pushed the cart through the swinging doors into the morgue work area. The other man— a rather stocky fellow with skin the color of madrone bark and short, thick, black hair dramatically streaked with white, making him look like a badger—picked up a clipboard to which he'd attached a pile of forms and followed them, motioning me along.

We went past doors to the autopsy rooms and back into the storage area. The chilly air of the cooler was actually warmer than the air outdoors—no one wanted to accidentally freeze the dear departed.

The van crew lifted the bag with care and transferred Jenny to a steel table. Then they unzipped the bag and left it to the man with the clipboard to do the rest. He signed a sheet and handed it to them to sign before ripping off a copy for them and keeping the rest.

"OK, I got her. You're done."

The two men from the van grunted and left with their gurney.

The badger-faced man looked me over. "Don't I know you?"

That threw me. I recognized him from the last time I'd been in the morgue, but I was surprised he remembered. "I'm a PI. Some of my searches end here."

He frowned in thought. Then he snapped his fingers. "Yeah! Back . . . October I think it was. How many Does do you have to look at every year?"

"A lot less than you."

He laughed. "I think I see more corpses in a week than most horror film freaks see in a year. So. You want to eyeball this one and we'll get the hell out of here? Don't know about you, but I'm cold!"

"Yeah, let's get it over with."

He put on indigo-colored latex gloves and peeled the edges of the bag down with big, gentle hands, as if to some silent ceremony he carried in his head. There was no sick delight in it, only a kind of sad reverence.

I looked down at Jenny's pale blue face and flinched at the surprise there. Whatever had killed her had come upon her too fast for screaming. The soft Grey strands I'd expected were curled around her face and chest, but frayed away as they went lower; they didn't form the same kind of tangled web I'd seen on the zombie but looked more like a moth-eaten shawl that was falling away in broken threads. There was very little blood and she looked as if she might have simply frozen to death—if not for her startled expression. I was pretty sure she wouldn't stand up and come looking for me later, and I breathed relief.

"Well?" the badger-man asked.

I shook my head. "Nope." I let him take the answer as he

pleased. I hated lying, but if I identified her, I'd have to sign a form that would bring Solis to my door in a hurry.

He nodded and leaned over to attach a temporary ID with a number to her. Then he gently closed the bag and led me out of the room.

"Have you seen any other bodies like that recently?" I asked.

"What do you mean, 'like'? They're all dead and we've had more homeless than usual, but that happens when the weather's severe."

"Another body came in on Thursday in a similar condition— very little blood, very cold, extremities missing. A Robert Cristus?"

We stepped out through the swinging doors and stopped by the desk. The morgue attendant looked thoughtful.

"Yeah . . . Now you mention it, very similar—at least at first glance." He turned a piercing gaze on me. "You're interested in that case?"

"And this one. Actually I wonder if there have been any others like that—similar condition and circumstances."

When he stopped to stare at me, I got a look at his badge, which read "Fishkiller" in large letters followed by two groups of smaller words I couldn't read before he moved again.

He scowled in thought and went behind his desk, putting the clipboard down. He looked at his computer screen and sat. "I think so. . . . I'm not sure without looking, but I think there have been a few others. All homeless, high blood loss with very little spatter or staining, chewed or missing extremities . . . We have a limb or two also. Similar condition, but no associated bodies."

"Would one of those be the leg discovered in the hotel excavation on Occidental near Royal Brougham?" I asked.

"That's the one. Very similar . . ." He was intrigued, squinting and staring to the side as he thought. I dangled some bait to see if he was the curious type he seemed.

"Do you think there might be older cases like this?"

His fingers slid to the keyboard without his looking at them. "Maybe . . ." He began to type, becoming absorbed in his search.

While he was a little distracted, I said, "That's odd. What does your badge say?"

"Um . . . yeah. Just call me Fish—technically it's Reuben Arthur Fishkiller, but . . . uh . . . Even for an Indian it's kind of an embarrassment. Means, you know, 'crappy fisherman.' You're not supposed to kill 'em, just catch 'em."

"You could change it."

"My mother would skin me. She hates what I do; she hates where I live and where I work. She says I'm a bad Indian for working with the dead—contaminated, you know. The dead and the living aren't supposed to mingle."

"I can understand the sentiment."

He bobbed his head while continuing to type in fits. "Yeah, but it's fascinating. I love forensic pathology. I'm pretty far down the food chain, but I feel like—now, this is hokey, I know—I feel like I'm helping the dead find peace, or justice or something. We just throw people away and then we cry over the hollowness of our own lives. Kind of a messed-up society."

"You mean American society."

"Yeah." He laughed. "See, I *am* a bad Indian. I get frustrated with my own people sometimes. I think some of them hold on too hard, too long. They get pushed around, but they take it because they don't want to have to change. The rez system, the welfare—it's messed up. But when we want to take care of ourselves we get told we can't by the government, or that we're destroying tradition by the tribal elders. Always in the middle. It's hard to be in touch with nature, in balance and thoughtful of tradition, while making a living in the bigger world. But that's what we all want—somehow. My family was so proud when I went to college. Then they were disgusted by what I chose to study—Ha! Yeah!" He sat back and grinned in triumph.

"What?" I asked, smiling back at him—he had that kind of grin.

"Got 'em! We did have some similar cases after the 1949 earthquake. Also Pioneer Square area—which was pretty badly hit, just like in 2001. Those old buildings are on fill over the mudflats, and they heave and crack and all kinds of freaky stuff shows up. Maybe it's my ancestors having a little revenge on you guys," he added with a wink. "You know, Doc Maynard paid Sealth to let them name the city after him—even though that kind of thing is bad luck and binds the spirit to the thing that has its name—and then when he died, none of the whites even came to old Sealth's funeral. Lousy deal."

"Didn't the chief say something about ghosts of the natives haunting the city?" I asked. I thought I'd seen some quote about it somewhere.

Fish leaned back in his chair. "Well . . . there's a pretty speech attributed to him, but I doubt he actually said it. I don't think he was that flowery a talker in real life. But the quote—they teach this in tribal school—is 'These shores shall swarm with the invisible dead of my tribe, and when your children's children shall think themselves alone in the field, the store, the shop, upon the highway or in the silence of the woods, they will not be alone. At night, when the streets of your cities and villages shall be silent, and you think them deserted, they will throng with the returning host that once filled and still love this beautiful land.' Almost sounds like a threat, doesn't it?"

I blinked at him and thought the old man knew a lot more

than he got credit for. Certainly the ghosts of his people did throng parts of Seattle—I'd seen them. "Sounds a little sad to me, for a people who don't want the dead and living to mingle."

"Oh, that's just the bodies. Ancestors and other spirits are around all the time—according to my mother and my old grandma anyway. Not sure how I feel about it, though. Not sure I'd want to hang around myself with nothing to do."

"Wouldn't know until you tried it, I guess," I said.

"Yeah. I think I'll put that off a little longer, thanks."

The noise of the day shift arriving distracted him and I made a quick exit before anyone asked me to sign any forms.

I was intrigued and disturbed that there was a matching pattern of deaths from almost sixty years earlier. The indications pointed increasingly toward a long-term paranormal element and the most obvious was the vampires. I wasn't at all pleased at the prospect of a private conversation with Edward Kammerling, but it appeared I had no other option. Asking the other vampires without consulting Edward first would rouse his annoyance. Our current relationship was one of deliberate distance on my part and occasional attempts to gain control over me on his. I suspected that I had a very small surprise to spring on him that would force him to keep his distance for our chat, but it would only be good the one time. I hoped I wouldn't regret giving it up in the future, but you can't horde all your assets forever.

With the information from Fish and a strong feeling that Jenny Nin would not be shambling out of the morgue, I left Harborview with a fair balance of good and evil before me: no immediate monsters and an emerging—if upsetting—pattern of bodies that might point to the cause of the recent deaths; but to learn more, I'd have to walk into my least favorite lion's den and have a talk with the head lion—who was distinctly a man-eater with designs on me for a side dish.

I drove back to my office past Occidental Park and saw that the police were already cleaning up and closing the crime scene down. Solis was nowhere in sight. I imagined he wasn't pleased with these deaths, but there might be very little he could do to keep the files active. Without the knowledge I had, the logical conclusion—even if the facts were a bit reluctant to fit perfectly—was simple death by exposure to the intense cold, followed by depredation by feral dogs. Ugly and unpleasant, but adequate for most purposes, and I'd come to know that an adequate explanation was often more desirable than a perfect truth.

From my office I called Edward's secretary. It was Saturday and I got an answering service staffed by an actual person. She assured me Mr. Kammerling would be in touch.

My mind wandered toward thoughts of Will and, as if summoned, my cell phone rang, displaying his number. I wasn't sure I wanted to answer, but I poked the button anyhow.

"Hi, Will." I was still irritable from lack of sleep and the ragged edge of pity for Jenny Nin. Not sure what he wanted, I wasn't too inclined to fill the empty air between us with words.

"Hi, Harper. I wanted to apologize," he started, "for being hasty—for freaking out the other night. I know things couldn't have been what they looked like."

Since they weren't so far from what they had looked like, I didn't say anything.

"This is pretty hard." I knew he wanted me to make it easier, but I wasn't going to. My misery and shock at the way our last date had ended were turning into anger, and I had no intention of letting him off the hook with a few halting apologies. "I was hoping," he continued, "that you might have breakfast with me. I'm down at Endolyne Joe's."

"It was snowing on the hill earlier," I said, "and I'm at the office now. Driving back across the bridge and down to Fauntleroy isn't high on my priority list."

"The snow's not so bad here and it's keeping the morning crowd away. We'd have some privacy."

I growled. Will was wheedling, which I'd never heard from him before and didn't like, but our business was unfinished and I supposed I should take the opportunity he was offering to either save our relationship or bury it for good.

"All right. I need to close up some stuff and I'll be there as soon as I can."

Yet another reason to love my rattly old Rover: four-wheel drive and aggressive tires. Not that they'd save me if I drove like an idiot, but I'd seen enough SUVs in ditches from the ice and mud after the storms to take care and assume nothing.

The Rover managed the trip fine, even with a few patches of ice pretending to be snow in the curvy shadows where Fauntleroy Way wriggles along the coast and then turns inland to climb the hill that I live on top of. There were plenty of parking spaces in Endolyne Joe's lot, and I could see through the restaurant's windows that the place was mostly empty.

Officially, the area is Fauntleroy, but the bit just south of the ferry landing is called Endolyne—pronounced "end o' line," since it used to be the end of the trolley line until sometime in the 1950s when the last of the Interurban service was shut down. The restaurant is supposedly named for a notorious womanizing trolley conductor called Endolyne Joe, but I wasn't sure how much truth there was in the tale.

Once again, Will was waiting at a table in a warm corner

while the few other customers in the place had chosen to sit at the counter in the immediate blast of heat from the blue-and-white-tiled kitchen. I was hungry, but I had very little desire to eat and shooed the waiter off with "Just coffee, please." Will reached for my hands and I let him take them without either resisting or aiding. I felt a cold that had nothing to do with the white dusting of snow outside.

"Harper, I'm sorry. That was just the stupidest thing I could have done."

"I don't know—freaking out seems like a pretty normal reaction to what happened. Abandoning me under the viaduct . . . now that was a little rough." It wasn't until the words were out of my mouth that I realized how pissed off I was, how saddened, how very disappointed. And how little I cared if I hurt him back.

He shook his head and looked upset. "I know. It was . . . rotten. I was so shocked by what I thought I saw. . . ."

The waiter returned with a thick-walled mug of coffee for each of us and a plate of coffee cake for Will. I pulled my hands back and wrapped them around the mug, happy for the extra heat and the escape from Will's grip. I glanced aside and didn't see any sign of the blue filament of Grey stuff I'd seen on his hands at our last parting, so my discomfort was purely human.

"What did you think you saw?" I asked.

He looked uncomfortable and I noticed that the glow of energy around him fluxed greenish and sank down. "It doesn't matter. It wasn't true."

I was out of patience with being diplomatic. "Maybe it was true. Maybe the thing you saw that you don't want to believe really was a zombie and maybe I really did tear it into pieces."

Will jerked back against the upholstery of his seat. "What?"

I pitched my voice down to a harsh whisper. "I don't know

what you think you saw—what sort of justification or confabulation you've made for it—but the fact is two monsters walked up to us on the street and I dismantled one of them. To you they looked like bums, but to me they were a hairy man and a walking corpse, and the zombie had to go. And that's what they really were and that's what really happened. I'm not crazy, before you ask. I'm telling you the unvarnished truth: I talk to ghosts; I work for monsters. That's the big, ugly secret you always wanted to know. There it is."

I sat back with my coffee mug and glared at him and waited to hear what he would say.

Will gaped at me, his face very pale. The light reflecting off the yellow walls turned his silver hair a buttery blond and he looked young and confused and charmingly nerdy behind his spectacles. I felt like I'd kicked a puppy.

"Why?" he choked out.

"Why what?" I replied in a milder voice. "Why work for them? Why tell you now? Why lie?"

"Why are you being like this?"

"I'm not 'being' anything but truthful—as ugly as it is. This is why I never discuss my cases and why I disappear and why terrible things seem to happen around me. I don't like it, but it is what it is. Usually it's not nice or pretty—it's brutal and damned ugly and I wish I wasn't stuck in it. But I do the best I can to keep the ugly from spreading. That's what I had to do Friday night."

"By . . . tearing that . . . creature"—Will fought to get the words out, and I could see the energy around him twisting and flushing with clashing colors—red, green, orange, and vivid naked blue—" . . . tearing it apart . . . you were . . . making something better?"

I had tried to explain it before and I knew he wasn't taking it in any better now, so why waste the breath repeating myself? "Yes" was all I said.

"But . . . what happ—"

"What do you think happened?" I demanded, leaning forward again, pinning his gaze with mine. I wished I could push on him somehow—at least stop the strobing, polychromatic storm around his body—but it wouldn't have been right.

"You— I don't know." He slumped in his seat. "I don't know what you did. I saw you reach into him and he . . . fell apart. And there was some light. And then he was gone."

I nodded. "Yeah, that's about it."

The colors around him collapsed to a miserable olive green that clung like toxic smoke. He looked shrunken and disjointed. "How often? How often does it happen?"

I started to say it wasn't common, but when I tallied it in my head, the number of disturbing and awful things I'd done or seen or had a hand in was too big, and the zombie was actually one of the better incidents—at least someone had taken some relief from it. My pause was too long, and Will saw me calculating the number of horrors.

He shook his head. "I can't live with that. I can't take on that . . . breakage."

I was torn between outraged silence and screaming, but I chose to speak calmly. "I don't have a choice."

"I guess . . . this isn't going to work, then. I am sorry. I am."

"Yeah, I know. I'm a great girl, except for the ghosts and the craziness." He shifted in his seat and I held up my hand to stop him. "No. I think it's my turn to go."

I got up, still holding my coffee cup. I handed it to a waiter as he passed. "I can't finish this." Then I looked back down at Will. It seemed like I ought to kiss him good-bye—a nice Hollywood gesture—but I didn't. "I am sorry, too, Will. I love you but I don't belong with you."

I left, villainous and caddish, because although I felt angry and wrecked and horrid I was also relieved. At least it was over and I didn't have to care about anyone but me. I wondered if by "breakage," Will meant mine. Maybe he thought I was crazy and that's what he couldn't bear. Or maybe he got it and he just couldn't face that. Even a tiny dose of the Grey was more than I'd wish on most people, and certainly not on Will, no matter how upset or brokenhearted I was.

Driving was difficult. My eyes kept tearing up and the fog of the Grey seemed worse with the snow light. The road was icy and treacherous—like me, I thought, and then got angry with myself for it. Anger made the tears stop, at least, and I thought I would not go home and feel sorry for myself.

I killed time going to the gym and then doing some research for Nanette Grover's cases before I headed home again, a little depressed and just wanting to be alone with the simple needs of home and pet. I did chores and played with Chaos for a while. The weather didn't seem to be agreeing with her, and I caught her shivering a few times. I wondered if I ought to turn up the heat in the condo, though it didn't seem uncomfortable to me. I reminded myself that she was six years old, so she was entitled to an occasional bout of crankiness, and offered her a raisin, which elicited a bouncing war dance and begging for more treats. She tried to steal any treats I might be hiding by climbing my legs and searching in my sweaters before crawling around my shoulders to get tangled in my hair and plant whiskery ferret kisses on my face and neck.

"Have you had that cuteness patented yet?" I asked. Annoyed at the lack of additional raisins, Chaos didn't deign to reply but scampered back down my body to tell her troubles to Nixon the Eggplant as she forced him—with a protesting blat—into a favorite hidey-hole next to the entertainment center. I could hear the toy uttering sporadic squawks and squeaks as Chaos bit and shoved it.

My attempts to rescue Nixon from the lair were interrupted by a phone call from Edward about a half hour after sundown. He purred his delight at my desire to meet. We agreed on eight o'clock at the After Dark—barely the shank of a winter evening for a vampire. I wished Quinton could come along as my bodyguard, but I knew Edward wouldn't approve and I didn't want him in a bad mood, however much I despised the necessity of going.

After dinner, I got dressed up as nicely as I could stand for the temperature—nice wool trousers instead of jeans and a better quality of sweater with dress boots instead of my usual urban hikers—and tucked the ferret back into her cage. I left her moping in her collection of old sweatshirt scraps as I headed out.

I had to stop by my office again before meeting Edward, and I needed a little extra time.

EIGHT

The After Dark club lies at the bottom of a circular marble staircase behind an iron gate that always seems to be locked. It's the social club, audience chamber, court, and coliseum of the local vampire community—or pack, as I prefer to think of them. I'd let Quinton know where I was going and when—just in case I didn't come back. I thought I could keep myself out of Edward's clutches, but everything's a bit of a crapshoot with vampires. They don't have the same motives, fears, or taboos that humans have, and it's all too easy to make a wrong assumption and end up a meal—or a toy, as one of my clients had discovered. I'd have to keep a tight rein on my recurring annoyance at the morning's scene with Will, too, or I'd be easy prey while distracted.

Even at a distance, I could feel their presence as a boil of fire and ice that sent billows of red and black into the Grey around the door. I took a couple of deep, steadying breaths of the frigid air and started down the stairs. The gate clanged shut behind me, cutting off a few hardy idiots who'd decided to come down to Pioneer Square to party in the densely packed clubs, bars, and restaurants the area was famous for. They wouldn't have liked the reception at the After Dark, even if they'd gotten past the doorman, who opened the black lacquered doors as I reached the bottom landing.

He wasn't quite a vampire, as far as I could tell. The usual aura of death, blood, and magic wasn't the right density and he didn't exude the psychic stink I associated with bloodsuckers. He was even a bit nondescript—which was something most vampires didn't bother to cultivate. He looked me over with a flick of his gaze and held the door for me. "Ms. Blaine." He put out his hand for my coat, but I didn't surrender it. I never had before and I wasn't going to this time, either; the undead don't care what the air temperature is and there wasn't much warmth to the air that crept from the open doorway. I didn't know how long it would take to get the information I needed, but I'd be damned if I'd court hypothermia for it.

After a moment of wondering if he should allow such cheek on my part, the doorman let me pass into the club proper.

Just stepping past the foyer doors made me feel a little ill. The low-lit room looked a lot like a nightclub from a forties-era film, but this one was populated with flickering images of the past as well as the vampires, wrapped in black-and-red energy coronas. They watched me cross the room with unconcealed curiosity, every stare a blade. I was pretty sure they all knew who I was and that I had some status with Edward. They also knew I was off-limits unless things changed. Some of them must have hoped it would.

The normal grid of the Grey's energy lines seemed slightly skewed and blurred, though I didn't know why, nor had I noticed it the only other time I'd been here. But I'd been a little busy on that visit and hadn't had the concentration to spare for studying the oddities of the ether. I also realized that there were very few ghosts, in spite of the thick presence of death. I pushed aside speculation and fear and headed deeper into the room, toward a corner booth where I'd spotted Edward and a few of his cronies.

I caught myself frowning as I drew closer. There were three people with Edward: two men in suits who seemed to be flunkies of some sort and a thin woman with long strawberry blond hair. They were all vampires, but the woman had a very dim aura devoid of the heavy blackness of most and she was dressed in a romantic sort of gown made of a floating white fabric—not Goth-y, but more like a costume from a Pre-Raphaelite painting. With that thought I recognized her and stopped a little short of the table, surprised.

Edward glanced up at me, already waving the men away. He still looked like a shorter version of Pierce Brosnan frozen at an unaging forty—and had the accent to go with it. "A moment, if you don't mind," he said. Then he turned his attention back to Gwen.

He may have been as fixed as Dorian Gray, but Gwen had changed a lot since I'd first seen her wafting, almost as insubstantial as a ghost, around the Grand Illusion movie theater. Where she had been colorless and fading in the Gray before, her energy signature was now taking on threads and swirls of red and black. It was still a very small aura, but it was discernibly there. She had been sickly and I hadn't then realized that she'd been starving to death in a strange way, slowing fading from both worlds and spiraling down to apathy, madness, and self-destruction. That was not the case now.

I didn't know if I was pleased at the prospect of any vampire gaining strength, but I wasn't entirely unhappy to see someone who had been so pathetic reversing the downward trend of her . . . unlife? I don't suffer the self-pitying too well and "Lady

Gwendolyn of Anorexia" had been among the worst. Boredom I could understand, but most vampires tend more toward arrogance than ennui, and a vampire with a total lack of interest in survival seems contrary to their nature—at least so far as I could understand it.

I watched Edward whisper something in Gwen's ear and then kiss the back of her hand before shooing her on her way. Gwen smiled and edged out of the booth, turning the expression on me as she stood. A sharp-toothed smile I didn't like one bit.

"Hello," she murmured in a breathy voice. "I'm so pleased to see you again."

I gave her a small nod. "You seem to be doing well," I observed in as neutral a voice as I could manage.

"I am," she replied, nodding with enthusiasm. "I am. I don't drink tea anymore."

"You still go to movies and play role-playing games?"

"Oh, no. I'm much too busy. I miss the movies, though. Before winter's over, maybe I'll go to some again. Long nights offer so much more to do."

"I'm sure."

She glanced back at Edward and chuckled, touching her tongue to her front teeth, before floating away.

I slid onto the nearest seat of the booth, keeping close to the outside.

"Taking on more projects?" I asked Edward, arching an eyebrow.

"Still mending fences—as you forced me to do."

"As if that was such a bad idea." The cold and nausea I experienced in the company of vampires was tempered with a roaring sexual heat Edward put out whenever he looked at me. I kept my distance both physical and emotional, maintaining a pointed cynicism as a ward against his routine manipulations. I didn't care to be the next plaything in Edward's collection. Gwen seemed to be recovering from that—depending on your definition of "recovery." Most of his casual toys didn't do so well.

He forced a sigh—very theatrical in someone who never breathes. "You are truly a demanding taskmistress, Harper." He drawled my name with a purring sound that stroked down my spine with an insidious, lulling warmth and distracted me a moment from his moving closer.

"You don't seem to suffer much on account of it," I said, noticing his sudden proximity and giving him a warning glance. There was no place to recoil to without standing up, but I couldn't do that; the interview would end one way or another the moment I let him get the better of me. I didn't have much tolerance for any male playing games with me at that moment, but I'd have to go along at least for a while in spite of my distaste. I thought a defensive chill of disapproval was a little risky, but safer than any false friendliness. I set my teeth and kept to my seat.

Edward picked up my hand and held it in both of his, studying it as if he'd find some secret in the shape and arrangement of the bones beneath the skin. "My dear, I suffer the lack of your skills and guidance."

I pulled my hand back from his with some difficulty, feeling a sickening, artificially induced reluctance to remove myself from his ramped-up heat. "If you lay that on any thicker you'll need a trowel," I said. I wouldn't have been so bold if we'd never met before—even playing the noble suitor, he still had an edge of malice and considerable power to exercise it—but I thought the score between us wasn't so uneven as he did. Yes, I had convinced him to do things he didn't care for and he'd suffered physical harm for it, but the end results had been much better for him than for me.

"I've been very patient," he started, letting his projection grow colder. The rolling unpleasantness of his annoyance made me queasy, but the chill was a relief. Still, I could sense him readying another tactic. "How long do you intend to pretend that your tiny existence, your tiny home, your tiny job, and your mayfly friends satisfy your talents? You could do so much more. And I grow extremely tired of waiting for you to earn out your debt."

I laughed. I hadn't expected him to be so clumsy about it. "What debt? As I recall we're pretty even on the who-owes-who score. I brought some problems to your attention which, if left alone, would have destroyed you, and in exchange I asked for no favors for myself, only for payment to those you already owed. You got to keep your fiefdom, you got to be a hero, you got to play magnanimous lord of the manor and clean house of your enemies in one swoop. And—let me see—you saved Seattle and got Carlos back into your camp, which were certainly unexpected assets for you. How is that a debt on my part?"

"You got your payment for it," he replied, his voice chilling further, even while I saw a gleam in his eye at the anticipated snap of his trap. I thought I'd play along just a little further before I disarmed him.

"I got nothing but survival, a new set of scars, and an association with you and your kind I could happily do without. Yes, my cases closed, but the consequences of them aren't anyone's idea of a reward."

He leaned in a little, trying to catch my eye. If I let him capture my gaze he'd set his hook, whether he had a real claim or not, so I turned my head, glaring at him from the corners of my narrowed eyes.

Frustrated, his voice dropped to a hiss. "There is the small matter of a check, which you accepted and which therefore binds you to me in debt, since, as you point out, I owed you nothing."

"Oh, yeah. Even 'gifts' come with a price." I brought the heavy cream envelope out of my purse, meeting his eyes now, and snapped it onto the table between us. The sound reverberated like a broken guitar string. "You mean this check?"

I'd kept the check in its envelope in the bottom drawer of my office desk since the night it dropped through my mail slot. There were a lot of zeros in the amount line, but the temptation they represented hadn't outweighed the servitude I'd been quite sure would come with it. I'd twigged to the real cost of unearned rewards at an early age when I'd been offered an advance out of the chorus line—if I'd submit to the unpleasant kinks of the musical director. I hadn't learned the lesson well enough, though, and had been caught few times before I'd had it hammered into my knowledge of the world like a spike—the final time with the back of someone's hand.

I approach all offers of free lunches with suspicion, and the more lavish they are, the greater my skepticism. After my initiation into the Grey and with the effects of magical bindings lingering still, I had imagined the price would be even worse where magic and vampires were involved. Judging from Edward's reaction and the feel of shattered magic lying between us, cynicism had been the right choice.

I watched Edward pick up the envelope and draw the check and its note—"for services to the community"—out. The temperature dropped until my breath left ice crystals dancing in the air between us. Fury isn't always hot—if it had been, the paper would have been rendered into ash too fast to watch.

Edward placed the papers on the table with a delicate touch, as though something might break if he exerted even a gram more force. "Ah."

"You should check your own bank statements," I suggested. "Your accountants fell down on the job. I've had that since last May, but you didn't notice it hadn't been deposited."

He raised his gaze to my face, neutral on the surface, but the aura around his head was shot with bolts of furious red lightning in a boiling black storm. Then he sat back, the squall of anger blowing out as fast as it had blown in. He shook his head.

"I should have known it wouldn't work with you."

"We're not all that venal," I said.

"Oh, it wasn't venality I thought might catch you." He didn't say what he had thought would ensnare me, though. "But I've wasted enough time with this. What do you want from me—and this time you may very well incur a debt."

"Don't try and rope me, Edward. I just need information; I'm not asking for a favor."

"Very well," he snapped. "What do you want to know?"

"Who is killing the homeless in Pioneer Square?"

He seemed surprised. "However should I know? And why did you think I would?"

"The deaths have been very odd—not much blood in the bodies, hands and legs apparently chewed off in some cases."

Edward scowled, sending a ripple of cold over me. "I suppose the seed of suspicion was planted by your unfortunately clever friend Quinton. I can't say I care for the company you keep."

"I'm not so fond of some of it, either," I replied pointedly. "You worked together just fine before. Why the animosity?"

He almost smiled. "If I told you, I'd have to kill you," Edward joked—not that it was a joke. "Why would you, cynical one, believe such a tale, even from a friend?" He put an unpleasant spin on the last word.

"I've seen some of the bodies myself. But I don't know if these are vampire victims—I haven't seen many, but none of them looked like this. So I don't know what's wrong with these— except that something magical killed them and took their blood and limbs along when it left. That *sounds* like your kind, but there are other factors. Besides the sleeping dead, there have been zombies seen in the area—one I think might be an earlier victim of whatever did this—and there's a pattern that goes back sixty years or more. It's not a human killing these people. But since vampires also walk after death, you can understand how I thought there might be a connection."

Edward's lip curled in disgust. "I assure you none of my people are responsible. We don't . . . rend, and we don't raise zombies. The occasional mistakes are dealt with, not allowed to roam the night."

"If I accept that no vampire did this—"

"None did!" His voice carried force that battered against my mind and body. I didn't quite stop myself from flinching. Edward seemed a little mollified by my discomfort. The rest of the vampires in the room glanced at us and then away with a ripple of surprise across the red-fired surface of the Grey.

"I don't know that. I don't know what becomes of vampires' victims or where zombies come from. That's why I'm asking you. Whatever nasty thing is doing this, it has to stop. I assume you don't want the police to start asking public questions about bloodless bodies in Pioneer Square or the *Weekly* to begin spouting sensationalism about the walking dead and slaughtered homeless people."

"Zombies are necromancers' business, not ours," he spat. "We turn our kills only rarely and with care—"

"Like the care you exercised with Cameron?"

The growl he made raised black waves in the Grey. "That is not the matter at issue here. These dead are not made to walk—nor to lie bloodless in the street—by us. It would be madness and none of mine are mad. If you wish to know more, you should speak to Carlos."

His anger left me dizzy and nauseated. I swallowed hard but held my outward cool—I think. "I probably will. I want to stop this—regardless of who may be responsible."

"Be assured it is not one of mine." He leaned away, indicating an end to the conversation. "I have no further information for you, but I shan't hinder you in its pursuit." Damn right you won't, I thought. "I'll even warn my people away from you and your lone wolf if that will help you to resolve this mystery."

"That would help, as would any other information that flows to you about it."

He gave a brusque nod. "You'll have it. Is that all?"

I looked at the envelope still lying on the table. "Are we square?"

His lips and nostrils twitched but he nodded. "Yes. Though you might wish to examine the oddities of your . . . friend before you trust him further."

I raised an eyebrow but said nothing. Then I slid out of the booth and stood beside the table. Leaving him angry wasn't the best idea, so I nodded my head in what could be mistaken for a very small obeisance and said, "Thank you."

I could feel a flatness in the heaving Grey behind me as I left, as if I'd managed to surprise Edward, though I doubted that was possible. My mind was whirling with disjointed bits of knowledge and questions trying to find each other, and I had to struggle to keep my attention on the dangerous path to the door. I assumed

Edward's word had some binding to it. I never trusted vampires, though I knew promises could have magical implications in such an atmosphere as that one. What I couldn't know was if any of the other vampires might believe we'd broken whatever pact lay between Edward and me and started to think I'd make a lovely snack once I left the protection of the club. I had to watch them as I went, seeing calculation in some shifted gazes, eyes gleaming with hunger and curiosity as they watched me go.

None followed me out or appeared on the street once I exited the gate.

I didn't know why Edward had been so disgusted and offended by the idea of zombies, but the weight of his words convinced me he'd been telling the truth about vampire involvement in the recent deaths of undergrounders. Not that he and his pack were innocent of preying on them under other circumstances, but I was reasonably convinced that they hadn't done this. Or at least none that cleaved to Edward's protection had. Which included Carlos.

Since Carlos was also a necromancer, it seemed the next logical step was going to him, which I dreaded even more than speaking to Edward. I did not wish to renew the despair and horror I'd felt at our last parting. Even more so I didn't want to end up in his debt.

An itchy little idea flitted at the back of my mind and I thought perhaps I wouldn't have to talk to Carlos after all. I'd helped his protégé, Cameron, a couple of months before with the problem of a dead man who might or might not wake up as a vampire. At the time, Cam had implied there were worse things the deceased might come back as—things that had made Cameron shiver with dread. Not much fazes a vampire, even an infant one. Whatever it was, perhaps it was connected to my current problem. I'd helped to straighten out the mess of Cameron's death and unlife, and I didn't find Cameron particularly threatening—yet.

I pulled my cell phone out of my purse and called Cam's number. He answered quickly.

"Hey, Harper."

"Hey, Cam. I have a problem and I think you might have a hint of the answer."

"Really? Well, then fire away."

"I'd rather meet in person. There may be a bit more to it than a quick Q and A."

I heard the static and fuzz of him putting his hand over the phone. The furry silence lasted a few moments before his voice returned.

"We'll be at the Big Picture in fifteen minutes. In the den. Go straight at the bottom of the stairs and turn left after the ramp. See you there."

He didn't give me time to object that "we" was what I'd been hoping to avoid. But at least the venue seemed safe. I'd never been in it, but I'd heard of it.

The Big Picture was a tiny movie theater in a bar under El Gaucho. It also rented space out for private meetings, so there was a good chance that we'd have privacy—unless one of them really wanted to see the film.

It was too chilly in my thinner dress clothes and with my knee reacting to the weather to walk so far or wait for a bus, so I took the Rover up to Wall and First and found a parking space in a surface pay lot that hadn't yet filled up with young drinkers insisting on braving the cold to have a good time at the swankier establishments in Belltown. I walked in El Gaucho's doors and turned right before the doorman could frown at my trousers, following the short corridor to the neon sign that flashed BIG PICTURE over the staircase leading down. For a moment, I was bitterly pleased I'd never managed to see a film there with Will, and then I tromped on that thought and went on.

There's something very odd about a cinema in a bar, though I had to admit that the idea of kid-free movie viewing piqued my interest. As I went down the stairs, the smell of perfect popcorn wafted up. If only they had played old noir films, I'd have been in heaven. I had a fleeting vision of popcorn, beer, and Bogey—or even a comedy like *Bringing Up Baby*—on a big screen and smiled.

The lobby was the bar with a few seating areas defined by collections of sofas, chairs, and tables like tiny living rooms without walls. The lighting was diffused and made the predominant golds and greens of the decor look rich and inviting. The soft effect dimmed the layers of time so the space seemed less haunted than most—which pleased me even more. A few potted palms were wound with colored lights. A handful of couples were snuggling and sipping drinks in various spots among the furniture, but I couldn't hear their conversations even at the relatively small distances in the room. Apparently the sound-proofing for the theater had been extended into the rest of the space as well, and there was no leakage of the swing dance band from El Gaucho's bar, either. I saw a couple of doors at the far end of the room and figured them for the theater and private meeting rooms.

The bartender glanced my way, smiling, and invited me to get my ticket, order a drink, and go on into the theater, since the show was just about to start. I returned the smile and said I was looking for some friends. . . .

"Harper!"

I turned and saw Cameron coming my way from nearer the

theater doors at the back. He bypassed the bar and came to my side.

He hadn't changed much in the past two months. He was wearing a black dress shirt over a gleaming white tee and gray trousers, his white-gold hair was still spiky short, and the darkness of his vampiric aura was still mild. I guessed he hadn't done in anyone else since his slip in October, which had left him in debt to me. I wished I wasn't calling in that marker. Although I still had a fondness for Cam, his developing habits and talents put me off. I had to reevaluate my feelings about the dead-guy incident, if I was going to be fair. I'd been disgusted and upset and wanted to distance myself from him over it, but going to the morgue on his behalf had introduced me to Fish the first time, and that was turning out to be helpful. I wasn't going to let him completely off the hook, though. Call me a stickler, but I still disapproved of killing people.

"Hi, Cam."

He grinned, flashing fangs. "I'm fetching drinks. What do you want?"

I hesitated.

"It's just a drink. You can buy the second round," he said.

What the hell, it seemed like a day that deserved a drink—to drown it in. "All right," I agreed. "Bushmills, neat."

He flashed the smile again and headed for the bar, and somehow no one asked me to buy a ticket. Bracing myself, I walked across the lobby and down three small steps to the den to meet Carlos.

The space was a small nook beside the theater wall with one large couch and an armless upholstered chair. There was also a small, glass-topped bamboo table and a sort of rattan ottoman lurking like a cat that hopes to get underfoot. Carlos—big, dark, and scary as always—had one corner of the sofa, which left me with the choice of sitting next to him—not too attractive—or of taking the least comfortable seat, which also put my back to the stairs but gave me more options if anything blew up. I took the chair.

Carlos nodded to me and the tiniest of smiles twitched one corner of his mouth. He looked healthier than I'd ever seen him and I hated knowing how he'd gotten that way. I nodded back and he seemed amused by my apparent discomfort. Neither of us had a chance to say anything before Cameron returned with his hands full of glasses, which he distributed on the table. Then he threw himself into the other corner of the couch. He'd had a college student's tendency to slouch and sprawl when we'd met, but now he lounged like a young tiger and picked up his martini. I wasn't surprised that Carlos's drink was red wine.

Cameron leveled his violet gaze on me and asked, "So, what did you want to know?"

"How crass can I be without losing a limb?"

Cameron snorted a laugh without actually choking on his drink and quickly put it down. He pinched his nostrils together and glanced at Carlos. "Oh, man. Alcohol up my nose still hurts."

Carlos raised one black eyebrow. "Lack of breathing through it didn't change the nature of your nose, boy."

"I'll remember that," Cameron replied in a dry tone, rubbing the end of his nose and wrinkling his face as if about to sneeze. In a moment, he turned his attention back to me. "I think I'm shockproof, so ask what you want."

I took a deep breath and plunged in. "When you were worried about your dead man, you said he might come back as something other than a vampire—if he came back at all. Would that have been some kind of zombie?"

Silence.

They both gave me blank stares and I felt the temperature in the room drop. Carlos turned his head and shot Cameron a look that could have flayed skin. Cam flinched.

"I don't know anything about zombies," Cameron said. "And after what *didn't* happen last time," he added, shooting a defiant glance back at Carlos that left a wake of red annoyance through the Grey, "I wouldn't have anything to do with any that might be wandering around Seattle. I assume you're not asking because you want to make a movie or something. Have you seen a zombie around here?"

Too late to back out, I nodded and explained in a low voice. Their expressions grew intense and frightening as they listened. I had to shift my glance between them as I spoke to avoid the slightly sickening sensation that came with locking eyes with either of them for long. "Yeah. I . . . uh . . . was presented with one a couple of nights ago. The . . . creature that brought it wanted me to . . . umm . . . The corpse's spirit was still trapped in it and it wanted me to let it out. It was pretty messy."

I didn't say there'd been a witness. I suspected Carlos would insist on doing something to Will if he knew, and while Will and I weren't together anymore, I didn't like the things Carlos did when he felt that his world needed protecting. I may have been angry with Will, but I didn't wish that on him.

Carlos leaned forward, ignoring his wine, and put his hands flat on the table. The bamboo groaned and I heard a sound like thin ice cracking underfoot. "Tell us what happened. What did you do and see?"

I felt the press of his will on me and squirmed away from it, pulling the edge of the Grey between us to cut it off. "You don't have to compel me," I growled.

Cameron sat back with pretended cool, pulling up his knees and resting his drink on them. "Hey, yeah. Bad form, Teach."

Carlos's furious glare was worse than before, but this time Cameron didn't cringe. He glared back. "What's that movie," he asked me without shifting his eyes from Carlos, "where Paul Newman says, 'You don't treat your friends like marks'?"

"*The Sting*," I replied.

"Right." His voice took on a strange resonance. "I remember Mara said the same thing to me when we met."

Carlos's glare narrowed further, and then he turned his head aside with a derisive snort, breaking the glance between them. "Improving," he muttered.

Cameron made a raspberry noise. "Sore loser."

Carlos cast a hooded glance back at him that hit Cameron like a blow. The younger vampire's head jerked forward and knocked against his tented knees, sending his drink to the floor. Carlos watched without expression until Cameron sat back up, putting his feet flat on the floor again.

Cam was parchment white. He closed his eyes and ducked his head, saying, "I apologize."

Carlos nodded back. "Improving," he repeated. Then he turned his gaze to me.

This time he made no attempt to pressure me, just asked, "Please tell us what happened. What did you do and what did you see?"

"The zombie was rotten—decomposing—but it was still moving around. It had a lot of tangled energy lines on and in it, which I figured must have been whatever was keeping it animated. I could see a lot of Grey threads all over it, like a net. They were odd things without any energy to them, just some kind of soft, neutral material." I shivered at the memory of the thing and swallowed the urge to gag. "I had to reach into the decomposing body to pull the energy strands loose and then it fell apart. The body fell apart. And I separated the strands, which broke into two distinct energy forms. One obviously didn't belong there and took off—it seemed familiar, but I couldn't say how—but the other seemed to be the ghost of the body. I think he was Native American and he faded out. I don't think he stayed. I think he's gone. The other one I don't know about, but I'll find out eventually. Once the energy forms were gone, the body decomposed to dust and blew away."

Carlos frowned like storm clouds. "Is there more?"

"I've seen those threads around a few other places lately. The soft ones. At the site of a recently dead body and hanging on another. Neither of those bodies stood up."

Carlos glowered as he thought. Cameron looked at me and shrugged, waiting, but still unearthly pale, even for a vampire.

"Were the soft threads in the same shape?" Carlos asked. "Like a net, as you said."

"No. The threads were just there."

"Ah. An unusual creation. Not truly a zombie, but the term will do, for now. Your threads trapped the spirit in the flesh so it could not rest."

"Not my threads," I objected, "and how do you know it's not a regular zombie—if there is such a thing?"

Carlos rumbled a chuckle and sat back. "There are several kinds. True zombies are forced into form—spirit forced into dead flesh—but their binding is energetic. This binding you describe wasn't. Only because the body was decayed were you able to remove the animating spirit from the shell of flesh. You destroyed the net that bound the body together when you reached into the body. So long as the body retained the shape of life, the spirit in the flesh could not leave. The soft material of the net is the casting of some creature that captured and killed the man."

"So it's a spell of some kind?"

"No, it's a remnant, like a spider's silk that wraps a fly. It has no energy of its own and draws none. It is dead material, not living magic. A true zombie can be bound only in a recently dead body."

Carlos's voice wove a dim image before me of a dark man kneeling in a cemetery, muttering words that shook him with bleak magic and brought corpses stumbling to their feet from shattered crypts and desecrated graves. I had to shake myself free of an uncanny lethargy as he spoke, as if I might fall asleep and tumble into one of the empty graves myself. I caught myself and shivered.

Carlos continued. "Were the body so decayed, it should have fallen apart on its own. The casting held it, otherwise you would not have had so easy a time removing the energy forms but would have had to rend the body apart." Carlos frowned again and the room seemed to grow dimmer. "The second spirit, though—that disturbs me. It should not happen. There is a third party using this for their own ends."

I shook off the last of my daze. "Using what to their ends?" I asked. "I'm not sure what's going on."

"These walking dead, these strands of material come from some magical creature that kills men. I don't know what its purpose is and can't be sure that the castings don't linger past its own death. If they do, then whatever zombies are created will remain even after the creature is destroyed."

"But there won't be more zombies without this . . . thing making them?"

"Correct. At least not this kind of zombie. And those that remain must be destroyed as you did this one—by removing the energy form trapped within the body by the threads. Some spirits may flee on their own once the net of the casting is destroyed, but that can't be certain. Removing the energy strand is the only sure way."

I shuddered and Cameron looked grim.

Carlos smiled a little. "It is magical entanglement. You know that the shapes of magic tend to linger," he said. "Destroying them requires dismantling their lingering shape. Were it a necromantic zombie, or a vampiric turning gone wrong, the case would be different. But this is neither of those. It seems to be random. The creature does not do it deliberately, consistently, or both your other bodies would have risen also."

"Then I suppose I'm grateful for that or the city might have more than cold and power outages to worry about. There've been at least four deaths and possibly more among the homeless in Pioneer Square. Do you have any idea what the creature is that's killing people and leaving these threads?"

"No."

"Could it have been the creature that brought me the zombie? He—it was a sort of hairy man."

"A shaggyman, I suspect."

"What's a shaggyman?"

He flicked his hand dismissively. "They are the old people— the creatures in between the native animal people of legend and the living people of the normal world. The legends of Sasquatch are tales of a giant among the shaggymen. They aren't very intelligent or dangerous."

"That's bull. The first time I met one it wanted to make me 'a little more dead' because Wygan told it to."

That obviously intrigued Carlos and I regretted mentioning Wygan or the shaggyman. "Did Wygan send it this time?"

"No. The shaggyman seemed to be on the outs with Wygan

for not harming me the first time. It was scarred and it said I owed it for those scars, which it apparently got from Wygan. Destroying the zombie was what it wanted as recompense."

Cameron leaned forward, looking worried. "You haven't seen any other . . . weird things, have you?"

"What sort of weird things?" I asked back. "Aside from vampires and zombies and ghosts and shaggymen."

"Not—" Carlos shot him a warning glance, but Cam went on. "Not us. Other creatures that prey on men . . . and other things."

"Are you saying there's something that eats vampires out there?" That idea sent my stomach to the floor in a rush. I didn't want to find out what was worse than Wygan and Carlos. "What? Werewolves? Demons from hell? How much worse does this get?"

Carlos shook his head and hushed Cameron with another glower. Then he turned back to me. "You have nothing to fear from the shaggyman. It did not succeed in harming you," he reminded me. "And they cannot wield things like the thread you describe. It brought the zombie to you for dissolution. It could not have made it, but it wanted to free the spirit. If it was, indeed, one of the natives, the shaggyman would have felt pain over the spirit's plight, since the two have long been bound together here. Since the very beginning."

"That doesn't help me with the problem of zombies and dead homeless people who might or might not be getting chewed on by some kind of giant, man-eating, paranormal spider," I sputtered. Christ, there really was a monster in the sewer! "I can't let it go on!"

"Agreed. You cannot. But we are not the ones to help you," Carlos stated. He seemed anxious to cut the conversation short, which struck me as sinister. Carlos was not easy to disturb or discomfit, and if he didn't want to talk he had no compunction to find an excuse. But now he stood and made it plain that he intended to leave. "This is not a necromantic matter, nor does it belong to the realm of vampires. I do not know what creature is causing this, nor how it makes its web nor why it casts it as it does. It falls to you to discover it and to destroy it."

He walked past me and left the den, heading for the exit. Cameron started to follow him.

"What the hell, Cameron?" I asked.

He stopped and glanced down at me. "I'm sorry, Harper. There's literally no power we can use on this . . . whatever it is. It's not even making enough of a stir in the Grey to bother any of us. We've got no power other than the physical in this situation, and that won't help you now. If you find this thing and need some muscle, that's another story, but this isn't something we're any help on."

"What are you afraid of? I can't believe you're scared."

"I can't tell you. But it's not your monster—whatever that is. Believe me. And don't ask about the . . . others. Please. Carlos is going to make me hurt for that one as it is, and you really truly don't want to know more."

Cameron slipped past and followed his master.

Dumbfounded, I sat and stared at the untouched wine and the spilled martini. I bolted my whiskey and left, knowing I would never catch them. Even if there was more they could tell me, they wouldn't, and it was pointless to waste what remained of my evening in that hope.

But what in hell or out of it had made them clam up? I sent silent prayers to any god who might listen that I wouldn't regret the lack of that knowledge.

NINE

I don't get hysterical at the sight of a spider, but I admit, even the hint of something arachnoid prowling the tunnels under Pioneer Square and snaring its victims like flies sent a frisson skittering down my spine. Carlos hadn't confirmed the idea of a monstrous spider, but the image was strong in my mind.

I cursed Edward for planting the idea in my mind, but I still wanted to ask a few questions of Quinton. He'd said enough about his reasons for going underground that my sudden suspicions of him earlier had been allayed, but Edward's hints bugged me. I thought Edward was just throwing shadows, but I needed to know for sure. And it wasn't yet so late that Quinton would be unavailable.

Not knowing where he might be, I paged him and he called me back as I was returning the Rover to its customary slot in the "sinking ship"—the tilted triangular parking structure across the street from my office building, which reared from the block like the prow of a doomed liner.

"Hi, Harper. What's up?"

"I'm done with Edward—and Carlos and Cameron, too. I need to talk to you."

"I'm at the Double Header with Rosa and Tall Grass—he's a bit freaked about Jenny. . . ." He paused. "Where should I meet you?"

"Not a bar."

"Only place still open is Starbucks. I'll be there in ten minutes."

I doubted the conversation would go well, but it wouldn't be any better in private and at least I'd have a hot drink. I trudged down the street to the coffeehouse and ordered a very large drip coffee "with room" for cream. You have to be specific, or the baristas fill the cup to the rim with the crude oil they call coffee. I'd just gotten my drink doctored with cream and sugar when Quinton joined me.

"Do you want coffee?" I asked.

"Not really."

"It's cold outside."

He blinked at me. "Yeah, it's twenty degrees out there."

"Do you want to talk about this business in here?" I tipped my head toward one of the patrons reading a newspaper in the front window corner. To my view he was cloaked in a swirl of blackness, and I knew he was a vampire without even seeing the fangs. "Some people have friends everywhere."

He sighed and shrugged. "OK, I'll get some coffee and we'll go to your office."

My turn to shrug. I waited while he collected a cup of something hot and then we crunched along the frosty sidewalk to my office building. I had to use my key on the outer door since none of the ground floor businesses were open after six. As I unlocked, I noticed that the shadows nearby moved and reshaped themselves around furtive watchers. It appeared that Edward was keeping an eye on me, though it seemed he didn't realize I could see his minions even when they thought they were hidden.

I'd assumed all vampires understood the Grey at least as well as I did—certainly Carlos and Wygan seemed to know a lot more—but it occurred to me that Cameron had once been surprised he was unable to hide from me by sliding into the Grey. Maybe most vampires didn't know what I did. . . . It was an interesting thought and it distracted me enough that Quinton had to elbow me and remind me to get inside out of the cold. I locked the door behind us and we went upstairs to my office.

It was chilly, but the space was small and would warm up quickly enough. I put my coffee on the desk and sat down behind it while Quinton took the better of the two client chairs and leaned back in it with his steaming cup cradled in both hands. He looked tired, the aura around him reduced to a small blue glow. I studied him for a few moments, wondering.

He returned a bland gaze and said nothing. Quinton was always good at silence.

Well, I thought, might as well get it over with. "Are you a werewolf, Quinton?"

He snorted a laugh, frowning at the same time. "No! Werewolves don't exist. What would give you that idea?"

I ticked them off on my fingers. "Vampires, ghosts, monsters in the sewer, why not werewolves, too? And the mutual dislike between you and Edward—who refers to you as a 'lone wolf' and warns me to check into your 'oddities.'"

He sipped his coffee and remained reclined in the chair. "You've been reading too many bad horror novels. Or playing dumb-ass RPGs if you buy the idea of a deep-seated, traditional animosity between vampires and werewolves. It's fantasy. Werewolves don't exist," he repeated.

"So you say, but a year ago I'd have said ghosts and vampires didn't exist, either. Do you have proof?"

"I have logic. And I've never found any evidence of real lycanthropy. Vampires, magic . . . yeah. Weres? No. It's not possible. At least I think not, from observation. Maybe I missed something, but so far, no evidence to the contrary."

I picked up my own coffee. "OK, then. Elucidate."

"All right. Everything I've seen tells me that magic tends to respect the laws of physics—kind of freaky physics, but lawful physics. For total form-shifting to happen in less than, say, a couple of days, max, it would have to break conservation of mass, conservation of energy, and the laws of thermodynamics at the very least. If shape-shifting does exist, then it's an illusion, not an actual form change—unless it happens very slowly, which doesn't seem to be the case. If someone were to change from human to wolf, he'd have to make a whole lot of physical changes very rapidly, shedding or gaining mass and using up a ton of energy. There just isn't enough elasticity in the system to allow it—he'd burst into flames from the heat of the energetic change alone.

"I've never burst into flame that I'm aware of. Besides, you've been out with me plenty of times when the moon was full and I don't even get hairy palms. QED, not a werewolf."

He drank more coffee and gave me his bland look again.

I had to chuckle at the perverse sanity of it—and at Quinton's expression. There was a hint of merriment in his eyes that made me feel a touch foolish but not enough to mind. It was kind of sweet, in a way, to be gently teased after the emotional whirlwind of my failed love affair. I smiled a little as I asked, "All right, but why does Edward call you the lone wolf?"

Quinton shrugged. "You're the one who calls him the leader of the pack. Early on he discovered I was useful, but Edward doesn't like contractors. If you're not one of his kind, he prefers you to be either cattle or chattel, and I won't play that game. I'm the stranger with teeth who won't roll over and show my belly. Since I know how to hurt him, he can't come at me directly. So he makes a show of being unworried and immune. It raises his stock with the rest of the pack and we have a sort of uneasy truce. That doesn't stop him from making attempts to control me, and he's not above making trouble for me if it's not out of his way—which is what he's doing with you. His time scale is much longer than mine, so he doesn't try very often, but he does try."

"He's persistent," I agreed.

"Yeah." He paused and looked at me, a half smile turning into a small, thoughtful frown. "So what about you? He'd consider you a useful piece to control. How do you keep him at bay?"

"Mostly by seeing the traps ahead of time. So far, he's been predictable, but he'll try harder eventually. He tried tonight and I backed him off, but it was the last card I had to play. Next time will be worse unless I learn some new tricks. It's possible I know things about the way magic works that he doesn't, but I'm not sure yet."

His gaze on me was quizzical. "I know you know things—see things—I don't, but I don't have any idea what your life is like, how you manage this knowledge. It must be strange."

I nodded. "It's not easy to explain. Ben gave me a theory once, but it's not entirely correct. But the upshot is I don't just see ghosts, I interact with them. I see magic—the sort of energetic stuff magic comes from. . . ." I found myself unable to go further with that thought. Someday I'd figure out why. I shook my head, frustrated, but resigned for now. "Anyhow. There's a lot of freaky between the here and the there and I see most of it. I can even walk around in it and do a few things with it, but it's not as impressive as it sounds."

"What sorts of things? Aside from talking to ghosts and seeing magic." He leaned forward with his cup in both hands between his knees, giving me an intent look.

I didn't mind the scrutiny. He seemed truly interested and maybe . . . something more? I didn't mind that either, but I put that aside and thought a moment. "I can . . . see layers of time if they happen to be in the right orientation at the right spot. I can pull a sort of shield between me and the magic stuff, sometimes. I—" I couldn't say I could pluck energy and move it around. Strange. I could talk about it with Carlos, but not Quinton. I filed that for future investigation. "Well, not a lot else aside from the ghosts and being able to see that some people—or things—are magical in certain ways, but I don't know what all the signals mean."

"That's how you spotted the vampire in Starbucks."

I nodded again. "Yeah. I can see he's a vampire. They're sort of . . . in both places at the same time and there's a look and a smell to them I've come to recognize."

"A smell? Aside from the bad breath?" he added, making a face.

I laughed. "Yeah, aside from that."

He smiled before growing serious again. "Edward must want you badly—a human who can spot vampires and magic and still go around in the daylight. Someone with enough balls to take him on and enough skill to survive it. And you're a pretty good investigator, too. Very attractive package." I wasn't sure if he meant that intellectually or in a more personal sense. Either way, I kind of liked it, but that liking made me a little nervous.

I ducked my head and felt my face get hot. "Yeah. Well . . ."

Quinton didn't leave me to twist. "So what happened tonight?" he asked.

"He denies anything to do with the deaths or the zombies."

Quinton snorted. "Of course he does."

"I believe him. He was pissed off about it and disgusted by the thought of zombies, and his denials rang true. He even offered to warn his people off of us while we look into it. He didn't have to. He could have said nothing and sent me on my way or tried to kill me if I was too close to a truth he didn't want me to know. But he didn't even try. He sent me to talk to Carlos, instead."

Quinton shivered but kept silent, encouraging me with an eager nod.

"The details are nasty, so I'll skip them for now, but between the vampires and Fish—the guy at the morgue—I think I've spotted an emerging pattern that goes back at least to the 1949 earthquake, assuming all the dead or missing were in the underground or Pioneer Square at the time."

"All the people who've died or disappeared were undergrounders sleeping in the tunnels or the alleys and streets above them," Quinton confirmed, thinking aloud. "Not in the shelters."

"Then we're on the right track," I said. "This thing is paranormal, but it's not a vampire and it's not a zombie. It makes zombies of some of its prey by coating them in some kind of paranormal web, but that seems to be incidental to the way it stalks people or captures them or something. I'm not sure of that yet. But, corny as it sounds, we really are looking for a creature that's crawling around somewhere in those underground tunnels. That makes every undergrounder a potential meal. We have to find it and get rid of it, or it'll just keep on killing people, and some of them are going to get back up and walk. And I don't think the cops are going to be too hip to that."

"No. We'll have to go down and figure out where it comes from or where it dens up. Then we'll have to trap it and kill it."

I was glad Quinton had automatically included himself in the solution—it made me like him even more; he could have left the baby in my lap as Carlos and Cameron had. I went on, making a face as I said, "It might not be mortal. It's very long-lived if it's the same thing that killed people in 1949. And there might be earlier deaths that aren't in the database or not in a way that's made them stand out. If we can figure out what happened after the earthquake in 1949, we might have some clues as to where it came from and how to get rid of it again."

Quinton looked thoughtful and finished his coffee. "Y'know . . . there are a few undergrounders who might remember."

I scoffed. "Anyone old enough to remember the earthquake would have to be approaching eighty."

"Not necessarily. They've resurrected the oral tradition down there—it's not like there's TV or great reading material in the underground, so mostly they tell each other 'back when' stories. Some of them might still be awake, if they have a fire to keep warm by and haven't been drinking."

He got up, fired with urgency. "Let's go find them before they crash. The sooner we find the thing, the sooner it's gone."

I finished off my coffee too and stood up, not really thrilled about going back into the cold, musty dampness of the buried streets. I didn't have a choice, though; I'd agreed to help and I couldn't—wouldn't—back out. I wished I had some decent gloves and warmer clothes, but at least there was no wind in the dead city below and I'd have a friend at my back.

Quinton showed me another way into the underground down a narrow stairway in an alley. Once again there was a nearly hidden door at one side, set into an arch of cement. Quinton jiggered with it and we slipped into a catacomb of brick and old steel girders.

Something grunted in the darkness and there was a thump. We both fell silent and turned our heads, trying to pinpoint the noise. Quinton pointed deeper into the gloom ahead and began down the sidewalk corridor. I followed him carefully over the dusty, rubble-strewn floor, brushing past ghosts, to a set of stone arches where wooden doors must have hung that had now rotted and fallen away. We edged into the a cavernous space and I felt a touch of cold nausea.

I whispered into Quinton's ear, "Vampire."

He made a low noise and a shaft of white light cut the blackness, showing a slice of a once-grand room. Near the door where we stood was a humped, wriggling thing: two human shapes, one slumped, the other holding that one, bending over it. . . .

A sharp crack of ozone and a burst of arc light came from Quinton's other hand and he jabbed a small lightning bolt into the bending figure. The vampire shrieked and spun toward us, fangs bared, dropping the ragged man he'd been trying to bite.

"Bastard," Quinton muttered. He jabbed a second time at the vampire with the small stun stick. The arcing horns connected with the creature's shoulder and slid up the curve to its neck. The vampire shrieked and jerked and then fell to the ground where he lay looking more dead than it probably had in a long time.

"Edward said he'd keep his people out of our way," I said.

"Yeah. Well, either he lied, or this one didn't get the memo."

I looked at the vampire and recognized his face from the After Dark. "He didn't say he wouldn't keep them out of the snack bar," I said, "and this one probably figured it was the last chance to grab a bite of marinated bum for a while. So . . . is this one . . . down for good?"

"No, unfortunately. Just out for a while. The current disrupts what passes for a bioelectrical system in these guys, but it'll reset after he's been out a while. With higher voltage I could probably kill them, but I don't want to be in that kind of trouble with Edward or let someone like Lass loose with a stun stick that might kill a human as well."

"And that's what keeps Edward at his distance?"

"Kind of. He stays away from me so I don't stick him. That way none of his pack will ever see that he's as vulnerable to the stun as they are. Right now they think he's immune. If they find out he's not, his strongman image will be on its ass."

"How did you figure this electrical thing out?"

He grinned and I saw the light of his flashlight reflected off his white teeth. "You'd be amazed at the things you can find out if you break into the right parts of the Internet."

The other man moaned and rolled on the floor. Quinton went to help him up. It was Blue Jay.

"Hey, Jay. Are you all right?" Quinton asked.

Jay rubbed his head. "Yeah, I guess. I feel woozy. . . ."

"Let's get you somewhere warmer." Quinton put his shoulder under Jay's armpit and helped him up.

Jay directed us down the sidewalk and around to a hole in a wall where we could dimly see a yellow glow deeper in the hole. We crawled in and found a room in what must have been some building's condemned and forgotten basement. A clutch of shape-less people sat in a huddle around a lit Sterno can, passing bottles and chatting in low voices. They welcomed Jay, one of the figures giving him a blanket while another asked what had become of his own.

"I—lost it. One o' them bad men."

"One of them stole it?" asked a woman—I assumed from

the voice, since it was impossible to tell gender by the shadowed hump of the form from which it issued.

"Nah. I dropped it. But I don't wanna go back for it now. Go in the morning. When he's gone."

The shapeless female nodded.

"You guys seeing more of those creeps down here?" Quinton asked.

"The bad ones? Not more'n normal."

"Anything else? Critters? Walkers?"

One of the shapes rocked back and forth. "I seen a . . . a crawling thing, long as a snake, hairy like a yak."

"A yak!" one of the other shapes said. "You ain't never seen no yak."

"Then hairy like a musk ox—I seen plenty musk ox when I was home in Alaska at that qiviut farm."

"And a buncha rats," another said. "We saw 'em. Rats running through here last night."

They began chattering, throwing in comments in a flurry, and I couldn't keep track of which lump of filthy cloth was talking when.

"Bugs. Been a lotta bugs for winter time."

"And the shadow people."

"Lotta rats, yeah. Big 'uns!"

"That's trouble—rats. Something's stirred 'em up."

"It's the cold."

"Maybe they's scared of the yak!"

"And the crows," said Jay.

They got quiet and stared at Blue Jay.

"No birds down here, Jay."

"I know that. But I seen a crow with Jenny last night and this morning she was killed. You saw it, too, Grandpa Dan. It was an omen."

"Why didn't you see no crow when Go-cart died?"

"I ain't no medicine man. I just seen the one crow."

"Do crows come out when people die?" I asked in a low voice. I didn't like the clutching feeling that rasped up my spine as I thought of those big crows and Go-cart or of the gleaming eyes of creatures in the tunnels, watching Jenny from the darkness.

There was a glimmer in the Grey around them and one of the other lumps spoke in a slow, old voice, the voice of Grandpa Dan. "Sometimes. Crows are the messengers of gods and the spirits of our ancestors. They speak of death and magic. They say crows flew all day over Battleground back during the last days of the People—before the reservations. I did see Jay's crow, but it said nothing I understood. Maybe it was a raven though. Ravens intercede for us in the world of the spirits—maybe that's why it came here, to fight for Jenny, and it lost."

There was an uncomfortable silence before one of the others added, "My old grandma said the animals used to talk to us long ago, but now they're afraid and they lose their power with all these white men around. You hardly see real animals anymore in the cities. 'Cepting rats and dogs and mangy cats and they don't talk so much."

Grandpa Dan nodded. "Down here near the mud where we used to fish, maybe they talk more. . . . Maybe they remember more what it was like to be real animals." Then he looked directly at me and something atavistic in me stirred and quailed at his fierce glance. "These mudflats, they were the life of our people. It is still ours, even if it is only a ghost place now, buried under this city. We can't leave it. We'd do anything to protect it, if we could. We will do so when the need is on us." Then he turned his filmed eyes back to Jay, releasing me to shiver a moment. "That's why the animals and our ancestor spirits still come here—to keep the land safe. Maybe that's why your raven came down here, Blue Jay."

"Maybe that's why Frank's yak come here—to talk," another voice bantered.

"Was a musk ox and musk ox don't talk."

"Do you remember what happened in 1949?" I asked Dan.

"When was that?" Dan asked. "That was after the war—the Second World War. I was just a boy then."

The people around the circle watched with suspicion. I'd come with a friend, but that didn't guarantee they'd trust me, especially interrogating an old man they respected. I pushed on, but I chose my questions with care.

"Did you live here in Seattle?"

Dan shook his head and shrugged, growing tiny and bent before my eyes. It seemed as if the wise old man had vanished with the movement, leaving a smaller, weaker substitute behind who mumbled in a quavering voice, "Nah, I lived on the rez. I never lived here then." He seemed befuddled and I wasn't sure it was an act.

"Did you hear about the earthquake here in April of 1949?"

"Oh, sure!" another piped up. "Buildings fell down. That's why they torn down the old hotel and built that parking lot."

"You suppose that's where all them ghosts the medicine man drove away come from?" another asked.

"What ghosts?" old Dan asked.

"Them old 'skins. You remember. Back in . . . what, 'ninety-four? They used to raise hell up 'n' down the tunnels here. Scared the tourists. Then they got some shaman down from Marysville to come and send 'em on their way."

The old man shook his head, deep in its blankets. "I don't remember that."

"Well, they did it. And he danced and chanted and burned some nasty-ass stuff and sent 'em on their way."

"Where was that?" I asked.

"First and Yesler. That's the baddest corner. There's an old dance hall girl there and her boyfriend. He was a bank clerk at the old bank there. Sometimes y'see 'em there. And down Oxy. There's a lotta ghosts down Oxy."

That I could attest to myself. But that was about as far as we got. No matter how we asked—or who, when we moved on to the next group and the next—no one had any useful information about 1949 or the ghosts of natives or of zombies or monsters that ate people and set the dead to walking. The natives had a strange sense of proprietorship for the place; several talked about it as Grandpa Dan had, saying it was the closest you could get to the "old land."

"Do you know what we called this place before your people came?" one had asked.

"No," I replied.

"Duwamps. Funny word, huh? But it means 'good fishing' and it was good for clams and collecting driftwood for fires. It was our life. Before the rez."

Another said something in a coughing, lilting language and the speaker answered back the same way. Then they laughed and the bottles passed again. And it was the same in every group that talked about the mudflats: a slightly drunken declaration of protectiveness and pride even as they huddled in the hollows of the ground, in the face of the amnesia and disdain of society that drew a pall over everyone down below and everything that crept there, consigning it to Lethe.

We had been up and down hidden stairs and through obscure doors, dragged or dropped or slid or crawled through holes and grates, and when Quinton and I finally reemerged at the end of our exploration, I was as ragged and filthy as any of the homeless.

And as tired. I tripped over a rough section of cobble and felt the heel of my dress boot snap off with a stabbing pain to my knee.

"Oh, well," I muttered as Quinton caught me. "I didn't really like these shoes." I did feel bad about my coat, though, since I'd torn one of the sleeves and it was so dirty that I doubted dry cleaning would save it.

Quinton held me upright for a second longer than he needed to, and I didn't mind it at all. "You OK?" he asked, his voice a little husky.

I pulled my gaze from his before anything could get out of hand. "You keep asking me that. I'm not exactly a fragile flower of femininity," I said, looking down at myself. I didn't have the athletic, whipcord body I'd had as a dancer, but I didn't think I'd lost much by adding a little padding over the muscles and trading in my jazz shoes for something more practical—if a bit clunky. And, of course, I now carried a gun as well.

"I know, but . . . I like the excuse to hold your hand." Then he diffused the moment with a forced grin. "I'm a guy who lives in a bunker, remember? I don't get to paw that many attractive women—any women, actually."

"Well, that makes me feel special," I answered back.

"I do my best." Then he frowned. "But, damn, you need to get home."

"Are you sick of my company already?"

"No, but you're barely keeping on your feet—I got you up pretty early today. And you could really use a shower. You smell like basements and alleys."

I wrinkled my nose. "I do. And my knee hurts and I'm too tired to tell you how utterly lousy it is of you to say so."

"Then I'm glad you're tired, because I'd hate you to have to tell me I'm lousy. I bathe regularly! No lice on me."

I caught myself giggling and pulled myself up. "I need to go home."

"Can you drive?"

"I can," I said, and I was sure it was true. I could make it that far, but if I'd had to go much farther than West Seattle I might have had to say no and I didn't want to know where that might lead. It was inappropriate—wasn't it?

Quinton walked me back to my car and handed me in. Before I could close the door, he leaned in and kissed me on the cheek. "Drive safe."

Then he walked off and left me to it.

Wow. Not a brotherly kiss, but not a pushy kiss. . . . My thoughts bogged down in wondering what that meant, getting tangled in the mess of bits and pieces we'd uncovered, and wandering back again to the press of his lips against my cheek. I mean, it was nice, but . . . wow.

This was ridiculous, I chided myself. It was just a friendly kiss. A good night. Maybe. I was so tired and achy my mind couldn't seem to sort anything. No one had had any real clues to the monster or to the events of 1949. The only things I could think of to do now were to look for the threads I'd seen before, try to physically stalk the thing, and start talking to ghosts. And not think about that kiss.

TEN

Sunday carillons and children's shouts welcomed another fall of feathery snow outside my windows. This lot was thick enough to stick, and the rare white stuff turned the thin morning sunlight into a diffused glow suitable for the instant holiday. I rolled out of bed, shivering, and turned up the heater while I took a shower and did some stretches to loosen up my cranky knee and shoulder.

I'd stayed up too long after I'd come home, petting Chaos and thinking things I shouldn't have, and now I was paying for it under the barrage of morning sanctity. Next time I moved, I swore I'd check for bell towers before I signed anything.

I just couldn't get my mind into job mode—besides which, I'd worked Nan Grover's cases on Saturday and knew where to find a couple of her wayward witnesses pretty much whenever I wanted. There wasn't much else to do on that score, so going to the office was pointless. I didn't want to moon around the condo all day, but all I could think of to do was replace my coat and I hate shopping. With a choice between hated activity or idle speculations and idle hands, I figured I'd be better off shopping.

I ended up in Fremont, lurking in the back office of Old Possum's Books 'n' Beans, wearing out my friend Phoebe's ears with tales of woe and wrath over Will until she decided I needed to eat and dragged me to the nearest restaurant.

I poked at my breakfast and Phoebe frowned at me. "If Poppy saw you treat good food that way, he'd talk you blue." Phoebe's family owned a restaurant and food was taken very seriously, especially by her parents, who considered my rangy frame a personal challenge to their aesthetic sense. "You know you better off without that man." Phoebe's mild Jamaican accent rendered it as "wheat-oudt dat mahn."

"Yes," I said, stabbing a potato. "I don't need anyone else's doubt and paranoia—I have plenty of my own."

She smacked the back of my hand with her napkin in a gesture exactly like her mother's dish-towel reprimands to anyone who tried to sneak a taste from her pots. "Don' start that. Doubt and paranoia are part of your job—you don' got to take them home. Besides, those rawboned men got no wind—how's he gonna keep up with you, all skinny like that? You'd wear him out. You need a man with some strength. Strength of character at least. Imagine saying you're too difficult for him!" Phoebe snorted. "Jackass."

I laughed. That was not a word I'd ever have applied, but the vision of slender, silver-haired Will with donkey ears à la Pinocchio was irresistibly funny.

Phoebe grinned at my laughter. "That's better. Now, what're you gonna do the rest of the day? Don' say you goin' back to work. Nor home mopin'."

"No," I replied, still chuckling. "I have to buy a new coat—I wrecked my old wool one last night and it's too cold to go without. You know how I shop for clothes."

She nodded. "You buy whatever's closest to the door and get

the hell back out." Which was exactly what I did, so I nodded, too. "All right then. You finish your breakfast so I don' be tellin' Poppy you starvin' yourself and I'll take you shoppin'."

I rolled my eyes. "Yes, Mom." That earned me a stern look that went completely awry on Phoebe's round, good-natured features, but I did finish most of my meal before we left.

We were shoulders deep in the racks at Private Screening—a vintagewear shop down the street from Phoebe's bookstore— when my phone went off and what passes for normal life reared its head.

"Hi, Miss Blaine. This is Fish from the morgue. Sorry to call on the weekend, but I found some stuff and I thought you'd want to know."

"You work on Sunday?" I asked, tangled in a mohair monstrosity from the fifties.

"People die seven days a week. And my boss usually stays home on Sunday, so I could search the database without him getting mad."

Phoebe glared at me. "Is that work, girl?" she asked, her voice rising and falling in annoyance.

"Yes."

She snorted. "I shoulda known from the way you perked up." She helped me out of the coat as I tried to talk to Fish.

"What did you find?"

"Some of the records are pretty old, but I've got a few other deaths with similar wounds and blood loss, and they go back to just after the fire, during the reconstruction. Not a lot of them, but a few in dated clusters. All Pioneer Square and the lava beds."

"Lava beds?"

"The area around the new stadiums was the red light district. They called it the lava beds. Most of the matching deaths were south of Yesler, and they coincide with periods of destruction or construction. Just like the recent ones."

"How many?"

"I got . . . eleven solid over the fifty years or so between the fire and the earthquake in 1949. There might be more, but they didn't come up specifically. I might find them if I did the search by hand."

"No, Fish, please don't bother. This is fine—it establishes a pattern over time and an area to search. Thanks."

"What are you going to do with this information?"

"Would you believe me if I said I was going to go hunting for monsters?"

He laughed. "I might. Could be anything down there, and with this long a pattern, it's not a human—unless it's a copycat, but they like to copy high-profile crimes, not obscure accidental deaths." Interesting: Fish was taking the idea of a nonhuman killer in stride—or seemed to be. I filed that mental note for another time.

"Is that what the coroner is calling them, officially?" I asked.

"Not officially. Misadventure is most likely, but he hasn't closed any of these except Cristus, so far—and only because the family pressured him. The deaths are strange, but they don't look like murder or accident or natural causes and there's not much else."

"So Robert Cristus had family."

"From what I saw, not the sort you'd want to snuggle into the bosom of."

"Maybe that's why he lived on the streets."

"Could be. Uh-oh . . . Gotta get back to work. Call me if you find any monsters. I want to get first shot at the necropsy."

Fish cut the connection and I stuck the cell phone back into my pocket.

"What you was saying about monsters?" Phoebe asked, holding out another coat.

"Oh . . . a joke."

Phoebe frowned at me. "Don't be tryin' that on me. You up to something."

"And I'm not going to tell you what."

Phoebe made another snort. "How's that one?"

I put on the dark wool coat and felt wonderful. The sleeves were long enough to cover my wrist bones and the hem came all the way down onto my thighs, both of which were rare for me. I gave it a suspicious stare, half expecting some Grey gleam, but it was just a coat—a nice coat—and that pleased me even more. Of course, it turned out to be an expensive nice coat, but that wasn't unusual. I bought it anyway, hoping it wouldn't go the way of the previous one.

Another fine flurry of snow had started up by the time we left the shop. I thought I had spent enough time feeling bad about my morning and the weather, so I thanked Phoebe and took off, much to her disapproval. I needed to get started on interviewing ghosts before the weather got any worse.

The voice from a coffee shop's radio assured listeners that the snow wouldn't last and the temperature would soon be rising, but it didn't feel that way to me. The kids I'd heard shrieking in the snow that morning were probably hoping he was wrong as much as I hoped and doubted he was right.

The darkening sky seemed bleak and portentous overhead as I headed for work. I'd have to contact Quinton; I needed someone to watch out for me down in the tunnels and out in the streets. I wasn't always sure how safe or visible I was when I went Greywalking. I'd dodged a ghost through the layers of time once, but I didn't want to repeat the feat, especially if there were other people

around who might cause problems—or get upset. I'd had my fill
of that for a while. And Quinton not only had a stake in the pro-
ceedings, he didn't mind my oddities, which made me downright
happy.

I called Quinton while I waited for the Rover's heater to kick
in, and he agreed to meet me outside my office so we could begin
hunting for long-dead witnesses to whatever was killing people in
the underground. I took off my new coat and redonned my old
leather jacket, missing the warmth but hoping the hide was tough
enough to withstand crawling through the Grey. Then I headed
back to Pioneer Square on foot. Quinton was waiting as expected,
wrapped in his stiff waxed duster.

I told him what Fish had discovered about the long pattern of
deaths. "So," I concluded, "we're looking for something that's been
down there quite a while. Questioning the living hasn't helped." I
drew a long breath. "So I'm going to start asking the dead."

"You mean . . . the ghosts of Go-cart and Jenny?"

"No. They don't seem to have left much trace. I'm going to
have to look for ghosts who are aware enough to talk and who
also were alive during the periods and in the places the . . . thing
has killed people in the past." I didn't want to get used to thinking
of the creature as one thing or another and risk closing my mind
to clues, but the vision of a giant man-eating spider still flitted
through my head and I shuddered. "The area of most activity has
been down here in what Fish called the lava beds, south of the old
skid road," I added, pointing at Yesler Way.

"The bricks."

"Is that the whole area? I never heard the term before you and
the undergrounders used it."

"Yeah, the corridor flanking Occidental a block on either side
from Pioneer Square south. The whole place is full of those big,

white bricks they used to pave the park and the Square. There's a lot of stuff under those bricks."

"Fish said most of the deaths had been south of Yesler, so let's leave the Square for later, when there are fewer people in it—it's a bit exposed for what I need to do."

Quinton looked at the sky, as bright as it would get all day, even with the cold white flakes still drifting down. "We'd better start in the alleys."

We walked around the corner and went down the nearest alley, plodding through the slushy filth of snow, garbage, and urine that had built up between the buildings. I let my hand run along the striations of time that tipped up near the alley wall and felt the edges of years ruffle against my fingertips. I stopped and peered at them, fanning the time shards out enough to look into them. I heard Quinton make a noise and turned back to him.

He gave me a curious frown. "What are you doing?"

"Remember I said I can see layers of time?"

"Yeah."

"Some places they're slanted up, like broken bits of riverbed—layers and layers of time—and they're easier to get at. They're physically displaced, though, so I may not be able to go very far before I run into an obstacle or the bit of time just breaks off."

He shook his head like a dog irritated by a flea. "You're implying you can time travel. . . ."

"No. I can wander around in a tiny *piece* of time associated with this location. Most of it's just a recording—a kind of persistent memory—of this place. If I'm lucky, I'll find a ghost who's awake enough to talk to me, but most won't even know I'm there. What I need you to do is keep an eye on me and the area so I don't freak someone out or end up banging into something out here. I don't know what happens at this end and I wasn't worrying about

it too much the last time I had to do this, but I can't see this bit
of time well while I'm in the other one."

Quinton narrowed his eyes. "OK . . . But what if I can't
see you?"

"Let's find out," I said, pushing one of the planes of time and
sliding onto it.

I slipped sideways into another version of the alley. There
were two young men in cloth caps and knee-length trousers who
paid me no attention as they sprinted along, darting in and out
of doorways and yelling to the proprietors something I couldn't
quite hear. I followed one of them a few feet before I heard a sharp
whistle blast behind me.

I whirled and was caught in a flood of policemen who poured
into the doorways just as a lot of civilians tried to surge out of
those same openings. The noise was deafening and the two groups
clashed, yelling. But none noticed me.

I slid back out of the fragment of time and found myself closer
to the opposite end of the alley than when I'd started. Quinton
was a few steps away, wide-eyed.

"What happened?" I asked. "Are we all right?"

"Yeah, but you were pretty hard to see. If I hadn't known to
look for you, I might have dismissed you as a shadow in this light.
Where did you go?"

"When. Looked like sometime during Prohibition. Not the
period I need. We may have to go down below."

"There's not much access on this block. Some places, the underground's been cut off or is in use. This is one of those bits.
What else can you find up here?"

"Not sure. Let me look around a bit more."

I reached for the fluttering edges of time and eased into them,
pushing and shoving, looking for an indication I'd found the right

time period. No luck in that alley. We moved on to another and I tried again.

I found a slab of 1949 that smelled of dust and dry red dirt, and I stepped into a street still littered with debris from the earthquake. The silvery shape of the hotel across from my office had rained ghost bricks onto the sidewalk and a handful of workmen's shadows were shoving them into piles with what looked like bristleless push brooms. A lighted sign from another business lay where it had crashed from its moorings. I started forward, feeling a sort of push against my body as if I was walking against the current of a river. Time was intractable there and I knew it would resist any efforts by me to do anything.

I walked past the workmen, who didn't acknowledge me, and looked around. The street was busy enough with the memories of people cleaning up, but I doubted any of them would be much help even if they could see me. I went on toward Occidental, looking for the ghost of one of the street people who might be more aware of me than the shades of solid citizens. A building stood where most of Occidental Park was in my time—rather it slumped there, decrepit and broken backed, clearly destined for demolition. I stopped, startled to see the old place.

A ghostly dog ran to me and barked, putting its front paws out and its rump up, tail wagging. A cloud of birds erupted from the shattered roof of the building. One of the workmen called to the dog and finally came to drag it away from me by the collar, but he never saw me at all, berating the dog for its strange behavior as they moved away.

Seeing a phantom man in shabby clothes at the end of the block, I walked across the littered street and down the sidewalk toward him. He also didn't see me, but I followed him a while, growing a little more tired with every step against the inflexibility of time. He stopped to talk to three other rough-clad male ghosts at the corner where Waterfall Garden Park would stand someday. One of the men lifted his head to look at me, though his gaze was a bit unfocused.

I walked close to him.

"Hi," I tried.

He hadn't been that old, but he had the worn and weary demeanor of the prematurely aged. He nodded to me and said, "Ma'am." His fellows ignored him as they carried on their memory of a conversation.

I wasn't quite sure how this would work. I'd never tried questioning a ghost in his own environment before. Would he be aware that he wasn't alive? That things had happened after this moment in which we stood?

"I'm trying to find out if anyone's been hurt down here."

"Here? In the skid?"

I nodded. "Yes. After the earthquake but not by the earthquake."

"Y'mean Chuck-o."

"Was he hurt?"

"Killed."

"What killed him?"

"Something chewed him up and spit him back." The ghost pointed to the southwest. "Down by the cowboy store. This morning . . . or when it was." He looked confused. "When it was. When was it? Not sure . . ."

"How long ago was the earthquake?" I asked. He seemed to be aware of time as more than one point simultaneously, but not too good at dealing with it.

He looked happier with a simple question. "Quake was two days ago. And Chuck was found today."

"All right," I said. "Do you know now or will you know what killed him?"

His face pinched in thought for a minute. Then he replied, "No. But not something human. Not a dog, either. Or falling bricks."

"How are you sure of that?"

He snorted. "How do you know water is wet? I just know."

I nodded, feeling drained. "Thanks."

He returned my nod and fell back into his conversation as if I wasn't there.

I walked back to a less conspicuous location—I hoped—and slipped back out of the fragment of time. I emerged in a different alley and saw Quinton nearby, watching me.

"It's hard to keep up with you in there," he said.

"Really? It seems like I'm struggling to move an inch at time. I would have thought I'd be easy to follow."

"You don't move fast, but you move through the edges of things and it's hard to see you. Sometimes you disappeared into walls, but you'd show up again in a second or two."

"Hm . . ." I mumbled, thinking. I'd had some earlier clues that I got a bit incorporeal on this side of the Grey, but I wasn't sure how much. I was too tired to muck around with the idea, though.

"Did you find anything?" Quinton asked.

"Huh?" I shook myself back to attention. "Not a lot. A tramp in 1949 who said a man named Chuck was killed near the old Duncan and Sons—the cowboy store, he called it. Sounded like the same cause, but he didn't know anything. And I saw the building that used to stand where Oxy Park is. I don't know why it seemed odd to see it. . . ."

It was getting later and I felt I'd discovered nothing new about the immediate problem.

"We should get going. There's nothing else accessible here."

It was already getting dark under the snowy clouds, so we stopped for lunch—I was ravenous from my exertions in the layers of time—and finished up our exploration of the ground level. Then we descended into the tunnels beneath the sidewalks and alleys in the bricks, and I slid and slipped in and out of fractured time.

The area under Occidental Avenue was thick with memories and with the spectral flames of the fire, but most of the shades I saw there were mere recordings with no ability to answer me. We went up and down the blocks under the street until one ghost caught my eye. I tried to get a better look, but she darted down the alley gallery into which Quinton and I had first dropped with Blue Jay. It felt like weeks ago.

Here, the layers of time were less disarrayed, and I thought I could stay within the current confines of the alley if I pursued the ghost into her own plane of time.

"Keep an eye on me," I ordered Quinton as I riffled the edges of time, looking for a glimpse of the face I'd spotted.

"Got your back," he said as I pushed into the bright shock of ghostly summer and slid into the silver fragment of time.

The place wasn't empty in the cold sunshine of a long-past summer evening. A thin crowd of incorporeal men walked along the mud-floored alley that even in the memory of heat and dry weather stank of waste and spilled alcohol and a sea-salt odor of something that had died in the mud long ago. The men wore the rough working clothes of lumberjacks and miners, and they peered into odd little lean-tos built against the backs of the new brick and stone buildings that soared out of the pit of the half-built sidewalks. A few thin girl ghosts sat beside the blanket-covered doorways of the shacks at the bottom of the buildings.

The combination of the masonry buildings and the pit made me think I had to be in a time after the fire but before they covered the sidewalks, so I must have been in the reconstruction— about when the deaths had first started. I knew they'd raised the street level to accommodate modern plumbing and get the roads above the high-tide mark, and I'd seen the original first floors of the buildings near Quinton's bunker, but it hadn't occurred to me until I was standing in it that the sidewalks and alleys had lain below the street for a while, forming canyons around every block until whenever the new sidewalks had been built to connect the new street level to . . . I glanced up and saw fancy doorways complete with lintels and footings just hanging from the sides of the buildings one floor above me, waiting for the sidewalks to come to them like sand washed seasonally onto a rocky beach.

This alley deep in the lava beds had become a row of cribs— cheap bunks for the lowest class of prostitutes to turn their trade in. Men too poor, too vicious, or too low-down to go to one of the many famed and infamous brothels of Seattle trawled this sunken, ghastly place for the most pitiful and desperate women, hidden from disapproving middle-class eyes by the sheer walls of the rising roads and stone buildings. I felt a little sickened. If one of the ghostly girls had any free will, then I'd found a possible witness right at the source. I'd have to talk to her—I couldn't back away from the job because I found the setting distasteful—but I did wish I didn't have to know this place.

One of the men stopped to bargain with one of the girls—a tiny Asian who looked about sixteen. The girl didn't seem frightened of the bigger white man in his rough clothes, just tired, and she nodded to him and they went into the lean-to behind them. I felt a flush of anger and disgust and had to remind myself that this was the past and there was nothing I could do to change it.

I'd noticed that the ghosts who could interact usually wanted to—almost seemed compelled to, as if the opportunity to break their endless routine of memory was like a flame to a proverbial moth. They had come to me in the recent past for help; now I'd come to them. I didn't like manipulating them, but I would do what I had to to get the information I needed.

I looked around and saw one of the young prostitutes flinch, startled at seeing me. She was the girl I'd spotted earlier, I was sure. I darted down the alley to the crib the girl was edging into and stopped a few feet in front of her, trying to catch her eye.

"Don't go. I won't hurt you, I just want to talk to you."

The girl shook her head, twin black braids flying outward, and stepped backward farther. She was wearing a thin, ragged calico dress that brushed over her bare feet. I looked harder at her. She was Native American and I was a strange-looking towering white woman in an alley full of ethnic child prostitutes. I shouldn't have been surprised she was intimidated.

I squatted down, smothering a wince, in the stinking memory of the unfinished alleyway, bringing my head down below hers. I was appalled at how young she looked—twelve, maybe? None of the men or other girls in the alley took notice of me—one of the men stepped right through me, raising a hard shiver on my back.

The girl backed up to the edge of the entry flap. "No, spirit, go. I should not talk to you."

I put out my hands, palms up, resting on my knees, so she could see I didn't have anything in them to hide. "I need your help."

She made a face. "What help?" she spat. She feared I was trying to trick her—I'd seen that in the living often enough.

"I'm trying to find . . . a creature. A monster that shouldn't be here. I want to make it go away. It hurts people—kills them. It killed people here, now."

The girl jerked back a little farther. "A zeqwa?"

I shook my head. "I don't know. It's a monster."

"A monster," the girl said, nodding and shuffling a little closer. Her English was accented and clumsy. "A zeqwa." She shook her head with exasperated pity and squatted down in front of me. "Foolish spirit, you. Many zeqwa. Some eat children." All right, so a monster was a zeqwa and there were a lot of different kinds. Which one was I looking for?

"Some do," I agreed. "This one eats anyone it can find. It can chew through rocks and it catches people and it eats some of them and some it . . . makes walk after death. Do you know about it?"

She shook her head. "Not eating or making the walker. But I see Sistu in the water and on the land. I see him in the . . ." She waved her hand to indicate the depth of the alley and the enclosing buildings. "In this place."

"What is Sistu? What kind of zeqwa?" I asked, knowing I was frowning with interest and the growing throb in my bent knee and hoping I wasn't frightening her.

"Monster. A . . ." She made a motion with both hands that I couldn't quite understand. Seeing my confusion, she stuck a finger in the mud and made a long, sinuous line and hissed.

"A snake," I said.

"Bigger than snake!" she snapped. "Big as you stand."

"A serpent . . . a sea serpent?"

"Yes! But he comes on the land, too. Three heads. One like a snake on each end, one like a man in the middle. Many, many teeth. Very hungry, very strong. His blood can turn you to stone. His stare make you freeze. I see Sistu in the dark here below."

"Where did he come from? Where does he live?"

The girl shook her head. "He lives in the pool. He come from the water." Then she looked over my shoulder and I felt the presence of a ghost nearly on top of me.

I stood, turning and stepping aside as the ghost of a man in work clothes stopped where I'd been crouching. He held out his hand, the phantom sun sending a spark from the coins in it.

The girl ghost stood up and took the coins, looking at them suspiciously. Then, smiling mechanically, she let the man follow her into the crib. As the curtain over the doorway fell, I saw her expression became unseeing and blank as the fragment of time curled on itself in the repetition of her endless loop of memory.

I backed away before I reached out, grabbing for the edges of the temporacline, and slid out of the slice of history, gritting my teeth against impotent fury, frustration, and the grinding ache of old injuries.

I stumbled back into the haunted corridor beneath the street and bumped into Quinton. I could feel the tension in my jaw as I brushed past him. "Get me out of here."

"What happened?" he asked, catching up to me in a few strides and then passing me to lead the way out.

"I found the ghost of a child prostitute—Indian. She said she saw a zeqwa—a monster—called Sistu about the time of the first deaths."

"Is it the one we're looking for?"

"I don't know. The timing's right, but she said it's a sea serpent of some kind with three heads."

"And you don't think a three-headed sea serpent is very likely to have done this?"

I felt myself growling and stopped to take a deep breath—or three—and calm down. "I don't know. Her description doesn't make sense to me. She must have been twelve! A kid!"

He put his hands on my shoulders. "Shh . . . Harper. She *was* a kid, but you can't do anything about that. Not now. Let's find out about this monster. Then we'll have something more to go on. Now, be stealthy or someone may catch us coming up from here."

I stifled myself and limped after Quinton.

I'd managed to avoid any dire filth this time, so we got a table in Zeitgeist Coffee. We cleaned up and sat down to figure out what to do next.

"I think we need to look at the newspaper archives at the library," Quinton suggested. "The central branch will be open for a few more hours today, and we might be able to find out more now that we have the info from the morgue."

"I need to call Fish and find out what he knows about this Sistu thing. Maybe it's got some signature or habit or something we can look for."

"And we can look it up and see if there's more information. If it's a local legend, there may be documents in the local folklore and Native American sections."

I nodded and got out my phone to call Fish. I was still bothered by the ghost, but Quinton was right that there was nothing I could do for her. She had died a century ago and her life couldn't be changed. I wondered what had led her to be selling herself in an alley, but had to put it out of my mind before I got angry all over again.

Fish was just about to leave the morgue when I called. I asked him about Sistu.

"Huh . . ." he responded. "No . . . don't think I've ever heard of a sistu, but 'zeqwa' is a Lushootseed word that means monster— any kind of monster from a man-eating seal to an ogre or a giant dog—so whatever specific thing your source is talking about has gotta be from somewhere around Washington or British Columbia. I'll ask my mom and my old grandma. One of them will know."

"Great. Thanks, Fish. Should I call you or will you call me?"

"I'll call, but let me give you my cell number—I'm off for a couple of days."

I wrote down the number he offered and disconnected.

Quinton was watching me and pulling a chocolate doughnut to pieces. "What's he say?"

"He doesn't know, but he'll ask some people who might."

"All right. You want anything aside from coffee before we head out to the library?" He pointed to the part of the doughnut he hadn't touched yet. "These things are pretty wicked."

I shook my head. "No thanks. I don't like chocolate much."

He just raised his eyebrows and nodded. I appreciated the restraint. Some men might have made a comment about how unfeminine it was not to be gaga for chocolate, but I'd never acquired much taste for sweets—especially chocolate—between my mother's belief that I was fat and my father's career as a dentist. I didn't mind skipping the doughnut, but I didn't want to abandon my coffee before we went back out into the cold to walk to the library. It was pretty dark and we wouldn't have a lot of time before the librarians threw us out—no matter what good friends they were with Quinton. I drank a little too fast as we headed out the doors, and yelped.

"What? Are you hurt?" he asked, following me to the corner.

"No," I mumbled, throwing the cup into the trash. "I burned my tongue."

"Really? Let me see. Stick it out."

I did stick out my tongue. And made a face to go with it.

"Oh, God, it's horrible! A zeqwa!" he cried, throwing up his hands and cowering in mock fear.

I pulled my tongue back in. "Nut," I said.

"Don't think you can butter me up with endearments," he replied, wagging a finger in the air. "I've heard that one before. Just before the guys with the straitjackets showed up."

We both broke up, stumbling a little on the icy sidewalk as we ascended the hill. We must have seemed drunk, giggling like children with me favoring my aching knee so I skipped and staggered unevenly, but we got to the library about an hour before closing time.

ELEVEN

Quinton knew his way around the library better than anyone other than an employee—and possibly better than some of them. I wasn't entirely thrilled with the Koolhaas building but I didn't think it an eyesore. No, the eyesore was the screaming-yellow escalator enclosure with its strange display of two faces and a giant eyeball projected on mostly spherical blobs that were seen through rough holes in the escalator's interior wall. Shafts of light seemed to transfix the misshapen faces and eye, making them look like alien trophies as they writhed, mouthing silent words and blinking with disembodied lids. I couldn't look at it for long. The wiggling, flickering faces reminded me too much of things out of my earliest Grey nightmares.

Quinton caught me turning away. "Disconcerting."

"That's a word for it."

He smiled and we came out of the escalator tunnel into the "mixing chamber"—a huge room that took up the whole floor with clusters of worktables, chairs, standing carrels, shelves, and counters where patrons and librarians were supposed to "mix" to find information. Mostly people seemed to gather in clumps and chatter among themselves, so the room had a constant low din like a tropical jungle. Quinton sought out one of the librarians who was wearing a wireless mic headset like a stagehand in a large, professional theater. After a moment's conversation the librarian shook his head.

"Sorry, can't put you on the staff computer right now. Leslie's got it. The regular computers are open and they're pretty fast. Here, let me grab you one."

He darted across the chamber to a computer in a standing carrel. I thought it was a good thing we wouldn't be using it very long, since the stand-up desk height was well designed to discourage lingering. In spite of the proximity to closing time, most of the computers in the room—and there were a lot—were in use. Many of the patrons looked high school or college age, and I guessed from the fevered looks on some of their faces that they were racing to find materials for papers due the next day. A lot of the library branches weren't open on Sundays, so this was the natural place to come if you were running late and didn't have Internet access at home. I wondered how many papers were being plagiarized outright in the last-minute panic.

Quinton ran a quick search and we made a list of newspaper archive dates and issues, which I carried back to the librarian with the headset. He called to someone using the device, and a stack of bound journals and microfiche cards was delivered to me in a few minutes. I put them on a table near Quinton and went to look at his progress before I dove into them.

He was glaring at a page full of prompts and code strings on the computer screen and typing with angry slashing strokes.

I put a hand on his shoulder. "What's wrong?" I asked.

He turned his eyes up to look at me. "I wanted to check some other sources—in case there's been anything like this elsewhere." He looked back to the screen and frowned. "This archive is being coy—it wants a bunch of login passwords it never asked for before. Someone thinks they're being secure but it's just a pain in the butt. I'll back-door it. . . ." He patted my hand and drew his away to return to the keyboard.

"OK. I've got a pile of stuff from the newspaper archive. Have you found any information about the Sistu yet?"

"Not yet . . . I'll finish this and get to the folklore section. . . ." His concentration was on the screen and the task of getting around the system's security. He didn't see me nod, didn't notice the withdrawal of my hand, so focused was his attention. I couldn't begrudge that—I was the same way on a case sometimes. But I wondered what archive he was getting into that fascinated him so, since I couldn't imagine anything in the library that would have that sort of security—or anything we were looking for that would need it. Quinton intrigued me, but it wasn't for his transparency or simple life.

I skimmed through the old *Post-Intelligencer* issues, taking notes on all the deaths or other strange occurrences that seemed to fit our pattern in the right date ranges.

The records before the fire didn't show anything that was a match—even a rough match. The first odd death happened in April of 1890, during the rebuilding, when the Kline and Rosenberg building on Washington between Commercial and Second collapsed during construction. One of the workmen had been buried under the falling bricks and was found dead and missing an arm and a leg once the bricks were shifted out of the hole. The missing limbs were never recovered and the collapse was blamed on piers that hadn't been sunk deep enough into the mud and sawdust landfill that made up that part of town.

I had to find a map of the original plat to realize that the site in question was now the northwest corner of Occidental Park—Washington Street was still the same, but at the time Oxy had been called Second Avenue and First Avenue was called Commercial Street. The same location where I'd seen the tumbledown building in the city's memory of 1949. I wondered if it could have been the replacement Kline and Rosenberg building.

Another project on Washington—the Brodeck and Schlesinger building between Third and Fourth—fell down a month later while its second floor was under construction. It was no wonder they'd turned the area into a park, since it seemed to be bad luck for buildings. Between the two events I spotted records of several more deaths with the same hallmarks. After the second building went down, though, the deaths had stopped. I didn't know what had put an end to them—the reason for the collapse was again given as unstable piers—but I knew from experience that it was possible for magic to bring down a building and wondered if that was the real cause of the second building's fall.

As I read forward, that period of Seattle's history was full of freakish events, from the city's project to raise the streets—but not the sidewalks—that had resulted in the deep corridors I'd visited, to the "inadvertent suicide" of an unlucky pedestrian who fell from the streets above. There were other odd deaths, but I didn't find another death by monster until that of a transient named Charles Olander in 1949. I assumed this was Chuck-o, and I felt pretty sure I was right when I read that his body had been found at the other end of Occidental, near the current football stadium, where some pipes had broken in the street during the quake. That would have been a block or less from the old Duncan and Sons shop with its life-size plaster horse standing on a platform over the sidewalk.

Quinton sat down next to me, brushing a hand down my back and jarring me out of my thoughts about whatever was feeding on people beneath the streets.

"Not much on the Sistu," he said. "A lot of the Native American and local legend books are at the Ballard branch. And the other archives didn't turn up anything like it outside the Seattle area for any time period, so it's not a moving phenomenon—nor is it government related or monitored that I could discover. It's localized."

"Why would the government—" I started.

A voice came from overhead, telling us the library would be closing in five minutes. I tried my question again, but Quinton shook me off. I picked up my notes and got ready to go back out into the cold.

Once outside he said, "The government gets into a lot of strange research, so I checked an old info source of mine to see if there was anything like this, but I didn't get a hit. What did you get?"

"Not as much as I'd like," I admitted, sighing. "But there is a matching geographic area and everything happened down on the street level south of the skid road—it used to be Mill Street, but they changed the name to Yesler Way during the rebuilding.

"The first related death was right after the fire. A couple of buildings collapsed down on Washington Street—the northern border of the bricks. There were several deaths in the area from Washington to what's now Royal Brougham between April when the first building went down and May when the second one went. I don't know what made the deaths stop, but it coincides with the second building's collapse. The southernmost body was found the day the second building fell, down in a dumping ground which was in the same location as the current hotel project at Occidental and Royal Brougham. Apparently that area had been used as a dump for a while—debris from the fire was hauled there too—and that wasn't the first or the last body ever found there."

"I'd bet that was the Seattle equivalent of dumping the bodies in the East River in New York," Quinton said, starting to walk. "You can't drop them into Elliot Bay, since they'd come back on the next high tide, or stick in the mudflats at low tide."

My own stride was slower than his, my knee now feeling stiff and swollen. "Yeah. Looks like a lot of stuff came back at high tide. The paper had the tide table on the front of every edition because the sewer backflushed whenever the tide came in so . . . you had to know when it was safe to flush your toilet. With that kind of tidal action, I doubt anyone dumped anything in the bay that they wanted to see the last of."

Quinton paused and matched his pace to mine. "Hell, no. What if Uncle Peter suddenly came back from his fatal fishing trip to embarrass everyone with a suspicious bullet wound or something?"

I smiled. "What if, indeed? But don't you think it's funny: they raised the streets for toilets? I wonder if it still gets wet down on the old street level at high tide. . . ."

"I can attest it does not. The seawall keeps Elliot Bay at bay. For the most part. There are seeps of course but the buildings have pumps and drains in the basements."

"Another undergrounder secret?"

"Nope. A Seattle utilities problem. It's a whole new definition of rising damp, considering the current downtown sidewalks are about thirty feet above the old sidewalks, so to keep the sewer lines at a good angle, the streets farther up the bluff must be about . . . seventy feet above their original levels, maybe more."

"Impressive engineering."

Quinton eyed me with a silly, self-conscious smile. "Yes, indeed."

I laughed and didn't even feel guilty. "Is that flirting?"

"That's what it said on the instructions. Did I do it badly?"

"No, but don't let it get out of hand," I warned with a lack of sincerity.

"No, ma'am," he replied, smothering a chuckle. He made his face serious. "All right, all right. Back to work. So we know the area is the same for all the significant deaths and that whatever is causing them comes and goes."

"I think our monster's trapped down there," I said.

"It seems to get around if it wants to," Quinton replied.

"Only up to a point. It doesn't wander far from the core of the bricks and never has so long as white men have been keeping records. We don't know that it's this Sistu, but it's the only monster anyone's come up with and it's of native origin and, as you said, the phenomenon is localized to Seattle's tenderloin. It seems to turn up when things get torn apart in the historic district, which used to be the mudflats—Indian fishing grounds. We don't know when or how it was last put to bed, but it does seem to have a limit or a way to box it up. This creature doesn't just run amok forever. We don't know enough about the history of the underground to know exactly what's been done down there or when that might have unleashed and later banished this thing."

"We need to take the tour."

"What?"

"The Underground Tour. I think they've got one late tour left today, if we hurry." Quinton grabbed my elbow to support me and began to jog down the snow-crusted street toward Pioneer Square. "Can you run? C'mon. The historian may know something if we catch him."

"The Underground Tour? It's a tourist trap," I objected, skittering and wincing along behind him.

"Yeah," he agreed, "but it's about real history. They spin it for the guests, but the facts are still the same. If anyone knows anything about the history of the underground and the strange things that happened in it, it'll be the tour people."

We slid and slipped down the hill to the Square and made it in at the back of the last tour of the day. We'd missed the introductory speech, but since the group was small, and the weather lousy, the woman at the ticket window let us join the group as they headed out to the totem pole. Our guide was a tall, lanky man in his fifties with one lazy eye and hair that had faded from red to gingery beige. His voice was clear and loud without being a shout and his patter was funny enough to distract the small group from stamping their chilling feet too much.

"I know it's pretty cold out here so I'm going to keep this part short and get us in under the street in just a minute. A lot of the area we're going to be walking through is condemned and of course it's all private property, so you'll want to stay close to me and not wander off. It's perfectly safe so long as you stay on the wooden walkways and cleared paths—our rats are all union here and they don't like to cross any lines, but they do occasionally pick off stragglers, so your best bet is to stay with the group and . . . are there any children here . . . ? No? Oh, well . . . usually we call 'em bait, but you adults will have to take your chances."

That got a laugh.

Our guide, whose name we'd missed, talked briefly about the totem pole—stolen by the city fathers on a trip to Alaska, burned in the fire, and replaced at the cost of the old pole plus the new one—and the pergola, which had been built as a trolley stop, knocked down by a runaway truck and rebuilt.

"Unfortunately," our guide went on, "when the repaired pergola was reinstalled, the city felt that the area needed more support and poured tons of concrete down into the space below to shore up the street corner—didn't know there was anything down there did you? But there is. The classiest underground restroom you will never see. Like the pergola, it was built for the Alaska-Yukon-Pacific Exposition of 1909 and was billed as the most luxurious 'subterranean comfort station' in the world at the time. Marble floors, murals, a shoe shine station, a barber, even a tailor's stall to make repairs to your clothes. People came from all over the world to inspect our restroom and build subterranean comfort stations of their own."

One of the tourists held up a hand and asked if the comfort station was still there.

Our guide shook his head. "Yes, but unfortunately it's now sealed behind that load of cement the city poured in. These large, decorative lamp standards around the Square are actually ventilation shafts for the comfort station down below—just like the uprights in the pergola. And speaking of down below, let's get in there."

The group trailed the tall guide across the Square and street and down First Avenue half a block, the guide talking at each pause about whatever the group happened to be standing near. The pace was slow enough and the distance short enough that I had no difficulty keeping up, in spite of my complaining knee.

The guide opened a gate and led us all down a flight of metal-framed stairs and through a metal door to an area of brick arches similar to the place where Quinton and I had found the vampire attacking Jay. We continued under the sidewalk on a walkway of creaking boards, past piles of discarded junk, while our guide filled us in on the history of the underground and how it came to be.

We followed him north, through a hole in the wall, to where

a sudden burst of light came down from work lights strung near the ceiling. A lot of broken furniture, pipes, cans, and other strange objects leaned in the far corner. We took a dogleg turn and came out into an L-shaped room with a door into a building on the inside corner. Flickering light came in through the ceiling and a once-fancy sign with lightbulb sockets and blue and white enamel stood canted in a corner spelling out "SAM'S——" something; the second half was missing. The guide stood in the middle of the room under the odd light.

I felt much colder in that area and got an unpleasant sensation of something crawling on my skin. I edged a little farther into the room, putting my back to the stone wall near the door in the corner, but couldn't escape from the feeling of dread. The room was fairly boiling with Grey and bright with blazing energy lines in hot yellow and blue, but I couldn't see an immediate source for my discomfort.

"We're now directly under the corner of Yesler and First," the guide began.

So this was the "worst corner" in the underground according to the Indians, where a native shaman had driven away a pack of ghosts. Maybe that was an explanation for the energy levels and my disquiet.

"You're standing now at the original street level of Seattle. Now, back in the 1860s through 1880s this was all mudflats, and as we told you upstairs, it got a little wet at high tide. So after the fire, the city had a great opportunity to raise the streets up from the tide line and make downtown safe, dry, and sewage free. But raising the streets was a huge undertaking—and undertaking is the right word here because although no one died during the fire, a few people did die in the streets and especially the sidewalks afterward."

He pointed up to the modern sidewalk above us. "This was all open for several years while the streets went up. So the people who wanted to get into the buildings to shop or do business would come down a ladder or stair at the end of the block and walk along the sidewalks down here. Unfortunately, they occasionally missed the ladders and fell to their deaths. This was about the same time miners on the way to the Klondike were pouring into Seattle. Heavy merchandise from the shops often ended up stacked on the streets and sometimes a box or barrel would fall into the open sidewalks and kill a pedestrian here below. So you can see it was a real adventure going shopping downtown in those days."

He smiled and the tourists smiled back until he continued, "Now, I hope none of you folks are afraid of ghosts, because this corner is reputed to be the most haunted part of the underground we're going to walk through today. But don't worry, we've never lost a guest. No matter how hard we try."

A few of our fellow tourists glanced at each other with shaky bravado and I, of course, didn't say they'd been shoulders-deep in phantoms since they'd parked their cars.

As he went on about the bank that had originally occupied the building, I found myself peering around with trepidation, staring more sharply at shapes and shadows than I might have.

"Now, I've never seen it," the guide continued, "but several of the other tour guides and the crew of a TV show that filmed down here say they've seen the ghost of a young man at this corner. He is thought to have been a bank teller who worked in this bank right here. The story goes that he was killed by a miner in a dispute over a . . . lady of negotiable affection."

The crowd tittered, but I recoiled as something that was definitely not a young man dead or alive loomed up in the icy cold, malforming the lines of energy that strung through the space like a net.

"Bitch," someone whispered in the silvered gloom of the Grey. I looked for the speaker but could only spot a moving columnar disturbance in the thin mist and bright lines. Whoever or whatever it was didn't have enough power to come any further out of the paranormal, and I was just as glad of that, considering the vicious tone of its voice.

Unaware of the uncanny member of our group, the tour guide was explaining the glass prisms embedded in the sidewalks above that cast light down into the buried level. As he talked about the manganese that turned the prisms purple over time, I felt the unseen thing halt in front of me, twined in lines of energy like an insect in a carnivorous vine.

"Don't interfere with me," it murmured.

Startled, I jerked back. "What?" I hadn't expected something so barely present to be aware of me, much less so angry.

"Meddler, busybody . . ." the thing whispered. The lines flared as it surged toward me, and fell back, restrained by whatever spell those strands of elemental energy wove. I racked my brain. I knew what this thing was if I could just recall. . . .

"Do I know you?" I asked. The woman on one side of me glanced my way then back to the tour guide when she realized I wasn't talking to her. Quinton touched his hand to mine but didn't make a bigger move—he knew I faced something he couldn't see or hurt.

"No," the whisper replied—I could hardly think of it as more—and the connection was made. It was a discarnate revenant. I'd met a manifest revenant before and not enjoyed the experience, but never a discarnate. Powerful in life and aware in death but entirely incorporeal, they were generally angry, frustrated, and malevolent. They're the things that whisper madness and suicide into the ears of the receptive and depressed. A shred of some powerful thing that had died or been exorcised incompletely, this one must have been the remains of something the native medicine man had tried to remove but could only weaken enough to bind it to this place. Nasty bits of psychic personality, all revenants were aware of everything around them, even if they couldn't affect it, and that made for a vicious and tricky ghost. Since this one knew who I was, it probably knew what I was looking for.

I edged away from my corporeal neighbors and muttered, "Tell you what, I'll leave you alone if you tell me where to find the Sistu."

I felt it laugh more than heard it. "Find death where there is no light, no comfort, between the tides, in a pool that is not a pool." It laughed again and faded away, letting the energy of the Indian's magic slide back into its warding shape.

Well, I thought, it had been worth a try. And at least the nasty thing was gone, I added with a shudder. Whatever it had been in life, it was one unpleasant customer in the afterlife. The unsettling feeling of the room eased when the invisible creature left.

Quinton shot me a questioning glance and wrapped my hand in his but I shook my head and mouthed, "Later."

Our guide was asking for questions and almost ready to move on. I put my hand in the air.

"Yes. The lady in the back," he acknowledged, pointing at me from his height over the heads of the tourists.

I put my hand down. "You mentioned the ghost of the bank teller. Are there other ghosts associated with this corner?"

"Well, not anymore," he replied, "although there are reportedly other ghosts in the underground. A lot of tour guests used to report seeing or hearing the ghosts of Native Americans here.

It was so disturbing and frequent that a shaman was called in around . . . 1997, if I remember correctly, to clear the place and send the ghosts away. It must have worked, because it's been pretty quiet since then."

The old man we'd talked to Saturday night had been right about the ghosts, but wrong about the dates. I wondered what the Indian ghosts had been doing down here, since Fish had said that the living and the dead didn't mix. What would have made them linger and why had they associated with the revenant? Did they have anything to do with the Sistu—if that was the monster we were chasing—or with putting it back in its box in the past?

As I'd been thinking, the group had begun to troop out and go on around the corner into the bank vault. Quinton and I trailed them but saw no other lingering shades as we rejoined the tour group and climbed some stairs to exit into the ragged end of Post Street.

We listened to more patter about the underground and followed our guide to cross First again and trailed up the street to enter a narrow building at 115 Yesler. Except it wasn't a building, really, but a door between buildings that held staircases going up and down. Down led again into the underground. This time we emerged inside a building—a former store showroom with a crazily sloping floor. The cement was warped, tipped, and pitched until it looked like a model mountain range.

The guide explained that the delicately stenciled plaster walls in the room led them to believe the shop had once been quite elegant. "At one time this building would have had a polished wood floor, but it's now concealed by this concrete you see. All this concrete throughout the underground was poured in at the city's insistence when plague broke out here in 1907." The crowd made an uncomfortable rustling as he went on. "They thought that sealing the wooden floors and sidewalks would stop the rats and their friends from coming up through the foundations, but they didn't think about the fact that all these buildings rest on oiled cedar pilings driven into the mud and landfill beneath, and that landfill is unstable." Unstable enough, I thought, to bring down buildings—and trap monsters? "Most of these buildings are currently sinking at a rate of a quarter of an inch a year and have been for some time. That settling accounts for most of the uneven floors, tilted doorways, and strange noises you may encounter as we continue the tour."

Well, that and the ghosts, I thought.

He talked a bit more about the room we were in, saying that it had been in a couple of films, including the original *Night Strangler* movie—a vampire story set in Seattle's underground—that had come from the TV series *The Night Stalker* that I thought I might have seen as a kid, but couldn't remember.

At last we'd exhausted the exhibits in the old shop and went out. We followed the guide past the shop's original window-filled frontage and around the corner of Occidental to a dark area of red-bricked arcades and deep terra-cotta walls. A few work lights in cages hung at random intervals to cast deep shadows into the mist-heavy corners. Once again the throngs of ghosts were thick—even thicker down in the underground than they'd been on the surface.

"Now we're under Occidental Avenue, but when this was originally built, it was called Second—notice the sign up there. Once the sidewalks were completed, people still used the underground sidewalks as a sort of covered mall to avoid the rain, and the doors on the old street level remained open until the underground was officially closed in 1910 due to a second outbreak of plague. But despite that, much of the underground never really closed at all; it just became the underworld. This stretch of Second, from where we are now to about where Qwest Field stands today, was the most crime-ridden, vice-filled, and profitable part of the whole city.

"Along this stretch there were several hundred women who listed their occupation as 'seamstress' and yet not a single one of them owned a sewing machine. For many years, Seattle's 'seamstress' tax paid for the fire brigades, police, streets, and schools the more upright members of society demanded without ever having to legalize Seattle's most lucrative trade—prostitution."

I suppose I should have been appalled, but after having seen their ghosts—both the adult women on the street and the sad girls in the alley cribs—I wasn't so much outraged as sad to hear my worst imaginings confirmed.

I missed something of the tour patter while I thought of those ghosts and only heard the guide say, "Once the sidewalks were installed, most of Seattle's vice, drugs, and gambling sank to the underground levels in spite of the official closure of the underground and was still in full swing when Prohibition hit and gave the old place an infusion of new blood—highly alcoholic blood—and crime. Prostitution ceased to be our most profitable underground business in favor of bootlegging.

"Now, let's move a little farther along here. . . ."

As we walked down the vaulted corridor, the space was raucous to my ears—filled as it was layers of time and packs of ghosts. We paused in front of a building labeled "107 Saloon" as the guide described later efforts to preserve the underground with earthquake-proof structures and shoring up the walls that were already up to six feet thick in some places. I thought any monster that could go make a hole in the four-foot-thick walls of the Great Northern Tunnel wasn't going to be much deterred by the stone and brick of the underground's street buttresses, no matter how thick. I listened with only half an ear to the tales of the city's halfhearted efforts to clean up the vice and crime in the underground—somewhat hampered by the involvement of police and politicians in the money-making end of the enterprises—while I looked around the section of sidewalk for possible phantom informants. The darkness inside the shell of the 107 Saloon wasn't dark to me—the space was thronged with a party crowd of speakeasy patrons whooping it up among the thinner ghosts of the Klondike's miners and lumberjacks. I glanced in at them and was struck by the sight of a familiar face.

Among the crowd of illegal drinkers, I spotted Albert—the ghost who inhabited the home of my friends Ben and Mara Danziger. For a moment, I tried to catch his attention, but I soon realized I was seeing a mere loop of history—a bit of the old building's memory of its past. I watched Albert with narrowed eyes and recognized the quick twist of his head and the gleam on his spectacles from a far more recent encounter. I ground the feeling of unpleasant familiarity through my mind until the image and idea clicked together. He was the second spirit that had been riding the zombie I'd released under the viaduct. Damn Albert! What was the bastard up to? I'd have to find out. I didn't like the idea that the unpredictable specter might be involved in the deaths of undergrounders. It might not be true, but I still needed to know.

I barely managed not to fall on the uneven slope of the floor as the guide led us out and up to the alley behind the Merchants Cafe. My knee made a popping sound as I stumbled to keep my footing. I'd need to ice it and do an extra set of stretches to keep it supple after this.

From the alley we could see down to Occidental Park—right

to the lot where the Kline and Rosenberg building must have fallen.

Our guide continued his speech. "During World War Two, the military used the underground, but once the war was over, it was abandoned once again. From 1946 to 1952, the underground became a dumping ground for trash and broken furniture as well as a scavenger's delight for antique collectors who stole most of the period bits and pieces including the doors right off the buildings. Without the doors, the underground became a highway for burglars, and most of the businesses in Pioneer Square were hit at one time or another by enterprising thieves who came up from the unprotected basements. It also became a haven for the homeless and several fires were started by transients trying to stay warm. In 1952, the underground was officially condemned and closed—supposedly for good," he said.

He pointed down the alley to the park. "Normally, I'd take you down to the park for a look at the totem statues of sun and raven, the bear, orca, and Tsonoqua—the ogress called "nightmare bringer"—but it's pretty cold and dark today. They are very interesting sculptures, however, and I urge you to come back when the light and weather are better. Now, follow me across the street and we'll wrap this up under the Pioneer Building."

As we crossed the street he told us we'd be going down one of the few original staircases still intact. "Most of these were removed in 1952 when the underground was sealed, but this one was preserved under its cover. When the lower levels of this building were reopened for business, the staircase was restored for our use. The original staircases had no rails, so try to imagine, as you descend, what it was like to use these steep, open stairs every day." We followed him down the stair and I shivered at the thought of taking those slippery steps without a handrail. Especially if I'd been drinking like a miner or a lumberjack. No wonder people missed them and became "inadvertent suicides."

We entered the final room of the tour, filled with strange objects that had been found in the underground. The guide pointed out a tin bathtub that had been found inside one of the walls—suspected of being used to brew up literal bathtub gin—and a bored out cedar log from the water system. There was also an early glass plate photo of a Madam Lou Graham and her "sewing circle" with a note attached that said Madam Lou's brothel—where the photo was taken—had been housed at First and Main, probably in the building that was currently the Bread of Life Mission. Quinton and I both smothered chuckles over it. Finally, the group moved on and followed our guide into the gift shop, where Quinton and I cornered him at the cash counter.

His name was Rick and he was the tour's historian. I introduced myself and said that we were doing some research into myths and legends of the underground.

"Well, I covered a lot of the more interesting ones on the tour," Rick said, "but, of course, there's more than a ninety-minute tour has time for. Some things don't play too well, so we don't use them on the tour, and others aren't exactly family fare. We make light of the vice and crime, but it was pretty rank. For instance, the age of consent was ten and not a few Klondikers disappeared and never showed up again. It's really safer to talk about toilets, rats, and political corruption in pursuit of the almighty dollar."

No doubt, but sewage wasn't my topic of interest. "We're specifically looking for anything about Indian activity in the underground, any legends about monsters or ghosts that were banished from the area and when those might have occurred."

Rick shook his head. "Aside from the story I told you about the shaman, I don't know much about that. The local Indians haven't had much pull with the city historically, so if they wanted to do anything or thought there was something going on, they were pretty much ignored until the eighties or later. Even the totems in Occidental Park were a pretty late sop to the native population."

"Was there any activity after the earthquake of 1949?" I asked.

Rick thought a moment, narrowing his eyes so the wandering one seemed to vanish. "Hmm . . . I think there might have been some kind of ceremony by the local Indians then, but I'm not sure. There was a lot in the papers of the time about the buildings that had been damaged and the repair or destruction of them, but the local natives didn't rate that kind of coverage. Some interesting artifacts were found in the mess, since it was the first time some of that ground had been excavated since the fire. I think they pulled up some of the original wooden sewer pipes then and found a lot of objects in the street fill, since the city dumped anything it could get into the streets to raise them—including dead animals and broken furniture. Most of it was just thrown into a different dump, afterward. People weren't very interested in the historical value of things dug out of the street then, and the local tribes hadn't yet convinced the state to treat Indian artifacts as important. If the Indians did some kind of ceremony to placate earth spirits or ancestors, you'd get a lot more information by talking to them."

I wasn't sure there was anyone else left to ask. I said as much to Quinton as we climbed the stairs from the tour shop to the Square.

"Not a total bust, though," he said. "We know the Indians were aware of things going on down there; we just don't know what they did about it."

"We'll have to hope we get some information from Fish on

that. And I'm going to have to go to the Danzigers' and talk to them about something."

"You think they'll have some ideas about this?"

"No. I saw something down there that might link up to something else, but I'm not sure. I want to check before I make an assumption."

Quinton stopped as we got outside the door and looked around. We both spotted Zip and Lass nearby. Lass chattered and punctuated his words with hard slashes at the air while Zip smoked. Across the street, I saw Sandy dragging her cart and watching something ahead of her that I couldn't pick out. Lass and Zip suddenly turned and started in the direction of the Bread of Life Mission—it was dinnertime—passing Sandy, who ignored them.

Quinton rustled beside me as he pulled his hat down a little farther on his head. The night was coming down with a sharp edge of ice, and we watched the homeless as they drifted toward food and shelter and respite from the short, harsh day.

"All right," he said. "I'll do some more asking around. I'll call if anything comes up."

"Hey," I said, putting my hand self-consciously on his sleeve. "Umm . . . This was kind of fun. Aside from the working part."

"And the creepy parts. What happened down by the bank? It got damned cold down there and you were talking to something."

"And that's about all. There was some kind of remnant of whatever the medicine man did at that corner—a real ugly customer. It told me a riddle about where the Sistu was, but it doesn't make any sense."

Quinton took one of my hands in both of his and chafed it warm. "What did it say?"

"It said I'd find death where there was no comfort, between the tides, in a pool that is not a pool. Whatever that means."

"Why would it be all cryptic like that?"

"Because it can. Ghosts want to talk to me, but that doesn't mean they want to say anything nice. The nastier the spirit, the more likely it is to want something equally nasty or just to want to do someone some hurt. Most ghosts don't know we're here. Of the ones who do, some are angry enough to want to do us harm. They're pissed off because they're dead and we're not."

Quinton nodded, making a thoughtful grunt and rubbing my other hand. "I get that. I might be pretty ticked off myself if I were a ghost."

"You'd certainly not be able to do that," I said, nodding at his hands around mine.

He blushed and let go. "No, and that would be a pity. God, it's cold out here," he added, looking around again, uncertain of himself for a moment. "I'll give that riddle some thought and I'll try to find some other information for you."

"Thanks," I replied. I admit I was thinking about his stealth kiss the previous night and wondering if he'd try it again.

Instead he blushed a bit more—thinking the same thing?—nodded, and walked off after Zip, Lass, and Sandy. I went back to the Rover, a little disappointed, and headed toward Queen Anne.

TWELVE

It was about seven when I called the Danzigers. Dinner was over with and their son, Brian, was winding down toward bedtime—of which Ben was in charge. Mara was happy to have another adult in the house for a while, though I didn't think she'd be as thrilled once she knew the nature of my visit.

For once, Albert did not show himself when I arrived. I wondered if he knew why I'd come, though I didn't see how. Ghosts didn't seem to be any better at reading minds than anyone else. Mara answered my ring of the doorbell.

"Harper!" she greeted, her Irish voice almost turning my name to laughter. "Come in, come in! Seems a while since you've visited."

I stepped into the entry hall, saying, "I got a little distracted over the holidays."

"Not surprising." She took my coat and hung it on a peg before leading me into the living room where a bright fire burned in the grate with the scent of pine needles. I could see a sparkling screen of blue energy in front of the fire. I wondered if it was the source of the odor or if Mara had put it there for some other reason. The interior of the Danzigers' house was always much calmer than outside, being cleansed of magical residues and protected from intrusions by Mara's witchcraft. I still wondered why she hadn't banished Albert when they first moved in, but then I seemed to be the only person in his current acquaintance who didn't find him charming.

"What was it you were wanting to discuss?" Mara asked, plumping down onto one of the pale green sofas that flanked the fireplace. Her coppery curls reflected the firelight as if born from it.

I looked around but still saw no sign of the resident ghost. "Is there a way to talk without your houseguest hearing us?" I asked.

Mara looked puzzled. "Well, yes. Why?"

"I don't want to say where he can listen in, but as I need your help and—in a way—his, I'd like to talk here and now, if we can."

Mara lifted her shoulders in a resigned shrug. "All right. How much time do you want?"

"I think thirty minutes will be enough to explain it."

"That's easy enough." She sat up very straight and began muttering under her breath in lilting musical phrases accompanied by the gleaming blue of magic that she caught on her fingertips and painted on the air in curling, vinelike shapes.

As the creepers of energy took shape, she rose from her seat and began to walk around the outside of the twin couches counterclockwise, still singing a little and passing her hands through the air, leaving gleaming trails of blue. The bramble followed her, growing around the couches faster than kudzu. She circled the couches three times, and the sparkling shapes of magic grew higher and denser with each pass until they were more than head high and beginning to arch over us as if they grew on some invisible arbor. Mara made one last gesture and the magic arbor closed over our heads. I heard a distant bubbling and murmuring, as if the magic were alive and talking to itself as we sat beneath it.

"All right, then," Mara said, sitting back down. "What has Albert done?"

"I'm not sure what he's done or what he intends, but I know he's been up to something and he may have information that will help me with a problem."

Mara leaned back and made herself comfortable, ready to listen. "Go on."

"A few days ago I was brought a zombie, for lack of a better word—literally a walking corpse. How it was animated I'm still not entirely sure and that's less important than this—when I broke it down, there were two spirits in the shell of the body. I've talked to Carlos about this and there should be only one. One of the entities seemed to be the spirit that had inhabited the body in life—and that was a while ago, considering the state of decomposition. But the other was Albert, and I'm pretty sure he hasn't been in a body of his own in a while."

Mara was appalled. "Heavens, no! Albert animating a corpse? Are you sure? I wouldn't have thought him capable—he's not terribly strong."

"But he is unusually strong-willed."

"Is he?"

"You don't think so? He comes and goes, he moves things as big and heavy as Ben's desk, he eggs Brian into all sorts of trouble, he got me to follow him into the Grey once before I even knew I could do it. . . ."

Mara bit her lip a moment in thought. "Yes . . . He does have an unusual activity level. He can do all that, yet he never speaks to anyone but Brian—I'm not even sure he speaks, so much as plants a suggestion, which is rather a strong action of itself. But it would take a necromancer to animate a corpse. Or some very black magic."

"I don't think Albert animated the corpse," I corrected. "I think the restless soul of the body is what kept it moving—although something else was keeping the body intact and causing the original spirit to be imprisoned in it. Albert just went along for the ride I think. Then I saw a memory loop of him in a speakeasy under Pioneer Square and that got me thinking that Albert may know more about the creature that caused the zombie. The walking corpse is connected to that creature, as are a spate of recent deaths of the homeless in the historic district. It also seems likely this creature's been loose in the area in the historic past, including the time since Prohibition, when Albert died. I need to talk to him about that creature. And just because I'm like that, I want to know what he was doing riding a zombie at all, but especially one of these zombies."

"And you think he's up to no good or you wouldn't have wanted this privacy spell."

"Yeah, I do. I just don't see how there's a benign explanation for what he was doing. And I'll need your help to question him. I may be able to talk to him and I may be able to hold him, but I'm not sure I can force him and I can't do all three at once. You made a tangle for me to capture the poltergeist with. Can you do something like that to hold Albert while I try to make him answer my questions?"

"Compelling a ghost seems a little extreme. . . ."

"Mara, I know you and Ben think he's a good guy, but I don't. I think there's something unpleasant about Albert and that he's got an agenda separate from yours. It's not just my personal grudge. Whatever he's up to may not be bad for you and your family, but

I doubt it's good. I haven't met a revenant yet who thought the ends didn't justify the means."

"True . . . They don't really think like we do—when they think at all."

"You and Ben know that the willful ones are manipulative by nature, and Albert *is* willful."

"You could try asking Carlos for help," Mara suggested reluctantly.

I shook my head. "Carlos and Cameron absented themselves on this, and I wouldn't want them involved anyway, now that I consider it. I think you and I can do this ourselves. Especially since I don't want to pay whatever price Carlos would be asking for the service. And this is your house and I won't be a bad guest in it by attacking and interrogating your pet ghost. But I have to talk to Albert."

"Pet!" Mara objected.

"You treat him like he's part guard dog and part favorite uncle."

Mara frowned. "Do I . . . ?" she murmured, and I knew she was reviewing the past at high speed, thinking hard about every interaction she'd had with Albert.

"I didn't come to accuse you of anything," I said, bringing her mind back to the problem at hand. "I just need to talk to Albert so that he has to answer. Can you help me do that?"

Mara glanced around. "I'd better work fast. This spell's almost used up. A tangle won't work so well this time—he'll see it coming. I'll have to use a net. This shan't be fun and we'll have to do it right here, since I can start the spell under this one, where he can't see it. If I cast too many spells, he'll be suspicious—he's always interested in my magic and comes poking in to see what I'm up to." She slid off the couch and dug in her apron pocket for a bit of chalk, beginning to make marks on the floor between the two sofas. She jerked her head up to stare at me. "I hope I shan't regret this."

"So do I."

"When I say so, go upstairs and tell Ben we'll need privacy in the living room for a while. He'll understand and stay out. And he'll keep Brian out, too, if the boy hasn't gone to sleep yet. Albert will probably follow you down, so when you come back here we'll see what happens."

I nodded and she went back to chalking diagrams that began to glow a dim gold as she advanced. When she chalked one that flickered to black, she sent me to talk to Ben. As I stepped through the fading blue vines of the privacy spell, they fizzed and fell away. Mara put one of the afghans from the couch over the markings on the floor and remained whispering over it for a moment as I left the room and went up the musically creaking stairs.

I could hear some murmurs from the room off the middle of the upstairs hall. I assumed that was Brian's room and tapped on the door.

"Come in!" Ben called back.

I opened the door and took a step inside. The room looked like fairyland after an explosion. Toys and books and clothes were everywhere in the room that was painted with pale streamers of blue, green, and violet on one wall, trees and meadowlands on the next. Tiny faces peeked from corners and hid in the grass of the field—including a less-pleasant face that glowered at me from behind Ben's shoulder: Albert. I ignored him and gazed around the room. A merry ceramic sun cast twisted copper rays over the railed bed where a giggling Brian lay listening to Ben read a story from a huge, leather-bound book. Brian looked toward the door and laughed, waving at me. "Harpa!"

I don't know why Brian likes me but I assume his tendency to throw himself bodily at me and shriek is supposed to demonstrate that. His parents say so, a least. I'm not a fan of children as a rule, but even with the head butting and howling, Brian was starting to grow on me a bit. Like mold.

"Hi, Harper. Come in and help us read a story," Ben said. Ben's curly black hair was standing up in static waves—a pretty good sign he'd had a long day of Brian-herding.

I came over to the side of the bed and waved at Brian. "Hi, rhino boy."

Brian stuck out his tongue and made a raspberry noise. "No rhino."

I twitched an interrogative eyebrow and looked at Ben. He sighed. "We're done with animals for a while. At the moment, we are an intrepid prince of Russia—no thanks to baba Irina, my mother."

Brian spouted something I didn't understand and Ben translated. "His highness wants his wolfhounds. No wonder they call this age 'the terrible twos.' "

"Does that make him Brian the Terrible?" I quipped.

Ben rolled his eyes. "Too true. Here I thought a break from the budding linguists last term was going to be a vacation. I'm supposed to be back in the classroom this quarter, but the cold is keeping the university closed."

Brian made a demanding Russian noise and patted the book in his father's hands.

"I'm to get back to reading Ivan Tsarevitch or suffer the consequences. Better tell me what you wanted before his highness has us thrown to the wolves."

"Mara and I are going to do some work downstairs. Just wanted to warn you it won't be Brian-safe until we're done. You probably want to stay out, too."

"Ah. OK. I'll finish up here and go upstairs for a while, then.

Mara can fill me in later." Ben was too tired to argue, even if there was a speculative gleam in his eye about what his wife and I might be doing. Ben's fascination with magic and ghosts was certain to get him in too deep someday.

"Thanks, Ben," I said, heading back out the door as Ben's voice, rolling Russian consonants like the sea coming to shore, continued with the story.

I could feel the cold presence of Albert at my back as I descended the stairs. The ghost followed me into the living room. I was careful not to step on Mara's hidden marks but to pass very close to them nonetheless. I stopped on one side of them and turned sharply.

"Hello, Albert," I said.

It's rare for me to startle a spirit, but he came to an abrupt halt and floated back a bit, stopping just over the afghan. Mara had once said she didn't see him but rather had an idea of where he was and what he was doing. I hoped it was a pretty precise idea.

A hostile approach wasn't my first choice, but if Albert fled, I'd lose my chance. I'd give him one opportunity to volunteer. "I need to talk to you about Friday night."

I saw the flicker of his shape and knew he was running. I pointed at Mara. "Grab him."

She flipped the corner of the afghan up and said some sharp word that plucked on the energy grid of the Grey like a harp. A gust of unfurling magic shot up from the floor and tangled over the invisible shape of Albert with the motion of a hurricane. Mara grabbed hold of the edge of it and nailed it to the floor with her chalk, marking one last sign in the revealed circle. The afghan drifted to the floor behind her as the net sang in the Grey, its almost-human sound raising goose bumps on my skin.

I sat down on the couch I'd occupied before and looked toward the shape beneath the net of magic. "Is this all right, Mara?"

She got up and sat next to me on the sofa. "Yes. It should hold him as long as I want to leave it there. I'm sorry, Albert, but you've got to stay and talk to Harper. I'd not have thrown the net if you hadn't tried to scarper off."

Albert's form sifted back to visibility. I supposed he didn't see the point in wasting energy to hide when he couldn't move. He glared at me.

"Knock it off, Albert. I just need information," I said. "Can you talk to me?"

He glowered.

"OK. I guess the mountain comes to Mohammed." I reached out and riffled through the layers of time, feeling for one that would have Albert in it as strongly as possible. Wherever his presence was strongest, that was where I thought I'd be most likely to get him to talk. Though it was also where—or when—he'd have the most power and latitude to cause me trouble. I hoped the net was enough. I found a hard, cold plane of time and slipped into it . . . and fell back out.

"What—?"

Mara turned a curious frown on me. "What's wrong?"

"I can't stay in the time plane Albert's occupying."

"But . . . you didn't slip at all. You stayed right here."

I puzzled on that a moment. "Then . . . this is the same place . . . ?"

"It must be a loop or a bridge of some kind that connects him to both that plane where his energy was strongest and to this one. I don't think I care for that. . . ."

I turned my eyes to Mara. "Then why isn't he talking?" Something cold brushed across my knee.

"Maybe he needs—"

"A voice." It was a reedy tenor and it came from Albert. I looked toward him and saw a thin line of the net touching my knee, connecting me to Albert. "It comes from you," he confirmed. "If you want me to talk, you have to lend me this."

"I'd rather not, but I guess I don't have much choice."

Mara stared at me. "I can hear you both! But Albert's so quiet. . . ."

I peered into the darkness of the grid, seeing Albert as a haze of light floating above the blazing energy lines. I thought I might be able to push a thin strand of that energy to him and boost his voice. . . .

"Yes!" Albert's thin voice urged in my head.

I yanked back to a more normal level where the Grey was ever-present, the neon lines of power and force dim glimmers that clung to the shapes of the world.

"No. I don't think that would be a good idea—giving you power."

The light silvered his glasses and hid his eyes. He moved restlessly in his mesh of magic.

"Mara, can you tighten that net up a little?"

"I can, but why?"

"Albert is playing games."

Mara gave a twitch of her hand and the reticulated spell cinched down, binding Albert into stillness. The illusion of light on his glasses faded.

"Better," I said, moving my foot so it touched the edge of the net to maintain my connection to Albert. I felt it like a static charge passing over my skin.

"I won't help you," Albert warned.

"You will if you want to get out of that net. Let's start with something easy. What's your full name?"

He was stubbornly silent. I didn't know if a geas—a magical compulsion—would work on a ghost, and I wasn't thrilled about trying it, but Albert wasn't cooperating. I plucked at a bit of the Grey and stared at Albert, catching his gaze as I pulled the buzzing, energetic material in front of me, forming the power connection that would allow me to make a binding demand on the ghost. Then I gave a mental push in Albert's direction and said, "Talk freely and we'll be done sooner. Then you can go." I could see the fast-multiplying black lines of pressure build and press on the ghost, forcing my demand against him. He jerked his head back, then he shuddered. The tiny black lines clung to him and sank into his form like needles, knitting a compulsion between us. I felt instantly cold to the bone—the chill of lonely death. Compulsion runs two ways, and I'd have to take care to remove the connection completely when I was done with Albert. But I'd have to maintain the pressure as long as we were connected; I didn't want him to push back and I didn't want the feel of unquiet graves lingering in my mind.

"Very well!" he snapped.

"What is your full name?" I asked again. I wanted to see what he did when the answers were nonthreatening. It would make it easier to know when he was lying—which I was sure he'd try. Unlike most of the people I saw, Albert had no aura to act as a tell of his emotions.

"Albert Wallace Frye," he answered, sighing a little with resignation.

"Any relation to Frye of the Frye Museum and Frye Meat Packing?"

"None. Had I call upon the fortunes of Charlie or Frank Frye, I'd hardly have been serving bootleg whiskey to whitter-brained flappers in a speak south of the skid." His tone stung with resentment, and I found I didn't need to push him to speak now that he was started. He wanted to spit out the lost story of his life. I might have more trouble keeping him to the point.

"Is that how you made your living—bootlegging?" I asked. I'd let him run a while, get comfortable, before I asked about zombies and monsters.

"I made what you call a living in the pharmacy trade. I made *money* by distributing booze—which I'd started out making myself when the bluenosed fools of Washington state voted in their goddamned dry law. A better day for a dollar never was had until the Volstead Act made the booze business a crime. Don't believe them when people tell you crime does not pay—it paid better than propriety. I only kept to the druggist's counter to give myself a front from which to dole out the bottles."

Mara looked shocked at this venomous recitation. I guess even Irish witches have foolish romantic notions about American bootleggers as some kind of alcohol-running Robin Hood and his Merry Men. It was no revelation to me that they were in it for the money and not for the thrill of twitting a stupid law.

"So you couldn't keep up with demand," I prompted. "Then you went into distribution on your own?"

"Hell, no. I partnered up with Olmstead."

"Roy Olmstead?"

"The same."

"I see. You did the distribution for Roy's boys. That explains why you walked me into a speakeasy on the bluff that time. Did you work that one, too?"

"No. I dropped goods. I only worked the One-oh-Seven."

"That's the place under Occidental, right?"

He peered at me. "Where?"

I racked my brain a moment. "Second Avenue."

"Correct. I had to recoup my losses on the shop—I bought an interest in a drugstore upstairs, but it wasn't going so well, what with Bartell and all, and my partner and I talked about opening a saloon instead." I knew Bartell Drugs was a major chain, but I hadn't realized it had started in Seattle.

Albert talked over my ruminations. "When the dry law came in, we busted. We tried a refreshment parlor, but everyone tried that—you can only sell so many phosphates and flips. I was stuck with half a bad bargain. So we brewed up some goods and sold them downstairs, where it was harder for the dry squad to raid us. That's how I met Roy—he was in on a raid and he told me I was a chump for going it alone. He said the way to make money was to run the liquor like a business—which is what he did."

"He also got caught."

Albert shrugged. "Small beer. He was back right after. Business as usual."

"I meant the Thanksgiving raid."

"What Thanksgiving raid?"

An incredulous chuckle escaped me that he didn't know and I did. "Roy Olmstead was arrested in 1924 and did four years at McNeil Island—it was the largest successful raid in the history of Prohibition. He appealed on a cause of unconstitutional process because the Federals tapped his phone. It's a very famous case—*Olmstead v. United States*. I'd think even a ghost would have heard of it." With my interest in mystery and crime novels, I had gobbled up the details of the case in a college law course.

Albert stared at me. "They jugged Roy?"

I gave him a bemused look to cover a sudden wash of tiredness and an urge to shiver. This interrogation was more draining than I'd hoped. "When did you die, Albert Wallace Frye? When did you die that you didn't know the Feds nabbed Roy Olmstead?"

"I don't know."

"How can you not know when you died?" I demanded, giving a mental push against the black needles and feeling them prick me, too.

Mara leaned close. "I'm not surprised—dyin's traumatic. Who'd want to be remembering that?"

I nodded and backed off. I'd try a different tack. "All right. What is the last date you remember?"

"I can't recall a date." He seemed to think, his eyes behind the tiny wire-rimmed spectacles shifting as he considered. "It must have been May. The weather was nice, but not summer-hot in the attic—I lived in the attic then. Nineteen twenty-two. The bar had been raided again and the supply was short. I didn't want to wait for the next run and my partner and I didn't want to close the speakeasy, so I was 'stretching' the booze."

"What does that mean?"

"I was cutting it with carbinol—legal stuff from the pharmacy stock. It smells sweet and no one would notice—they certainly wouldn't complain," he added with a laugh, "and I wasn't using a lot, just enough to eke a couple of extra bottles out of the lot we had to make it through till Sunday—that's when I'd have the next shipment. I'd done it before when we ran the speak on our own, but you have to be careful with carbinol—it's got nasty effects if you sauce it up too much."

Mara was choking on outrage. "Carbinol? That's methanol—wood alcohol. It's toxic!"

"I know what it is, Mara. Sit tight." I turned my attention back to Albert. "So you cut the whiskey with carbinol. What then? You sold it to someone who died?"

Albert radiated confusion. "No . . . I don't think I did. I can't recall what happened. . . . A couple of Roy's boys dropped in to see me. Things get a little fuzzy here. . . . I remember T.J. saying something about the whiskey in the sink, the carbinol . . . and then . . . and then . . . I can't remember."

"They drowned him in it," Mara said, her voice icy and her accent thickening under suppressed rage. "I cleared that memory from the place when we moved in. I didn't want a murder lingerin' in my house."

"But you let the victim stay."

"I thought that's what he was," she replied, her face and voice gone hard. "A victim."

"Apparently a worthy one."

"The lieutenant was a businessman and this was just business. He wouldn't have had me killed," Albert objected. "He didn't. I'm sure of it."

"No, you're not," I corrected. "You don't even remember."

"Roy didn't let his men go armed! He said he'd rather lose the liquor than a life!"

"That may have been Olmstead's rule, but his underlings seemed to have decided it was too big a risk to let you poison people on his booze. It wasn't good business to let that happen. They held you under and drowned you in your own sink."

Albert looked shaken and I could feel his distress in waves through the Grey. "No! Those skunks! Those rat bastards! I'll kill them!"

"They've all been dead for years, Albert."

"I'll find their descendants. I'll make them pay for killing me.

I knew I'd been murdered. I knew it wasn't an accident!" If he could have, he'd have stomped his foot and thrown a fit. "When I get a body of my own again, I'll hunt them down and pay them back for what their fathers and grandfathers did."

"Ah. That's the thing I want to talk to you about."

"What?"

"The body. Is that why you're still here? Looking for a body to take over?"

"Of course! I was murdered, you dingy broad! I deserve to get my life back one way or another."

"So you caught a ride on a zombie."

"They don't last long enough to keep. I thought I could set a few things in motion, but the damned redskin fought me and then that hairy thing meddled and brought you in and that was the end of that idea."

I felt tired and stiff with cold but went on. Now we were getting to what I needed. "You've tried to get into one of those before?"

"Couple, few times, yes. They turn up in the tunnels after earthquakes or construction. There were a lot of 'em for a while after the bootleggers broke through some of the walls down below to make escape routes and to stash barrels from the dry squads."

"Do you know where they come from? What causes the dead to walk like that?"

Albert rolled his eyes. "They come from the snake thing that lives down there."

"What snake thing? How does it make them?"

"I don't know! Why ask me? I only borrow them when I can. The snake comes up into the tunnels sometimes when there's a hole in the right place—and don't ask where because I don't know. It came up when I worked the speak. It stays away from crowds, but it's a hungry bastard and sometimes we'd find its leavings in the sidewalks or tunnels we'd cut between the basements and have to bury 'em quick or have the cops all over the place. You don't want the customers to know there's a monster downstairs, so we tried to chase it off. We couldn't do it, but the old Indians could. When we came up with enough firewater and cash, they made it go away.

"I thought I'd never see another one of those walking dead, but they came again after the big quake and that's when I thought I'd try to get one. But either I didn't have the strength or it didn't and it fell apart, but I knew I'd find a way."

"Have you found one?"

"I might have," he said, going cagey and avoiding my gaze. I could feel him wriggling in the Grey. "Why d'you think I wanted that bottle you had?"

Mara whispered, "I think he means the flask Ben made for you that Brian broke."

I nodded. "Why'd you make Brian break it?"

"Because I didn't want the witch to use it on me. I didn't like seeing that other one in there and it didn't like being in there. It wanted out and it said it would help me get the boy. But you killed it before it could help me."

"What do you mean, 'get the boy'?" I asked, and leaned on the black needles of the compulsion until Albert winced, feeling them against my own skin as burning cold that spread into my flesh.

"The witch's son," he babbled. "He listens to me. Since I've gotten stronger, I can talk to him—his mind's more like yours—but he's pliable. Even if I can't have him, he can help me find a body I can have. He'll be powerful when he's older. Don't look at me like that. It's her own fault. She made the house stronger. She made me stronger. It's only fair! I was robbed of my life!"

Mara made an angry, snatching gesture, shouting, "Take yerself off, y'toad!" and a string of furious epithets I didn't understand. Startled by Mara's outburst, I jerked back from Albert, ripping the black threads that lay between us and feeling the cold flood away. Then the net that contained Albert flushed furious red and collapsed into a hard knot of magic that was flung up through the ceiling, dragging the ghost, screeching, into the ether. Mara muttered after him for a minute, glaring up at the ceiling where he'd disappeared. "Y'scheming gobshite! Shaggin' bastard!"

I slumped into the couch, gulping warm air into my frosted lungs and shivering until the chill faded. Without thinking, I rubbed at my stiff knee. I felt drained and the injured joint ached, but I got better as I warmed up.

A clatter sounded on the stairs and Mara swallowed her curses before a befuddled Ben trotted into the living room blinking and wondering what had happened.

"Something came through the floor upstairs and went out the roof! I couldn't see it but it felt like acid on the wind it made. What have you been doing down here? Are you OK, Mara? Harper?" He took a good look at his wife's face and leaned back. "Uh-oh . . . What did I do?"

"Nothing!" Then she bit her lip and stood up, sighing. "Oh, love, I'm sorry. Nothing you've done. 'Tis that wretched Albert. He's—well, I've made a terrible mistake letting him stay. He's not a good thing to have about. I've sent him off for a while until I can collect what to do with him."

"What to do with him?"

"I think I may need Carlos, after all. . . ."

Ben and I stared at her. "I don't think that's the best idea . . ." Ben started.

"That foul thing has designs on our son! And it's my fault! My fault for not probing deeper to find his true nature. That—that—" Mara nearly choked on her re-stoked fury.

Ben closed the distance between them and rolled her into an encompassing embrace whose comfort I envied. "Shhh . . . Don't feed the gobshites."

Mara hiccuped a laugh and punched him weakly on the side—which was all she could reach. "You!"

"Yes, me. I get that you're mad and that Albert has been up to no good with Brian. So, what's he been up to and have you stopped him?"

Aside from the riot of her hair, I couldn't see Mara over the tops of Ben's shoulders even as I got a little unsteadily to my feet—I felt like I'd run ten miles in snow. Her voice seemed to come from his chest. "I've corked him up for a while," she said, "but it shan't last. I'll have to find a way to send him away permanently. I've been so foolish. I let him stay and he used the magic I poured into the house to protect us to plot vile things and grow strong enough to attempt them. We can't allow that to go on. And he won't give up his plots if he remains, even if I can limit his ability to execute them."

"Then that's why you thought of Carlos," Ben concluded.

"Yes," she sighed. "I know, I know—it would be bad to call upon him. I may simply have to imprison Albert until I can find a solution. Though I can't say I fancy being a prison warden."

"How long can you leave him where he is?" I asked.

"Oh, he's spiked on the roof now. I suppose I can throw a dome of the Tender's Lace over him and keep him in his little hole a week or so."

"Can you come up with a solution to him in a week?" Ben asked.

"I can come up with something. . . ."

"Good. We'll put him in his box for a while and not worry about it this second. Tomorrow will be soon enough if he's no threat to Brian tonight. You're too upset, Mara, to do the best you can do right now."

"Hark at you. Voice of reason."

"I learn from exposure. What about you, Harper? Get what you came for?"

"Yes, I'm sorry to say."

Ben shrugged.

"I should go," I added, making myself walk forward without any show of the wobbliness I felt. It wasn't pain so much as shock and exertion.

Mara started to object, pushing herself free from her husband's embrace, but I knew pro forma when I heard it and I got out of the house as fast as decent manners would allow. I'd really tipped over the Danzigers' apple cart. I felt bad about it, especially since I'd been right about Albert. There is, sometimes, more solace in being wrong, and I had to leave them to grapple with the problem of Albert alone for the time being.

I didn't want to inflict my bad feeling on anyone else, so I didn't call Quinton or drop in at Phoebe's place but went home to the ferret who ignored me in favor of her squeaky eggplant.

THIRTEEN

The temperature was up to thirty degrees when I rolled out of bed Monday morning. The snow was still sticking, but it didn't look so impressive once it had been plowed and shoveled into dirty piles only a few inches high at the curbs with the rough shapes of shrubs and grass poking through in the fields and yards. It was still too cold for most of the schools, though—some still operating without electricity or heat—and kids would be loose on the remaining snow before noon. Otherwise, it was an average Monday. I did the morning routine, working on my knee and shoulder for a while before heading to my office to dive into neglected work for Nan Grover.

At twelve minutes past eleven the door alarm Quinton had installed months ago pinged me and a matronly woman walked into my office, followed by two men with the look of guided missiles. The woman had chin-length gray hair naturally streaked with white and looked about fifty. She wore a charcoal gray suit with black running shoes and a black wool swing coat under an aura the color of battlefield smoke lit by gunfire. The men didn't match: both fit and thirtyish, cloaked in rain-colored energy co-ronas, one wore a pair of slacks and a sport coat under an East Coast–style overcoat; the other had on jeans and a padded sta-dium jacket. They sent off a cool psychic stink of no personal stake in whatever had brought the woman to my office. They came to follow her orders.

All three had their coats undone over the telltale lumps and wrinkles of concealed pistols. I thought I'd seen damn near every variation and rip-off of this group that existed, but never one headed by a grand-old-lady type before. The disconnect between the woman's appearance and her energy bugged me—not to men-tion the gun. I didn't bother asking if I could help them and stayed put behind my desk where my own pistol and the panic button on the alarm were a handbreadth away.

"Are you Harper Blaine?" the woman asked. Her tone was bored, as if she really didn't need my answer but she would stick to the form.

I didn't see a point in skirmishing over it. I gave her a bland look back as her attack dogs stationed themselves on each side of my door. "Yes, I am. And who are you?"

She didn't carry a purse, so she brought a leather ID folder from her coat pocket. She flipped the folder open, saying, "I'm Fern Laguire. I'm with the NSA." She closed the distance between the door and the desk and stood so close she loomed over me as if it was just an accident of my cramped office space. Then she flapped the folder closed before I could read it properly. I'd done that a few times myself, so I looked up at her and put out my hand.

"May I see that again, please—a bit slower? I don't speed-read."

Laguire clucked her tongue and showed me the ID again, not releasing the folder but just holding it open in front of me, as if I was kid with ADD and she a harried teacher. She did seem a little teacherlike, in a smile-and-yardstick sort of way, but I noticed she narrowed her eyes as she held the folder for me. The washed-blue irises gleamed like ice chips.

The ID wasn't helpful. It did have her name and the agency name, seal—an eagle standing on a key—and office address in Maryland, but it didn't have any indication of rank or deployment beyond the words "Field Liaison." She could have been a secretary or the director for all the card said, though I guessed she was probably as close to an actual spook as "No Such Agency" had. The great mystery of intelligence agencies: a cryptology unit with more tentacles than a school of squid and more pull than anyone wants to admit. I'd have bet even money that the backup were on loan from the CIA or FBI because they certainly didn't look like mathematicians or computer geeks.

I let the card go and Laguire flipped it closed, dropping it back into her pocket. Her New England schoolmarm personality seemed a perversely appropriate choice for an NSA field operative, but it didn't really go with the glacial eyes and the disturbing energy cloud around her—the effect was creepy, like seeing your grandmother whip out a flick knife and dispatch the cat for spitting up a hairball.

"I don't do wiretaps or foreign data transmissions," I said, "so I doubt I'm going to be much use to you."

"We're not interested in you, dear. Not in any professional capacity, at least," Laguire replied. "We want James Jason Purlis."

"Who?" I wasn't faking ignorance; I'd never heard the name before in my life.

Her voice was soft and refined, but it left a hard wake in the Grey that would have caused most people to toe her line. "Oh, but you do know him, Ms. Blaine. You were in his company yesterday. Caucasian, brown hair, brown eyes, thirty-five years old."

I'd been in a lot of people's company Sunday and about half answered that description. "You have a photo?" I asked.

Laguire pulled a five-by-seven black-and-white from her pocket and put it on my desk, pushing it across the blotter to me with both index fingers. It was a blowup of an ID photo, grainy and bland. Judging by the clothes, it was about ten years old. The young man in the photo was a generic white-bread nerd—as if he'd tried to be unmemorable—short hair, clean shaven, overweight, slightly sullen or just bored. Aside from everyone else, I'd talked to Fish, Quinton, and the Danzigers, as well as a few waitstaff, librarians, and a gas station attendant yesterday, and many of them could have been the man in that photo, given different hair, weight, glasses, whatever. I knew who she wanted, but I wasn't going to turn.

I shoved the photo back across my desk. "I spent all day tracking witnesses and evidence for investigations and for cases going to trial. I spent a lot of that time with some homeless people who don't exactly hand over their business cards, and the rest of it in a glorified trash dump. Which one of the hundred or so people I talked to or stood next to do you think I should recognize from that picture?"

"Only J.J. Purlis. He went to ground years ago and we've been waiting patiently for him to show up on our radar ever since. Yesterday he did. Now he's vanished again, but you were IDed and here you are." She seemed to imply I soon might not be.

"Who told you I was with this Purlis, and where?" I asked. "You give me a clue and I might give you your man."

She shook her head with a disappointed smile. "I won't name our source. That would be ill-advised. Purlis is a danger to national security and to the health and safety of people like you. He has knowledge, skills, and the mind to cause harm. You have a duty to turn him over."

"You make this guy sound like a terrorist," I said, flipping my hand to dismiss her drama.

"As information is the real source of power and since crypto systems are now defined as matériel, he well could be. I imagine you think you're protecting a witness or an informant, but all you are doing is standing between us and a fugitive."

"Fugitives are the purview of the federal marshals' office and law enforcement. Not Fort Meade's carnivores."

A palpable hit. Laguire's mouth tightened at the reference, but her voice stayed calm, if a bit chillier. "Mr. Purlis is our asset. We will reacquire him. You will not stand in our way." She leaned in a little. "I don't need to play games with you. I can get what I want other ways, but you won't like them, Ms. Blaine. It's very simple. All I want is Purlis's location."

I stood up and Laguire had to tilt her head up to meet my scrutiny. She didn't like it, but she didn't want to step back and even the distance—it might look like retreat. "I don't have your mystery man's location, Ms. Laguire. I don't know a J.J. Purlis and your photo is worthless. You can—"

My suggestion was cut off by my cell phone—lucky for both of us.

"Excuse me. I need to answer my phone, but since the nature of my work is confidential, I'm sure you understand my asking you and your associates to leave now." Then I shut up and gazed at her without blinking or hostility, just blank and expectant.

Her smoky aura flared with frustrated explosions of orange and red, but she laid her card on my desk, turned silently on her heel, and strode out of my office. Her bodyguards followed her.

It was possible she'd left a bug or had some kind of tap on my cell phone or something, but I doubted she'd set up any such thing. If she'd caught a late-night flight, she'd have been on me the night before—surprising a subject when they're tired or disoriented from being jarred out of bed is a classic tactic for interrogators. So chances were good she'd caught a morning plane and come to me less than an hour after picking up her escort at the federal building. Even the Feds play turf wars, and she would have had to check in with the local office first.

By the time I'd finished the thought, I'd missed the call but I picked up the message. Fish had found some info on the Sistu.

"My old grandma said she'll tell you what you want to know but she'll only talk to you in person. She's old. I mean old, like Kennewick Man old, so she doesn't leave the house. Call me back and I'll set it up, but it has to be today."

I called his cell phone.

"I had a client in the office and couldn't answer the phone," I explained after exchanging greetings. "What's the deal?"

"We have to go to the rez. I'll take you up there and introduce you, then you're kind of on your own. Grandma's an old she-wolf and she's still got teeth. Hope you've got a few hours, 'cause she doesn't do anything fast."

"I have the day, if that's what it takes. I need to bring someone along, though. Will your grandmother have a problem with that?"

"Depends on whether she thinks she can scare him."

"I don't think she can."

"Then she'll probably be OK. She respects strength, so long as she gets respect back. Real old-school."

"Where do I need to pick you up?"

"I live up in Montlake, near the arboretum."

"We'll be up at your place in forty minutes. I'll call for directions when we're on the way."

"OK. See you then."

I agreed I'd be seeing him and paged Quinton. Then I went out to find a noisy place to grab some lunch I could wolf down in twenty minutes. The drive to Montlake was usually fifteen minutes from my office, but it sounded like a long day ahead and I both needed food and wanted to minimize Laguire's chance of picking up any of my conversations. Some things are worthy of paranoia, and she and her agency gave me the chills.

My phone rang again as I was crossing the Square. In the frosted cold, the area was mostly deserted except for the snow drifts and ghosts, and I glanced around for any sign of surveillance or monitoring. Not even the phantoms were interested in me.

Spotting nothing, I still answered the phone in a sharp bark unlike my usual tone. "Blaine."

There was a pause. "Um, this is your alarm company," Quinton said. "You left a message for us to return your call. . . ."

"I have three nines and I'm running late because of an official visitor." Three nines was the pager code Quinton had programed to indicate a break-in at my office—it was also the UK version of 911. "Tell the installer I'll meet him at Bakeman's in a couple of minutes." I hung up without waiting for a reply and hoped Quinton knew me well enough to guess my meaning and show up both quickly and discreetly.

Located on Cherry in a basement row of little lunch spots that mostly catered to local office workers, Bakeman's was determinedly blue collar in service and atmosphere. The odor of roast turkey and meatloaf wafted out the sunken door along with the clang and shout of the staff passing orders and moving customers at New York speeds. The hard, slick walls and Formica tables reflected the noises of the busy kitchen and the hurried diners into a rattling cacophony. No one lingered over a cup of joe at Bakeman's or "took meetings" at the no-nonsense tables without risking the owner's notorious sharp tongue. If Fern Laguire or her mismatched muscles wanted to snoop, they'd have to come in, order up, and join us at our table to have any hope of eavesdropping or getting in without drawing attention.

I'd barely sat down with my food when Quinton popped in through the lunchroom's back door from the building above.

"Hey," he said, sliding in next to me to facilitate a lower-volume conversation.

"Hey. Two things first. We're going to Marysville to talk to Fish's grandmother about the Sistu, which should take a few hours so you better grab some food if you're hungry. And I got a visit from the NSA about thirty minutes ago."

Quinton looked thoughtful. "I'll be right back."

He returned in ten minutes with one of Bakeman's famous sandwiches and a can of soda. "I always think I'll have the pie next time and I never do," he said.

I finished my soup and glanced at him as he wolfed his food. I was glad he hadn't run, though I hadn't really expected him to. "You know anything about this Fern Laguire?"

He nodded and swallowed. "I hear she was heartless at twenty and had passed 'ballbreaker' in her thirties. Ten years ago she'd advanced to vitrified in all human emotions except anger. The scale appears to be logarithmic."

"She has two assistants who smell of Fed, one probably CIA, the other local Feeb."

Quinton nodded acknowledgment.

"Do we have a problem?" I asked.

"There's a hole in something. I don't want to discuss it right now. In fact, considering communication is the name of the game with them, probably best to get moving and talk as little as possible. Fern may not have you bugged yet—if she just hit town she hasn't had much time."

"Unless she came on a private flight, I'd guess she couldn't have arrived before eight-thirty this morning—assuming flights landed on time with the snow."

He hummed, thinking. Then he asked, "Do you need your cell phone for this trip?"

"I need to call Fish for directions to his place."

"Use a pay phone—it's safer. I'll have to disable the cell—otherwise they may use it to track or bug us." He put out one hand for my phone and picked up his soda with the other, draining it in three big gulps.

I handed him the phone, which he looked over and put on the table.

"Remove the battery, will you?" he asked, rummaging in his coat.

As I pried the battery out, Quinton pulled a big folding knife from his pocket. I started to snatch my phone back, but he stabbed the side of the soda can near the upper crimp and cut the top off. Then he wiped the remaining soda out of the can with a napkin and dropped my phone in before squeezing the can into a flatter shape and folding the ragged edges down, making a sort of tight metallic envelope. He handed me the phone and the battery, and the tiny spark that seemed to pass between us when his fingers brushed mine had nothing to do with the phone. "Hold on to these, but keep them apart and don't put them back together until we're back in Seattle—unless you have to. I want to check the Rover before we go. Call Fish and I'll meet you at the parking garage."

Quinton folded the paper over his remaining half sandwich

and stuffed it into one pocket of his coat and the knife into another pocket. Then he left through the door he'd come in by. I figured that Laguire was probably still waiting for me at the Cherry Street door, if she was watching, so I used a pay phone across the street to call Fish, buying Quinton time to get to my truck unseen—I hoped—while I got the directions.

Quinton was lurking in a dark corner of the garage and slipped into the Rover's backseat when I unlocked it. He gave me a thin smile. "No sign of spooks or bugs."

We picked up Fish and headed for the Tulalip reservation west of Marysville. Fish told us about his grandmother as I drove and Quinton sat in the back, scowling at his own thoughts.

"We're going to see Ella Graham. Now, she's not actually my grandmother," Fish explained. "We call her Grandma as a term of respect because she's old and wise—and kind of scary. I'm not sure how old she actually is, but my mom says she's about a hundred and I wouldn't be surprised if that were true. She's also . . . crotchety, I guess is the word, so you have to cater to her a little. Pretty old-school. If she had her way, she'd live in a long house with her whole family and smoke salmon over the fire. But she knows all the stories and legends and she's got a good memory for stuff she saw or heard when she was younger. She said she'd talk to you, but she wanted a gift." He held up the large gold-wrapped box he'd had on his lap all this time. "My mom tipped me she's a sucker for chocolate, so I got some Fran's."

"Give me the receipt and I'll reimburse you," I said.

Fish chuckled. "Heck no. I want to see how she eats them— they're caramels. We'll have to stop at the casino and get some cigars for her, if you want her really happy."

"Cigars? You're kidding."

"Nope. She doesn't smoke 'em. She just likes to smell 'em

burning—says they smell like the old days. If we get lucky, Russell will have some Cubans he got from his cousin in Whistler and let us have one or two."

I shook my head. "Cuban cigars and handmade chocolates. Not exactly the combo one expects to bring when visiting elderly ladies."

"Not just any old lady—Grandma Ella. It won't seem so strange when you meet her."

I shrugged. "If you say so. Who's Russell?"

"Russell Willet. He's a buddy of mine from, hm . . . preschool, I guess. We ate mud together. He decided to work for the tribe. He's a good manager, but he gets bored when things go well for too long, so he keeps changing jobs. At the moment, he's working in the casino, but he's always got contacts in everything."

"Willet, Graham . . . I know one of the bigwigs in the tribal council is named McCoy. How come you ended up with the stereotyped name?"

"That's my mom for you," Fish replied, shrugging. "I think she was mad at me for giving her so much trouble in the womb. She didn't even give me a name for three years—some Indians wait to name their kids until they do something of merit or 'find' a name themselves. It's not a very common practice, but it's still around. Mom just called me 'dirty boy' for a while—'cause I was really good at getting filthy and tracking it all over everything. My original birth certificate just says 'boy, Williams.'"

"You could have changed it," I suggested.

"Nah. It was a little rough when I was a kid, but now I kinda like being Reuben Fishkiller. 'Reuben Williams' would have been boring."

I was a little confused. "But you call yourself Fish, not Fishkiller."

"Not all the time," Fish said. "Most of the kids I grew up with have a totem name of some kind—an Indian name we earned—but we don't usually use them outside the tribe. It takes some explaining and . . . well . . . it sounds kind of pretentious on most people. I mean, you'd look funny at some guy who came to hook up your cable and his name tag said 'Swimming Bear,' right?"

I chuckled. "I'd look pretty funny at anyone whose name was 'swimming naked.' "

Fish sputtered and laughed. Quinton snickered and fell silent again as Fish and I chatted on, but Quinton's mood didn't have the same brooding feel after that.

When we got to Marysville, the casino was easy to spot. The Tulalip reservation started just to the west of I-5 and went all the way to the waters of Puget Sound around Tulalip Bay. The area was beautiful once you got away from the highway, and when I'd first moved up to Washington, only a few billboards advertising bingo and cigarettes had given any indication there was commerce tucked away in the tree-covered hills of the rez. That wasn't the case anymore. The consolidated tribes of the Tulalip reservation had replaced their kitschy old casino and "trading post" with the largest casino complex in the state and a pair of massive malls—one anchored by a Wal-Mart and the other filled with designer-goods outlets—right up against the freeway where there had once been nothing but fields of creek-fed bracken and marsh grass. Now there was hardly a sign of the overgrown fields behind the new buildings and the massive lot that hosted the Boom City fireworks market-place every year from mid-June through Independence Day.

Fish directed me to the main casino, which featured a pool with a realistic, life-size orca—the reservation's emblem—rearing out of it and an imposing bronze statue of a native spear fisher-man about to get his point across to a smaller creature a little farther up the driveway's artificial river. I parked off to the side of the massive, triple-peaked portico with its colorful pyramid lights on top. Construction of a hotel tower had begun beside the casino, and the site had a lightning-struck look in its winter weatherproofing.

"It's almost too bad they're going to put up the hotel," Fish said. "Until recently, you could see those lights on top of the casino for miles when they turned on the show. Drives the Marysville people crazy." He chuckled and got out of the Rover, stepping carefully onto the ice-crusted asphalt of the parking lot. Quinton and I followed his example.

In spite of the development, the parking lot had a fair number of ghost images, flickering like film projected on smoke. Several of the spirits, both human and animal—and some were a bit of both—turned their night-sky eyes on us as we passed and watched us with curious expressions.

Quinton and I followed Fish into the building, through a soaring lobby of stone and murals and colored lights where the hotel's reception desk would someday greet guests. Then down a wide corridor and into the gaming rooms with a ceiling of twinkling stars and sudden simulated thunderstorms. Circular banks of slot machines stood in treelike groves around the periphery, raising neon branches into stylized Art Deco canopies. The walls swam with murals of salmon, orca, otter, and trout, and the carpet was patterned with water currents and stones. The space felt disorientingly like a drowned forest in which the patrons floated in a watery twilight. The building itself was so new it hardly had a ghost, but a few were there, as were the silvery striations of time and the blue and yellow lines of the Grey's power grid. A pair of sly eyes in a vague, misty shape kept a close watch on us from beside a tree of nickel slots as Fish led us over to a small gift shop against one of the river walls.

A burly man in a three-piece suit rearranged a group of expensive watches under the glass countertop. He looked up as we entered and grinned, his eyes taking in everything in quick twitches. He had the hot, gold-sparked aura of a man with boundless energy. "Hey, Fishkiller!" he cried, closing up the case and dropping the keys into his vest pocket.

"Heya, Willet."

"So, what is it?" Russell Willet asked. "Your mom's birthday or something?"

"Nah. Taking these white eyes out to see Grandma Ella."

"Whoa!" Willet peered at us as if we were exotic beasts. "What do you want to see Grandma Ella for— No, wait. Don't tell me. I don't want to know."

"Nope, y'don't," Fish said.

"But I bet I know what you want." Willet turned and ducked down under the counter, rummaging through a cabinet. He brought out a wooden box a little larger and flatter than a shoe box. When he opened it, the smell of tobacco, cocoa, dark soil, and pepper floated up into the air. A red triangle around a little gold crown adorned the white label inside the lid, with the word "Montecristo" under it. Neat rows of cigars about as thick as my thumb and twice as long nearly filled the box. Willet carefully removed two of the cigars, which made an oily crackling sound as he touched them, and slipped them into a bag before he put the box away again.

He handed the bag over to Fish and admonished him with a raised finger and a twinkle in his eye, "All right, then. Those are for Grandma Ella—because I swear she'd put a curse on me or something if she knew I didn't hand them over. That is my personal high roller stash for buttering up the big winners. If you want your own, there's plenty to choose from," Willet added, pointing to a humidor cabinet on the back wall of the tiny shop.

"I don't smoke," Fish objected.

Willet looked at Quinton and me again; we both shook our heads. "Too bad," he muttered. I started to reach for my wallet, but he put up his hands. "No, no. Can't accept payment for a gift to Grandma Ella. Just tell her I sent them. I want to start off the year on her good side."

Willet shooed us off to deal with a couple of other customers and we continued on our way.

Back in the Rover, Fish directed me deeper into the reservation. We headed down toward the water, into an area called Priest Point, where the Snohomish River emptied into Puget Sound. The building I parked near, at Fish's command, was quietly lunatic—a collection of additions and repairs under which the original building couldn't be detected, the whole perfectly painted and clean in the midst of its frost-withered yard and a fog of spirits. A narrow dock stuck out into the water a few dozen yards behind the house. I could make out a trail of Grey habit worn down to the end of the dock where generations of fishermen must have sat or stood to cast their lines.

The path to the door looked odd—frosted with Grey and wandering through sudden dislocations of time that looked like fence posts of neon yellow and sparkly blue. As I stepped forward, the smells of brackish water, cedar smoke, and some kind of hot fat sizzling over flame wafted over me in alternating waves. The short walk felt like miles across one of those fun house floors of sliding planks and bouncing, slipping slabs. I was grateful Fish was in front and couldn't see how hard I concentrated on every footstep. Quinton stayed just behind me and when we reached the comparative stability of the front stoop, he touched the small of my back and caught my eye, giving me a questioning look.

I felt a little dizzy, but I murmured, "It's all right. There's just a lot of ghost stuff here."

He nodded and redirected his immediate attention to the house, though he left his hand a moment longer on my back and a little spark of orange leapt from him in my direction and tingled a second on my skin like the brush of a blackberry leaf.

The front door lay up some steps and behind an enclosed porch with a deep overhang. Inside the porch, several sets of fishermen's bright yellow foul-weather gear hung on pegs above a bench with two pairs of muck boots under it. Next to the foulies someone had hung a basket that looked like the oversized bell of a French horn and a shaggy cape of some kind with bits of shell sewn on in patterns obscured by the folds. Fish saw me studying the hairy garment.

"That's a cedar cloak—it's made of shredded cedar bark. I'm not sure anyone wears it anymore, but I don't want to ask."

I nodded, sure it would be a bad idea to remove the cloak and basket while their ghostly owner was standing and glowering beside them. The specter was clothed in the memory of the cape and wore the basket on his head, which made him look remarkably like the shaggy creature who'd brought me the zombie Friday night—if the shaggyman had been wearing a truncated cone for a hat.

Fish knocked on the door.

A voice like a chorus of seagulls called out in incomprehensible syllables. Fish called back and waited.

"Let yourself in!" the seagull voice screeched. "I'm an old woman, you young fool!"

Fish sighed and opened the door, waving us through ahead of him. The interior was bakery-hot and smelled of sage. Another row of hooks waited for our dry coats and we were glad to use them.

Fish pointed to a slatted wooden tray on the floor. "Take off your shoes and leave them there—she'll rant for hours if we track mud on the floor."

I was relieved to sit down to remove my boots—it gave me a moment to get used to the tumbling, twisted state of the Grey inside the house. Planes of time and ghosts of trees stuck up or out at tilted angles and a flight of salmon swam past, disrupted by the jerking loop of an owl that swooped through them in multiple exposure. Bits of people appeared, moved, and vanished as if seen in shattered shards of mirror hanging in the air or scattered across the discontinuous floors of every version of the house and land that had ever existed. Animate sparks of colorful energy broke from the grid and scampered loose through the chaos like animals and mythical sprites. I could barely separate the real house from the illusions, so odd was the construction ahead.

Finally, sock-footed and undressed of outer layers, we trooped through a pair of offset doorways, down a hall, and into a sudden calm—the energy within the Grey snapped into a grid of gleaming threads and all the riotous dislocation and overlapping phantasms vanished, leaving only a thin silver sheen to everything. The nearly bare living room we entered must have been as large as the original house and a wall of windows faced south to show the Sound outside. There was a stone fireplace on each end of the room and both of them contained blazing logs of cedar and fir that perfumed the air and lent momentary shape to swirls of cold memory. Rugs covered the wooden floor that supported a couple of low, heavy chairs, a rocker, one sofa at one end of the room, and a scattered herd of red-and-black wool hassocks at the other.

The ancient woman sitting on a hassock near the western fire must have been huge once. Now her skin hung in folds over the jagged frame of her bones, and the long twin plaits of her hair looked like two white snakes coiled on the floor beside her and rising to whisper in her ears. Shapes like the wings of giant birds folded around her in the Grey, glinting with gold tips. She was wearing baggy, old, gray sweats and pink socks. A carved wooden cane poked out from under her cushion on one side. She stared at us, her gaze sweeping over each in turn. Then she put out her hand.

"For me?"

Fish seemed startled, as if he had forgotten she could talk, and stumbled a step forward, holding out the gold-wrapped package with the bag of cigars on top. "Yes, Grandma. We brought you some chocolate and Russell Willet sent you some cigars."

Grandma Ella cackled. "Hah! Buttering me up." Her sharp glance cut to me and Quinton. "You two. Go in the kitchen and fetch out that bread and coffee. Can't tell tales without food and drink." She pointed with her skeletal hand from which the skin hung loose as tattered fabric.

Wordlessly, Quinton and I went to the kitchen, leaving Fish caught in a net of Ella Graham's cawing in Lushootseed—the language we'd heard so often among the Native Americans, both living and dead; the same language the young prostitute's ghost had spoken to me.

Coffee and freshly baked bread were sitting on the kitchen counter. We gathered things together and put them on a tray, while Quinton said, "She's . . . kind of scary, though I'm not sure why."

"There's a lot of uncanny stuff around this house. I don't think she's bad—I'm not even sure she knows about everything that's gathered around her—but she is a bit unsettling."

"That's a word for it. Fish really jumped when she took notice of him."

"Wouldn't you? I mean, even if she's not some kind of witch, the ghosts around here are paying her a lot of attention and there's a bunch of other things—magical things—running around in here."

"In here?" Quinton asked, his eyes a little wide as he pointed at the floor.

I thought about lying to ease his nerves, but instead I said, "Not so many in here and none in the living room." OK, so I'd downplayed the number of things in the kitchen a little. "In the entry and outside there are a lot of bits of magic and . . . elemental things, I guess. They don't seem to be interested in us except that we're visiting Mrs. Graham and they're interested in *her*."

"Hurry up in there!" The old woman's voice rang in the air of the kitchen without her raising her volume in the living room.

We both started a little, and then I took a deep breath and picked up the tray. "You know, I flunked food service in college," I said. "Let's hope I don't drop this thing."

"I can take it," Quinton offered, his hands full of other bits and bobs.

"I have the impression she expects it to be me. Remember what Fish said about catering to her old-school attitude."

Quinton nodded. "Yeah, right."

We marched back into the living room and put the tray down on the floor near the fire, which earned a gap-toothed grimace from Grandma Ella. There was no place else to put it at that end of the room and no place else to sit but on the strewn cushions, so that's what we did. Fish sat beside the old lady—apparently to play the part of translator and servant—while Quinton and I sat across the hearthstone from her. The whites of Fish's eyes were showing.

"Hmph!" the old woman grunted, and I realized she was

sucking on one of the chocolate-covered caramels from the now-opened gift box. "Salty. Good." Fish breathed a sigh of relief and loosened a little.

There was a ridiculous amount of rigmarole with distributing the bread and coffee and getting one of the cigars lit, putting the coffee pot near the fire so it stayed hot, finding just the right spot for the cigar so the smoke curled into the air properly and the tobacco stayed alight. Mrs. Graham grinned at us the whole time. Then she turned her sharp, dark eyes—barely etched by age—on me and I shivered even in the sweltering room.

"Sisiutl," she said, her voice a mixture of serpent hiss and bird cry. She glowered as she said it, as if she'd just noticed something about me she didn't like. The wing shapes around her head in the Grey heaved slowly upward and fell back down, folding tight around the old woman. "Sisiutl zeqwa . . ." She continued in Lushootseed for a sentence or two, and Fish translated while she stopped for a sip of coffee.

"You call him Sistu, but he's properly called Sisiutl. A zeqwa—a monster—Sisiutl is a creature of the water—a sea serpent—that lives in the waters of the Sound," Fish said. "He is the emblem of warriors who may bathe in his blood to harden their skin against the arrows of their enemies. He is the death of many seals and many men."

"Sisiutl?" I asked, unable to keep an edge of amusement out of my voice at the sound of the word.

Fish looked nervous and the air near him turned the color of light through ferns. "That's his proper name. It's a Kwakiutl word—"

"Funny, is it?" Grandma Ella shrieked. "If you respect the creature you call him by his true name! He won't heed your call if you name him something else. Sisiutl is crafty and cruel and hungry. He tells the warrior, 'Bathe in my blood and be strong,' but he must not, or he'll be turned to stone! A single drop is enough for strength. A foolish, greedy man will become a rock and Sisiutl will laugh at his fate. He will become a canoe and offer to take the hunter to the best seals, but if the hunter does not pay him a seal, the canoe becomes Sisiutl again and will devour the man. The man cannot escape him. Sisiutl is strong and fast. Three-headed is Sisiutl—the double-ended serpent."

"Three heads?" I asked, not sure how a double-ended snake could have three heads.

"One head at each end like a snake—as quick and as vicious, with a viper's tongue and horned brow. In the middle"—she covered her sunken belly with one hand—"a man's face with mustaches like a sturgeon, horns, and two clawed hands beside it. This is its true head, from which Sisiutl speaks. Between his scales grows hair like cedar strings and he can change his form at will. In water, he swims faster than the seal, faster than orca, but on land he is slower and moves like a snake. He is the guardian of Qamaits's pool outside the house that leads to the land of the gods, and worthy men may call upon his help, but if they fail to pay him, he will eat."

"Who or what is Qamaits?" I asked. You'd think I'd be pretty used to the weird and unsettling by that time, but the oddity of the house and its occupant threw me and left me feeling a bit at sea.

Grandma Ella waved my question aside and glared at Fish as she helped herself to more bread.

Fish bit his bottom lip before replying. "She's another zeqwa, an ogress who eats children. She's kind of like Baba Yaga and she lives in a magical house. She's got a bunch of other names, too, but all her aspects are kind of half-magic, half-monster. Umm . . . I'm trying to remember the rest of the legend about the house. . . ."

Ella Graham snorted. "See what leaving your people causes? Ignorance!" She returned her glare to me as Fish blushed and lowered his head. "Inside the house of Qamaits lies the staircase to the sky—where the gods live. You can climb to the sky through a hole, like the sisters who married stars did, but that won't bring you to the gods. If you want to talk to the gods in the sky, you go up the stairs, past Qamaits and past her guardian, Sisiutl. If you please the gods, they will bless your hunting with his help. But if you anger them, squander their gifts, or do not feed their helper well, the gods will be angry and let Sisiutl eat *you*."

"Is there more than one Sisiutl?" I asked.

She scoffed. "No! He is *the* Sisiutl."

Now came the crazy bit, but I figured there wasn't much crazier than three-headed sea serpents that eat people and turn into canoes, so I dove in. "What would happen if the—if Sisiutl got loose from his pool?"

"He would eat. As he ate after the earthquake."

"Which earthquake?"

"After the Second World War. I had been worried for my sons but they came home safe. Then Sisiutl shook the ground and ate the men he found there. Horrible. To survive the killing in Europe only to be eaten at home. We didn't have the casino and the houses and the shops then. Many people went away from the reservation to work. When Sisiutl came, our people were the only ones who knew it was him. It was difficult to find Qamaits and make her call Sisiutl back to the pool. If Sisiutl had been hunting men, the gods would have been furious, but he was only hungry after so long asleep. No hunters were fed to Sisiutl that day and only Qamaits could put him back into the pool."

"Where was Sisiutl's pool? Where did your people send him?"

"It was in the garbage dump, then. But there's no water there now. When you fight Sisiutl, you'll have to find another pool for him or send him back to the gods."

I was taken aback. "Why would I fight Sisiutl?"

Ella Graham spat into the fire and started to get up from her cushion. Fish jumped up to help her to her feet.

Clutching her cane, she glared at us, batted Fish aside, and hobbled to the fieldstone mantle above the eastern fireplace, her white braids dragging on the floor and her loose flesh swaying like weeds in water. She took something off the shelf and returned. Fish helped her down.

"Get me another cushion, Reuben," she ordered, and Fish gave her his. She sank down and over, so she was reclining on her side, her face gone waxy from some pain. She held out a long brown and gold feather toward me. "You take this, Pheasant Woman. You'll need it to unpick the knots of dead things."

I was flabbergasted and shot an irritated glance at Fish. He shook his head rapidly, eyes wide, scared. "What makes you think—?" I started.

Grandma Ella cawed a nasty laugh that made me bristle. "You're just like Pheasant. Pheasant's daughter died but he loved her so much he went to the land of the dead to bring her back. He couldn't see the dead with his open eyes, only when he closed them, but he couldn't keep his eyes closed and he stepped on the dead and made them angry. They tried to send him away, but Pheasant didn't want to leave his daughter. He wanted to stay, but the land of the dead is not for the living. So one eye died, and Pheasant sees the dead through one eye and the living through the other. Like you. Take this," she repeated, thrusting the pheasant tail feather at me again.

Reluctantly, I took the feather and felt her shudder as I touched it. It didn't seem special, but I could see the wings that folded around Ella Graham unfurl and refold, glittering—they reminded me of something. . . .

"You remind me of Grandpa Dan," I whispered, unable to keep the words back.

Ella Graham snorted. "Dan! A horse for spirits to ride. He cannot stop Sisiutl," she sneered and pulled away from me, glowering. "You think I don't hear the whispers of our ancestors saying Sisiutl comes to the land between? Hm? Our people have grown weak and small in numbers, and Sisiutl feeds on too many. Who but you to gather spirits and send him and his spawn away again, Pheasant? Now you go away. Get out of my house. You, too, Reuben. Come back when the dead sleep properly." Her voice began fading and her eyes dimmed as she continued. "Bring more chocolates. And tell that rascal Russell I forgive him for sinking my boat." She dropped her cheek onto the cushion and let out a sigh, closing her eyes, and the house seemed to sigh also, becoming subdued and darker inside than the darkness falling outside would account for.

The three of us exchanged startled glances. Fish put his hand in front of her mouth and looked terrified. Then he slumped in relief.

"She's just asleep. But we'd better go."

We all agreed on that point, struggled to our feet, and shuffled out through the topsy-turvy Grey and the cloud of spirits to my truck in nervous silence. No one said a word until we were back on the main road out of the rez. Quinton had returned to his brooding and Fish kept casting nervous glances at me as I drove.

When I had the truck safely back up on I-5, I shot him a look. "What?" I demanded, half irritated but mostly curious what made him so skittish now when he'd gone along so well before.

"Do you really think Sisiutl is killing those people?"

"What do you think?"

"I don't know. I mean—wow. Uh . . . ancient Indian monsters . . . umm . . . chowing down on homeless people in Pioneer Square? It's kind of . . . kind of . . ."

"Outlandish?"

"Nuts."

"It's your monster, Fish; your culture. If you and Russell really think Grandma Ella can curse you for sinking her boat—even if you only think it a little bit and late at night—is it more nuts to imagine that a monster might be real—just a little bit and late at night—down in the Square where things get strange?"

He didn't look at me. "And you . . ." He gave a nervous giggle, which was pretty funny coming out of a stocky guy who looked more like an outlaw biker gone straight than a doctor. "You see dead people?"

"I hate that movie," I said, truly nettled and frowning—I knew that was unfair, but still . . . Then I nodded, keeping my eyes on the road. "Yeah. I see dead people. Things that linger, things that go bump in the night. Mostly harmless."

"But not Sisiutl."

"If it is Sisiutl."

"You seemed pretty sure."

I made myself shrug. "It was the only lead I had. The information isn't a complete match, so it's not an absolute."

"Let's assume it is," said Quinton from the backseat. "For the sake of discussion. A legendary, three-headed sea serpent that likes to pretend to be a canoe and eats people, and he lives in a pond outside the house of some kind of goddess ogress who has a staircase to the gods."

"That sounds pretty damned dumb to me," I said.

"You're just stuck on the name."

"It's silly." I realized that it really bugged me. "Something that eats people and gnaws on the remains, leaves zombies in the underground and breaks through four-foot-thick cement walls ought to have a scarier name than 'Sisiutl.' "

"It's up there with 'Son of Sam' and 'Baby Face Nelson,' right?"

"All right, Mr. Physics—what about the shape-shifting? You're the guy with the 'there are no werewolves' conviction. If Sisiutl is responsible—if we accept that this legendary, three-headed sea serpent is eating homeless people and spitting out the parts—don't we have to accept that it turns into a canoe, or a dog, or a . . . rat the size of Cleveland, too? How does that fit?"

"It doesn't change shape."

"Whoa! Come back?"

Fish wrenched his head around to stare between the seats at Quinton. "What?"

"It doesn't actually change shape," Quinton reiterated. "Not if it has a corporeal form. It can't—or at least not quickly and safely. We have to assume a corporeal form, since it makes holes in things and has teeth that can and do rend flesh. It eats people—doesn't seem to be much doubt it gnaws on them, so the missing have probably taken a visit to the literal belly of the beast. So if we assume 'Sisiutl' as the cause, we assume 'corporeal' as the default expression. With me?"

"Yeah," said Fish.

"Since it cannot change shape, it follows that it does not change shape, but it may create the illusion of shape change. It wants you to see a self-propelled seal hunting canoe and, if you're the right kind of person to see Sisiutl at all—and it probably knows if you are—then you see a canoe."

"What if you're not the right type to see Sisiutl?"

"Then you see death. It eats you while you're freaking out about seeing a giant two-headed, three-faced snake god with horns and a mustache like a bottom-feeder."

"Sisiutl isn't a god . . ." Fish objected.

"No, but if you weren't a Tulalip Indian—"

"Tulalip is the name of the reservation," Fish corrected. "There's a group of Salish tribes on the rez, but it's named for the bay, not the tribes. All the tribes from Vancouver Island down to the middle of Oregon are some kind of Salish—even Sacajawea's tribe back in the Lewis and Clark days—so you can't call the place 'Salish' or the other tribes would be pissed."

I could see Quinton nod in the rearview mirror. "All right. Sorry."

"No problem. Go on."

"OK. So, what would you think Sisiutl was if you were like me and it came slithering down an alley looking hungry and saying 'I'm a canoe!' in Salish?"

"Lushootseed—that's what we call our language. Hm . . ." Fish mumbled, thinking. "Yeah, I see your point. I'd think I was see-ing a giant mutant snake, probably, 'cause that's what I know—snakes, not sea monsters and not Sisiutl. Huh. But no one's said anything about giant mutant snakes in the alleys around Pioneer Square."

"No, they haven't," Quinton agreed. "Because the people who see it either die or think they must be hallucinating. It only comes out at night when there aren't a lot of people and it hunts in the tunnels under the streets or in the alleys where it's dark. Grandma Ella said it was clever. It must be clever enough to stay away from high-risk conditions."

"What if it's not Sisiutl?" I asked.

Both men frowned.

"Hm . . ." Quinton muttered. "That could be, but there haven't

been any leads to other monsters and Sisiutl as Ella Graham described it fits the facts we have without throwing any out—two
big steps in the right direction. Its appearances match the pattern
we noted in the paper and that Fish found in the morgue records
and the fact that the patterns of deaths halted when Indians took
action lends a lot of credence to the Sisiutl theory. And the ghost
said it was Sistu."

I nodded this time. "She did."

Fish goggled at me and I feared he was getting a little hysterical. "A ghost told you about Sisiutl? You called me because a ghost
told you to?"

"No. I called because an Indian told me there was a monster
that ate people during the right outbreak of historic deaths. She
happened to be a ghost and I find ghosts to be very unreliable
sources—they lie a lot. I needed a living Indian to tell me what a
Sistu—that's what she called it—was and what it was capable of,
so I could decide if I thought the lead was viable."

"She wouldn't call Sisiutl by name where he might hear her!"
Fish cried, on the verge of panic. "Didn't you get what Grandma
Ella said? If you call him by the wrong name, he won't come, but
if you use his real name . . ."

I glanced at him and then through the mirror to Quinton.
"Maybe we shouldn't then."

We found ourselves casting nervous looks at each other and
out the windows, suddenly paranoid that we'd attract our death.

FOURTEEN

The sun had gone long before we reached Seattle and the road was feeling slicker under the Rover's tires as I drove. We had fallen silent as we reached the edge of the university, and in the hard sparkle of streetlights on frost, the road had seemed like a tunnel through a mysterious land.

Fish had calmed down a bit by the time I'd dropped him off at his place again, but it was obvious he was still working through some of the hits his worldview had taken. Yet another comfortable reality I'd managed to knock holes in for someone. I hoped Fish would bounce better than Will had. Wistfulness at the thought of my trashed love affair washed over me and faded as we drove away from Fish's house.

Quinton had moved up to the front seat but was still frowning a little.

"What do you think?" I asked.

"About what?"

"This monster thing."

"Not sure."

"All right. What about the guests I had. this morning? You think we're still clear?"

"The Rover is. I don't know about your office or home. Depends on how much they think you know and if they have the resources to do much about it. I think it's likely the available resources and time are limited."

"Why would you think that? Ms. Laguire gave me the impression she was going to put out whatever effort she had to—"

"She may be willing to put herself out," Quinton interrupted, scowling, "but there is no way the NSA thinks it's worth unlimited resources. Trust me—it's Fern alone with whatever assistance she can pull in by leaning on the local Fed office. It's her personal failure. They're giving her a chance to redeem it, but that's all."

"Then just what the hell is it between you and Fern Laguire . . . J.J.?"

He turned and glared at me. "I don't want to discuss it right now."

"This is nice. Usually I'm the one who gets accused of being all mysterious and closed off, but you—"

"I'm not that jackass you date!"

I pulled the truck over into the nearest parking lot—which happened to be the Group Health hospital's main entrance lot. I put the car in the nearest empty slot and yanked on the parking brake so I could turn and yell at Quinton directly—I could never be called coy in my anger.

"Not that it's any of your business," I spat, "but we're not dating anymore!"

"Good!" he shouted back and swung out of the truck.

I shut down the engine and scrambled after him.

"What does that mean?" I demanded, catching up to Quinton near the main hospital doors.

He shrugged elaborately, as if throwing something off his shoulders, and turned back. The corona around him in the Grey flared a moment before pulling in tight to a pale line of rapidly flickering colors. "What I mean," he said, his measured tones coming out in puffs of frozen breath, "is that you shouldn't be dating someone you have to lie to."

"Well, I'm not."

"No. I guess not. Or not anymore at least." He stood there looking uncomfortable. "Why not?"

I heaved a sigh that made a long white column in the air. "Remember I told you about a zombie I was brought on Thursday?"

"Yeah," Quinton replied, shuffling his feet against the cold welling from the cement beneath our feet.

"Well . . ." I was finding the subject difficult to talk about—though not in the same way that I found myself unable to speak of the nature of the magical grid to normal people. "Will was with me at the time and he freaked out a little."

"I can understand that. Most people would."

"Yeah. Well. I had to . . . dismantle it . . . and he didn't deal too well with seeing that."

Quinton stared at me and shivered, though from cold or from his own imagination's conjuring, I wasn't sure. "Ugh. That would be pretty hard to take. Did he . . . umm . . ."

"Dumped me," I said, nodding. "Not that I don't understand it, but it still hurts. We tried to patch it, but . . . You're right—I can't date someone who can't deal with what I am or what I do and has to be lied to or shielded or wrapped in ignorance."

"I'm, uh . . ." he stammered, biting his lip.

"Don't say you're sorry. Because you aren't. Things just don't work sometimes." I found I couldn't look at him and turned my glance off to the side. Something bright flared in the Grey, but by the time I'd turned my head back, it had gone and Quinton was still just standing there, looking a little too bright and too pink.

He grinned and the energy around him went pinker. "OK, I'm not sorry it didn't work out." Then the pink faded down. "But I do wish it hadn't happened that way. Zombies and shaggy things . . ."

"They're still out there," I reminded him, feeling somewhat uncomfortable and wanting to change the subject away from my broken love life. "And even if we think we have a likely monster, we aren't any closer to stopping it or figuring out why it's doing this."

A small group of grim-looking people came out from the main lobby, talking about someone's prognosis and the risks of surgery. It had seemed so late in the frozen dark, we'd both forgotten it was only a little past five.

Quinton caught my eye. "You want to get some hot food and try to figure out where to start looking for answers?"

I gave a crooked smile. "Yeah."

Dinner was about as un-datelike as you can get: hamburgers at the Kidd Valley across the street from the hospital. But it was hot food and the windows of the building were steamed with moisture. Quinton and I huddled with our food as far from the doors as we could get.

"You think we're really looking for Sisiutl?" Quinton asked.

"Yeah." I sighed. "Much as I feel silly saying it."

"Then we'll stick to 'Sistu' for now, I guess. Even if it doesn't notice, seems like there's points in favor of not using the formal name."

I agreed. "We need to figure out where it's hiding and what it's up to—is it just hungry or is there something else going on?"

"Start from where it came from," Quinton suggested. "Ella

Graham said something about a dump. Wasn't there something else about a dump in one of the papers or something?"

"Yeah. There was a dumping ground south of downtown."

"Right. About where the stadia are now."

"Which is where the hotel construction is. Think it's the same spot?"

"High probability. If the construction broke through to wherever Sistu was imprisoned, he'd escape, and it's likely he'd eat the first thing he found."

"Probably one of your missing homeless."

Quinton nodded. "But is he doing something specific or just rampaging around at random? Right now, the pattern is just homeless people who were down in or near the bricks. The bricks isn't very far from the breakthrough point, but Jenny was found father north, so he's moving his territory closer to the Square itself—there hasn't been anything south of the stadia."

"Maybe there's something special about the Square—it never seems to have gone beyond the northern boundary at Cherry Street—or maybe its hiding place is near there."

"Between the Square and the bricks is where the most activity has been. That puts Oxy Park in the middle of the pattern. I think we should start there."

"What about the ogress Grandma Ella mentioned? She's Sistu's keeper, so she'd have to be nearby, too. Ella said Sistu had been returned to . . . what was her name?"

"Zeqwa?"

"No . . . that means 'monster.' " I thought a moment. "Kammits?"

Quinton brightened up. "Qamaits! Right. Ella said Sistu had been returned to the ogress in 1949. She's his keeper and she'd keep him down, unless she had some reason to let him run loose."

"Like punishing someone for pissing off the gods, as Grandma Ella said—or repaying a favor."

"And the undergrounders aren't the sort to avoid someone just because they look a little scary—they're a scary bunch themselves—so it's not like they'd refuse to give a god a drink or something," Quinton said.

"So . . . what do you think? Someone helped Qamaits out of the construction pit and the first thing the monster did was eat someone whose leg was found in the excavation?"

"Seems like a possibility."

"Even if I were an ogress, I think I'd be more grateful than to let my pet eat my rescuer."

"Maybe she couldn't stop him. Ella Graham said Sistu's a hunter. . . ."

"I guess he's graduated from seals to people, then. But if he's hunting for a reason, maybe there's a pattern to who's been killed. We'll have to start at the beginning of this spate of deaths. We need to find out who was at the excavation the night before the leg was found. If they're still alive and not a monster's lunch, we need to talk to them."

"And Qamaits."

I nodded. "Yeah, but I think she'll be easy to spot—after all, she's a legendary monster, too, so like Sistu, she'll look like one thing to some people, and something else to others."

"Like you."

I pulled a face. "Probably. But I don't know what she'll look like, and a lot of people and things have shadow shapes. She could be anyone. We have to find her, or anyone who saw Sistu come out of the hole—anyone who might have an idea what it's up to, what it might be 'hunting,' or why."

"We'd better get downtown before it gets too late and everyone's asleep."

"But it's most likely we'll get information from people who don't sleep in the shelters all the time—people like Tanker and Lass."

"And Sandy—she's sharp-eyed and crazy enough to sleep rough a lot more often than most women down there."

I shook my head. "She's nuts all right, if she's doing that."

"More than half of them are—it's protective behavior." He slurped up the last of his soda. "Let's go."

I regarded my half-eaten food and decided I didn't need to finish it—the burger was huge—but after talking about the homeless I felt bad about throwing it away.

Quinton saw me looking at it. "Wrap it up. If nothing else, we can give the burger to Bella."

For a second, I wasn't sure whom he meant, then I remembered Tanker's dog. As I hesitated, Quinton reached over, wrapped the burger in its paper and tucked it away in one of his capacious pockets.

We went back to the Rover and drove down to Pioneer Square. I didn't park in my regular spot, though, just in case the NSA had been doing their homework. Instead, I put the truck into a slot under the Alaskan Way viaduct and we walked in from the western edge of the historic district. Coming up beside Marcus' Martini Heaven, Quinton nudged me and pointed into the dark alley on the other side.

"Looks like Tanker," he said. I recognized the shape of the stocky dog, and as we crossed the street, Quinton shoved the wrapped food into my hands. "I'll talk, you feed."

Tanker turned with a jerk as we got close and Bella stiffened for a moment until she recognized Quinton. Then she went all over wags and friskies. "Heya, Tanker," Quinton said as he knelt to pet the dog.

"Hey Q. Miss Thing." I guessed he was feeling a little more sociable than last time but hadn't quite forgiven me for apparently accusing him of lying.

"Hi, Tanker," I said and held out the packet of leftovers. "Mind if I give this to Bella?"

He eyed the wrapper. "What is it?"

I peeked into the wrapper. "It's a . . . meatloaf sandwich." I'd forgotten about Quinton's unfinished lunch—he'd switched packages on me.

Tanker laughed. "Damn, woman, you gonna spoil my dog."

"She's a good dog. She won't spoil. Can she have it?"

He waved a casual hand at the dog who was looking in every direction, trying to figure out who she should be paying most attention to. "Sure. Go ahead. She don't like to eat out of hands, though. Gotta put it down in front of her."

"OK," I said, crouching down near the dog with a creak from my knee as Quinton stood up and moved closer to Tanker, pulling out the leftover burger and offering that to the man, getting back into his good graces.

"Hey there, Bella," I murmured. "Got a treat—I think." I'd never had a dog as a kid and as an adult I'd never had a lifestyle that lent itself to the kind of care dogs need. I took my neighbor's pit bull for walks once in a while, but that was about the extent of my dog contact. I was just a little nervous of Bella's powerful jaws as I put the opened wrapper down on the brick alley floor in front of her. The dog licked her lips and wiggled, looking at the food, but didn't move to snap it up.

"It's OK, Bella, eat," Tanker said, eyeing his own leftovers.

The dog let out a happy yip and dove in on the food. I scratched her ears as she ate and I listened to Tanker and Quinton talk.

"Tank, I'm kind of worried. Do you remember when Tandy disappeared?"

"Why'd you be worried about that old drunk?" Tanker asked around a mouthful of burger.

"Just bothered. I mean . . . bad shit's been happening, and I think I haven't seen Tandy since before it started."

"Man, Tandy ain't smart enough to do nothing but raise a bottle."

"Not much, I agree, but have you seen him—or Bear or Jolene?"

Tanker swallowed a bite of burger. "Hmph! I think I saw Bear a while back before Christmas. Jolene I don't know—she don't stand out much. And I don't give a crap in a paper bag about Tandy. Him and Lass drink together all the time. You should ask that peckerhead where his friend is, 'cause I don't know and I don't care. He could fall down a sewer and drown in shit and I couldn't care any less than I do."

Quinton nodded as Bella finished off her sandwich with a joyful smacking of her jaws, her master only a few bites behind on his own food.

"Huh," Quinton grunted. "I wonder if something could have happened to them. You think anyone would hurt one of them?"

"Everybody likes Bear and Jolene! And nobody give enough of a damn about Tandy to do him hurt. I don't know why anybody'd kill poor ol' Jenny, neither. She was kind of a stupid woman, but she wasn't mean 'less she was needing a fix." He chewed the last of the burger and swallowed with a smile.

Bella felt I needed my face washed with meatloaf-scented doggy tongue.

"Bella, off," Tanker said. "Don't go slobbering all over the lady." Apparently the food had bought some goodwill from the owner as well as the dog.

Bella stopped licking me and gave me a half-apologetic look with her tongue hanging out one side of her mouth.

"That's all right," I said, getting back to my feet after a final scratch behind the dog's ears. "She's a nice dog."

"I trained her myself," Tanker said with pride.

"You did a good job."

"Dogs like to know who's boss, else they get in trouble. But if you're a good boss, they'll do anything for you. Anything. I swear, I'm gonna let her eat that damned Lassiter next time we see him. Don't know why I didn't let her this last time. That damned asshole done something to her and it's only 'cause I don't want her eating on nothing so trashy as him I didn't let her rip his leg off. Can't trust no man'd hurt a dog." Tanker had begun to glower and the aura around him had gone red with his anger.

Quinton patted Tanker on the shoulder. "Bella'd get a stomachache from Lass. Better not let her get a good bite."

Tanker snorted. "Keeping away from him, for sure."

Quinton nodded. "You seen Sandy tonight?"

Tanker scratched his head through his hood. "Yeah . . . Round on Second Ave. Extension by the Quick Mart. She might have gone back to the park, though—it was getting cold and I think she was watching someone."

"We'll find her. Thanks, Tank."

"Yeah. You the same." Tanker nodded at us awkwardly and clucked at Bella, "C'mon, girl." We walked back out of the alley as he continued deeper into it.

We slunk around to Occidental Park, staying out of the sight lines to my office building. Quinton pointed at the bear totem.

"John Bear used to like to sleep under that. That's what Blue Jay meant when he talked about Bear sleeping with the bears. You can see there's no one sleeping under it now."

Just beyond the totem, a trash can fire burned to warm the hands of a small circle of homeless. The obese woman at the foot of the other carving scowled at us as we passed and pressed herself into the dark. I couldn't see much of her in either the Grey or the normal, cowering as she did in the black fold of the totem's shadow. It occurred to me it wasn't a nice totem—Nightmare Bringer. I wasn't too surprised it cast a very dark shadow and I certainly wouldn't have wanted to sleep near it with such an association. The woman pulled a black blanket over herself and hunched into a shapeless mass.

We walked on down to the burning trash can and found Zip, Sandy, and the man I often saw pacing and talking to himself. We were offered cigarettes by Zip and drinks from an unseen bottle in a paper bag. Sandy nodded and the talking man told us the voice of the turtle would be heard in the land.

"God, Twitcher. In't no turtles here 'bouts," Zip complained. "In't likely to be talking noways."

"Even the End of Days must have an end," Twitcher replied.

"I think that's supposed to be the Final Judgment," Sandy said. "I don't think we've quite got to that yet."

"Aren't the dead supposed to rise up and be counted or something?" Twitcher asked.

"Yes," Sandy replied uneasily, giving him a sideways glance.

"Ah. Then I guess it's not time after all, or the streets would be full of 'em." Twitcher nodded to himself and settled into nervous jiggling from foot to foot and flapping his arms.

"Perhaps," Sandy said.

"Hey'm, Harper," Zip said. A waft of beer and rotting teeth made me turn a little away as I answered.

"Hey, Zip." I put myself closer to Sandy and upwind of the incredible stench Zip had acquired.

"How's your case?" Sandy inquired.

"Could be better. How's yours?"

"Gone to ground for a while I think. Lost him earlier today. Hope to pick up his trail later tonight, maybe tomorrow. What brings you here?"

"Trying to find out who was down by the hotel construction in the last few months."

"We've all been down around the hole," Sandy said, but she had a thoughtful frown on her face.

"Yeah," Zip added. "Sometimes t'ey got wood scraps we kin winkle out. Lockin' up t'garbage since that leg were found, though."

Quinton poked Twitcher in the ribs. "Hey, Twitcher. You know anyone's been down there, or who had a mad on for any of the lost?"

"Not to mention all of them," Twitcher replied. I noticed that he stopped jiggling if he was talking or doing something, but when he had nothing to say, he twitched. His spasms were less controlled when he tried to stand still and I realized he walked and muttered to keep some control over his body's incessant movement.

"Try that again," Quinton requested. "Are you saying every one of them was someone someone else wanted to hurt? Who?"

Twitcher shook his head rather violently and bounced on his toes. "No, no. Nobody didn't like Little Jolene or Jan and we all didn't like Hafiz. So that's everybody and nobody. Go-cart got a lot of people mad, but they didn't usually stay that way. Well, Tanker never did forgive him for running over his foot that time. . . ."

"An' Bear were good, but he weren't allus a easy fella t'be

friendly wit'," Zip said. "Him 'n' Lass'd go around—you'd think they hated ch'other."

"Can't go by Lass—he doesn't like anybody," Twitcher said. "You call *me* twitchy—hah!"

"Lass in't twitchy, he jes crazy."

"But . . ." said Sandy, "I'd rather be on Tanker's bad side or Bear's than Lassiter's."

"Oh? Why?" I asked.

"He's sneaky. Tanker and Bear both let you know when they're mad."

Zip hooted. "Lass in't so good at keepin' his temper on the QT. Remember when him'n Hafiz got into it? Hoppin' at ch'other like frogs on a griddle."

"Not that everyone didn't get into it with Hafiz sometime, the mouthy so-and-so," Twitcher supplied.

"What about Tandy?" Quinton asked. "Anyone ever get into an argument with him?"

"Nah," Zip said. "Couldn't git inta nothin' with him. He's allus drunk and happy."

"Drunk and sloppy," Sandy corrected. "He'd drink with anyone who could keep him upright enough to tip the bottle."

"When was the last time anyone saw Tandy?"

The three undergrounders fell silent, thinking.

"Thanksgiving," Sandy finally said. "Before the windstorm."

"Where did you see him?" I asked.

"Down near the football stadium."

"Near the hotel construction?"

"Not that close, but he could have walked there. He wasn't too drunk at that point."

"Was he with anyone?"

"Actually, he was with John Bear and Little Jolene."

I glanced at Quinton, who shook his head. "Bear and Jolene were seen later than that."

"But Tandy wasn't," Sandy added.

"Are you sure?"

"Well, I never saw him after Thanksgiving and I watch."

"When was Hafiz killed?" I asked.

"He was found the Monday after Thanksgiving, but I think he'd been dead a day or two," Sandy said, thinking aloud. "The body was under some tree limbs that fell off the plane trees here in the windstorm."

"He was killed by the falling boughs?"

"Oh, no. They just hid the body."

We kept chatting with the three until our toes were numb in our boots and we couldn't feel our faces, but nothing else useful emerged. As Quinton and I walked on to find more undergrounders, he said, "Tandy and Lass used to drink together a lot—but Tandy did drink with pretty much anyone, as Sandy said."

"So he could have been with Bear and Jolene or he could have been with anyone else whom we haven't talked to yet."

"But the fact that he disappeared just before the leg was found makes him prime suspect to be the owner of that leg."

I shivered. "Ugh. So that would make Tandy the first to disappear, then Hafiz was killed—but he seems universally disliked—then what?"

"After that, Jan and Go-cart were both found dead—in that order. But there was a good lag between Hafiz and Jan."

"Who disappeared between those?"

"I'm not sure. I'd guess the order was probably . . . Jheri, then Jolene . . . then Jan was killed . . . then Bear and Felix disappeared, and Go-cart died. And Jenny."

"That's about one a week, average. Pretty hungry monster."

"Yeah."

I paused, frowning and thinking there had to be a connection I wasn't making. "I want to talk to Lass. His name keeps coming up. Then we might want to go back to Tanker."

"You think Tanker knows something he hasn't told us?"

"Someone knows something, and the only people who can be ruled out are the confirmed dead."

We walked around the area for a while but didn't have much luck finding Lassiter, so we went below.

Down in the bricks, we found Tall Grass, raging in a corner and waving a soft brown object in the air. When he spotted us, he raced down the crumbling floor and shoved the object into my hands. "You wanted it! You take it! Take it away!" He shook me, shouting into my face.

"Grass, Grass, calm down," Quinton murmured. "They'll hear. Be quiet."

Tall Grass turned on Quinton. "You brought her down here. She wanted the hat. It's your fault! It's your fault Jenny's dead!"

Quinton pulled his face back from the other man's. "Grass, you're out of your head. It's not our fault. Something or someone killed Jenny, but it's not me or Harper. And it's not you."

"It's that hat!"

"Damn it, Grass, get a grip. It's not the hat."

"It was Bear's hat. Bear's dead. It was Jenny's hat. Jenny's dead," Tall Grass babbled, his voice cracking toward hysteria.

"Grass. How do you know Bear's dead? We don't know Bear's dead. He's just—"

"I saw it! I saw his spirit! And the creature—the monster—I saw! I saw!" He was hyperventilating. Then he began to scream, staring at nothing at all, bellowing in terror, his eyes rolling up to show too much white.

"Damn it," Quinton muttered. Then Tall Grass gulped, fainted, and slumped to the floor.

Quinton looked down at him. "I was never glad to see someone faint before."

"Hey . . ."

We both looked around. Someone had stuck their head around the corner. When we caught sight of it, the head pulled back.

"Don't run off, Lass!" Quinton hissed. He motioned with his head for me to catch Lass.

I sprinted down the rough walkway, feeling sudden twinges in my bad knee, and collared Lass less than ten feet down the Occidental side. "C'mon and lend a shoulder, Lass," I suggested. "We have to get Tall Grass out of here."

Lassiter goggled at me, shaking. His hands crabbed for his pockets.

"Don't reach for that," I told him. "I don't go down easily and I'll take you with me. Not going to hurt you if you come help Quinton and me out."

He shuffled reluctantly ahead of me to where Quinton was trying to get Tall Grass up. The Indian was unconscious and limp.

Quinton looked hard at Lass and told him, "Put your shoulder under his armpit and get him up. We'll have to carry him up the Cadillac stairs and hope we can find a place to leave him."

"Why not here?" Lass whined. "Who cares? Why are we risking our necks for him?"

"Because if he stays down here while he's like this, he might die. I helped you. Now you help me. Or I won't be doing you any favors in the future, Lass. Get me?"

"OK, OK. I got you."

Lass helped lift Tall Grass and the two men carried him like a sack between them to the bottom of the stairs that came up beside the Cadillac Hotel. I scouted up the stairs and peeked out, waiting until I was sure the street was empty to hiss at them to come up.

Tall Grass was making noises and trying to move by the time we reached the street. Quinton set him on the sidewalk and hunched down beside him. I grabbed Lassiter's wrist before he could hare off.

While Quinton checked on Grass and muttered to him, I interrogated Lass a bit.

"What were you doing down there?"

"I—I live down there."

"Not right there . . ."

"Not all the time, no. I—I heard something. I heard Grass talking to himself. He's on drugs, man!"

"Surprise, surprise. He thinks he saw a monster eat John Bear."

"I told you—he's flipped out."

"I'm not sure he didn't see a monster down there."

"What?"

"You see monsters. I heard you say so."

He looked startled and glanced around but I was blocking his only line of escape.

"Did you see the monster that ate Bear?"

"I seen things. . . ."

"What did you see and where did you see it?"

"I seen—I seen a . . . lot of scary dudes. They hurt us. . . . That's what Q-man gave me the stunner for."

"Yeah, but I'll bet you've seen more than that, or you wouldn't be so scared."

"I seen . . . a snake. Big snake."

I looked skeptical—not that I didn't believe him, I just wanted to make this insecure man talk, and nothing starts some people off like the idea that others don't believe them.

"I did! It was as big as a car! It had a whole man in its mouth—like when a rattlesnake tries to swallow an egg."

"Where did you see it?"

"Uh . . . Under the Square."

"You can't get under the Square."

"Yeah, you can! Behind the Pioneer Building there's a grate down in the alley. You just lift it up and go in the hole!"

"When did you see the snake there?"

"I can't remember! Leave me alone!" He shoved at me and bolted past my shoulder. I could have stopped him, but he needed to salvage some pride and I didn't mind letting him think he'd gotten away with it. I thought I knew where to find him later.

I turned back to Quinton and Tall Grass, who was fighting his way back to his feet.

"Get away," Grass snapped.

"You gonna be all right?" Quinton asked him.

"I'm fine."

"You were pretty hysterical. . . ."

He glared at Quinton and stared around. Seeing me with the hat still in one hand, he darted over and snatched it from me. "That's Jenny's hat."

"You said it was Bear's hat."

Tall Grass looked trapped, his eyes shifting restlessly between us. "It's not."

"C'mon, Grass," Quinton went on. "We all know it was Bear's hat. You said you saw him get eaten by a monster."

"I didn't say that!"

"Yes, you did. We want to stop it. We want to find the thing that ate Jenny."

"I didn't see the S-s— . . . I didn't see it eat her!" Grass wailed. He leaned against the nearest wall and buried his face in the cap in his hands. "We were sleeping and it came in the dark. Like rushing water. And she made a noise and then . . . then I felt something cold and it smelled rotten and stinking. I opened my eyes and saw it swimming away through the walls. It swam through rock! All I had left was this stupid, stupid hat! And tonight I saw John Bear. Bear's ghost. Walking through the bricks and he stopped and looked at me and said, 'You keep the hat.' Then he left. He left me with this hat. He cursed me with it." Even with his voice muffled by the fur of the hat, I could hear him sobbing, and his shoulders shook with the spasms.

"It's not the hat, Grass. Believe me, that's not what got either of them killed," Quinton said. "Bear wouldn't curse anyone. He just wanted to make sure his things went to the right people. You know how Bear was."

Tall Grass shivered and raised his head. He didn't look at us, but he spoke to us nonetheless, stuttering as he caught his breath. "The z-zeqwa . . . took her. S-s—"

"We know what it was. We want to find it and find out why it came."

"I don't know," Grass whispered fiercely. "If someone sent it to eat Jenny, I'll tear his head off!"

"We'll find out. You go find a fire to sleep near tonight. Don't sleep in the bricks. Don't sleep in the skid at all. Hear me?"

Tall Grass nodded mutely, still dazed at his own outburst of grief and anger. We walked him up to Occidental Park and left him with a scowling Sandy while we went on to try to find the grate that led under Pioneer Square.

"Why would he say that?" I asked. "That someone sent it?"

Quinton shrugged. "I don't know. Maybe he believes it came hunting her."

I frowned and let that tumble in my head.

We discovered a grille loose in the alley floor between the Seattle Mystery Bookshop and the back of the Pioneer block. A steel frame and hinge marked where it had been embedded at one time, but now had been twisted out of its frame and laid back on top of the hole. To my eyes, the whole area was clogged with cold silver mist, the grating outlined and blazing in neon red and yellow—not the most comfortable combination.

Quinton glanced around as if making a mental note of the place. "I never knew there was anything under this."

"Me, either." I bent and pulled on the grille. It swung up and revealed a narrow vault, barely one person wide, that led to a tunnel angling down sharply to the west, leading under the Pioneer Building. Narrow steel-clad doors stood shut before what proved a steep metal staircase. We eased down the ancient stairs by the beam of Quinton's flashlight. Something about the location and disposition of the narrow stairs made me think of a servants' or workers' entrance, even though we'd reached it through the alley. It looked as if the area had been rebuilt at some point, cutting off the original access, but I couldn't decipher the tangled time planes of the Grey at that location to see what had once been there. The Grey was in complete disorder here, as if layers of time and memory had been heaved about by magical earthquakes.

At the bottom of the stair was a very short corridor that logic told me dove under the edge of the sidewalk in front of the Pioneer Building. And ended abruptly in a wall.

"Dead end," I said, but there was something wrong about the wall. . . .

I let everything normal slide away from me as I stared at the wall, moving deeper into the Grey until the wall was a black shape crazed with red and yellow energy threads and wisps of pale gray. I crouched down and inspected the gently waving pale threads.

As my face drew near, I felt the thin breeze that animated them, thick with age and mud, salt water, and things gone rotten. The threads weren't just gray in color, they were Grey in substance. I grabbed onto the web of it and pulled it apart.

A hole had been chewed through the real wall, leaving a narrow tunnel. I turned back to Quinton, who looked more like a bulk of steam around a bright tangle of energetic strands than a person at that moment.

"I guess it's time to get dirty," I said.

He looked nervous and his eyes shifted from a spot just above my head to the rift in the wall that had been hidden by the Grey threads. I realized he was looking where my head would be if I were still standing—he couldn't quite see me in the gloom as I crouched near the energy grid of the Grey, just as I wasn't seeing him normally, either. I wondered if this was how ghosts saw us, but I doubted it, since most of them don't seem to exist as close to the grid as I did.

I pushed my way back up to the world as I normally saw it: the normal, living world, slightly misty, shot with gleams of energy and ghostlight and the watery currents of time and memory.

Quinton jumped a little and adjusted his gaze down to me. "Where did you go?"

"Not far, just far enough to find this. Want to see what's at the other end?"

"Yes, and no. It gives me a creepy feeling."

"Can't say I'm thrilled with it myself, but Lass said he saw a 'snake' down here, and the camouflage is the same material I found before."

Quinton took off his hat, rolled it into a tube, stuffed it into a pocket, and started to climb into the hole.

"Hey," I whispered, feeling a little oppressed by the place—

even a touch scared—and protective of my companion. "I see better in this stuff. I should go first." I didn't want to, but it was smarter. If there was something otherworldly waiting at the end of the tunnel, I'd have a better chance of seeing it than Quinton would.

I crawled into the hole, getting unhappy signals from my shoulder and knee that no amount of working out would compensate for stupidity. I took a deep breath and crept forward into the silver-skinned gloom of the burrow. I felt the ghostly material brush against me as I went, and I could hear Quinton rustling along behind me.

The rough bore was wide enough for us to pass through without squeezing, but the dank, dark feel of it and the smell of watery decay ahead lent our journey the feeling that we were crawling through the closing grip of a stone fist. I could hear the gentle slosh of water ahead, echoing as if we were approaching a subterranean swimming pool. A low moan, like distant wind, came and went in the hollow tone ahead and sent a shiver over my skin that left goose bumps in its wake that had nothing to do with the cold.

I could see a hard line ahead at knee level—just a micron of harsh yellow energy against the Grey-swathed blackness of the tunnel. I felt forward with one hand, a few inches at a time, patting at the chewed floor of rubble, dirt, and crumbling cement and sliding my knees along to keep pace. My hand found a smooth platform that ended in an abrupt squared-off edge. Reaching down, I felt another smooth face and another platform. . . . Steps.

I dragged myself forward until I could tuck my hips under and sit on the edge of the first step. My boots made a tiny splash as they touched the surface farther below me.

I turned my head and whispered back to Quinton, "There's a

room here. It's big, from the sound of it, and there's water on the floor. There might be something moving around in here, but I can't tell yet."

"Right behind you."

I stood and moved forward, sliding my feet gingerly on the slick floor. I felt liquid lap over the tops of my boots and wet my ankles. Something muttered and sloshed off to my right. Peering into the depths of the Grey, I saw the room seem to brighten with the filmlike light of ghosts and the flicker of energy.

The floor stretched away under the water, showing marvelous geometric patterns in colored marble and stone. The walls were white marble streaked with veins of pink and gold, dividing the space into rooms and corridors of stalls with polished wooden doors. The wreck of an old oak chair bobbed slightly in deeper water way across the room. The murmuring thing lurched toward me and I caught a sharp breath in surprise.

It was a zombie. Before it could make its way closer, I shot a fast glance around, looking for any shape that might be Sisiutl, but there was nothing above the surface that looked like a snake or a sea serpent. I shuffled farther into the water until it was up to my thighs and, wincing at the thought of what was in it, ducked my head down to look below the surface of the brackish, smelly water.

Dimly I could see how the marble floor had subsided, allowing water to seep in at high tide through the cracks that must have formed over time. One end was misshapen by a mass of cement— probably the stabilizing material that had been poured in when the pergola above had been rebuilt. But even with the best concentration I could expend, I couldn't see any sign of Sistu in the depths of the water and I couldn't hold my breath much longer. I stood back up, soaking wet, and threw my hair back, gasping for

air. The "subterranean comfort station" was festooned in webs of
Sisiutl's Grey stuff, as was the once-human creature that struggled
nearby. Where the soft Grey strands hung, the shapes and colors
of the surfaces beneath were hard to see clearly. I could see the
gleam of the dead man's life tangled in the Grey web that held
his flesh in form, but I couldn't see deeper. The moisture had attacked his skin, and where his legs had been soaking in water, they
were bloated and soft, the rest of the body being slack, darkened,
and exuding the rotten smell I'd whiffed in the hole. In the corporeal dark, I couldn't make out more than its form—no face was
visible—but it definitely wasn't as close to total decomposition as
the last one I'd been this close to.

"Quinton," I said in a low voice, "there's a zombie here. I need
light."

He didn't hesitate but swished through the water to my side,
clicking on his pocket flashlight and finding the sad, dead thing
with its beam.

He caught his breath in shock and his footsteps faltered a moment before he finally stopped beside me. "That's Felix. He was
the last to disappear before Go-cart and Jenny were killed."

"If Si— the monster had Felix, why did it kill the other two?"
I wondered.

"I don't know. Maybe . . . this is sick . . . maybe he's saving
him for a snack? Maybe he's like an alligator and he prefers his
meals . . . aged?"

"He didn't really eat the others. . . ." I said, thinking aloud.
"He just killed them and left the bodies behind."

Felix's ambulating corpse stumbled toward us, making low
noises in its decayed throat. An idea was struggling to form in my
mind but crumbled away as the zombie seemed to cry out and

fall to its knees, tangled in the mess of Grey threads and mud that spun across the flooded floor.

Quinton's light wavered and moved off the weakly struggling zombie. "Harper! Do something!"

I admit I hesitated. Once again, I'd have to deconstruct a zombie in front of a man I liked. The last one hadn't handled it very well. . . .

"Get the light back on him," I snapped. "I can't see what I need to do."

Quinton directed the light onto the moving corpse and I closed the distance between us. I squatted down in the water and, shuddering with disgust, I put a hand out to touch the remains of the man. It was soft but solid, and even with the light I couldn't see any way to hook out the trapped threads of its life. I did not want to hack the poor thing apart with a pocket knife—revulsion made me turn my head aside and gag at the idea.

"There has to be a way," I muttered, shivering in the chilly water that had set my damaged joints to aching. I studied the zombie as I shoved it back into a more upright position.

The dead thing slumped against the wall, possibly exhausted, but making no more large movements and few sounds now. Where it leaned against a drapery of the Grey threads, it seemed to vanish into the wall. That was interesting. The neutral Grey stuff must have been as much a form of camouflage as of holding its victims. Or was the trapping just incidental?

The more I looked at it, the more I thought the latter was the case: the Grey web stuff was Sisiutl's camouflage. It probably spun a web of the stuff over itself and that was how it seemed to change shape as it slithered across time and space. It was smart enough to use the same material to cover the door to this place.

"This is its lair," I gasped.

"What?" Quinton asked.

"This webby stuff—"

He interrupted, "What webby stuff?"

"There's some magical material I've been finding around the Sistu's sites. I told you about it. It's all over the place here, and all over this poor bastard. I think we must be in the lair. Sistu's hidden it with the webbing—that's why you couldn't see the hole until I tore the web away. And that web is all over this guy—Felix. I think that's why his spirit can't leave—the magical web has his energy trapped in his dead body."

"Well, get it off him then!"

I really didn't want an audience, but we had no way of knowing when Sisiutl would be coming back for his dinner and I couldn't stand the idea of leaving Felix to be released from his prison of rotting flesh only by the bite of the monster's jaws.

"Damn it, damn it, damn it," I muttered, shivering in the cold water. I needed to get the web stuff off of him and get a better look at the threads of his energy. I tried pulling it off with my hands, but the web was thicker and more reluctant to part than the other examples had been. It was as if the stuff had been knotted together, not just spun like spider silk. I'd have to untie it or find a way to cut through it. . . . My mind ground through possibilities for a moment. . . .

Something about knots . . . Then I thought of Ella Graham's feather: She'd said it would help to untie the dead—no, she'd said "unpick" the dead things. She'd lived through the Depression and raised grandkids during the war, and she'd learned frugality the hard way, remaking clothes and salvaging bits and pieces by picking them patiently apart with a bodkin or needle. Maybe I could use the pheasant feather the same way to loosen the knots of the

Sisiutl's snare? Pheasants had one eye on death and one on life, so maybe the feather did have some affinity for the Grey, as Ella had implied. It was nuts but so's the Grey and, when in doubt, crazy sometimes works.

I still had the feather in the pocket of my jacket and I pulled it out. It was a little bent and wet, but it seemed OK. Feeling like an idiot, I held it by the quill and brushed it at the zombie's head.

The Grey web split a little. I brushed more and the web began to loosen and fall away. I could see seams opening up in the fabric of it, like faults or runs in a nylon stocking. I swiped and swabbed until the web was loose. Then I tore the last of it away with my free hand. The dead man's form grew softer and slacker as the web fell away, but it was still knitted together too strongly to pull apart as I had the first time.

Quinton's light wavered. "I think . . ." he started.

A distant swishing sound had started up.

"I think something's coming. . . ."

Hurry, hurry . . . My mind felt jellied by the cold—I needed to finish and get the hell out of the water before I got hypothermia. The feathery end wasn't doing any more work. My heart pounded and, in spite of the cold, I'd begun to sweat.

If there were any gods watching, I hoped they were on my side. Desperate, hoping the picking-apart analogy would keep working, I flipped the feather over and teased the quill over Felix's slumping shape until the tiny ridges on the tip caught on a thin yellow strand of energy. I resisted the urge to panic and dragged it toward me with a steady pull. A visible loop of energy sprang up out of the density of his form and I snatched it on the little finger of my free hand. Then I reeled it in against the growing pressure of the knot inside him.

The strand popped free and I rocked backward as the hot

yellow skein of Felix's trapped life spun out faster than film from a runaway projector. There was an odd shushing sound and the body fell down, boneless and loose.

A flash of white shot from the body and cut the gloom in two.

The swishing sound stopped and something hissed. Then it roared, and the swishing became a hailstorm sound of scales on stone.

I cast one last glance at the rotten body at my knees. Gone, dead, nothing but decaying matter now. Felix no longer inhabited his corpse.

Quinton grabbed my elbow and yanked me to my feet, my knee protesting with a ratcheting sound I felt through my whole body.

"C'mon!" he shouted, dragging me toward the fissure in the wall through which we'd come.

A gigantic head with a pair of horns like a Japanese war mask's thrust from the hole, roaring and flicking a forked tongue as long as my body into the air in front of us. The horrible sound shook through my chest and rattled us both back a few steps as adrenaline lit a fire in my sluggish blood.

"Other side!" I shouted, pulling Quinton at a right angle to the monstrous head that was coming deeper into the room on a neck as thick and shaggy as a hundred-year-old cedar. A jaw full of glittering teeth snapped at the air where we'd been.

We bolted south across the floor, staying out of the deep water to the west. But any door there had been buried in a cascade of cement, and we found ourselves in a dead end.

"There's no way out of here!" Quinton yelled.

"We can't get out until the hole's not full of monster! We just have to get out of its way until the tunnel's empty. Then we can bolt for it," I gasped back, dragging him around the edge of a marble toilet stall.

The hailstorm sound of the creature entering the room petered out and we could hear it thrashing the water near Felix's body. It shouted something and I thought I recognized the sound of Lushootseed, though I didn't know what it had said. We peered out.

At the far end of the room coiled Sisiutl, gleaming in the Grey. In the dark, I judged it about thirty feet long and thicker than the totem pole outside. Its shape flickered and melded from one serpentine thing to the next—Medusa's coils, a dragon, Cerberus with three heads on snakelike necks. . . . Something moved a bit at one end and, with a slithering sound and a splash, a monstrous serpent head reared up and turned our way. I could see the curving shape of its horns and some kind of frilled shape just behind the jaws. The forked tongue that had almost tasted us before shot out and the snake end hissed. Another shifting snake head rose and the whole, huge creature settled into a solidly ophidian form that lay in both realms at once. Then it flipped itself violently into a sort of W shape, and the booming voice shrieked again, coming from the center of the body that now looped toward us like a sidewinder, splashing and hissing through the water at a furious speed.

"Rur! Thief! Ladro! Vohr!" it roared, flickering through its many shapes.

"Light!" I ordered Quinton. "Let's see if we can blind it for a moment."

Quinton snapped on the beam of his flashlight and waved it at the beast. At its center we caught sight of a horrid face with dripping fangs and strands of fleshy hair around a wide mouth that shouted the words as the serpents at each end hissed and spit in rage. The center face yelled as the light caught in its dark-adapted eyes. Two clawed hands pawed at the dazzled eyes and the face screamed a cacophony of languages as we dashed past it.

One of the snake ends whipped after us and I yanked a bit of Grey shield between us, my shoulder protesting the quick movement. The snake head thrust through the shield but let out a sharp hiss and recoiled, shaking as if confused and raising its frilled ruff in a lightning-quick motion that cracked the air with a boom.

The hole lay just past Sisiutl's body. I shoved Quinton ahead of me as the next head came around and snapped at us with a mouth full of needlelike teeth flanked by venom-dripping fangs. I shoved the point of the pheasant feather at it, hoping it would have an effect, but the thing just pulled back, shadows of its varied seemings wavering over its body like a heat mirage for a moment. Then it firmed again to Sisiutl, the head drawing back in confusion. But the human face with its slash of a mouth shouted some more and the two snake heads writhed as the massive body whipped about, trying to track us.

Quinton dove into the hole as I unholstered my pistol. If the feather didn't work, I was willing to try anything. The HK made a hard click as I squeezed on the cocking lever.

As the first of the serpent heads darted in, I fired at its eye. In the speed of the moment, I missed the plunging orb, but the bullet hit the head's nose and the central face shrieked as the whole creature jerked back from us.

I leapt for the crack in the wall and scrambled up, ignoring the complaints of my limbs as Sisiutl screamed and threw itself against the hole in fury, shaking the wall. It appeared I'd done no more than piss it off, but I was still ahead and I ape-scrambled up the tunnel as fast as I could, tearing my shoulders, knees, and gun-filled hand on the rough surfaces of the rift. I heard the hard-rain sound of its scales and the furious hissing of one of the serpent heads as Sisiutl shoved itself back into the tunnel.

"It's on my heels!" I shouted to Quinton, buzzing from the fight-or-flight chemicals flooding my system. "Get out into the alley and hold the grate for me!"

Fangs bit at my boots and I kicked free viciously.

Ahead, Quinton pounded up the metal stairs and through the steel doors.

I flipped out of the tunnel and into the open space at the base of the stairs. I rolled onto my back, bringing my gun up as I tried to gain my feet. A snake head shot out of the hole and I kicked it hard as I got up.

It recoiled only an instant and then whipped forward again and met a volley of lead as I fired at it as fast as I could. Shrieking, it fell back a little, and I jumped and ran up the steps, kicking the doors closed as the bleeding head snapped upward from the pit.

Quinton grabbed my hand and we bolted down the narrow tunnel to the vault beneath the alley. My shoulders throbbed from the effects of recoil and my weak knee dragged me sideways. Quinton reeled me back in and hauled us both forward.

With Quinton holding my hand, I couldn't reload, but I wasn't sure how much good shooting Sisiutl was doing. It seemed to shock it, but it certainly wasn't more than that.

We flung ourselves out of the vault and slammed the grille down over the hole, hearing the rush of the monster behind us. Panic-driven speed pumped heat into my limbs and I ignored the twinges of joints, didn't even notice my soaked clothes as we tore out of the alley and onto the street.

"It's fast," Quinton panted.

"Then run faster!"

We dashed into Pioneer Square and down Yesler. "Stay in the

open," Quinton yelled. "It's keeping to the alleys! If we can force it into the dead end of Post at the Fed Office Building, we might be able to slip it!"

We ran past Post and turned at Western, keeping the tall old brick warehouses between us and Sisiutl. My knee protested every step, but I didn't dare slow or limp and Quinton seemed to be having more trouble than I was, since he kept looking back to keep an eye out for Sisiutl.

I didn't need to: the roaring and hissing of the zeqwa was as loud as traffic to me. I could hear its enraged babble as it pursued us, spitting words in dozens of languages. We had a lead of about a block, since it had had to go several blocks out of the way to stay out of sight while we just ran as straight and hard as we could. The cold air burned my lungs and I could feel the instability of ice forming on the bricks of this stretch of road. Sisiutl had kept to Post, as we'd hoped, but we couldn't know if we'd be able to keep ahead long enough to lose the monster at Marion.

We shot out of the narrow confines of Western at Marion and into the open ground behind the Federal Office Building. We heard Sisiutl's shriek of frustration and the ground shook as it slammed into the building's wall at the end of the cul-de-sac. Quinton's tugging on my wrist didn't let up.

"He'll avoid the open. He'll dive for the sewer."

"He'll be pushed toward the bay," I gasped.

"Right!" Quinton yelled, and jerked me in that direction, up Madison on the other side of the federal block, and then body checked me to the left onto Post. We pounded along for one block before pausing.

"We lose him?" Quinton panted.

I couldn't hear the roaring of Sisiutl's curses so well, but they weren't gone and they seemed to be getting closer under the street. "No," I gasped back.

Quinton nodded and dragged me out of Post Alley and up Spring Street to the door under McCormick and Schmick's side entrance without even checking for observers. He wrenched the faked lock open and shoved me through the door, pausing only long enough to close the door properly behind us before we were pelting down the ghost-thick passage under First Avenue to the last wall at Seneca—the wooden wall between Quinton's lair and the rest of the underground.

Quinton grabbed something from his pocket and pointed it at the wall, which twitched and sagged a little as we dashed closer. Quinton dug his hand into a crack in the wooden structure and heaved his back door open, throwing me through and following just as fast before slamming the door closed again and slapping at a few bolts and switches to secure it.

My knee started to fold and Quinton slipped one arm around my waist, drawing me close as he leaned against the wall and stared at his security monitor.

Both our chests were heaving as we panted for breath, trying to keep our noise low and not alert the monster if it should find the passage. Quinton kept me pulled to his chest and I noticed one or both of us were shaking. I kept my ears cocked and my sight tuned to the Grey—just in case.

But the roaring and multilingual cursing had moved away and was fading toward the waters of Elliot Bay.

"He's not coming," I panted.

"Looks like you're right," Quinton replied, pulling his gaze away from the monitor. He leaned his head back against the wall, his chest still heaving. "I thought we were gonna buy it. Holy crap . . ." He looked back at my face and wrapped both arms around my shoulders like he didn't plan to let go for a long time. "I thought he had you. I thought that thing was going to eat you. You kept pushing me out of the way and I thought you were too worried about saving me to get out of its way."

"You had to save *me* at the end. Let's not get stupid here," I admonished, at least as much to me as to him. I was trembling and it wasn't all from flight adrenaline and imminent chill. Some people get a rush of excitement from surviving a near brush with death. I'd never been one before, but this time I was sweating and restless and throbbing with heat.

Quinton's eyes in the dim safety lights of his refuge looked smoky and hooded as he looked at me, still breathing too fast. "Oh, no. Let's," he said, and brought his mouth hard against mine.

I clutched him and pushed into him, kissing back and feeling the quickening of desire between us and some tiny voice telling me to stop stop stop. . . .

"Stop," I panted, pushing back.

"What?"

I looked him in the eye, terrified I wouldn't see the mate to my own emotion, and tried not to laugh with delight. "I want to be sure this time. . . ."

"I was sure the minute I met you."

Catherine wheels of pink and gold sparks spun off of him, lighting my world with the glow of his affection and desire. I laughed and dropped my mouth back onto his, pulling and shoving at his wet clothes and warm body, wanting him against me and in me and right now, damn it!

We staggered as my knees gave out and tumbled onto the narrow pallet of his bed under the stairs, tearing each other's damp clothes off and scattering the pieces everywhere as we fought our way to bare flesh. We tangled together roughly at first in demanding sexual frenzy, relieved to be alive and frantic to be together. Crying out and laughing ran one into the other as we gentled, finally, into making love, coming to a shattering peak, and falling, finally, against each other, exhausted and wet.

Then we rolled apart and blinked at each other, my sight filled with the afterimages of flashbulbs and fireflies. Before I could get cerebral about it, I stumbled off the bed and grabbed his clothes, throwing them to him. Then I started snatching and donning my own, grinning like a maniac, even as I fought to stay upright on my abused knee.

"Let's do that again. At my place," I said.

Quinton dropped the wet things I'd thrown on the floor and yanked on dry jeans from a pile by the bed. He grabbed me by the shoulders as I went by, a blaze of gold and pink around his sweat-gleaming body.

"What?" he asked, shaking his head, bemused.

I leaned over and kissed him. "I want to take you home and ravish you, idiot."

"When?"

"Now!"

I did not care that my clothes were damp, torn, and dirty, that I ached all over, or that the drive to West Seattle was long enough to restart the chill on my skin. Quinton didn't let me keep the wet things on once we were inside my condo and I heartily approved of his methods of warming me back up. The electricity of our coupling lit my world in giddy swirls of hot pink and gold light until we both curled into my devastated bed, quivering with happy exhaustion that dropped us into deep, contented sleep.

FIFTEEN

I tend to wake up grumpy. I am not a morning person in spite of years of rolling out of bed early to hit the gym or practice hall or to pound out a few miles of calorie-burn on the street before breakfast. Tuesday, I woke up downright effervescent—even if I did have to ice my knee and take pills to relieve the swelling. I'd never "done" bubbly before that I could remember—not since being a little kid bouncing out of bed in anticipation of holidays and Christmas packages—not even with Will. Warm, mellow, glowing, yes, but not, as my uncle put it, "bright eyed and bushy tailed"—which I always thought sounded a lot like a squirrel, and considering my uncle's .22-caliber reaction to squirrels, I found the phrase horrifyingly ironic.

I let Quinton get up at his own speed while I started coffee and took a shower. Chaos had been irascible, dancing around in fury and then throwing herself on the floor like a bratty child pitching a fit. She was bouncing around, trying to get a bite of my bare toes, when Quinton emerged from the bathroom, pulling his shirt on over his shower-wet hair.

"Hey there—" I started, but he put a finger to his lips and then leaned in to whisper in my ear.

"Ignore me."

Puzzled, I bent down to pick up the ferret before she could get too badly underfoot. Chaos bit my thumb. "Ow!" I yelped. "What was that for?"

Chaos made a high-pitched barking sound and fought to escape my hand. Quinton stopped rummaging in his backpack and turned an expression of mixed concern and curiosity on us. I loosened my hold on the ferret a little but didn't let her go, and she settled down a bit, but still wanted out of my hand. I put her down again and she darted for her cage.

I followed and bent down beside the cage to look in at her while Quinton began to walk around the room with some kind of electronic device in his hand.

"Hey, ferret-butt," I cajoled my pet. "What's up with you?"

She poked her head back out of her nest of old sweatshirts and heaved a ferret sigh. I reached out a finger and stroked her ears and she rubbed against my hand, but as soon as I tried to pick her up, she squirmed away.

"What a contrarian you're being today. Are you sick or something? You don't look sick. . . ."

Quinton put his things down and joined me on the floor, peering into the ferret's cage. "How old is she?"

"Six."

"Huh. That's getting kind of old for a ferret. Maybe she needs a checkup."

"She's due for shots in a couple of weeks. If she keeps acting up, I may take her in early," I said. Then I looked him over and asked, "You done with whatever you were up to?"

"Yup. No bugs in here," he answered, keeping his voice low. "There's always a possibility of passive bugging through the phones, tapping at the central station, or using parabolic devices at a distance, but they're a pain, so it looks like Fern's either not too interested in your home life or she's on very short rations. We should check your office, too. Has your alarm called the cell phone since she turned up?"

"Oh, damn it—my cell phone!"

I got up and found my purse and dug for the phone, tossing other things out as I hunted: keys, feather, spare pistol clip, wallet. . . .

Quinton knelt down in front of me and picked up the feather, and then offered it from his kneeling position with teasing reverence. "Your spear, m'lady zombie-slayer."

I laughed and he grinned, encircled instantly in little pink and gold sparks with the feel of champagne bubbles as they crackled through the air. Wow, pink sparks . . . My face felt hot and my fingertips were trembling from the sudden flush of giddiness.

I turned away, putting the feather back in the bag, and tried to resume my hunt for the phone, but Quinton wasn't having it. He stood up behind me and touched my shoulders very lightly.

"Harper. I don't want to make you nervous. Last night was wonderful—well, after the sheer terror—but it doesn't have to mean—"

"Shut up," I suggested. "Don't say it doesn't have to mean anything." I turned around and faced him, standing very close, and the small difference in our height in bare feet let me look hard into his eyes without having to tilt my head down much. "I didn't drag you into my bed just because I was scared or excited about being alive or . . . rebounding or whatever. I like you. I trust you—with my life. And I don't have to lie to you. I love being with someone who *knows*! I think it's better than the sex—which was damned fine."

He started to smile, but it kept on spreading wider until he grinned and laughed and gave me a fast kiss on the lips. I thought my blush would set us both on fire and had to look back down at my purse and make busy to keep from babbling like a fool.

I got the phone out—still sealed in its crushed can. Quinton put his hands over mine, stopping me from unpackaging the phone.

"Hang on. As soon as the battery is back in, the phone can be tracked and used as a bug. Right now, you're the only lead to me and the cell phone is the best lead to you. Fern's friends will definitely be monitoring it for her. For now, let's assume the office is bugged until we can check the phone from someplace other than here."

I bit my lip and looked at him, taking a long, bracing breath before I said, "I think I need to know a little more about Fern Laguire's motives. You've said several things that make me think this is personal between you two."

"Oh, it's personal," he replied, nodding, the colors around him fading down to a constrained amber glow, "in an impersonal sort of way." His tone verged on amused. "We only met a handful of times, but I know her pretty well by observation—better than she does me—and she hates me. I am the huge black blot on Fern's otherwise stellar career. I was on loan from another agency to do some work for Fern's group at the NSA—my previous supervisor wanted to hide the embarrassing evidence of the project I'd been working on once it blew up. I had the right mix of odd skills, so they seconded me to Laguire's group. The NSA's nickname around Fort Meade is 'Never Say Anything.' It's a great place to hide someone with tech skills from prying investigators." Quinton paused and looked around. "This is going to take a while. Let's sit down."

We parked ourselves on the sofa, leaning into opposite corners so we could see each other without one of us having to resort to sitting on my coffee table.

"All right," Quinton resumed. "I ended up at Fort Meade because the guys I had been working for were an embarrassment—it was their project that first got me started looking at the cracks in reality—and the agency wanted to keep it quiet, but I was already starting to think I was in the wrong working world. I'm just not of the mind they are—well, you know that. But working for Fern Laguire was not the best place to nurture a sense of the rightness of big central government and its actions.

"You know about the NSA . . . ?"

I nodded. "Crypto specialists, intelligence gathering by electronic eavesdropping. Supposedly, they don't work on domestic systems or run covert ops."

Quinton snorted. "Yeah, and if you believe that there's a pointy leftover from the World's Fair up in Queen Anne I'd like to sell you. Mathematicians and their algorithms don't care about political boundaries. The crypto-geeks at the server farms of Fort Meade do it because they love the game—the intellectual challenge of breaking the system—and very few of them know the source or final disposition of the intelligence they decode. But I did and so does Fern.

"I had an attack of conscience over it and I wanted out. But there was no way Fern would let me go, because her idea of freedom and mine were not even in the same philosophical universe."

I narrowed my eyes. "You're not going to say they retire people to six-foot dirt apartments, are you? Because I have a hard time buying that."

Quinton shook his head. "No. Fern's not homicidal as far as I know, but retiring from intelligence or any classified service comes with monitors and strings. They don't just let you walk out and go your way and that's what I craved. Fern didn't want to let me go at all and she's very good at finding ways to make people stay. It's a big key to her success within the agency—people work for Fern until they drop. But I left. I didn't say I was going, because I knew how she worked. I just made myself disappear, in spite of their security measures, and they didn't know how. I think they still don't. That alone must just boil Fern's brain, but that I slipped the chain completely is even worse. I proved her fallible. She's never going to forgive me. If she can get me back, then she saves face—which is all-important to Fern at this stage in the game. She's nearing retirement and she has to be totally nonstick armored on her way out the door or she'll get the same treatment she's given plenty of others."

"Ugh," I said with a shudder. "Sounds like she wouldn't mind if you *did* get killed."

Quinton shrugged. "So long as she could show I'd never compromised her, she'd be good with it."

"I wonder if she could be persuaded that she's hunting for a dead man. . . ."

"It's a remote possibility I could switch records with one of the missing undergrounders—I know most of them well enough to get at the right records—but she'd never buy it without a body."

"And you don't really match up to any of the bodies that have turned up, so far."

"True. Nice thought though—never had a woman offer to kill me off before."

"Well . . . they say friends help you move and good friends help you move bodies. Just a different kind of body."

That got a laugh out of him, which pulled a smile from me, in spite of the subject matter. He sobered and looked at me with a tinge of blue in his energy corona.

"Harper, you don't have to be in the crush between me and Fern Laguire. You can roll over on me. I'd only ask that you tell me ahead of time, so I have a head start on her. I can disappear again and she'd leave you alone."

I gave my head an adamant shake. "No way. I'm sick of being left. I'm not throwing you to the dogs like a bone to save my own skin. I wouldn't even if— And I need your help, because I'm not going to abandon the dead, either," I added, letting my eyes turn aside as I felt a hot blush on my cheeks.

"Umm . . . yeah," Quinton said, looking pleased before his expression sobered with the subject. "There's still our three-faced friend in the sewer," he added with a shudder.

"Not to mention Detective Solis—so long as we're on the topic of people of interest."

"Maybe Sistu will eat Fern and we can blame it on a secret government project," Quinton speculated, half-seriously. "The Feds would step in and Solis wouldn't be allowed to pursue the case any further no matter how he felt about it."

"We should be so lucky," I scoffed. "It's not as if we have any control—" I stopped, cut off by an intersecting thought.

"Control of what?" Quinton asked.

I frowned, concentrating, trying to get a hold of the slippery idea that had run through my head. I put up one finger to hold back his questions as I thought. "We postulated a pattern. What if the pattern is determined by a person—not a god masquerading, but an ordinary person and their ordinary drives? Ella Graham said that if the gods were pleased they might send Sistu to help a petitioner hunt. Maybe . . . Qamaits can lend out her pet herself. She's got power over the monster, so why not hand him over to someone who did her a favor? Like . . . getting her out of the construction pit?"

"Then the person who helped her out is still alive."

"And using their monster-on-loan to settle scores. But Sistu needs to eat more frequently than his hunting buddy wants to whack someone, so . . . he grabs a snack and takes it to his lair for later."

"So Felix was a snack, but Jenny or Go-cart were revenge?"

I nodded. "That's what I'm thinking. Separate the zombies from the disappeared, and the ones who were found dead are the key to finding out who's responsible. We're not looking for anything supernatural on that score—just a human with a grudge."

I shuddered and thought about the necessities of the normal world. "This isn't going to fly with Solis. He might buy the idea that someone killed some of the undergrounders, but the chances are good whoever it was has an alibi for at least one of the deaths—he doesn't have to be nearby if Tall Grass was right about Jenny's death. I'm not sure how I'd point the finger, either. Solis is not my biggest fan since the poltergeist business."

"It's more important to get rid of the monster than to lock someone up for it."

I nodded. "We'll have to catch up to whoever it is first since the monster must be hanging around him . . . or her. It won't be easy, since the monster might decide we look like lunch and whoever's directing it might not even know what's going on if they don't speak Lushootseed or whatever the thing speaks. I wish I knew what it was saying last night. . . ."

"What who was saying?"

"Sistu. Didn't you hear it yelling at us?"

"I couldn't make anything out of it. It sounded like screaming or speaking in tongues."

"Many tongues. I think I caught a few words, but the rest was mush. It talks. And it flickers through a whole closetful of shapes as it does. Ella Graham said it was clever and sneaky. Maybe we can slow it down if we can just figure out how to talk to it. . . ."

SIXTEEN

Mara let us in. She nodded to Quinton and gave me a keen look that wasn't a smile but wasn't anything else, either. I didn't know what had brought on this distance—unless she was still upset about Albert—but her invitation inside was distracted and formal.

"Do come in. Ben's upstairs. I'll be keeping Brian busy down here, so he'll not trouble you."

I gazed hard at her, trying to figure out what was wrong, but she'd cloaked herself in deliberate blankness. I glanced deep into the Grey for any sign of Albert—thinking he might be the cause of her coolness—but I could find no sign of him in the house and only the hard, red ball of the trap Mara had wrapped him in the last time, still clinging to the roof under the twisting gold lines of her protective spells.

"Thanks. Mara," I started, but she waved the rest of my words aside.

"Not now, Harper. I've a lot to think on," she said, and hurried off, worrying her bottom lip.

I looked at Quinton and shrugged. We headed for the stairs and up to Ben's office beneath the eaves.

Ben was doodling and drinking tea when we entered the attic. He jumped up from the desk, not quite knocking his head against the low ceiling.

"Oh, hello! Sorry, sorry—kind of jumpy since the Albert incident."

"Why?" I asked. "Has he done something else?"

"No, no, no," Ben babbled. "But I keep thinking he will and I'm a little stir-crazy anyhow. I feel like I'm in Mara's way. I thought I'd rework my lesson plans since we've lost almost a week of classes, but . . . I just can't concentrate on them. Oh, who's this?" he added, finally turning his attention to Quinton.

"This is Quinton. He brought me a . . . an interesting case and we could use your help. It's likely to be dangerous, though."

Ben seemed to perk up. "Is it a Grey thing?"

"Yes. We've been looking into the deaths of some homeless in Pioneer Square—"

"I saw some news articles about that," Ben said.

I nodded. "The ones that said bodies had been found apparently chewed by dogs, right?"

"Yeah. Not dogs, I take it?"

I shook my head and sat down on a clear spot on the office sofa. "Not dogs."

"Tea!" Ben exclaimed.

Quinton and I both stared at him, startled by the outburst.

Ben blinked back. "Sorry. Tea. Would you guys like some? I have a pot up here; I can get more glasses."

I considered saying no, but it was a little chilly in the office and Ben seemed to want to do something. "Tea is great, Ben. We can wait."

"I'll be right back," he said, ducking out and bounding down the steep steps so the stairwell rang behind him.

I tugged at the elastic knee brace under my jeans as Quinton cleared some space beside me. He looked at the spines of the books as he lifted them off the seat. "I can't even read half these titles and it's not just because they're in German and Russian and . . . I don't know what language that is. . . . He's got some really old books here." He had a gleam in his eye as he flipped opened a venerable leather-bound tome stamped in faded gold Cyrillic. "Wow. The publication date on this is 1789. That was a hell of a year."

"Oh?"

"Yeah. The French Revolution started in 1789—among a lot of other events that changed the world." He caught my bemused look. "Hey, I was always good with dates and numbers. Mom was an engineer and Dad was a spy—you pick up skills," he added with a shrug.

"So, the spy thing . . . that's the family business?" I asked.

"Dad's side," he said, putting the book down with care and sitting next to me. "I was kind of my mom's kid and I got into computers and science and math early on because of her—got the nickname because of her, too. I didn't see my dad much, so the spy thing seemed sexy and exciting—which you can't say for engineering—and that's how I ended up working for the government in the first place. I wish I'd stuck to electronics."

The sound of Ben's heavy feet on the stairs cut the conversation short before I could ask, "What nickname?"

It took a bit of faffing about to get everything distributed and settled again—Ben's Russian tea habits being almost as fussy as any formal Brit's—before Quinton and I could get Ben's attention.

I curled my hands around the hot glass in its metal holder and noticed the scabs and scrapes from the previous night's narrow escape. It seemed strangely distant until the memory of fear rushed back in for a moment and made my gut twist. I sipped my tea and caught my breath as Quinton cast a questioning glance my way.

I shook him off with a small, reassuring smile. Ben was watching me, too, but his look was more plainly curious.

"All right. So. These poor homeless folks," he prompted.

"Aside from the dead, there are several missing and they all seem to be victims of the same thing. They're being eaten by a legendary Native American monster and, aside from killing people, it also makes zombies," I said. Ben was capable of rambling for hours, so I figured I'd better nip that tendency in the bud by cutting straight to the bone of the matter.

Ben's face lit up. "Really?" Then he shook himself and his face went white under his dark beard. "Oh my God, that's horrible!"

"There's a lot more to it," I said. "This monster, Sisiutl, seems to be under someone's control—partial control. We need to catch both the monster and the man and get rid of the monster. But we're here because we got up close and personal with Sistu—it's a safer name to use—last night and it seems to talk in a whole glut of languages, bits and pieces all at once. I think we'd be a lot safer if we can talk to it. It's clever enough to pull pranks and make deals to hunt in exchange for food, so if we can talk to it there's always a possibility we can bargain with it—if it doesn't eat us first. It also seems to cast illusions of shape-shifting. I'm not sure what's going on and I'd like to be better equipped the next time we run into it. So I thought we should ask you for any ideas about the nature of the beast."

Ben glowed gold and sparky with intellectual pleasure. "You've both seen it?"

"Not just us. Plenty of people who didn't know what they saw, or who died right afterward," I said.

That made Ben a little grimmer as he asked, "What does it look like? What kind of forms does it throw?"

"It's a two-ended sea serpent—kind of like a hairy snake with a head at each end and a human face in the middle. It's the human face that does the talking. The snake ends just hiss and bite. It shows various forms—I saw Ouroboros, a gorgon, a multiheaded dog with snakelike necks for each head, a dragon, and a kind of snake with hands. Oh, its default form seems to have clawed hands near the human face and horns on the snake heads. And it sometimes acts as a guard to the house of the gods, sometimes helps hunters and warriors, but it's also a bit of a trickster and very, very hungry."

I thought Ben was going to dance with glee, once again caught up in the excitement of his favorite subject. "Let me think, let me think," he muttered, scrabbling in his books and papers. He found a pen and made a bunch of quick notes on the back of a legal pad that was already full of other notes on the pages. "Repetition of the snake theme . . . guardian . . . warrior . . . helper . . . hungry . . . multiheaded . . . Oh, man. It's the universal monster."

"Huh," Quinton and I both said.

"Well, you know your Campbell, right? His ideas about monomyth—universal themes in myth and religion—and universal heroes?"

We both nodded—it's hard to avoid Campbell's *The Hero with a Thousand Faces* in college.

"OK, well . . . he's a bit overblown and people always forget his sources—Joyce, Mann, Frobenius, Spengler—but there is good support for the idea of universal—or at least widespread and recurring—themes in myth. What you've encountered is a great example. The guardian, the serpent god, the helper and slayer of warriors. It comes up again and again. So . . . my guess is that the shapes it shows are the various forms by which it's known in different cultures and it can speak the languages of all of those cultures which call it into being."

Quinton interrupted. "I only saw the one form—the double-ended snake with the head in the middle."

"Oh?" Ben looked puzzled. "Why is that do you think?"

Quinton scoffed. "Because that's the shape I was expecting. Harper is the one who sees magic things. I just see what's there to be seen."

"Did you have any idea what you might see before you encountered it?" Ben asked.

"Yes," Quinton replied. "We'd been told by an old Indian woman what it was and what it looked like."

Ben grinned. "Clearly the monster's appearance fulfills the expectations of the viewer. Of course Harper sees multiple forms—she sees the magic, so she sees it all. Wonderful! I hadn't thought of it."

"Well, it's fine to see it, just not too close," I said. "It's big and it's got lots of teeth in those heads. If we run into it again—and we have to if we're to get rid of it—we need to keep it from eating us before we can send it away. It understands English and speaks a little, but mostly it spews words in dozens of languages at once, which makes it hard to understand."

"I'm sure it would pick just one if you get its attention long enough," Ben suggested.

"That's kind of tricky," I protested. "Its default form seems to be the native legend—the double-ended sea serpent—and that version doesn't speak English. Also, I don't think any of those forms are really native English speakers. Unless it turns out to be Grendel in disguise, too."

Ben shook his head. "No, Grendel isn't that archetype and he would have spoken Old English at best, not modern."

"Well, then . . ."—I hesitated to ask, since I was already in the doghouse with one member of the Danziger family—"would you come with us to talk to it? Assuming we can catch it? We need to figure out where it came from and who controls it. There's also an ogress around somewhere who can call it back to her side, and we'd like to send the whole bunch back to the gods and keep any more homeless from being lunch."

"Well, you can't compel gods or their helpers; you can only argue with them and get them to agree to leave," Ben said. "You'll have to gain the agreement of this ogress to send the monster home after you separate the monster from whoever is currently using its powers."

"We're not sure who controls it," Quinton reminded me, "but we can find out. But we'll have to catch the thing eventually and it's not likely we can just throw a rope around its neck and drag it to the zoo. We may need to persuade it."

"Legends are full of that kind of lawyering—you can't just banish power from the gods and you can't kill gods or their guardians. If it's a clever monster, bargaining will appeal to it," Ben agreed, nodding. "Yes, I'll go. I'd be stupid not to. I've never seen an incorporeal beastie before."

"This thing is not incorporeal," I warned. "It's got real teeth and they chew through real concrete walls. And if anything happens to you on this excursion, Mara will probably kill me."

"She's not like that."

"She seems plenty upset with me at the moment."

"I think she's more upset with herself—we both feel a bit like

Ted Bundy's neighbors. 'He was such a nice ghost, so quiet. . . .' It's unsettling and we both wonder what else we may have missed seeing." Ben raised his eyebrows at me.

I shook my head. "I don't know of anything else. And I only suspected Albert because his behavior didn't add up in my mind. So far, my experience with lively ghosts has been predominantly unpleasant."

"I know. . . ."

"I don't think this monster business is going to be a lot more fun, but it's at least something I don't have to chase on my own. So," I added, standing up, "you guys ready to go catch monsters?"

Ben stood up and put his glass aside. "I don't have anything I'd rather be doing. I'll let Mara know I'm going. I'll meet you in the hall."

Quinton and I nodded and we all trooped down the first flight of stairs. Ben peeled off to find Mara on the second floor while Quinton and I continued to the first.

As we stood in the entry hall, I concentrated on buttoning my coat. "So . . . what about the nickname?" I asked.

"The—? Oh," he said, remembering our interrupted conversation upstairs. "My mother's name is Quinn."

"And you're Quinn's son. Quinn's son becomes Quin*ton*. . . . That's a terrible pun."

"It stuck for a while. But my dad never used it—I don't know if he even knew it existed—and I never used it around my employers. Everyone there called me J.J."

Once again, Ben's appearance was ill—or perhaps well—timed and we dropped the conversation to pile into the Rover and head to Pioneer Square in search of Sisiutl, or his hunting buddy— whichever we got to first.

I let Quinton and Ben out at Second and Cherry so I could scout a parking space Laguire's watchers wouldn't pick up instantly and Ben and Quinton could walk down the Cherry Street side of the Square. I found a space on Western and sat in the truck a few minutes to check my cell phone for the first time in twenty-four hours.

I wasn't surprised to see that the intrusion alarm had signaled my phone about six p.m. on Monday. They'd probably walked into the building and hidden until most of the offices cleared out, and then picked my less-than-stellar locks and been on their way in minutes. I'd have to be very careful what I said in my office for a while. I made note of the other numbers and messages on a pad of paper and shut the phone down again, removing the battery as Quinton had instructed. It was a pain, but I couldn't risk being stalked by Laguire and her minions. With no other way to find me—and through me, Quinton—I hoped they'd keep their eyes on my office and not start prowling around, stirring up trouble.

I walked up into Pioneer Square and found Quinton and Ben standing by the Chief Sealth bust, talking to Fish. I joined the cabal.

"What are you doing out here?" I asked.

"Grandma Ella called. Which she doesn't do. So when she said I should come down here and find you, I figured I'd better . . . come looking for zeqwas." He blushed and the blanket of color around him flashed in swirls of yellow and green—nerves and uncertainty. "I was thinking . . . y'know . . . it's crazy, but . . . there's some power in belief and if . . . someone thinks there might be a monster after them, maybe, in a way, there is. Maybe . . . maybe there are things I could do to help you. With my people down here. I'm a bad Indian but I speak Lushootseed, at least."

I nodded, not sure what to say.

"Fish has been talking to Grandpa Dan and some of the other Native Americans down here," Quinton said. "They don't think we're crazy."

"Grandpa Dan said it was their duty to be attentive—whatever that means," Fish added. "And that we'd be granted the aid of the spirits to stop the killing."

"Someone besides us thinks Sistu is eating people?" I asked.

Quinton replied, "They're not sure of that specifically yet, but they do think there's something magical going on—they're getting superstitious and scared."

"They're not all scared," Fish corrected. "Some are mad. They don't want a monster on the loose. It's a bad sign. They want it to go away. They"—he looked a little embarrassed again—"they said they'll help when the time comes. I don't know what they think they can do. . . ."

"Did any of them have a crow with them?" I asked.

Fish gave a nervous laugh. "There are crows all over around here, with all the garbage from the restaurants. Of course there were crows." The apple green color of his aura got brighter as he got more nervous. I'd have bet money there had been crows—and ravens, too—in the thick of that discussion, listening in like crafty old women and carrying off their information afterward. It appeared that Quinton and I were no longer the only people taking this seriously. I also wondered how a single phone call from Ella Graham had convinced him we weren't nuts and wound his nerves so tightly—he'd been on the verge of rejecting the whole thing by the time we'd dropped him off Monday night.

I smiled at him. "I'm glad you came. Let's go find a monster."

Ben and Fish stood watch while Quinton and I popped in and out of the underground, looking for any sign of Sisiutl. We had no luck. Even in the monster's lair, there was nothing, though there was some sign there might be more zombies somewhere around. Recent casts of the Grey zombie nets and a hand that was still fresh enough to ooze blood made me fear someone else was missing and unable to give up the ghost properly. We came back up into the alley knowing time was against us; Sisiutl was moving.

"It doesn't look like it's abandoned its den," I said as we rejoined Ben and Fish, "but where does something like that hide in broad daylight? Where is it now?"

"I don't know," Quinton replied. "Just guessing, I'd say it's sticking close to its master, so we need to find him."

"Who, what?" Fish asked, looking from one to the other of us.

"It's not down there. We think it's on the move," I explained. "It's been cagey so far, so if it's moving, it's either following its master, or following his orders."

"Master? I'm confused. Qamaits is Sistu's mistress," Fish said.

"I should say we need to find whoever currently has Sistu on loan from Qamaits. We think someone did her a favor and she lent them the monster's aid in hunting—like Grandma Ella said. But so far, I haven't seen any of our likely choices for the role."

"That's kind of unusual," Quinton added. "Most of these guys usually hang out right around here or over in Oxy Park."

We all walked down to Occidental Park. Under the glass picnic house, enjoying the beam of the sun through the panes in the comparative heat of 34 degrees—the warmest day since the storm—we found Zip and Sandy still standing watch over Tall Grass, who was babbling and looking sick by turns.

"Hey," Quinton greeted them. "Have you guys been here all night?"

"Of course not," said Sandy. "Grass didn't want to sleep inside, so we took turns."

Fish muttered something in Lushootseed and Grass jerked his attention to him, letting out a torrent of the language too fast for my uneducated ears to make out as anything but shushes and trills. Fish was taken aback and stared at the older man, crouching down beside him to talk.

We all watched a moment as the two Indians conversed in rapid harmonies of speech.

"I wonder if he knows where it went," Ben said. "That's a pretty intense conversation."

"Where what went?" Sandy asked.

"Um . . . Tanker. Or Lass," I supplied, speaking the first names on my tongue, pretty sure I didn't want to ask Sandy if she'd seen any snake monsters with her zombies.

"Lass took off," Zip said. "Tanker, too."

"Took off for where?" Quinton demanded.

"I dunno. I in't Lass's buddy; dun't go drinkin wid im much. Not like Tandy."

"Hey . . . Do you know if Lass was with Tandy the night Tandy disappeared? Thanksgiving I guess it was," Quinton asked, forcing himself to lower his intensity, which roared around his head in tangerine spikes.

"Sure was. Hit me up for smokes—traded me a swig on t'J.D. Dunno where they got it . . ."

Ben and I didn't know which conversation to watch.

"Did you see them later that night?" Quinton asked.

"Nah. They dun't come by me. I was down to the Union fer some turkey afore, but I's long gone to bed whenever t'ey finished off that bottle."

Quinton shot me a glance. Then he turned back to Zip. "And you don't know where Lass is now?"

"No, I dun't! I said so, din't I?"

"He said he was going to the Showboat," Sandy said. "I don't know why he'd say that, though. They tore it down in '94. But Tanker was taking Bella to the U, so maybe Lass was following them. I can't say I like Lass's behavior lately. He's obsessed with that dog!"

"Showboat?" I wasn't as familiar with the campus as I was with Pioneer Square and some of the neighborhoods.

"Showboat Theater. On Showboat Beach on the south end of the campus," Sandy explained. "It burned in the eighties and they left it for years because of the asbestos. They finally tore it down in 1994."

"Why would Tanker go to a torn-down theater?"

"He didn't go there," Fish said, looking up from his conversation with Tall Grass. "He went to the University dock. Grass says Tanker was going to try to get a job on the research vessel's dock crew. He says Lass and . . . Sistu followed him. Grass's pretty freaked out. He says he saw it following Lass like a dog. . . ."

"Shadow of a dog," Grass corrected. Then he hid his face in his hands and started shaking.

"Oh, shit," Quinton muttered. "It's Lass."

SEVENTEEN

We bundled into the Rover and went after Lass. The three of us who'd seen the bodies had no desire to see another. Ben caught our fear and started blurting nervous questions. I just concentrated on getting us there as fast as possible in the fog that was boiling up from the icy water of the lakes and canal, muttering pleas to whatever gods might bother to listen that we not find another body.

"What's going on?" Ben demanded. "Who are we chasing?"

"Lassiter," I replied, making the connections. "He's one of the homeless guys and the monster is trailing him around like a faithful hound. He also sent Quinton and me to Sistu's lair last night, and neither of us—who spend a ton of time around the Square and thought we knew every inch of it—knew about the back door to the comfort station," I started, reconstructing my thoughts out loud.

"What comfort station?"

"The one under Pioneer Square." I turned a glance at Quinton.

"That's what the revenant on the tour meant—a place with no comfort, between the tides. What are the chances that Lass, who came to you worried about monsters following him in the underground, would know a bolt-hole you didn't know about? The hole was camouflaged and there was no evidence anyone had ever used that bit of the underground as a flop. And if Lass—the paranoid—knew about such a snug little hole, why would he be sleeping in the bricks and risking the wrath of Tanker and Bella—whom he is now chasing?"

"How would he get control of Sisiutl?" Fish asked. "There has to be a gift made, not just a favor."

"A gift? What sort of gift?" I demanded.

"A token from Qamaits to signify his command of— Sistu."

"Well . . . if it's following him like a dog, maybe Qamaits gave him the thing's leash—it must have a leash of some kind; that's how these things work," Ben said.

"Why would he want the stunner if he had the monster's leash?" Quinton asked.

"If he doesn't speak Lushootseed, he might not know what the ogress had given him. He might not understand that Sistu meant him no harm since he wouldn't understand what she told him," Fish said.

Quinton shook his head. "If Lass understands Lushootseed, that's news to me."

"So he wouldn't understand the monster was a gift, not something stalking him."

"Probably not. But the stun stick wouldn't have been much help against that kind of monster. So why did he come to me?"

As we turned in near the oceanography buildings, I made a suggestion. "Given Lassiter's erratic behavior, I'm not sure he knew it wouldn't help, or that he understood how Sistu operated. He might have thought it just ate whoever it wanted but hadn't yet attacked him for some reason."

"He seems to have gotten the hang of it now," Quinton said in disgust. "He's bringing the monster right to Tanker and Bella—he hates them—and you know he'd harm them both if he thought he had the tool to do it."

"I agree. It's the known dead who are Lassiter's victims—those are the ones Sistu killed for him. The others, they were just food for Sistu. The legend says you have to keep the monster fed or the gods get pissed off," I thought aloud.

"It also says you shouldn't abuse their gifts," Fish added as I turned into a parking lot. "Qamaits isn't a goddess, but she still lent out their pet. A couple of days ago I wouldn't have taken this seriously, but . . . I may be changing my mind. These legends are kind of specific. This Lass guy will have to answer to the gods for messing up or there'll be hell to pay."

The area was under construction here and there behind the medical center—the inevitable expansion of a growing campus— and once I'd parked the truck, we had to run around the west end of the South Campus Center buildings to get down to San Juan Road and the oceanography dock. My cranky knee protested the whole way.

There was no sign of Lass or Tanker at the dock. Quinton skidded to a halt beside me in the thickening mist seeping off Portage Bay. "Where is he?" he snapped. "That damned Lass . . ."

"Where did the Showboat used to be?" I asked.

Ben came panting up behind us. "To the west a little . . . that open area we passed . . . near the gate. We'd have seen him as we came down the street."

Fish joined us, looking a little ill from the exertion. He bent and put his hands on his knees to catch his breath.

A dog yelped and growled in the gathering mist.

"That's got to be Bella," Quinton said, pointing east toward the salmon fishery.

I pushed normal aside and bolted forward into the Grey that was for once easier to see as the normal filled with thick white vapor. I ran toward two knots of bright life circling each other in between the hard lines of the fishery's upright towers. Quinton and Ben followed with Fish trailing behind. As I pounded across the ground, I put my hand behind my back to check my pistol and couldn't put my hand on it. It was there—I could feel it pressing into the back of my right hip—but I couldn't grab it and panic spiked through me—it seemed as if I was too far into the Grey to grab hold of something as normal as a gun. If Lass had his stunner I stood a chance—though unpleasant—against him, but I had none against Sisiutl without the gun to drive it back long enough to run like hell, and I didn't think anyone but Quinton had any other weapons on them.

The dog let out a yelp as a white arc dashed between the two bright figures ahead. One of the knots of light spun and began to dart away. The other started to chase it.

In the whispering and muttering of the Grey I heard someone else call out in the normal. "Lass!" Quinton shouted beside me. "Lass, don't!"

I slammed back into the normal with a jolt and skidded to a halt just beyond the spawning pool and a few feet from Lass, who was turning to stare at Quinton and the rest of us. I started to try again for the gun, but Quinton put a light warning hand on my elbow, keeping his eyes on Lass the whole time. He took a slow step toward him while Ben and Fish stumbled to swaying stops nearby. The power grid of the Grey hummed with tension and seemed to color even the normal mist red.

Lass, half crouched and tight as a spring, had whirled to stare at us, his eyes darting over each of us in turn. The little shock stick he held arced and crackled spastically as he twitched with fear and drug withdrawal and squeezed it in his unsteady fist.

"Q-man," he mumbled, as if he'd struggled to put the name and face together.

A cloud of sickly olive green shattered by bolts of orange swirled around him in the Grey, and he seemed to have a pair of dark shadows where Quinton had none. I wondered for an instant about Ben and Fish, behind me, but I didn't turn to look. Lass straightened up a little, his fear easing a touch at seeing a familiar face. "Man . . . I—what you want?"

"Where's Tanker?" Quinton asked.

"I don't know, man! I was—I don't know. That dog. That dog, man, it was trying to kill me! All dogs try to kill me. They hate me! They follow me around!"

Quinton eased closer to Lass, the long sweep of his coat meeting the creeping fog and concealing his movement. "The dog's gone. She won't be bothering you for a while. I don't think you'll need the stunner any more." He held out his hand, still at a distance. "You can give it back to me now."

"No! The other one's still out there!" he shouted, stumbling a step backward in fright. "The big . . . the big thing, the snake-dog! It's gonna eat me, man. It's gonna tear me up like Tandy! Got its eye on me. It's gonna eat me!"

Quinton shifted to the right, herding Lass into a blank wall. "That why you sent me and Harper to its nest? So it would eat someone else instead?"

"I didn't mean to! But, but . . . y'know . . . it's hungry all the time," Lass whined, pinging between terror and self-justification. "Gotta keep it fed. And I thought . . . I thought you knew about the others. It's not my fault! I didn't *make* it eat 'em!"

"I know you didn't, Lass. It's been a good hunting dog—it ate your enemies for you. Why would the dog eat its master?"

"I'm not its master! I don't want it! I didn't know what it was. It ate Tandy! And then it started following me around!"

Lass had run out of room and bumped up against the wall. He jerked to look at what he'd bumped into and Quinton closed the gap between them, snatching the stun stick from his hand and locking his other arm around the quivering junkie's shoulders, pulling him in tight against his side. "It's OK, Lass. I won't let it eat you," he said, crouching down and bringing the other man down with him. "We're much too small for it to see."

Quinton waved the rest of us closer, to make a fence between Lass and any immediate ideas of escape. We gathered around in an arc with the dark wall of the fishery building at Lass's back and the spawning pool at ours.

"These guys will keep the monster away while we talk. Now, how did you end up with the snake-dog?"

Lass shook and huddled under the edge of Quinton's coat, like a child. "The fat old squaw woman—you know, the one in the park who laughs at everyone. She was stuck in the pit, so we went to help her out. Tandy was pretty drunk. He fell in. I got the old lady out and I was going to get Tandy when this big thing came out of the hole and ate him! It bit him in half! I got the hell out of there. I figured the old lady could run away her own self."

"Did the old lady give you anything?"

"Yeah, she was all happy I'd helped her and she said she was going to give me something, but all she gave me was a piece of string. I had it in my pocket for a while, but I threw it away."

"Why?"

"I figured it out," Lass said, squinting as he tapped the side of his head and tried to look clever. "It was the string that tied the snake-dog to me. I wanted to get rid of it, so I threw the string away. Smart, huh?"

"Where did you throw it away?"

"I'm not gonna tell you! You might go get it. . . ."

"I think the old lady probably wants it back, don't you?"

I wished Quinton would hurry—the cold fog was crawling into my clothes and making me shiver. I also didn't much care for Lass and found myself impatient to be done with the creep.

"It's a bad thing!" he insisted. "It's the only thing I had—I ain't got nothing in the world but my clothes, not even family, not even friends—but I didn't want that piece of string. It's bad!"

"I agree. But you don't want it lying around where someone will find it," said Quinton. "If you tell me where you dropped it, I'll take it back to the old woman. OK?"

"You would?"

"Yup."

"In the bricks . . . After Jenny . . . I had to get rid of it! You understand?"

Quinton nodded and began to say, "I understand—"

The spawning pool erupted behind us and we all spun to stare as Sisiutl leapt into the air with a rush of water and a shriek like metal tearing apart. Twisting and flickering through a dozen appearances, it screeched its polyglot language and dove through the air toward us.

Fish shouted in Lushootseed as Lass screamed and jerked out of Quinton's grip, dashing for a hole between the fog-bound buildings. Confused, Sisiutl whipped toward Fish and roared a string of angry Lushootseed. Fish, bug-eyed with terror, stumbled and fell backward, babbling uselessly.

The face in the center looked disgusted and the serpent heads at each end snapped at the air in fury as the creature whipped around to go after Lass.

Ben waved his arms in the air, shouting out words in as many languages as he could, until the zeqwa turned its attention to him, snapping its various jaws near his head. Ben flinched but didn't run, continuing to shout and seeming to demand a response.

At last Sisiutl roared a reply and ceased thrashing the air so violently to concentrate on the man between its two hissing heads. As man and monster spoke in a rattle of Latin and several other languages I could almost catch, Fish crawled to me in a daze. He looked sick and shocked.

"Are you going to be all right?" I whispered.

"Yeah . . . I just . . . I guess I wasn't ready for . . . this," Fish said.

"No one is. I wish I knew what they were saying. . . ."

"Sisiutl says he wants to eat us. Ben is saying we're not to be toyed with. . . . Umm . . . something about powers and the favor of gods I'm not really getting . . ."

I stared at Fish. "How do you know that?"

"I can hear him. It's weird. I know he must be talking to Ben in whatever freaky mix of languages they're using, but I get Lushootseed in my ears. Some of the words are muffled though. Probably concepts my language doesn't have."

Sisiutl rolled like an impatient whale and shrieked.

"He's losing his temper. He's hungry. He says the man with the dog wasn't enough food. He says we're enemies of the man he helps, so he should eat us."

Ben frowned and shook his head, making a flinging gesture with his arms as he replied in fast syllables. Then he yelled in English, "I'm telling him he's free, so he doesn't have to eat us—we're not his master's enemies. He has no master now but Qamaits."

Sisiutl reared up into a U, the snake heads snapping at us and the main face screaming.

"Uh-oh . . . he's going to eat the other guy—Lass. The one who ran off," Fish exclaimed, scrambling to his feet. "Sistu says he will take him to the sacred ground. Oh, shit . . ."

Sisiutl sprang into the air and dove into the fog-shrouded water, leaving a knife cut in the rising mist.

"Sacred ground? What? Where?" I demanded.

"There's a marsh on the other side of the bridge. You know?" Fish burbled, starting to run in the direction Lass has gone. "Foster Island—it used to be sacred to the Duwamish people—they used it as a burial ground! That's where he'll go! He'll herd the man there to kill him! We can't let him do it!"

"It's heading for the arboretum!" Ben exclaimed, starting after Fish.

"We can't catch them on foot," I said, grabbing Ben as Quinton went after Fish. "We'll take the Rover and catch up, but we'll have to be faster than Sistu—Lass has a lead but the monster won't kill him in plain sight if the marsh is close," I thought aloud. "He'll carry him there in one of his webs."

"You can't let him be killed," Fish said. "He has to answer for his crimes. I—I have to believe those legends. I've seen them now! He has to make it good—that's what the legends say!"

"How?" I asked, starting to run for the truck, thankful for the brace on my knee that kept it from collapsing, and hauling Fish along with me. "The cops won't believe it."

"Not them. The sky gods! He used their gift to kill other

men—it's evil! He has to apologize, make good, or they'll unleash the storms."

"Storms?" I shouted, incredulous.

"The winds, the rain," Fish panted as he ran. "These gods . . . drowned villages for less . . . in the days of the People. If their . . . monster exists . . . the gods must, too. I told you—there will be hell to pay . . . if this man doesn't . . . apologize. Dead or alive."

EIGHTEEN

We caught sight of Lass running at the end of the bridge before he bolted down the stairs to the greenbelt that ran along the canal edge to McCurdy Park. Sisiutl leapt from the water and looped across the ground like a giant sidewinder. I turned sharply onto the grass and rammed the front of the truck into Sisiutl's side. The monster whipped around to glare at me with all its eyes, setting one head to snap at the Rover's headlights, ripping into the metal around them. The monstrous serpent bit and struck at the truck repeatedly, gouging chunks from the steel body, shrieking in a chorus of languages as Lass dashed farther away.

Roaring when it noticed its prey escaping, Sisiutl lashed one last, hard time at the truck—denting the hood and rocking it on its tires—and bolted back into the water. I turned the truck and gunned its engine, jolting across the grass and into the parking lot beside MOHAI—the Museum of History and Industry—that lay next to the park and the pontoon bridges through the marsh that linked Marsh and Foster Islands to the arboretum beyond.

I left the scarred Rover parked awkwardly at the edge of the fog-filled lot, as close to the footbridge as I could. We all spilled out and started for the bridge, hoping to catch Lass before he entered the marsh, but we were not as fast as the terror-driven speed of his flight and he slipped through ahead of us, making no more sound but the panting of his breath and the slap of his broken-down shoes on the wet boards. He disappeared into the grasping mist, pink tinged as swift winter sunset pierced the clouds.

We pounded behind him onto the bobbing planks of the bridge to Marsh Island. We plunged into the tunnel of fog, stumbling on the uneven, wet ground of the marsh trail in the eye-dazzle of the sunset-colored murk.

Cold, wet mud sucked at my boots where the cinder trail had been washed partially away by the winter storms. The noise of Lass floundering through the marsh, startling animals from the reeds ahead, led us forward. Cattails and knife-edged grasses rattled like bones and slashed at us as we passed. The mist muttered with the voices of water and lost souls. Behind me I heard a splash and a cry.

I spun back, finding Quinton and Fish just a handbreadth away, half obscured in the fog. We'd stumbled right to the very edge of the island's ragged, flooded shore without knowing it. Ben was partially in the lily-choked water, clawing at the muddy trail.

"Help," he gasped, his teeth already chattering from the cold.

Quinton threw himself down and caught Ben's hands. Fish and I started to anchor him and pull Ben up when the water of the lake heaved and broke over us.

A cloud of hidden birds startled into doomed flight as Sisiutl launched from the water with a Fury's scream. Its rush ripped the fog aside, showing a clearing where the trail opened into a lakeside viewpoint. Lass was a dark shadow on the far side and Sisiutl crossed the clearing in a handful of sidewinder bounds, its heads snapping at the man who had so recently controlled him. Lass snatched up a branch thrown onto the swampy shore by the storms and batted at Sisiutl.

We yanked Ben out of the mud and I darted toward the monster as soon as my hands were free. I grabbed my pistol, taking care to keep the lethal muzzle pointed away from Lass as I aimed at the zeqwa. I yelled at it and fired at the first snake head I got in my sights.

Sisiutl shrieked and whipped one head to bite at me. I ducked, sidestepping into muddy water to the knees.

Ben dashed past me, waving and shouting, "No, no!" before relapsing into a blur of languages that sang in the double mist of Grey and normal in raucous raven cries. Ghosts circled and gibbered around the clearing in some macabre dance of death as the fog drew in close again. The remaining three of us surged closer to Ben, but were still a length behind in the darkening haze.

One gigantic serpent head cut through the mist, jaws agape, and snapped down into the distance, bringing a short scream from Lass. Another reared closer, hissing in anger. Ben's dark hair showed against the pale fog and the head darted for it, the maw opening to strike.

"Ben, down!" I yelled, hearing the echo of my cry from Quinton and Fish.

The booming voice of Sisiutl shook the marshy ground and the gust of its breath opened a window in the fog as Ben tried to duck away. The teeth snapped onto Ben's side. I fired into Sisiutl's grinning middle face as Quinton darted forward and shoved the arcing stun stick against the nearest bit of the monster's body.

Sisiutl screamed and hissed, jerking sideways and dropping

Ben into the muck with a wrenching flick of one head. I corrected my aim and kept shooting.

Fish yelled at the zeqwa, darting back and forth in frustration and fear.

The other head rose into the thinner fog, Lass's form writhing in its mouth.

"Put him down! Fish, tell him to put the man down!" I shouted. "He has to answer to your gods, remember?"

Fish bellowed the words in Lushootseed. The far serpent head shook its prize like a dog with a rat, and the horrible face in the middle, its catfish barbels dripping water and blood, roared a defiant reply.

Fish cried back, pounding the ground with his hands, nearly spitting with rage and fear. The spirits of the island rose into the air at his pounding and keened silvery shards of recrimination.

I let off my last shot and Quinton jabbed the shock stick one more time into the lurking serpent face that hung over us.

Sisiutl screeched and flung Lass down nearby. Then it dove back into the brackish water. A wake of bubbles moved fast and straight toward the canal and we were alone with the ghosts.

Fish swore and threw himself on Ben—lying still and quiet— feeling for a pulse and pressing on the bright red wound that covered his side and shoulder. "Oh shit, oh no," he muttered, and began ripping at Ben's clothes. "Go look at the other one!" he ordered. "I'm going to work on Ben. And call the medics!"

I stumbled to my aching knees beside Lass, but I didn't need to touch him; his eyes were already dim and glazing as his breath dribbled out in a long, slow sigh. Sisiutl had snatched gullies in his flesh, leaving bone and muscle exposed and wet with gushing blood. I could see his spirit loosening from his mangled body with no hope to stop it.

The shades that roamed the island circled us in the fog, whispering and crying, teasing the tenuous threads to snap and dissipate into the pulsing swirl of the Grey. "Oh, no, you don't," I muttered.

Quinton caught my arm as I started to lean forward and reach for the tangle of energy that was slowly rising out of the shell of flesh. "What are you doing?"

"I have to catch him. He has to fix this—remember what Fish said about there being hell to pay? Lass has an appointment with some gods, and I'm not letting him duck out just because he's dead. You need to call 911 for Ben. There's nothing else to do for Lass."

My hands closed on the burning cold of Lass's soul.

NINETEEN

I'd never tried to hold on to a knot of Grey energy before. I'd always let them fall from my hands and ravel away, being more interested in breaking them apart than holding them together, until now. My fingers hooked into the knot of brilliant yellow fire that broke from Lass's body and sharp shocks racked my frame, shaking grunts of pain from my mouth and keeping me swaying on my knees.

Outside of his body, his remembered shape formed in my grip, and Lass glowered at me and tried to twist away. I clutched him hard. His mouth began to move—

A noise like a train wreck wiped out all other sound and rocked me back onto my heels. Sisiutl's screech of defiance rose on a black plume of smoke from where my Rover had been—the pissed-off monster had taken out my truck. Quinton, holding an unfamiliar cell phone, shot a look toward the parking lot and then back to me.

"Harper?"

Shuddering from the contact, I fought to my feet, never

letting Lass's specter go. "It's going to be a long walk home with this bastard."

Quinton peered at what must have been empty mist between my hands to him. "What . . . ?"

"It's Lass—the incorporeal part, at least," I growled from the flashing heat/cold its touch wrought on my bones. "I wish I had a bottle to put him in. . . ."

Nearby, Fish was struggling with Ben, making pads of fabric and strapping them over the bleeding wounds on his side. "One of you call 911, damn it! I don't want this guy back on my table tomorrow!"

"Already done," Quinton said. Time had passed without my notice. "We lost Lass."

I glared at him before I realized he was talking to Fish.

In the murky distance, sirens wailed toward us. I stumbled a few steps to where Fish was working, shirtless in the cold. "How bad?" I asked.

"Bad," he snapped, tying off another strip of fabric from what had been his shirt. "We might get lucky—his body temp was already down and heading for hypothermia from the dunking so he's not bleeding as fast as he should be, but he's shocky and he could collapse. I hope I remember how to save a life instead of studying the remains of one. . . ."

I backed away, giving a speculative look at the struggling ghost in my hands. If Albert could do it . . .

"Don't," Quinton said, putting his hand on my shoulder.

"What?"

"I can see you thinking it. Don't try to save Ben by putting Lass in his body. Even if it worked, it would be wrong."

Carlos's words to the same effect echoed in my head and I found the irony painful.

"I can't keep holding on," I said. "He's . . . slippery."

"You could let go. . . ."

"No! There's something undone here, and Lass is the one who has to do it—to put it right." I shuddered, hating the idea that had come into my mind. "I'll have to hold him myself."

The sirens were closer and distant strobes of red and blue bounced off the fog. Time was running out.

"Quinton," I said, catching his eye as he tried to watch everything. "I'll have to be a little . . . thinner. I don't want the medics to see me do this."

Quinton was a little confused. "Do what?"

"Take this . . . inside," I said, shaking the protesting ghost of Lass.

"No! Harper—"

"Only choice left. Keep an eye out," I added, taking the wet pheasant feather from my bag and sliding into the Grey with the fingers of one hand twined in the knotted energy remains of Lass.

The shape of the dead man grew more solid as I sank deeper into the Grey until the silvered mist gave way to the burning black and colored light of the grid. Lass was a blazing gold wire frame of a man in my grip, twisting and writhing and more immediate than the merely bright knots that were Quinton and Fish . . . and the dimming skein of Ben. Wygan had stuck a bit of Grey into me once. Now I'd have to see if I could do it myself and hope it wasn't so permanent this time.

I pulled the living fire of Lass's ghost into a tight ball as it fought and twisted to escape. Then I stroked the feather over my own face and chest, feeling my shape loosen as the grid thrummed with fury and the screams of something in the grip of terror.

Time tilted and spread in a pool of mercury and rust. Heavy in the slowing of time, I pressed the harsh light that was Lass against my chest, pushing it deeper with the feather and my hands until I felt something crack and yield. We floated half incorporated, half apart, and mad with excess of life and death until the pain drew a whimper from my throat and then flared up in a blaze of agony as my own shape closed around the bindle of the dead man's energy.

I reeled back to the normal, panting and crying with the pangs of Lass's dying ripping through me. Quinton caught me but only barely in my still-thin state. I sucked breath in between my teeth, gritting them against the slashing agony of the dead man's presence.

"Harper . . . ? Are you all right?" Quinton asked, his face creased with fear, the Grey swirling around him in swathes of anxious green and orange.

I shook my head, not trusting my voice to remain steady, not to rise to a scream. The flashing lights of the Medic One unit were static near the smoking spire that rose from the Rover and the sirens had stopped. I could barely hear the splashing of feet through the mud above the screeching feedback whine of the Grey in my head as the paramedics headed toward us. I staggered toward Ben and Fish who knelt beside him, shaking his head.

He looked up. "What have we done? What happened? I don't know what to tell them. 'A monster came out of the marsh and killed them'?"

"Ben's . . . dead?" I ground out, feeling my head spin and my guts drop in horror. The worlds shook me between them and I felt like a banner torn by the wind.

Fish shook his head. "Not yet. But Sisiutl—and that man. My God . . . What did we do?" Then he glared at me. "What did *you* do? This is because of you."

I shook my head. "No. Sisiutl—"

"It's a legend! It's a story, like Qamaits and Tsonoqua bringing nightmares and eating children! It doesn't exist!" He clasped his head in his hands as if it was going to explode while he groped for sanity in the face of what he'd seen. "It can't! Oh, God, it can't! This can't be happening!"

Lass tore at me and screamed in my head and I tottered, trying to keep my feet but falling to my knees beside Fish. I grabbed the babbling man by the shoulders, partially just to steady myself, and shook him, stuffing down the shrieks of Lass's fury and my pain. "Then," I gulped, choking out each word, "blame . . . me."

Fish's eyes went wide in horror as he stared at me, as if I, too, were a nightmare. His lips trembled to form words, but they didn't come out.

"It's . . . all me," I ordered, and Fish nodded stiffly, shaking.

I tried to turn, but weakness dragged at me as the raging torment of Lass imprisoned in my head and body tore through me, blinding me with red veils of agony, so that I didn't know where Quinton was—where anyone or anything was.

"You have to go," I gasped, hoping Quinton was still nearby. "Don't let them get you."

I didn't see him beside me or feel his touch through Lass's stabbing and slashing inside, but I could hear Quinton say, "You're out of your mind."

"Yes," I started. Then the pain broke me and I screamed, falling into the bleeding blackness between the grid and down, shrieking, to oblivion.

TWENTY

Swimming in the dark and the residual pain with Lass half heartedly cursing me made the bed very uncomfortable. I didn't like the bed: it had too many pillows and it smelled of too much bleach and something metallic. A discomfiting languor had fallen on both of us—Lass and me—and I felt I would never surface from the wreck of sleep. It was the way my fingers tingled and burned that got me to open my eyes.

The room was a soft mint green and my heart jumped with fear. I remembered the room. The last time I'd been in such a room I'd just finished being dead. I jerked up—or, rather, I didn't, as my left arm twisted and yanked me to a stop with a yelp. Someone's hands pressed against my right shoulder.

"Shhh . . . Don't jump around like that. You'll hurt yourself."

That was Quinton's voice. I blinked grit and gummy tears from my eyes and turned my head toward him. With no hat or coat and his long hair brushed down around his shoulders, he didn't look himself. A battered and jury-rigged palmtop computer sat on the side table between us, and he put a stylus down on top of it as he leaned toward me.

He gave me a thin smile. "Hi."

I tried to bring my hands together to rub my tingling fingers, but the left one didn't move more than an inch and that with a sudden stop and a steely clank. The right had an IV needle in the back and a patch of tape holding the feed line in place. I rattled the other hand again, still a bit disoriented. This was Harborview . . . wasn't it? A hospital bed . . . So why couldn't I move? I hadn't broken anything. . . .

"They handcuffed you to the bed," Quinton explained. "The cops are a bit upset about Ben and . . . the other guy, and Fish wasn't making a lot of sense. Detective Solis just thought it was better to hang onto you as a material witness—or a suspect— until he knew what happened."

"What—" The sound that came out of my mouth didn't qualify as speech. I had to swallow and try again. "What are you doing here?"

"I said I'd keep an eye on you, didn't I? So I am. You were a little scary there before you passed out, but once you were unconscious you looked normal, so the medics weren't freaked out by that. They weren't happy though—you give really strange vital signs. I don't know what's up with Ben yet. He was in surgery earlier and I've been—"

The room door swung open and admitted Solis, cloaked in a violent boil of red and orange. He glowered at us and walked to the other side of the bed to do it up close. He shot a sharp glance at Quinton.

"You can go, Mr. Lassiter," Solis said.

Quinton looked at me, a line forming between his eyebrows. I rolled my eyes back to Solis. "I prefer he stay," I replied, fighting the feel of slipping deeper into the Grey as other words tried to push into my mouth.

The detective's lips tightened in a hard line. Solis simmered but finally shrugged ungraciously. "As you like. Residue on your hands shows you have recently fired a gun. Multiple shots. At whom were you shooting?" he demanded.

"At whom do you imagine?" I asked. I didn't mean to be flippant, it just came out on the drift of whatever drugs the hospital had given me. Reality seemed terrifyingly remote, especially with Lass struggling inside my head. "Has someone been shot?"

Solis's expression was volcanic. "No. But shots were fired and one man is dead, another critically injured. Previous bodies in the historic district are dead of similar wounds, and you at the scene of the last three—imagined I didn't spot you? Do I care that they are not shot? No! I care that this coincidence cannot possibly *be* a coincidence. There is a linking cause and you know what it is. Of this I am sure."

"What . . . did Reuben Fishkiller tell you?" I asked, fighting Lass who screamed in my head about dogs and snakes and monsters. "I only remember something big . . . from the fog . . . and trying to drive it away."

"Mr. Fishkiller says"—Solis paused to snort in derision—"'a monster attacked you all. Throughout this investigation I hear 'a monster came from the sewer.' Now it's a monster from the fog.'"

I shrugged, one-sided, tilting my head and raising my eyebrows. "That's what it was!" Lass blurted through me. I pushed him back down, feeling sweat start on my face. "But maybe . . . a dog?" I added. "Or a bear? A bear ran amok in the University District last year. . . ."

Solis snorted. "Where is the body if you shot it? Why is it that where your cases touch mine, hell breaks loose and the mysterious becomes common?"

I shrugged, choking Lass's shrieks of terror.

"Bad karma," Quinton suggested.

Solis retrained his gimlet stare on Quinton. "Is that your explanation, Mr. Lassiter?"

Quinton shrugged also. "Don't know. Maybe it's just that Ms. Blaine attracts strange things."

Solis nodded and looked sour. "Indeed. You were there? You saw this monster from the fog?"

Quinton shook his head. "No."

"What did you see? You were there when the Medic One unit arrived."

"Nothing—there was nothing to see."

Solis shook his head in disgust. "Why were you all in the marsh to begin with?"

"My fault," I croaked. "Following . . ." I cast a look at Quinton and hoped I was guessing right—and could keep Lass quiet long enough to finish. "Purlis."

"Who is Purlis?" Solis snapped.

"The dead man. I think," I added. "Identity was clouded. The link you wanted . . . may have been him."

Solis calmed and the fire that ringed him banked to a tight, hot gleam. "Clouded . . . You'll say he was part of an investigation, no doubt."

"A tangent. Mucking in your sandbox, Solis. Sorry."

"What do you know about him? How did he connect to this?"

I felt exhausted from my aches, from restraining the dead man raging in my head, and from trying to keep myself in the normal. "Present at the crimes. Ran when asked about them. No more than that."

"No background?"

I shook my head; sweat stung my eyes. "Broken, blocked. Government-sealed files. Why I wanted to talk to him."

Solis grunted to himself, the colors around him shifting more to yellow and away from furious red. "I am to turn this case over to a federal officer," he said, as if to himself. "Classified. None of Homicide's business."

I wanted to tell him to leave me alone if that was the case, but I kept my mouth shut.

"I wish I knew . . ." he muttered, and fell silent for a long moment.

"Am I under arrest?" I asked at last.

He had seemed distracted but snapped back to a ferocious focus on me as he answered. "Not yet." He leaned over and unlocked the cuff from my wrist and the bed. Then he straightened again. "But if Benjamin Danziger dies, it's you I will come for first—Federals or no." He looked at each of us, his eyes narrowed. He saw something that satisfied his scrutiny and left the room without another word, tucking the handcuffs into his coat pocket as he went.

I slumped into the bed, feeling Lass fall back down from his fighting and clawing now that there was no one to cry to. The Grey was thicker and more present than usual and I hoped Lass was as exhausted as I. I glanced at Quinton.

"You changed files?" I whispered.

Quinton watched Solis leave. "Yes. If they check, it's officially J.J. Purlis who's dead. I hope Fern will let it go, not try to convince someone I'm still out here. It's the easy way out for her and once she's retired, she may not care, so long as I never turn up to embarrass her. And I don't plan to." He looked at me and frowned. "You look horrible."

"Thank you. Lass . . . fights."

"It's bad, isn't it?"

I nodded. "The sooner I'm rid of him, the better."

"We have to get out of here. They didn't know what was wrong with you, so they said shock. I think you can check yourself out, now that Solis has removed the handcuffs."

I let Quinton help me get up and get dressed. He pressed a kiss against my temple as I leaned on him. I was tired and rubber-legged, even as we crept down to Critical Care to check on Ben. It wouldn't matter to me if Solis could hang me on a felony murder hook; if Ben died it would be my fault and I'd wish I was already dead.

We came out of the elevator and headed for CCU. I stopped cold at the sight of a figure in a black coat swishing into the CCU nurses' station. I caught Quinton's arm and pulled him back behind the corner to listen out of sight.

"Yes, dear. Has Detective Solis come down to look in on Mr. Danziger?"

"Naturally, it's Laguire who's stepping on Solis's toes," I muttered. I couldn't hear the nurse's reply as more than a mumble, but I'd recognized the coat's owner, even from the back. Quinton's face went stiff and white at the sound of Laguire's voice.

"Really? Well, thank you, dear. I'll look for him upstairs. And I understand the morgue is also in this building . . . ?"

"Always tasteful, Fern," Quinton muttered. "The coroner's fingerprint check sent up a flare. Don't know why I thought she'd be slower off the mark."

"She wants to see your supposed corpse," I hissed.

"She won't recognize it, since she hasn't seen me in years. It's not a great patch—it may not hold—but for now, the file swap will keep her off me and might convince her bosses to consider me dead. They'll recall her to Fort Meade for now whether she likes it or not. Fern may not buy it, but she can't argue that the body doesn't line up with the file info—Lass was actually a decent match, once they scrub off the filth. She couldn't tell us apart if I walked up and kissed her."

"Kiss that icicle and all bets are off." A shudder of the ghost thrashing ripped across my frame and almost brought me to my knees. I guessed Lass didn't like being a decoy. I could feel him trying to crack me open and escape and I didn't think I'd enjoy the process if he did. I gasped from the twisting pain. "We need to get out of here and get rid of Lass."

TWENTY-ONE

We evaded Laguire and escaped from the hospital to a taxi that took us to my condo in West Seattle. The temperature was nearly normal for Seattle in winter, and it wasn't until we were outside I realized it was Wednesday—I'd been in the hospital overnight. Laguire hadn't been as fast to respond as I'd thought.

At the condo, the ferret huddled in her nest and refused to have anything to do with me, twitching her head and backing away as if I smelled bad when I offered her a hand. Couldn't blame her—me smelling of ghosts and monsters, carrying an angry spirit that lashed at me and screamed continually. I had to let Quinton take care of her while I took a shower. Chaos didn't seem to mind that—being fond of him and his many interesting pockets.

Once I was out of the shower, Quinton tried to put me back to bed.

"You need some rest."

"Not as much as I need to get rid of Lass," I countered.

He made a face. "You don't look good. You shake, you twitch . . . and you're not too solid all the time."

"All the more reason to get this ghost out. We need to find the string Lass mentioned—the leash—and take her pet back to Qamaits."

"How do you expect to find one piece of string in Pioneer Square—whatever it looks like?"

"Lass will help—if he knows what's good for him." Lass writhed and kicked, sending pains through my legs and shouting obscenities in my head.

"You can't rest even until it's dark? I could go to the Women in Black vigil and come back for you."

"There's no way I could rest. Not without drugs—and anything strong enough to knock Lass out will take me down for another day." Lass didn't seem to mind that idea, cooling his ire for a moment in contemplation of a fix. "Besides, if the undergrounders are at the memorial and Solis and the Feds are busy at the hospital, they won't be in our way in Pioneer Square. If I can find the leash, I think I can control Sisiutl and put paid to this whole sorry mess." The boiling fury inside me shrieked and struck in terror at the thought. I stumbled and had to sit down. I pretended it was just to put on dry shoes.

Quinton looked resigned and rolled his eyes in mock horror. "Rosa's going to kill me for missing the vigil."

"She can't kill you—you're already dead," I teased, but it didn't come out too well as my voice broke in the middle and I barely restrained Lass's epithets against Quinton.

"Behave," I muttered. "I can find other places to put you and they won't be as pleasant. Cooperate and you get to go. Mess this up and we'll both be in hell for eternity."

The raging thing settled down to a mutter of bitter words and the sensation of being dissolved by acid.

Quinton frowned at me. "What?"

"Talking to Lass," I growled. I checked my bag for the pheasant feather and found it looking ratty but intact.

"You think that's still useful? It looks pretty sad," Quinton said.

"Don't know. Better to have it, just in case . . ." My limbs burned and my guts felt like I'd been punched repeatedly in the stomach. "Quinton, can you drive?"

He blinked, frowning. "Sure. Why?"

"I'm not sure I can."

"Drive what? The Rover—"

I cursed the air indigo as I recalled that my truck was a smoking ruin in the MOHAI parking lot.

I wound down in a minute. "Are you sure it's wrecked?" I asked, foolishly hoping.

"Yeah. It was . . . flat in the middle and pretty crispy. Sisiutl left some nice tooth marks in it, too."

"Terrific," I muttered, hearing Lass's malicious laugh in my head. As living pond scum, he'd been creepy; as a dead passenger riding in my skull, he was a real bastard.

Both the bus and borrowing my neighbor's car sounded like bad ideas in my current, twitchy condition. I wasn't thrilled with the expense of a cab, but it seemed the only reasonable option and it got us back to Pioneer Square with minimal fuss, though the cabby shot disturbed glances at me the whole way. I was sure he'd seen me flicker.

We went to my office building and Quinton stayed downstairs, watching, while I went upstairs to find some rounds for my pistol and reload the magazines. Even with Laguire distracted, we couldn't assume her friends weren't still listening and a misplaced voice would destroy Quinton's cover among the dead. We'd have to sweep for bugs and clear the place, but it would have to wait until Fern Laguire was out of town and we were out of monsters.

We started the search near Sisiutl's lair—the alley being so overlooked we figured to get in and out without being observed. The snow and ice that had accumulated in the sun-deprived alley was still drifted in the shadows, in spite of the temperature's rise toward forty. It certainly wasn't that warm in the tunnel.

Quinton had to help me down, but once I was at the bottom of the stairs, I let the normal slip away and looked for any hot shape of magic that might be the monster's leash. I saw nothing that seemed right. I also didn't see Sisiutl.

"C'mon, Lass, where did you drop it?" I asked.

"Not here!" he shrieked in my head, bashing himself around my head in panic. "The bricks! Get out, get out, get out, get out!"

"If you're lying I'll feed you to it."

"No! No, no!" He was shaking so hard I shook, too, and his dismay drove me back out into the cold gloom of the alley.

Quinton lowered the grate behind me, raising querying eyebrows.

I shook my head, wobbling a little and catching myself on the nearest icy wall. "He says the bricks."

"Which part? Occidental's three blocks long there and it's two blocks wide—that's six blocks, and most of it's exposed at this time of day. And you're barely staying on your feet."

I ignored the last and tried to rouse Lass to answer, but he kept his mouth shut for once in a smug silence. I damned his contrary paranoia in harsh whispers and got nothing from him but snorts and giggles. He was enjoying making me scrounge for it—petty revenge for my threats, I assumed; for holding him to earth and the obligation he'd incurred. Fine. I could out-stubborn a junkie's ghost any day—I hoped.

I walked out of the alley and around to Pioneer Square's chilly wooden benches in front of the Underground Tour and the neighboring bars. We were passed by a flock of tour guests following Rick, the guide, out to the totem pole. Zip was chatting and smoking with Blue Jay and they waved to us, listing from a few early beers.

I sat on a bench and tried to think. It was easier with Lass being stubbornly silent, but the stinging pressure of his presence made my thoughts shatter and fall away. I tried thinking aloud.

"The bricks. It wouldn't be the First Avenue side—that lets out the whole three blocks there. There's no access to the underground at the park end except through the arcade, and that's public and well-locked at night. Not Oxy Park, then."

"Two blocks left."

"Lass said . . . he threw the leash away after what happened to Jenny. We found Lass in the segment under the Cadillac Hotel block when we found Tall Grass down there a couple of days ago. That's when Lass sent us to Sistu's lair under . . . here. It's the same place we met Grass and Jenny and the place where Lass had a run-in with Tanker and Bella. He said he lived there. . . ."

"What if it's the other block?"

"Burn that bridge when we come to it."

We stood up and headed for the bricks, my knees stiff from the cold and a sudden tremor from Lass. He hadn't thrashed when I'd gone down to the mouth of Sisiutl's cave, but now he was flipping out. His anxiety was like a dowsing rod. I hoped I could use that to my advantage while I searched the bricks. The time of day might make it difficult to get in and out and I dreaded the

sensations that might come in such a haunted place with my uncanny passenger, but I wanted this over with, and waiting would
make it worse, not better.

As we walked—I shuffled, really—it seemed the area was less
trafficked than usual. The homeless and undergrounders were
fewer—attending the vigil, I supposed—in spite of the warming
weather. Neither had the regular pedestrians yet returned like swal-
lows, still driven off by the chill of the salt-laden wind that came
up the streets from Elliot Bay. Yet as we went along, a small group
of Indians—normal and Grey—and the shadows of animals began to follow us, emerging from the underground, from alleys and
doorways, the animals morphing from trees and cloud shadow. A
few real birds joined the flight above us and a stray dog trailed well
behind, curious but wary.

Grandpa Dan was at the head of this bizarre procession, seeming to draw them forth—real and spirit—dancing and making
curious, graceful motions with his old, gnarled hands. He'd said
they'd come if there was a need, and I guessed there must have
been one. Whatever brought the Indians and their spirit compan-
ions, I was glad to have them nearby.

The Klondike Gold Rush park's doors were closed, though
a sign said they were open for business. The cold kept the rang-
ers and their visitors inside, and we had no difficulty in slipping
down into the bricks, leaving our odd entourage behind.

Down below the sidewalk, pain blossomed; in the sea of ghosts,
Lass seemed to expand inside me, pressing unbearably on every
joint and organ. I gulped air, swallowing the silvered mist of the
Grey and sweating in the cold.

I let myself drop deep into the Grey, to the point of the grid.
Searing lines shot off in hard geometric shapes and sudden ba-
roque curlicues that flung energy through the invisible world like

catapults. Quinton grabbed my hand; his grip felt remote and thready like a handful of empty plush, but it seemed to hold me in my own shape, rather than spinning out into the blackness of the grid in a million burning strands. He turned on his pocket flashlight whose beam looked like smoke on water. We went forward by inches as I looked for something that didn't belong—a line too hot, disconnected, wild among the busy conduits of the Grey's power lines. Lass kicked and writhed, making me jerk in Quinton's grasp.

We rounded the first corner, coming to the alley colonnade. I turned into it. Lass settled and sighed. I turned back out, toward the distant corner where we'd first seen Tall Grass and Jenny Nin sitting in the light of a small fire with Grandpa Dan and his shadowy wings. Lass moaned and twisted, clawing at my back, trying to escape. I shuddered and took another step and another. Each footstep was a struggle against the unwilling ghost.

Progress slowed more the farther we all moved into the darkness under the street and Lass became increasingly hysterical, shrieking and throwing himself against me. I stumbled over nothing time and again, forced to stop and hold on to a bit of wall in order to look around, searching for the leash, feeling ice-cold stone I couldn't see beneath my hands.

Down the farthest corridor—where Lass had hidden while Grass tried to give me the hat that had belonged first to Bear and then to Jenny—I saw a gleam as richly colored as pure emeralds and scintillant with old magic that smelled of water lilies and smoke. I crept closer against the thrust and panic of the ghost, who screamed, "No, no, no, no!" and slashed at me with bitter cold and the barbed edge of terror.

I gritted my teeth against the spurt of agony and felt hard, crumbling stone beneath my knees and hands. Quinton's thin, warm touch moved up onto my back as I crawled toward the green line that grew thicker as I neared. Its length coiled away into the distance, as thick as my thumb, impossibly cutting through walls and looping over the vibrant lines of the grid like a mad vine over a trellis. I could hear it singing in a hundred languages. I reached for it and my incorporeal prisoner shrieked, gibbered, and lashed me blind. I shut my eyes, gasping and shaking my hanging head, my hand falling short of my goal. Tears gushed over my lashes and ran blood-hot down my face.

Quinton's touch drew away and I felt a twist of my own fear tightening the grip of Lass's terror on my body. I moaned as Lass howled in despair and sank into a dull blankness in my head. I blinked my vision clear and rolled back to sit against the nearest wall, trying to focus again on the normal.

Quinton was looking at something in his hand under the beam of his light. He held it up and I could see its true shape as a green shadow around its thin and ragged manifestation outside the Grey.

"It's just a bit of string. But it feels heavy."

The long green tail of it snaked away into the mist of the Grey, shivering like a live thing. I put up my hand.

"Give it to me, please."

He handed it over and I felt the weight of something far at the invisible end. I tugged it. The green line went taut, singing. I pushed myself back up onto my feet but kept my back to the wall for support.

The wall across from me rippled and the rings of disturbance spread outward through the Grey until they vanished in the edges of vision. The singing blended to a roar and Sisiutl swam through the wall on a slice of time, shouting in a dozen languages, drowning Lass's horrified keening. The snakelike heads snapped and hissed, and the whole monstrous serpent rolled to bring its screaming center face to glare at me, gnashing its teeth and bringing its other heads close to strike.

I knew it understood at least some English—it had listened to Lass and had called me a thief—so as it raged and menaced us, I grabbed the feather from my bag and yanked once more on the leash. It reared up and I poked the central face with the long plume of the feather.

Sisiutl recoiled and snorted, its appearance rippling as the wall and the Grey had done before. I gave one more sharp jerk on the string and, thinking of Tanker's commands to Bella, ordered, "Peace, Sisiutl. Be quiet."

The monster seemed surprised, blinking all its eyes. Then it made two coils of its snake ends and raised the central head to my own height, staring with yellow eyes from the nearly human face. Meeting that gaze was like looking into a restless kaleidoscope. I had to shake myself and cling to the sobering pangs of Lass's pressure in my head to keep from falling into that stare.

We looked at each other as Lass went rigid and silent in my head. Quinton kept as still as the stone walls.

"I have your leash. That makes me your master for the time being," I said, not giving it a chance to argue or bargain. "I'm going to return your leash to Qamaits so you can go back to sleep."

"Hungry!" it roared.

"You've had enough to eat. Don't be greedy. You will stay here and be patient while I go to find Qamaits."

Sisiutl growled and snapped at us.

I yanked the string. "Enough! You *will* stay until called for."

Amazing me, Sisiutl lowered itself to the ground and sulked like a reprimanded dog.

"Now to find Qamaits," I said, starting to turn for the exit. Too soon. At the sound of her name, Lass twitched violently, making me jerk and stumble. Quinton grabbed my arm and steadied me, casting a nervous glance at Sisiutl.

"Do you trust it?"

I gave an unsteady nod. "Rules. It has to follow them. Now, you," I said, turning my attention inward to Lass. "Where can we find Qamaits—the old Indian woman who gave you Sisiutl's leash?"

Lass went still and stubbornly silent.

"Tell me or I'll cast you out and let the monster eat you."

Lass jerked and writhed. "Don't know where she is!" he whined in my head. "She's just a fat old squaw!"

"Bull. You know her. Is she in the crowd that followed us here?"

I could feel him sulking. "No."

"Then tell me who she is and where to find her!"

"Beside herself," came the rolling voice of Sisiutl.

I shot a glance back at the zeqwa. It merely blinked innocently. Then it grinned with all its sparkling teeth, the forked tongues of its snake heads flickering. It chuckled as we retreated but stayed where I had ordered it. Trickster.

We rushed out of the block, careful to check before bursting out of the door to the street. A rush and flutter of wings swished into the air as we emerged, making crow shadows on the sidewalk beneath the waking streetlamps.

The crowd we'd left behind had grown—natives and ghosts, human and animal. They stood in the new-fallen night and watched us with patient eyes. Then they fell into step behind us as we began to walk.

"Beside herself . . . ?" Quinton muttered.

Ogress, eater of children, nightmare bringer . . . Tsonoqua was also an ogress. Fish had said Qamaits went by many names. Maybe one half-goddess, half-ogress would cleave to another. . . . I knew where she was.

TWENTY-TWO

The temperature had dropped with the sun. A pair of trash fires sent out yellow light at each end of Occidental Park and carved the shadows into broken, moving shapes. There were few people in the park and those were gathered around the heat and flicker from the burning cans. When Quinton and I entered the avenue of plane trees, the bizarre parade that had come to Grandpa Dan's beckoning had tripled and followed us from the Cadillac Hotel to Oxy Park.

Lass had begun to stir again as we crossed Main, but I ignored him, peering into the jigsaw darkness toward the giant totems at the far end. In the erratic light, the black wooden statue of Tsonoqua—Nightmare Bringer—seemed to breathe and move, spreading her arms farther than usual to hold an oil-slick-edged hole in the air. The shape of the world seemed a bit warped at that spot. I headed straight for it, confirmed in my opinion that Qamaits and Tsonoqua were, like Sisiutl and Cerberus, just different names for the same thing. As we got closer, I could see a large, dark shape at the feet of Tsonoqua, bulking even larger with eerie shadows that moved independently of their object.

I stepped over the low rail that separated the totems from the walkway and stopped, facing the massive carving of Tsonoqua, whose arms reached out as if to pull me into an embrace—the better to eat me I supposed. The face, highlighted with red and green paint, pursed its lips as if to kiss, while a darkling gleam played in the hooded eyes. Another pair of dark eyes looked up from the face of the huge woman seated at the carving's feet.

The Grey was more present around the totems and I didn't bother to hold on to normal. Whatever happened next would take place in the thin space between the worlds. But as I let go, little changed, and I found Quinton still beside me and the strange audience of ghosts and humans, spreading around us in a circle, still visible in the Grey. The shimmering edges of the hole in the totem's hands seemed to spread and hold the worlds together in the presence of the gathered spirits, animal and Indian. The real Indians and the birds were there as well, watching, encircling us and completing the sphere of magic that contained us all.

"I want to return your pet," I started, "and the man you lent him to needs to account for his actions."

Qamaits laughed, showing needle teeth in her spirit form, and shook her head. "No dog."

"I didn't say it was a dog. I don't think your gods will be pleased that Sisiutl's been killing people who never threatened them on the whim of this man you gave his leash to. I only want to send the man up the stairs to account for it and return Sisiutl to his post—neither of you should be in the human world." Lass shrieked in my head and I winced as he began to claw and fight to escape.

Qamaits noticed and her laugh was dismissive. "I like it here. Sisiutl shares his meat. I do not have to hunt or gather food. It is cold, but I have many blankets and the people do not chase me away. Why should I go?"

"You have a duty," I said, sickened, knowing the people Sisiutl had netted must have gone down the maw of this creature, too. "The man has done wrong and Sisiutl is tainted with it. I only ask you to show me the stair so the man can answer for that."

As she considered, I looked at her collection of eclectic trash: the colorful blankets, discarded children's toys, fancy liquor bottles . . .

She stood up, easily three times my bulk and a hair shorter, yet she loomed, double-shadowed. She stared at me with odd eyes that gleamed yellow and red and shook her head, baring her pointed teeth. "If Sisiutl goes back to the realm between, I must go, too. Why should I?"

"You have a duty to the gods and you don't belong in the human world," I repeated as I threaded the pheasant feather into my buttonholes to free my hands. "You must go back."

Qamaits recoiled at the sight of the feather, her eyes staring. Then she roared and swelled even larger than her looming totem, the double shadows behind her filling and solidifying into a hulking shape from nightmare: wide and black and seemingly made of teeth and claws. "Meat!" she shrieked. "I eat you all!"

I jumped back, dragging Quinton with me and jerking on Sisiutl's leash, calling for the serpent-headed creature. The double-ended monster rushed into the park, casting a wave of color through the Grey and screeching as it came.

The crowd shuddered, gasping or muttering strange words and issuing angry animal cries. The huge sea serpent stopped between

Qamaits and me and glared at each of us with a different head. Qamaits drew up short, glowering.

"Who will it answer—me or you?" I asked, feeling weak-kneed and anguished as Lass battered against me in terror. "It says it's hungry. Want to find out which of us it prefers for dinner?"

I wasn't certain how much longer I could stand up, let alone bluff on instinct alone. I felt sure I was bleeding inside and tearing apart like a rag doll with ripped seams. It wasn't as bad as being beaten to death had been, but it was bad enough.

Qamaits moved back half a step, teetering on the edge of the hole in the worlds. Her glare shifted back and forth between me and Sisiutl and she gnawed her lip until blood flowed over her chin.

"Show us the stairs," I demanded, forcing my old dance-gypsy bravado to the surface.

Sisiutl grinned and snapped one snake head at the ogress. It would have been as glad to snap at me, I imagined.

Keeping a wary eye on me, Qamaits dug into her cart of discarded treasures and pulled out a strangely folded thing of plastic and cardboard, coated in filthy, torn, and peeling pink vinyl. She unfolded it: a dollhouse.

I heard Quinton snort beside me, but I wasn't about to cast stones—I was holding a legendary monster by a piece of frayed string and arguing with an ogress who looked like a homeless woman. Belief and appearances were only nodding acquaintances, it seemed. Qamaits lifted the house so it passed through the ring of oily gleam between her effigy's hands, and as she brought it down the ring expanded, the world rippling and warping to accommodate the house. Even Lass grew still as we were enclosed in the second bubble of Qamaits's realm.

The dollhouse grew and the ring of some sort of dimensional

rift flowed out to encompass the park, which became the yard. It unfolded until the house had become full-sized, its open front leaving the interior revealed and raw. The smell of water lilies and black mud rose into the frosty air as a pool formed from a puddle at my feet, a sturdy stone needle rising from its shore nearby. I walked unsteadily to the post and tied the piece of string through the eye of the needle.

Sisiutl rolled in the grass where bricks had been a moment before, snorting with delight. Then it stopped and slithered across the ground, back and forth, as if pacing in some strange, reptilian way. Qamaits stood aside and watched me with narrowed eyes.

I took the feather from my buttonholes and teased Lass loose from me. He shouted and fought to stay with me and not to be thrown into the realm of the zeqwas. I tore him out with a keen of agony and stumbled to my knees, pushing the last trailing threads of him away with the plume. Once outside of me, he recovered the memory of his shape but cleaner and younger than I had known him—and he did have a mild resemblance to Quinton. I shivered to see him looking so solid and familiar.

With a hunted look, he glanced around, as if seeking an escape, but there wasn't a way out. The world of the house ended in a band of rainbow beyond which the normal world of Occidental Park lay in a thin mist. The crowd still stood around it, their movements suspended. Sisiutl prowled its yard and snapped at Lass while muttering to itself.

Lass started toward Quinton and turned up his hands. "Q—"

Quinton looked a little dazed, but shook his head. "No. You messed up and I can't help you this time."

"But—I helped you. You took my identity to hide from those . . . people."

"I know. I'm sorry I had to, but there's nothing I can do for you now."

Lass slumped. "I don't—I can't . . ." Trepid and shaking, he eyed the surreal house of Qamaits and then the ogress herself, who grinned at him with bloody teeth.

Qamaits called to Sisiutl, who leaped toward Lass, biting at the air. "Choose!" she commanded. "Sisiutl hungers."

Lass stumbled back, remembering fear, and shot a supplicating glance at me. Then he looked at the long, vanishing stair that wandered up into the depths of the house and back to me again. "Please . . . can't you come with me? I don't want to go by myself!"

I was tired and aching and I wished I could hold on to my disgust of him, but I felt impotent pity as I looked at Lass's spirit. I don't know how I knew it was true—maybe the way Qamaits licked her lips or the shift in Sisiutl's pacing—but I was sure one step across the threshold would have the monsters on me and I didn't like my chances against them both. "I can't go with you," I replied.

Qamaits gnashed her teeth in frustration.

Lass hung his head and shuffled his feet. "All right," he mumbled, and began to walk to the house like a guilty child to his punishment. Sisiutl and Qamaits let him pass.

As he mounted the stairs, the house shuddered. With each step Lass took up the risers, he seemed to get farther away, and the house shrank into distance and dimension, shivering smaller and smaller. It dwindled, sparkling and rippling as the rainbow sheen of the rift spiraled closed until Occidental Park flowed back into place and the only sign of Lass's journey or of Sisiutl was the battered dollhouse—still glimmering prismatically—sitting on the ground at the feet of the totem.

Qamaits had dwindled back to a more normal size, but she

still bore the aspect of the ogress. She glowered at Quinton and me, shuffling toward the little house, drawing closer, cursing, and stooped to pick up the dollhouse.

Then she twisted, leaping at Quinton, snarling, her hands outstretched into talons.

I dove between them, pushing Quinton back and yanking a bit of Grey between us and the ogress. She rolled against it. Then plunged through with a shriek, swiping at me and bringing blood to my cheek. Her gory fangs gnashed an inch from my face. I shoved her back, snatching for the frayed feather, hoping to loosen her monstrous aspect and reduce her to a more ordinary opponent.

She thrashed forward, flickering but unhurt, slashing at me. She moved like an eel and I couldn't keep her at a distance. Quinton scrambled to help, but we only tangled together, stumbling. I shoved him back again, shouting, "Stay away! It's you she wants! No one wants to eat me," I added, muttering and glaring at the ogress. "I'd give you indigestion, wouldn't I?"

Qamaits feinted left and lunged right to clutch at Quinton's flapping coat. I caught her sweeping arm and whipped her back, jabbing the feather at her shadows with the other hand. The dark shapes crumpled a little, but she spun swift as a dervish and lashed back, forcing me to duck and catch my balance with one hand on the ground before swinging over my own feet and spinning a kick at her as I came back up before my shoulder could give up on me.

I had no time to reach for the pistol and didn't think it would do any more damage to Qamaits than it had to Sisiutl, so I continued with fist and feather, trying to dislodge her shadow selves and break her down.

But she was fast and enraged. She charged at me with teeth

bared as if to rip my throat out, her arms spread to grasp and crush.

I twisted aside, dragging the feather over her. She pivoted, using one arm as a counterweight as she flailed at me with the other, buffeting me into the ground again. I wasn't breaking her as fast as she was breaking me.

I screamed for help and the crowd of Indians, animals, and spirits stirred around us with a rush of wings and a distant chanting. A cloud of crows and jays swooped down, lashing the ogress's face with wing and claw. I lurched to my feet and scored the pheasant quill down her side, ripping a chunk of her Grey shape away.

Qamaits howled and shook off the birds, lurching toward me again. Ghostly shapes of foxes darted beneath her feet, knocking her down, and I tore another slice out of her shadow.

I was panting, worn down by the long ordeal of the past two days and now by the ogress's blows. I turned and was awash in a crowd of chanting ghosts that threw themselves between Qamaits and me.

I scuttled to the side, seeing the dollhouse still coruscating nearby. I braced and ran at the shadow-cloaked ogress, ramming my shoulder into her side at the cost of rent clothes and flesh, but driving her backward toward the shimmering house.

Qamaits fell back but dug in as I dove for her one more time.

We rocked into the verge of the house together, the rift between the worlds tearing at me and sending a feedback screech through my head. She was half in but fighting the draw of the house with her talons piercing into my shoulders.

Dark wings, gigantic and glossy, dozens of them, clattering with pointed beaks, beat into us, driving the ogress back, ripping at her face and striking us apart. Ravens with hot yellow eyes flocked and stooped, distracting the zeqwa. I twisted, shoved . . .

And she fell away with a shriek, tumbling into the miniature house, spinning and dwindling until she vanished.

The house collapsed on itself, dragging the rift and the Grey sphere with it, folding into a sad pile of dirty vinyl and cardboard again, dull, discarded, and sparkling with only a dim Grey light. The normal world crashed back into us with a roar of modern noise.

Quinton pulled me back to my feet, wrapping me in his coat and drawing me away from the dollhouse on the bricks. I shuddered and gulped air before I shoved my weakness aside to look back at the abandoned toy.

Grandpa Dan shuffled forward and picked up the house, folding it down until it was flat. Then he carried it, a procession of his people—material and incorporeal—forming around him as he went to the nearest fire and carefully dropped it in. The flames rose up in a rush of white and yellow and red, and the Indians watched the dollhouse burn, whispering songs until it was a white drift of ash.

I looked around, seeking a sight of the animals, but they were gone—every one but a dog that limped from the darkness, shaggy coat matted with mud and head hanging.

"Bella?" Quinton called.

The dog turned and ran to him, whimpering in relief. He gathered her up and took us both home.

EPILOGUE

I slept more than I worked for the next few days and didn't notice that Seattle had returned to normal temperatures and normal business while my attention was turned aside. Quinton had kept a covert eye on Fern Laguire and Detective Solis, and their actions were about the only thing—aside from rushing through work for Nan Grover and wrestling with the insurance company over my destroyed truck—that I was aware of for a while.

Laguire had managed to wrench all investigation into the deaths of the homeless and any possible monsters in the sewer away from Solis and bury it in a national paperwork tomb from which I doubted it would ever emerge. Solis had kicked at first, but a spate of shootings pulled him into other work that no one wanted to hide or interfere with. He didn't forget about the bizarre deaths, but he let them lie for the time being and roused no stink about me or the mysterious "Mr. Lassiter" I was spending a lot of time with.

In spite of worries that his cover was dangerously rickety, Quinton remained in his Seattle hideaway and in my life. He stayed in the condo for three nights after patching me up and clearing my office and home of bugs, further ingratiating himself with Chaos in the process—the fickle little beast—before returning to his own place. We were both loners at heart and Quinton was still wary of Laguire's local radar, so playing house was out of the question. But we found plenty of other things to do in between cleaning out the last of Sisiutl's zombies.

Quinton kept Bella with him for a while, but eventually he handed the miserable, orphaned dog over to Rosaria Cabrera of Women in Black. The dog became her constant companion. Though prone to bristle and growl at strange shapes in the fog, Bella proved to be a fine mascot.

Of Tanker there was never a sign, dead or alive.

Ben survived Sisiutl's attack, though not without scars. Being Ben, however, he was downright ecstatic about his tussle with an eldritch beast. Mara felt differently and took him to task about foolish risks while she struggled with the question of what to do with Albert. Eventually, the net full of ghost vanished from the rooftop of the Danzigers' home, but Mara didn't reveal what she'd done with it.

Chaos forgave me for stinking of monsters after a while and went back to climbing the bookshelves, stealing my shoes, co-opting my breakfast, and attacking my toes anytime they were bare. One day, she dumped the wooden puzzle ball Will had given me onto the floor, making her victory chuckle as she chivvied it around and stopped to dance about it in mustelid glee. I'd put Will forcibly out of my mind, and seeing the thing gave me a pang. I was happy with Quinton, but I would always have a soft spot for Will, in spite of our harsh breakup.

As Chaos played with the puzzle ball, the battered pheasant feather slipped from the shelf, caught a draft, and drifted, spiraling down to land quill first against the ball with an otherworldly chime. The puzzle shifted and the Grey rippled with a hush like someone cracking the seal on an airtight door that I could feel in every hollow of my body. The feather fell away and drifted to the floor, but the breathlessness in the Grey remained. Chaos leapt and spun, waving her toothy maw at the disturbance before she declared victory over whatever unseen thing had ruffled her fur. Then she bumped the ball back into motion and continued with her game, chuckling.

I watched the Grey-gleaming thing trundle across my floor and wondered what fresh hell might be contained at its core.

AUTHOR'S NOTE

In this book I've played faster and looser than I usually do with Seattle's real-life geography. In fact, the underground is mostly condemned, inaccessible by anyone but utility workers, or in use by the tenants of the various buildings that rise over it. If you aren't on the Underground Tour or don't have legitimate access to a building's cellar, you won't get into it without breaking a law or perpetrating a miracle. But the idea of the underground—with monsters—was so intriguing that I threw a lot to the wind and plunged into it anyway.

I did try to keep as much of the reality intact as possible, however, and I got a lot of help with the history and the layout of the area from Rick Boetel, the chief historian of Bill Speidel's Underground Tour. I've presented the history and fact of the underground as truthfully as I could: toilets really did flush backward at high tide before the streets were raised; people really did fall to their deaths from the streets to the sidewalks; a shaman really did exorcise the ghosts of native spirits from the underground corner at Yesler and First; and prostitution and other crimes and vices really did thrive in the darkness below the city streets right into the

1970s. There really was a Roy Olmstead (though I hope not an Albert Frye), who really was both a policeman and a bootlegger. And, yes, there really was a dumping ground near where Occidental crosses Royal Brougham.

Rick's help was invaluable, but I was also able to get additional information from books and Web sites. Surprisingly, one of the most useful books was *Distant Corner*, by Jeffrey Karl Ochsner and Dennis Alan Anderson, an architectural treatise from the University of Washington Press on the influence of architect H. H. Richardson (no relation) on the rebuilding of Seattle after the Great Fire. This book details the buildings; who built them; where and when; what they were made of; as well as their original purposes and what had previously been on the site. It contains a lot of photos, drawings, and maps, and it often discusses what became of the buildings in later years. This book provided the information on the buildings that collapsed during construction and some information about others that were damaged in the 1949 earthquake. It was also a surprisingly fun read.

With some idea of the history and geography of the underground in mind, I then needed a monster. It's harder than you might imagine to find a really good man-eating monster that isn't already working its fangs off in a half-dozen other series or films or TV shows. After several false starts, I settled on the Pacific Northwest Native American legend of the Sisiutl. And promptly got teased by both my agent and my editor. No one, they said, could take seriously a monster with such a goofy-sounding moniker. Being a stubborn cuss, I swore I'd make it work. I hope I did, but if nothing else, I got a great argument out of it that made it into the book as the discussion between Harper, Quinton, and Fish as they drive away from the Tulalip reservation. That's not quite how it happened in real life, but it makes much better reading.

As with many legends, Sisiutl's tales are occasionally contradictory and change with the telling or the teller. I ended up picking and choosing in order to make the monster suit my story, but I hope I was true to the spirit of the creature. The mythology and legends of the Pacific Northwest Salish are rich and weird, and I owe a lot to the Seattle Public Library's collection, which includes a reprint of *Mythology of Southern Puget Sound: Legends Shared by Tribal Elders*, which was collected and translated from the Lushootseed principally by Seattle historian Arthur Ballard. It's a great book, and it offers a wonderful peek into the culture of the local tribes at the time. I was also able to find audio recordings of spoken Lushootseed online at the *Seattle Times* Web site (seattletimes.nwsource.com/news/local/seattle_history/about_audio).

As I was writing the story, Seattle experienced one of its coldest winters on record—with overnight temperatures in the single digits. The drama of the unusual weather was an irresistible addition to the book. Yes, it was that cold.

Of course, I consulted a lot of other sources for my background research, and I hope I utilized the information well—or at least haven't enraged the authors by clumsy handling. I've made every effort to neither plagiarize nor distort, and to present as realistic a picture as possible of my rather fantastical Seattle, but this is still a work of fiction and isn't intended as anything else. Where I've twisted history, fact, or geography, I've done it for artistic reasons, meaning no malice or insult, nor any attempt to present my story as fact. Where there are errors, they are entirely my fault.